The Tigress
- - - -
The Exotic
- - - -
Angel!
- - - -

Three Novels by
Carter Brown

INTRODUCTION BY
ANDREW NETTE

Stark House Press • Eureka California

THE TIGRESS / THE EXOTIC / ANGEL!

Published by Stark House Press
1315 H Street
Eureka, CA 95501, USA
griffinskye3@sbcglobal.net
www.starkhousepress.com

THE TIGRESS
Originally published and copyright © 1961 by Horwitz Publications,
Sydney, Australia. Reprinted in the U.S. by Signet Books, New York, 1961.

THE EXOTIC
Originally published and copyright © 1961 by Horwitz Publications,
Sydney, Australia. Reprinted in the U.S. by Signet Books, New York, 1961.

ANGEL!
Originally published and copyright © 1962 by Horwitz Publications,
Sydney, Australia. Reprinted in the U.S. by Signet Books, New York, 1962.

Reprinted by permission of the Estate of Alan G. Yates, and licensed via
The Carter Brown Foundation Pty Ltd, Australia. All rights reserved
under International and Pan-American Copyright Conventions.

"Carter Brown and the Australian Craze for Faux American Crime
Fiction" copyright © 2020 by Andrew Nette as published by CrimeReads.
Reprinted by permission of the author.

ISBN: 979-8-88601-075-6

Cover design by Jeff Vorzimmer, ¡caliente!design, Austin, Texas
Cover art by Bernard Barton
Text design by Mark Shepard, shepgraphics.com
Proofreading by Bill Kelly

PUBLISHER'S NOTE
This is a work of fiction. Names, characters, places and incidents are
either the products of the author's imagination or used fictionally, and
any resemblance to actual persons, living or dead, events or locales, is
entirely coincidental.

Without limiting the rights under copyright reserved above, no part of
this publication may be reproduced, stored, or introduced into a retrieval
system or transmitted in any form or by any means (electronic,
mechanical, photocopying, recording or otherwise) without the prior
written permission of both the copyright owner and the above publisher
of the book.

First Stark House Press Edition: February 2024

The Tigress

In which Lieutenant Al Wheeler is called upon to unravel the mystery of
♦ the murdered secretary found in the coffin of her grieving boss's wife
♦ the insolent maid and the questionable "club" she works for
♦ the dead wife's nympho best friend and her wildcat-taming lover

The Exotic

In which Lieutenant Al Wheeler is confronted by
♦ a corpse delivered to the front door of Sheriff Lavers' by a clueless cabbie
♦ the two wily thugs who put the man in the taxi
♦ the dead man's daughter, who sheds not a tear for her departed dad

Angel!

In which Lieutenant Al Wheeler investigates
♦ the sudden death of a stunt flyer when his plane explodes in midair
♦ the rest of the flyers and the man for whom the bomb was *really* intended
♦ their sexy mascot, Angel, the good luck charm with the heart of ice

Contents

7
Carter Brown and the Australian Craze
for Faux American Crime Fiction
By Andrew Nette

13
The Tigress
by Carter Brown

89
The Exotic
by Carter Brown

173
Angel!
by Carter Brown

264
Carter Brown
Bibliography

Carter Brown and the Australian Craze for Faux American Crime Fiction

By Andrew Nette

Alan Yates was a mid-century Australian crime writing phenomenon, 300 plus books over a career that spanned the late 1940s to his last novel, *The Dream Merchant* in 1977. Published in 35 countries and 27 languages, he was the most reprinted Australian writer domestically and overseas until the early 2000s. Yet he is almost completely forgotten in his home country and was little known even at the height of his success.

'Rated third in the big five of mystery writing (John Creasy and Erle Stanley Gardner in front, Agatha Christie and Simenon trailing), Alan Yates is quite a mystery himself,' went the opening of a 1963 article in the then popular Australian tabloid magazine, Pix. 'At 39, he is far and away Australia's top-selling novelist with 40 million copies of 110 books appearing in 21 languages. Yet nobody in Australia really gives a spent .45 about his work... Few people realise he's even Australian.'

While Yates was a big seller, the lack of critical recognition given to his books flows mainly from the fact he wrote mysteries and private detective novels for Horwitz Publications, one of the largest of a group of Sydney based pulp publishers that emerged in Australia after 1945. Although reaction to Yates's work was better in America where he was published by the Signet imprint of the prestigious New American Library, even so, these novels are arguably recalled now more for their stylish and alluring covers by veteran illustrator, Robert McGinnis, than for anything to do with Yates.

Virtually all of Yates's prodigious output was faux American crime fiction, the most popular genre of pulp published in Australia in the decade and a half after World War II. These books featured mystery and private investigator tales, set in largely mythical versions of US cities such as New York, Chicago and Las Vegas, and heavily influenced by American crime authors such as Raymond Chandler, but perhaps even more so by the stories in the pages of remaindered American pulp magazines dumped in large numbers in Australia before the war.

Its success not only spoke to the country's increasing American acculturation, but deeper social changes underway after 1945.

♦ ♦ ♦

Australia's most successful 20th century author was born in the United Kingdom in 1923. He first visited Sydney on leave from the Royal Navy during the war, where he met his wife, Denise. They married in 1946 and lived in the UK, where he unsuccessfully submitted stories for magazines such as *Argosy* and *Strand*. He returned to Australia in 1948, worked as a publicist for the national airline Qantas by day, and at night wrote science fiction and romance for a number of local pulp publishers, including Horwitz.

His first Carter Brown crime novel for Horwitz, *The Lady Is Murder*, appeared in September 1951. On the strength of its sales the company immediately signed him up to pen an ongoing monthly series of two 20,000-word novelettes—a hybrid of the pulp magazine and the novel—as Carter Brown. He subsequently signed a 30-year contract with Horwitz. By the mid-1950s the front cover of his books boasted that he was "the slick story-telling sensation whose [sic] sold ten million copies." Although it is impossible to verify the claim, when Pix interviewed him in 1963, he was earning £25,000 pounds a year from writing full time (the annual male wage in Australia at the time was £728).

Yates's international success came after Stanley Horwitz, the entrepreneurial head of Horwitz Publications, pitched his work to NAL publisher, Victor Weybright. Weybright was in the market for a replacement for Mickey Spillane, who became a Jehovah's Witness following the publication of Kiss Me Deadly in 1952, resulting in a 10-year publishing hiatus. Signet signed the Carter Brown series in 1958, new books and US releases of work previously published in Australia. This helped Yates to get published in France, where the books were released through the crime imprint of prestigious Editions Gallimard, as well as Japan, Mexico, and numerous Scandinavian and Latin America countries.

The Lady Is Murder is remarkably hard boiled by early 1950s Australian standards. American private investigator, Mike Staynes, travels to London to accompany an attractive, rich, art loving widow to recover a painting, part of a valuable set she owns. There he becomes embroiled in a four-way tussle between the police, a vicious criminal gang, members of the underground Nazi movement, and a group of art heisting ex-GIs.

As the series grew in popularity its style become more playful and humorous. By the time *Walk Softly Witch!* was published in 1955, Yates had perfected his formula. The book, one of the early stories to be re-released in America, finds Carter Brown's best-known character, Al Wheeler, a lieutenant in the sheriff's department of the fictitious California town of Pine City, investigating the hit and run death of a local businessman. Suspicion falls on the man's wife, who could benefit from his generous insurance policy, but there are numerous suspicious suspects. The prose is assured, if not spectacular, and the tone is less hardboiled and more tongue in cheek. The sex is inferred rather than overt, and everything is drenched in 1950s Americana: leopard skin print, scotch whisky, Lucky Strike cigarettes, and Frank Sinatra.

Throughout the 1950s, Yates worked hard, occasionally at his typewriter for 48 hours straight with help of a then legal amphetamine Dexedrine. This pace only increased once he was taken on by Signet. They saddled him with an additional layer of editorial supervision and started pressuring for changes. In particular, his US editors wanted more sex. While Yates was not personally squeamish about matters carnal, Australian censors in the 1950s and early 1960s were, and his books had been banned in the northern state of Queensland and termed obscene in the New South Wales parliament. His US editors were also critical of the authenticity of some of his American settings and Yates's inability to meet deadlines, concerns which saw US crime writer Frank Kane drafted to rewrite parts of at least four of Yates's books.

♦ ♦ ♦

Carter Brown's success spawned many Australian imitators. From 1953 until the early 1960s, Calvert, a local pulp outfit about whom little is known, published the Carl Dekker series, penned by a number of writers and featuring an American freelance writer and detective who travelled the world solving crime. In 1954, Cleveland Publications bought the rights to a popular local radio show, 'I Hate Crime', about a PI called Larry Kent, moved the setting to New York and turned it into a series of books that would continue until the 1980s. Horwitz also commissioned two additional faux American crimes series. Melbourne tabloid news editor, Bill Williams, wrote 80 books as Marc Brody, the name of the main character and narrator, an American newspaper reporter who investigated crime, the first of which *Big Shot's Final Edition*, appeared in 1955. Sydney Journalist Audrey Armitage and teacher Muriel Watkins, wrote a series of 22 books in the late 1950s about a tough New York insurance investigator Johnny Buchanan, under the pseudonym K. T. McCall.

Queensland academic Toni Johnson-Woods, one of the few people to have examined the Carter Brown series in detail, argues its popularity is based on its irreverent take on the prevalent style of detective fiction popular at the time. One Australian magazine account in the late 1960s, noted Horwitz was keen "to devise a mystery series which would have Chandlerish overtones but would feature more light-hearted detectives, less kinky and with more liberal sex [by Australian standards], as well as an air of ritzy living. But Lieut. Al Wheeler and other Brown heroes were not to be glamorous or unusually gifted: they had to have a realistic, slightly seedy air to ensure readership identification among males."

In addition to engaging with the social climate of post war optimism and the growing demand for light-hearted entertainment, the success of faux American crime fiction can be viewed as a proxy for Australia's growing military ties with Washington in the post-war period at a time in which British political and economic power was on the wane. As local crime fiction scholar Stephen Knight put it in his 1997 book, Continent of Mystery, "The American-based novels of 'Carter Brown'... followed the culture brought by the American fleet into Sydney, a new imperial force that arrived here with the purposes of defending America's Pacific dominions, rather than the free world."

Underlying this was a deeper acculturation to American influence, underway in Australia since the 1920s, when jazz and US films started to appear for the first time. This continued in the 1930s, and accelerated after World War II, when the country hosted up to a million US service personnel. Yates did not visit the US until 1958, when Signet published the first Carter Brown novel, The Body. His 1983 autobiography, *Ready When You Are, C.B.!* records his wonder at what he saw: the huge food servings, watching Sammy Davis Junior perform at the Sands in Las Vegas; and the Manhattan cocktail party thrown in his honour by Weybright and attended by luminaries of the New York publishing world.

The least analysed but perhaps most interesting shift underlining the success of faux American crime fiction in 1950s Australia is the degree to which it was associated with changes in Australian sexual culture. The war and its immediate aftermath played havoc with traditional notions of sex and gender. Australian scholars have written about how close contact with American soldiers loosened conventional morality for women. Men similarly had their horizons expanded by their wartime experience. As was the case in the US, this period also saw more explicit publications move from the margins to the mainstream of Australian culture, including the pin up and local men's magazines modeled on magazines like Esquire.

Carter Brown's breezy, fast-paced Americanised narratives and salacious full colour cover art, infused with thinly veiled sexual narratives and consumerist abandon—much of it targeted at males—tapped directly into this new sensibility. His success can be seen as an early manifestation in Australia of a more masculine hedonistic consumer culture underway in the US since the 1930s, but far slower to reach Australia: a heady, imagined world of travel, adventure, and sexual independence, which allowed men to reclaim a sense of masculine space, free from the post war constraints and responsibilities of family and work.

[originally published online in *CrimeReads*, April 17, 2020]

Andrew Nette is a writer of fiction and non-fiction, reviewer and pulp scholar. He is the author of two novels, *Ghost Money*, a crime story set in Cambodia in the mid-nineties, and *Gunshine State*. He is co-editor of *Girl Gangs, Biker Boys, and Real Cool Cats: Pulp Fiction and Youth Culture, 1950 to 1980*, published by PM Press, and *Sticking It To the Man: Revolution and Counterculture in Pulp and Popular Fiction, 1956 to 1980*, also from PM Press.

The Tigress
- - - -
Carter Brown

CHAPTER ONE

I braked the Austin Healey to a stop outside the immaculate bronze gates which were locked, making a kind of symbolic threshold between life and death. We got out of the car and Sergeant Polnik jabbed his thumb against the night bell for a couple of seconds, then shivered suddenly.

"Graveyards always give me the creeps, Lieutenant," he said plaintively, "even when they're as ritzy as this one!"

"And you a cop?" I said, genuinely surprised. "Stiffs are your business, Sergeant."

His forehead wrinkled into a maze of furrowed lines. "Stiffs I don't mind," he growled. "The morgue don't worry me none, either, but graveyards—" he shivered again "—they worry me, Lieutenant, like anytime I'm going to look right through some guy who shouldn't be there in the first—Yikes!"

For a split second I was about to agree with Polnik—the guy who had suddenly materialized on the other side of the gates looked for sure like he shouldn't be there—but then I realized I couldn't really see through him; it was just a trick of the early morning sun, and I felt a little better.

The guy was old, with a shock of gray hair, and wizened up, as if the blood that had once run in his veins had long since dried and shriveled away to dust. Squinting hard, he glowered at us, then spoke in a piping treble that made me fervently wish I'd had at least some coffee before we started out.

"What do you want?" he demanded irritably.

"I'm Lieutenant Wheeler, from the County Sheriff's office," I announced loud and clear, hoping that I sounded at least as important as J. Edgar Hoover. "This is Sergeant Polnik. Somebody phoned a while back and said they'd just found a stiff. It wasn't some guy with a big sense of humor, I hope?"

"You'd better come down to the office," the old man said reluctantly. "Mr. Williams is waiting for you." He unlocked the gate with a key big enough to fit eternity, then gestured down the white concrete strip flanked by verdant grass on either side. "Just follow the road and you'll find the main building a half-mile along. I'll call Mr. Williams and let him know you're coming."

"Be sure you tell him who we are," I said. "We're in no mood for a sales pitch on his real estate at this hour of the morning, see?" If the old gent heard me, he gave no sign of it.

Polnik squeezed his bulk back into the Healey and I got in beside him, then drove through the open gates and down the concrete strip. About a minute later we stopped outside the impressive concrete building with its pointed Gothic arch framing two massive bronze doors. The sergeant looked at them dubiously as we climbed out of the car. "Cheez!" he said feelingly. "Once you're in, you're in, huh, Lieutenant?"

I looked at the large bronze lettering above the pointed arch—it spelled out *Eternal Refuge*— and nodded sympathetically.

"But everything's so hygienic here. You'd like that, wouldn't you?"

Polnik shuddered again. "I figure if my old lady ever bust out crying in here—which is real unlikely—they'd toss her out for making a disturbance."

A small man, neatly dressed in a dark suit, came hurrying down from the main steps toward us.

"My name is Williams," he said agitatedly, "I'm the superintendent here. This is a terrible thing, Lieutenant, terrible! We've never had anything like this happen here before."

"You trying to tell us this is your first stiff, pal?" Polnik grunted suspiciously. "What is this joint? An ice-cream parlor, or something?"

The superintendent's face contorted suddenly, then his hand dived inside his coat and scratched urgently. A look of bliss showed briefly in his eyes and his face smoothed out again.

"But this—this one is entirely unscheduled!" he protested in a shocked voice. "I must admit I found it hard to believe myself when Jordan reported it."

"Jordan?" I queried.

"The man who opened the gates for you," he explained. "He was on the job early this morning—to finish preparing the plot—we have a ceremony scheduled for eleven." His eyes squeezed tight shut in anguish. "The wife of one of our most distinguished citizens. I don't know how I'm going to explain to—"

"What happened exactly?" I asked patiently.

"I think you'd better see for yourself, Lieutenant—er—Wheeler?" His hand jerked upward like someone had pulled an invisible wire, and scratched the back of his neck with a faint rasping sound. "Jordan called me right after he found it and I warned him to touch nothing until the police arrived. It's not very far from here—if you'll follow me?"

He led the way down the side of the main building, across a lawn so lush you couldn't help wondering what gave it all that vitality. We passed a fountain with arcs of crystal-clear water gently playing from the open mouths of bronze cherubs, then headed down a tree-lined walk which had glimpses of impressive marble headstones on either side. They had done a real job on death in the Eternal Refuge; smoothed out all the unpleasantness, and if they hadn't quite managed to get over the permanence, they'd cloaked it with an expensive elegance that could change savage grief into trite philosophy in no time at all.

"Here it is, Lieutenant!" Williams stopped and pointed dramatically.

There was a large empty space between a soaring granite monolith on one side and a sculptured angel with bowed head and folded marble wings on the other. The hole was neatly dug in the exact center of the empty space, and the earth was neatly piled beside it. I took a couple of steps closer and peered down into the six-foot-deep cavity.

"Cheez!" Polnik said in a strangled voice beside me. "It ain't real, Lieutenant, it can't be!"

At the bottom of the hole lay a casket—a real expensive casket with what looked like gold handles and all. The lid was missing, and inside, resting comfortably against the plush velvet, was the body of a girl. A brunette, with long swirling hair that came well below her shoulders. She wore an evening gown of black faille which was very elegant, and strapless, showing the almost luminous quality of her white skin.

Her hands were neatly crossed over her breast, her eyes were closed, and there was a tranquil smile on her face. A golden bracelet on her right wrist was studded with rubies which winked in the sunlight.

"I don't understand how this could have gotten here," Williams said in an anguished voice. His lean fingers raked his forehead vigorously. "I don't see how it was possible. The gates are closed and locked by seven every evening, Lieutenant!"

I half-climbed, half-slid, awkwardly down into the hole beside the casket, then gently touched the bare arm just above the bracelet and found it was icy to the touch.

"She's dead, Lieutenant?" Polnik asked harshly, above my head. "I mean—she just ain't in a trance or something?"

"If that's a trance, someone should make a fortune with it. You'd better call the Sheriff's office and get Doc Murphy over here."

There was no sound for the next few seconds except for Polnik's heavy breathing. "The phone, Lieutenant?" he finally croaked. "It's inside that—that building?"

"You'll find a side door on your way back, Sergeant," Williams volunteered. "It opens into the janitor's office. There's a phone in there."

"Just so long as there ain't nothing else!" Polnik mumbled, then lumbered away like a circus elephant reluctant to balance on the big rubber ball.

I took a closer look at the girl in the velvet casket; at the hands folded so neatly across her breast—someone had gone to a great deal of trouble to achieve all that symmetry. A small, rust-colored stain showed faintly between the first and second fingers of her right hand. When I took hold of the wrist and lifted away her hand gently, there was a neat bullet hole through the bodice of her black faille dress, surrounded by a ring of dried blood.

So there was no deep trance that Polnik had hoped for—and we didn't need Doc Murphy to tell us she was dead, only how she had died and when. From somewhere above me I heard a faint, distracted moan.

"Lieutenant," Williams' voice cracked despairingly, "isn't that a gun wound?"

I scrambled back up the steep side of the hole, and stood on the lush green grass beside him. His hands had gone temporarily berserk—one scrabbling furiously at the back of his neck, the other seeking privacy inside his coat to pluck at his fine white linen shirt.

"The dreadful publicity!" His eyes rolled at the thought. "The newspapers will have a field day, Lieutenant! I don't know what the directors will say—nothing like this has ever happened to us before!"

"You amaze me, Mr. Williams," I said gravely. "You mean this is the very first casket—"

The scrabbling fingers suddenly deserted his neck and seized hold of an ear lobe with frantic desire.

"This is no time for bad jokes, Lieutenant!" His face was a putty color. "You don't seem to appreciate what a dreadful tragedy this is for us!"

"And for that girl in the casket," I snapped. "She's been murdered."

"Yes—yes, of course." His fingers relaxed momentarily. "I'm sorry—one can lose one's perspective at times like this."

"Have you ever seen her before?" I asked without any real hope at all.

"Oh, yes," he nodded. "Many times, Lieutenant."

"You mean you know her?" I goggled at him for a moment and now it was my turn to start scratching. "Who was she?"

"Miss Kains," he spluttered. "It was she who made all the arrangements."

"Arrangements?"

"She was Dr. Thorro's personal secretary," he said, as if it explained everything.

"What arrangements?" I snarled.

"For his wife's—ah—ceremony, this morning," Williams said painfully. "I told you earlier, if you remember, Lieutenant? The ceremony is scheduled for eleven—this plot was being prepared for the late Mrs. Thorro."

Sheriff Lavers sat in back of his desk and scowled at me in a kind of bewildered way, like he had to blame somebody and I was the nearest. "What time is it?" he snapped.

I checked my watch. "Five of eleven."

"So five minutes from now, Mrs. Thorro is buried in the same grave where we found the corpse of the doctor's secretary?" He shuddered at the thought and I didn't blame him. "This is going to leave everything else for dead the next two weeks in Pine City, you know that, Wheeler? People are going to be so goddamn busy talking about it, that if World War Three hits, they won't even notice!"

"Yes, sir," I said, because there wasn't anything else say.

"Thorro, as that superintendent already told you, is one of our more prominent citizens." Lavers bit off the end of a cigar and, with brooding precision, spat it into the metal trash basket beside his desk. "He's the leading psychiatrist in town, belongs on around seven or eight different committees for all the worthiest worthy causes. My God! They'll crucify us if we don't break this case real fast."

"You got any suggestions, Sheriff?"

He gave me a strictly hostile glare. "I'd like to make one but right now I need you, Wheeler, however repulsive the thought is to me! I want you to concentrate on this case to the exclusion of everything else, and that does include women. You can have anything you want—just name it—and I'll see you get it. Maybe we should call Homicide in on this?"

"That cemetery's in your county, Sheriff," I said mildly. "I don't figure we need all those big flat feet tramping over it the whole time."

"The lone wolf—the unorthodox cop?" he sneered heavily. "You'd better live up to your reputation this time—or else you're all through, Wheeler!"

"Yes, sir," I said patiently. "I did ask, you might remember, if you had any suggestions—and not for a handy set of rules on how to be a good lieutenant and eat my wheat germ regular every morning. Suggestions—like, anything I should know about approaching this hot-shot headshrinker? Any ideas about him, his wife, and his secretary—any juicy morsels that everyone in town knows but me? I figure if there's any dirt there, you're the guy to know it!" I finished admiringly.

There was a faint pinkish tinge in the Sheriff's eyes for a moment, but three quick puffs on his cigar, plus a timely recollection of what the doctor told him the last time, kept his voice almost mild.

"I sent Polnik to tell him about his secretary," he said, ignoring my questions. "So by the time his wife's funeral is over, he'll have gotten used to the idea—well, it won't be a shock anymore. That makes it easier for you to go and ask questions, doesn't it?"

"Maybe I should join him at the wake?" I snarled. "Sorry to hear about your wife, Doctor, real tough! And your secretary got herself murdered, too? Ah, well, that's the way the analyst's couch crumbles. Have another drink, Doc, and tell me all about it, huh?"

By the time I'd finished, Laver's head was shrouded in cigar smoke. "You handle it any goddamn way you like, Lieutenant!" he said in a choked voice. "But either you handle it, or Homicide does—it's your choice!"

"Okay, okay," I said hopelessly. "That offer of yours about me having anything I want—I guess you wouldn't include a three weeks' vacation in the offer?"

I was halfway to the door already by the time he'd shouted, "Out!"

CHAPTER TWO

Doctor Jason Thorro was a tall, lean guy, somewhere around forty, with an ascetic face and a close-cut head of prematurely gray hair. He wore a beautifully tailored dark suit that must have cost him upwards of three hundred dollars, and the accessories matched. The strong hands, with long, sensitive fingers, moved around the desktop in front of him incessantly while he talked.

"I appreciate your position, Lieutenant," he said quietly. "God knows who could want to murder poor Bernice Kains, but someone did apparently, and there has to be an investigation." He shrugged his shoulders helplessly. "I don't have to tell you what a shock it was to me when your sergeant gave me the details—a half hour before the funeral. And they left her body in Martha's grave!"

He got up from his chair abruptly and walked over to the window, standing with his back toward me.

"That couldn't be coincidence, could it, Lieutenant?" His voice sounded muffled.

"It doesn't seem likely," I said politely. "Do you have any enemies, Doctor?"

"My God!" He shuddered violently. "I hope I don't have any enemies who could hate me that much!"

"How about the girl—your secretary? Did she have any enemies?" I asked.

"Not that I'd know of," he said dully. "Bernice was my personal secretary, as you know, Lieutenant. A charming girl—a highly efficient secretary. What she did before or after office hours I wouldn't know."

"It was strictly a working relationship you had with Miss Kains—nothing personal at all?"

He swung around to face me, his mouth set in a taut line of disapproval. "I don't care for your innuendo, Lieutenant!" he said harshly. "I already told you—she was just a secretary."

"Sure," I said mildly. "How long had she been with you?"

"A year—maybe a little more. I can check my records if you want."

"Maybe later," I said. "How did you come to employ her?"

"My last girl left to be married," he said stiffly. "One of the employment agencies sent around five or six applicants. Bernice looked like the best of them so I hired her."

"She wasn't married?"

"Not to my knowledge."

"Did she have a steady boyfriend?"

"How many times do I have to repeat myself, Lieutenant?" he almost snarled. "I told you before—I knew nothing of her personal life!"

"If I don't ask these questions, Doctor," I said patiently, "a hell of a lot of other people will—including the newspapers. The girl's body being left in your wife's grave can't reasonably be coincidental. So it looks like whoever did it had good reason for hating not only the girl, but you also—or your wife, maybe?"

His face whitened again. "I don't have to tolerate this kind of slanderous suggestion, Lieutenant, and I'm not about to start. If you try and maintain this line of questioning, I'll see my lawyers right away!"

"That's your privilege, Doctor," I agreed. "But the deliberate placing of the girl's body in your wife's grave must have some significance, wouldn't you agree?"

He sat down and his fingers moved restlessly across the desktop. "I—I guess so," he said in a subdued voice. "I'm sorry. It's only natural you should ask these questions—it's just that right now I find them intolerable."

"Sure, I can understand that," I said. "But they have to be asked."

Thorro lit a cigarette to give his hands something positive to do, then puffed at it nervously.

"My marriage was not a success, Lieutenant," he said speaking very quickly. "It was a mistake. We both realized it after the first year but somehow we never got around to doing anything about it." A bitter smile turned down the corners of his mouth for a moment. "I guess my professional and social standing had a lot to do with it, and Martha enjoyed the luxury and social prestige she had as my wife, naturally. For the last five years we just drifted along.... We had a certain amount of mutual tolerance and that was all."

He crushed his cigarette savagely into the glass ashtray on the desk, then rubbed his hand across his forehead.

"What's the use?" he asked himself despairingly. "You want it straight, Lieutenant? We were lovers, Bernice and I—had been for the last six months!"

"And you still can't think of anyone who'd have a motive for killing her—like jealousy, maybe?"

"No," he said, shaking his head decisively. "No one. She came from Denver, and she didn't have any friends or relatives here in Pine City."

"How about your wife?" I suggested. "Maybe there was somebody who knew about you and Bernice Kains, and they figured your wife was getting a raw deal—then her death could've been the incentive for murder as revenge."

"I don't know whether Martha knew about us or not," Thorro said tiredly. "Even if she did, I doubt it would have worried her so long as I was discreet. Martha was a woman with a very practical sense of values—and if there was another man in her life, I certainly didn't know of it, Lieutenant." He shrugged again. "But when I come to think of it, I didn't know very much at all about Martha's life, outside of where we coincided."

I pulled out a cigarette of my own. "You're not being much help at all," I said gloomily as I struck a match.

"I'm sorry," he said mechanically. "Right now I can't think straight—you can understand that. Maybe if you talked with Tania Stroud, she could tell you more."

"Tania Stroud?" I queried.

"She was Martha's bosom friend and confidante." His mouth twitched in distaste. "They were always together—lunches, cocktails, dress showings, beauty parlors—I sometimes figured that Tania knew almost more about me than Martha did! She has an apartment on Lakeside

Drive. She's a widow with all the time in the world to indulge herself—and enough money to do it. Her late husband made the proverbial million and maybe he would have eased off enough to enjoy spending some of it, but a coronary prevented that!"

He scrawled the address on a note pad, then tore off the sheet and handed it to me.

"Tania was very emotional at the ceremony this morning," he said with a touch of dryness in his voice. "She cried loudly and hysterically from the moment we reached the cemetery—the chief mourner by right of assertion!"

"I bet Mr. Williams didn't approve of that kind of scene," I said.

"Williams?" Sudden interest showed in his eyes. "The superintendent out there, you mean? Interesting—very interesting. Quite advanced vermiphobia, I think!" He caught the blank look on my face and added, "Infestation of worms—an anxiety phobia, Lieutenant. You noticed how he keeps scratching himself the whole time?"

"I noticed," I said.

"A guilt complex, I would suspect." Thorro's voice was much crisper with professional enthusiasm. "I'd like very much to analyze him. I have a theory about people in his profession—they deal with the dead and those who mourn the dead the whole time. I feel this may very easily arouse a strong guilt complex. You see, *they* are still living and after a time it must strike them as being most unfair—in their world everyone else dies but them!"

"It's an interesting theory, Doctor," I said cautiously. "I figured Williams just has a bad case of eczema!"

"Really?" he snapped. "I doubt that very much, Lieutenant!"

"You prefer the infestation of worms jazz?" I twitched a little at the thought.

"The maggots of death eating away inside him," Thorro said, nodding enthusiastically. "It's a compensation, don't you see, a kind of squaring away with the guilt complex about being alive?"

For the first time since I'd entered his office, his face was animated. "'All right,' this man's subconscious mind says, 'I am guilty of living in a world of the dead, but the truth is I'm also dying like the rest of them.' Don't laugh, Lieutenant. Logic has no place in the darker recesses of the human mind!"

"Who's to laugh?" I asked nervously. "You just put me off spaghetti for life!"

I left the doctor's office on the sixth floor of the near new and so chic medical building, wondering how anybody who was real sick could have the effrontery to tarnish the soft pastel colors and shiny vinyl flooring with anything that so obviously didn't belong there, like disease.

For a couple of seconds on the drive out to see Tania Stroud I thought about taking a lunch break, but the vivid memory of Thorro's theory concerning the real trouble behind Williams' perpetual itch was more than enough to kill the pangs of hunger. Lakeside Drive did actually front a lake, a placid expanse of water complete with wildlife—ducks during the day and necking couples at night. In the early afternoon, with the still waters bright blue and covered with a sheen of sunlight, the lake had a lazy, timeless look about it that you'd automatically associate with the people living a life of leisure in the opulent apartment buildings and houses surrounding it.

I parked the Healey at the curb out front of the address Thorro had given me, and walked inside the building. I rode the automatic elevator alone and unwanted, locked in a wood-paneled, steel womb that would never rate a Mother's Day gift from me—until I was suddenly reborn on the twelfth floor. It took the pit of my stomach around five seconds to rejoin me, and by that time I was thumbing the buzzer outside the apartment door.

A vision in technicolor opened the door almost right away, and stood there looking at me—I think—but it took a while for my eyes to sort out all that dazzle. Finally I managed to get most of the colors into their right perspective; the flamingo-red was the color of her hair and lips, the gelid blue belonged to her eyes, and the lime yellow to her orlon sweater and matching tights.

She was tall, and what my old man, with a reminiscent gleam in his eye, would have called well built. Her bosom was a magnificent edifice, a superstructure, a monument to her femininity—and the hourglass concaveness of her waist made a delightful division between the jutting breasts and the breathtaking swell of her hips. There was a taut, lithe firmness about each one of those curves that produced a corresponding tautness in the back of my throat.

Her face—I finally got around to it—was pleasantly plump and, tearstained as it was right now, almost childlike. The coldness in her eyes thawed a little as she stared back at me almost as hard as I was staring at her.

"I'm glad you came," she said in a husky voice. "I was just thinking about you—come in!"

She turned and walked back inside the apartment and I followed her, enjoying the gentle roll of her lime-yellow bottom. We got into the living room with its picture window view of the lake, and its lush Oriental furnishings which were so hot a couple of years back.

"Sit down!" she commanded, pointing toward a long, low couch that flanked one wall.

I did like I was told. She moved over to the picture window, and pulled a cord so that heavy drapes rustled and slid together, cutting out the sunlight and the view of the lake. In the shadowy intimacy she moved back to the couch.

"Do you believe in telepathy?" Her voice vibrated slightly as she slid onto the couch beside me, pressing the length of one beautifully modeled thigh against mine.

"Thorro told you I was coming?" I asked the obvious question.

"Thorro?" Her mouth made a generous *moue* of distaste. "Please!

Don't spoil everything by mentioning that fiend's name!"

"But if he didn't tell you I was on my way, how else could you know?"

"You're being difficult, darling!" she sighed moodily. "I was just feeling like I needed a man when the buzzer went. I opened the door and there you were! You understand, *man?* It doesn't matter about a name—whether you came to fix the plumbing or sell a magazine subscription—thirty minutes from now you'll be on your way. A little numb maybe, but happy, and I'll have forgotten you ever existed!" She wriggled closer, so the weight of her breasts rested firmly on my chest, closed her eyes, and murmured, "Kiss me!"

"Maybe I'm a little numb already," I said hoarsely, "but I doubt if I'll be on my way rejoicing thirty minutes from now—and I doubt if you'll forget a cop so quick!"

Her eyes opened suddenly and wide. "A—what?"

"A lieutenant from the Sheriff's office," I said. "Al Wheeler. You are Mrs. Stroud, I hope, and not just one of my daydreams gotten out of hand and materialized—" I patted her nearest curve respectfully "—so delightfully solid?"

She moved away from me, putting a couple of feet between us real fast in a flurry of lime-yellow legs.

"The nerve!" she said indignantly. "Why didn't you say you were a police officer in the first place?"

"Well," I said with a small, sad smile, "cops are also human, they tell me—and something like you doesn't happen very often in our dull, routine life."

"You'd better state your business, Lieutenant!" she snapped. "I have a busy afternoon ahead of me."

"I could see that from the moment I walked in," I agreed sincerely. "I'm investigating the murder of Bernice Kains."

Tania Stroud squeezed two glistening tears gently from the corners of her eyes and I watched, fascinated, as they rolled slowly down her plump cheeks. "That's what I've been trying to forget!" she said in a broken voice. "My best friend in the whole world—dearest Martha—buried this morning—and even her grave had to be sullied by that dreadful woman!"

"Bernice Kains?" I checked, trying to keep abreast of events.

"The woman who made life a living hell for Martha!" she flashed at me. "But I don't blame her as much as I blame Jason Thorro—the fiend! He's to blame for everything—Martha dying the way she did, so young and all, and this other girl being murdered. It's all his fault!"

"How do you figure that?"

"You wouldn't understand," she sneered. "You're just a man like the rest of them."

"Wasn't that what you were looking for five minutes back?—a man?" I asked innocently.

She shrugged her shoulders irritably. "You damned well know the difference, Lieutenant. One is a purely physical urge, and the other is a question of understanding."

"Try me," I suggested. "I'm the sympathetic type."

"Do you know how Martha died?" she asked in a brittle voice.

"No," I admitted. "I haven't had time to find out yet."

"Then make time," she rasped. "It'll be well worth your while. She was deliberately driven out of her mind by that—that headshrinker—her husband! He got her into such a state that she just didn't know which end was up!"

"You mean she killed herself?"

"Oh, no," she said and smiled coldly. "He was much too clever to allow anything like that to happen. She had an accident. Poor darling, she was so confused all the time—and driving that wickedly fast sports car, it had to happen sooner or later, and that monster knew it!"

"You mean she was killed in an automobile accident?" I said blankly.

"That's what they called it," Tania Stroud said darkly, "but I know better! *He* planned it!"

"It's an interesting story," I mumbled. "I'll look into it."

"You don't believe me, do you?" The red hair billowed in rippling waves as she tossed her head.

"A little, maybe, but not too much," I said honestly. "I've got one murder for sure already, and I'm not in the market for another one, Mrs. Stroud."

"Men!" she moaned. "If you don't believe me, you ask Frank Corben—he'll tell you!"

"Frank Corben?"

"He was a good friend of Martha's," she said bitterly. "About the only one she had except for me."

"Sure, I'll ask him," I said. "Where do I find him?"

Her firm white teeth bit down on her full lower lip pensively while she looked at me for a long moment.

"Maybe he won't like it," she said. "You wouldn't tell him you got his name from me now, would you?"

"Cross my heart—cop's honor!"

"His place is the other side of the lake," she said. "It's called the Retreat, and it sits plumb in the middle of five acres of beautiful parkland. You can't miss it."

"I'll go talk with him," I said.

"You'll like Frank. He's got a great sense of humor, always kidding," she said. A plump hand rested on my thigh and a moment later the long nails dug sharply into my flesh. "But please be discreet, Lieutenant," she whispered. "Frank's a very lovely guy but sometimes he's got a nasty temper. Don't annoy him with too many questions or anything like that, will you?"

"I'll handle him with kid gloves," I promised, "and that reminds me—do me a small favor and take your claws out of my leg, huh?"

She got up from the couch in a sinuous movement, then stretched her arms over her head and yawned gently. The lime yellow sweater seemed glued—like my eyes—to that magnificent curved edifice for a couple of seconds, then she exhaled slowly.

"My!" There was an almost coy expression on her face as she looked down at me. "You're in such a rush, Lieutenant, you don't give a girl time for a second thought, even. Why don't you stay awhile and have a drink—or something?"

"I'm tempted, Tania," I said as I got to my feet. "But not right now, thanks all the same. Maybe some other time, huh?" I edged toward the door as I spoke.

"I don't think so," she said indifferently. "Now or never, that's my slogan. It's a funny thing, you meet so many guys who look like men but they all turn out to be rabbits in the end!"

"The last time I was in Hollywood I got Bugs Bunny's autograph," I explained regretfully. "It kind of changed my whole outlook."

CHAPTER THREE

"Retreat" it was called and retreat it was—sitting plumb in the center of five acres of parkland just like Tania Stroud had said—the sylvan glades so idyllic I figured any moment a crew-cut twosome, with one wearing a skirt for sex identification, would pop up from behind a bush and declaim excitedly that it's the mint-fresh taste that makes the real difference in a filter tip. When they finally manage to impregnate the tobacco with a touch of Scotch, then maybe I'll give up smoking the old-fashioned kind.

The house was a massive pseudo-Tudor, looking like a poor imitation of an English pseudo-Tudor, and they were pseudo enough, as I remembered from the long-ago wartime days in London's surrounding counties. I left the car on the gravel driveway and pulled the string that hung beside the massive oak front door. The antique bronze bell swung vigorously, acquainting those within that somebody awaited without.

Before the sonorous sound of the tolling bell had died away, the front door opened, and a maid gave me no welcoming smile. The smile she didn't need—not with that pert, slightly wanton, and nearly beautiful face. On top of her mop of short-cut blonde curls there was an honest-to-God frilly maid's cap that might have come out of a Hollywood French farce of 1935. Even if the face didn't say welcome with a spread of lips and flash of teeth, the slim body with its taut curves thrusting against the tight black uniform surely did. *Welcome, stranger—you're home*, it said to Wheeler, if not to the whole wide world.

For maybe five seconds then, there was no conversation while we looked at each other. I figured it was up to the maid because she'd opened the door and if she couldn't come up with a "Yes, sir?" I was happy to settle for a "It's about time, Bill Bailey!" Just as long as I got something. Another five seconds and I couldn't stand the suspense any more.

"If you don't have any attachments," I said confidentially, "my company will be happy to supply them—along with the vacuum cleaner."

"Whatever you're selling," the maid said flatly, "either we got it or we don't want it. Drive slowly on the gravel when you turn around—skid marks are a nuisance."

"That's what I always say," I said, nodding sympathetically. "But this face lotion I'm selling is guaranteed to remove anything, including the guy you got tired of last week. It comes complete in its own little vicuna flask with a camelhair stopper and you can—"

"What are you?" Her upturned nose wrinkled distastefully. "A kook, or something?"

"Maybe a kook, for sure a cop," I said happily. "Lieutenant Wheeler from the Sheriff's office, but you can call me Al."

"I wouldn't call you long-distance," she said with a disappointing lack of originality. "If you're a cop, then I'm a—"

"Don't say it!" I warned her, then showed her my badge. "I want to talk with Frank Corben."

"You're a cop for real?" She stared at the badge a few moments longer, then lifted her head and looked at me again reluctantly. "Wait here, I'll find out if he'll see you." The door closed in my face before I had time to argue.

I lit a cigarette while I waited, and thought wistfully that if this was one of the newer type maids, I should be running a domestic help agency and not wasting my time with law and order. Then the door opened again and she looked at me dubiously like she'd hoped I would have vanished before now.

"Mr. Corben will see you, Lieutenant," she said blankly. "I can't figure out one good reason, but I guess it's his problem, not mine!"

I stepped into the wide hallway, waited while she closed the front door, then followed her tightly bouncing black-satined rear until we came to a paneled door. She knocked, then opened the door and stood to one side. "You'll find Mr. Corben inside," she said briskly. "I bet he figures you for a kook, too!"

It didn't seem worth the time to argue, so I walked into the room and right away you could tell: in this kind of house, it was called, self-consciously, *The Den*. A large room that was self-consciously masculine with dark oak paneling, hunting trophies, and a couple of glass cases full of antique firearms. Four leather armchairs were arranged in a neat semicircle around the massive, empty fireplace, and sitting in one of them was a tweedy character smoking a pipe with a long stem and oversize bowl.

He climbed onto his feet as I came toward him. A genial smile combining with the transparent skin stretched taut over his facial bones gave the heart-warming impression of a screaming skull.

"Lieutenant Wheeler, isn't it?" He held out a gaunt hand and the cold spatulate fingers touched mine briefly. "I'm intrigued, Lieutenant, I don't often get a visit from the police." He made a low glug-glugging noise deep in his throat, in strict contrast to the previous reedy voice, so I figured it had to be laughter and someplace he'd made a joke I'd missed. "That is—" he glug-glugged some more "—this is the first ever!"

"I'm investigating the murder of a girl called Bernice Kains," I said formally. "Mrs. Stroud told me you might be able to help."

"Tania said that?" He removed his pipe from beneath his bloodless lips and stared at me with what looked like genuine surprise. "I wonder what made her say that!"

"Maybe she figured me for a kook the way your maid did?" I suggested coldly.

"Oh, dear!" He tapped the pipestem against his upper teeth and the sound rasped across my nerve ends. "Has Betty been rude again?"

"If Betty's the maid, you're right," I said. "I'd guess she's a little unique in the domestic help set?"

"She's all of that!" He glugged for a while—at least it was a break from that stem-tapping routine. "But she is a great help around the house, you know. I suppose that's why I put up with her idiosyncrasies. Please accept my apologies, Lieutenant!"

"With so much to look at, who hears what she says?" I asked gallantly.

Corben puffed good-humoredly on his pipe and nodded. "Yes, she is rather attractive, isn't she? I've noticed."

"Did you design the uniform, too?" I said.

His prominent, soft brown eyes hardened just a little as he glared at me. "I don't think that was in good taste, Lieutenant," he said reprovingly. "I shall ignore the remark."

"Bernice Kain's murder I can't ignore," I said. "The way Doctor Thorro tells it they were intimate friends, and he can't believe he's got an enemy who'd kill the girl, then plant her in the open grave waiting for his wife. The way Tania Stroud tells it, the doctor is nothing but a fiend who drove his wife to her death anyway, and she wouldn't be surprised if he killed the girl, either. How do you tell it, Mr. Corben?"

The skull in back of the translucent skin rearranged itself a little so that a look of mild bewilderment showed on his face.

"Tell what, Lieutenant?"

"You were a good friend of Mrs. Thorro's—you must have known something about her private life?"

"Oh—that?" He shrugged his sloping shoulders delicately. "I knew she and the good doctor didn't get along, of course. Poor Martha was a very emotional woman and at times, I confess, she could become quite boring with the detail of her domestic misalliance. But I never actually met her husband, and most certainly I never met this Kains girl, either."

He replaced the pipe between clenched teeth and sucked vigorously. "I'm sorry, Lieutenant, but you see I can't help you at all, I'm afraid."

"How about Tania Stroud?" I persisted. "What do you know about her?"

"The tigress, eternally stalking a mate through the jungle of life," he said lightly. "A temporary mate, of course. One could perhaps compare Tania more aptly with the Black Widow spider! She was certainly a close friend to poor Martha Thorro, and I don't think the doctor was ever one of her prey—but I could be wrong about that, Lieutenant."

"Yeah," I said, without much real hope. "Well, thanks anyway, Mr. Corben, for your time."

"My pleasure, Lieutenant. I'll have Betty show you out." He pressed a button beside the cavernous fireplace, then just stood there sucking his pipe contentedly.

The door opened a few seconds later and the blonde maid took a couple of steps into the room, then stopped and glared at Corben.

"You want something?" she asked shortly.

"Lieutenant Wheeler is leaving, Betty," Corben said evenly. "Please show him out."

Her mouth puckered disbelievingly. "You mean you called me in here just for that?"

"Certainly!" he snapped. "It is one of your duties, you may remember?"

"What's the matter with him?" she said, jerking a thumb in my direction. "He's forgotten how he came in already?"

"Betty!" Corben's lips clamped hard over the pipestem. "I want no more argument—show the lieutenant out!"

"Gee!" She looked at me with a derisive smile spreading across her face. "You want to hold my hand, Lieutenant, in case you get lost on the way?"

"It'll do for a start," I said enthusiastically.

Once again I followed the taut swing of her black satin hips out of the den and down the wide hallway. She opened the door for me with an exaggerated gesture. "You sure you can find your way to your car okay, or you want I should get you a seeing-eye dog, Lieutenant?"

"I wonder about you, Betty," I said. "A maid you're not—and Corben doesn't look the type to run to a mistress—but I could be wrong?"

"You got a great imagination, Lieutenant," she said easily. "Maybe there are times when a maid gets made, but not this one. I'm strictly the domestic help around here and if he don't like my party manners, he knows goddamn well this house would fall apart without me around—so I'm what you could call privileged."

A faint humming noise rose suddenly to a roaring crescendo, and I turned my head in time to see a white Mercedes come to a gravel-spraying stop beside my Healey. The driver climbed out and walked briskly toward the house, bouncing on his toes with an athletic vigor in keeping with his husky build. As he got closer, I saw he was young, maybe twenty-five, a couple of inches over six feet tall, and around one eighty in weight.

His shiny black hair was brushed back from a heavy, sun-tanned face and his alert dark eyes crinkled as he grinned at the maid.

"Hi, Betty!" he said in a cheerful bass. "How's the club's most successful hostess this bright and beautiful afternoon? Still playing tag around the kitchen table with old Corben the lecher?"

Finally the blonde's frozen expression penetrated and he looked at me for a moment, then back at her with an apologetic grin.

"I know—I should mind my manners. Well, introduce me, honey. This a new member?"

"This is Lieutenant Wheeler from the Sheriff's office," Betty said woodenly. "Lieutenant, meet Mr. Hal Baker."

The grin grew lopsided, then slid off his face altogether as he stared at me for a moment.

"Lieutenant?" he gulped. "Nice to meet you."

"And you, Mr. Baker," I said politely. "Does Corben really play tag around the kitchen table? I wouldn't have figured he had the strength, but I can appreciate the incentive just fine!"

"I was kidding, of course," he said, smiling uncertainly. "I'm always pulling the wrong kind of gag at the worst possible time."

"Any gag's okay if you're a member of the club, eh?" I suggested casually.

The smile got a strained look about it again. "That's just one of my more stupid running gags, Lieutenant," he explained much too carefully. "This house of Frank's is so goddamn big I always call it the country club—you know? And the other half of the lousy gag is pretending Betty's a hostess and not a maid."

"Sure," I said with an understanding grin. "I can see a running gag like that never misses, the way it broke up Betty just now."

"The one thing this girl lacks—a sense of humor," he nodded eagerly. "Well, if you'll excuse me, Lieutenant?"

"Go right ahead, Mr. Baker," I said politely. "I was just leaving, anyway."

He brushed past Betty into the house and headed toward Corben's den. I walked out onto the front porch, then turned for a moment and grinned at the maid.

"Thanks for showing me out, doll. Like it's been a real pleasure."

"Make it a Thursday next time you come visiting, Lieutenant," she said flatly. "That's my free day—I won't be here."

I heard the front door close in back of me just as I reached the Austin Healey; before I slid into the driving seat I made a note of the license plate number on the white Mercedes. Then I drove through five sylvan acres back onto the road again. My watch said it was three-thirty and there was still a whole big piece of the day left and maybe lime yellow was about to become my favorite color after all.

CHAPTER FOUR

Life, I figured profoundly as I rode the automatic elevator to the twelfth floor, gets more and more confusing. There was a time when a guy knew what he was, or figured he did, anyway—but these days it's hard to stay hip. I never did figure myself for an organization man exactly—I could have settled for being a status seeker—but now you got so many alternatives, from waste maker to hidden persuader, that it gets real hard to make a definite decision. When the vertical casket disgorged me finally on the right floor, I guessed I'd settle to be a sex-sampler and I didn't give a damn if Kinsey had put me out of date by close to a decade. If a guy liked his work, then what the hell? I figured as I thumbed the button beside the door of Tania Stroud's apartment.

Five seconds later I was so confused I'd forgotten the philosophy. I'd been expecting a technicolor vision, with a predominantly lime yellow theme, to greet me but somebody had pulled a fast switch and I'd gotten a big gray monotone instead. A big guy with a dark brooding face and his shirtfront unbuttoned showing a mat of coarse black hair on his chest. A guy who growled deep in his throat when he saw me, like he was starving hungry and I was hung from a hook in the butcher's window.

"I was hoping you'd come sneaking around while I was here," he said with heavy satisfaction. "All them lies she told me there wasn't any other guy at all! You know something, creep? By the time I'm all through with you, she'll be goddamn right!"

He gave me no time to argue the point. His left hand grabbed a fistful of my coat as he jerked me toward him, and his right hand rearranged itself into an ugly bunch of knuckles, poised ready to hammer into my face. I reacted fast, mainly out of respect for my teeth, and stomped hard on the instep of his nearest foot a couple of times. He opened his mouth to yell and I gave him a stiff-fingered jab in the solar plexus to confuse his vocal cords, then the side of my hand across his throat as a bonus.

I had plenty of time to detach his hand from the front of my coat while he just stood with his mouth wide open, eyes bulging, and his cheeks slowly turning a dull blue color. All in all, he had enough troubles already not to notice even, when I moved around him and walked into the apartment.

Tania Stroud was in the living room, sitting on the couch with her eyes open too wide and her flamingo-red hair about as disheveled as her lime-yellow sweater. The heavy drapes were still drawn across the picture window, giving the room that shadowy intimacy enhanced by the two glasses companionably touching rims on the small table beside the couch. It was the classic occasion for the clean-cut hero to blush modestly and ask if he was intruding.

"What—what happened to Benny?" she asked blankly.

"You mean the one with all that hair on his chest?"

"Who else?" she gurgled.

"He's having a little trouble with his breathing," I told her. "Either it's asthma, or he's been getting a little too much indoor sport lately. He'll be okay—I think."

The sound of heavy feet confirmed my forecast, and a moment later the big guy trampled into the living room with a red haze of contemplated murder and mayhem veiling his eyes as he came toward me.

"Tell him who I am, Mrs. Stroud?" I suggested while he was still ten feet away. "Tell him I can get him ninety-nine years for attempted murder even after I've shot him twice in the stomach in self-defense, huh?"

"Benny," Tania said in a strangled voice, "he's a police officer!"

"I don't give a goddamn what he is," Benny said thickly, "but right after I've finished with him, he'll be a—" He stopped suddenly, both voice and feet frozen at the same time. "A cop?"

"Lieutenant Wheeler from the Sheriff's office," Tania gulped. "I told you there isn't anybody else. Why don't you pin your thick ears back and just listen once in a while!"

"A cop!" Benny's face underwent a series of rapid and convulsive changes which finished in a lousy imitation of a smile.

"Well!" he croaked feebly. "Excuse me! I'm sure you understand, Lieutenant, I just made a mistake, that's all. I mean, I guess I had you figured for—"

"Sure," I said. "Let's forget it—you didn't hurt me any so I'll accept your apology."

"Thanks!" He closed his eyes for a moment while his body shook violently. "Thanks a whole lot!"

"I want to talk to Mrs. Stroud," I went on casually. "So why don't you get your coat and blow?"

"Talk?" His eyes disemboweled me and dropped live coals into the empty space left. "How long you going to be?"

I shrugged. "Who knows? An hour—a couple of days maybe. Why don't you call Mrs. Stroud sometime next week and find out?"

"Listen!" he bellowed frantically. "You can't—" Then he figured a lousy bastard like me maybe could and would. His massive shoulders sagged pathetically. "Sure," he mumbled. "I'll call you, Tania, huh?"

"Yes, Benny," she said, and carefully avoided his anxious gaze until he finally collected his coat and shuffled out of the room.

The front door slammed behind him and silence descended upon the apartment. I lit a cigarette and watched Tania Stroud straighten her rumpled sweater with two sharp tugs, then primp her hair for a while until she quit trying to rearrange it back into its original hairdo.

"You sure do call at the wrong times, Lieutenant," she said eventually. "Do you have something on your mind, or should I install a parking meter?"

"That Benny is an impetuous guy," I said idly. "What does he do for a living?"

"He drives a truck," she said casually. "I don't really mind what happened just now—he's gotten to be a nuisance lately."

"Where did you meet him?—at the club?"

"One night in a bar downtown," she said listlessly. "I was bored and he—club? What club?"

"The country club—Corben's place," I said.

Her hand touched her plump, smooth cheek nervously as she looked up at me. "Frank Corben told you about the club?"

"Sure," I nodded. "No secrets between Frankie-boy and me. I even got to meet the number one hostess—Betty."

"That bitch!" she snarled.

"It didn't show while I was there," I admitted, "but maybe you're right."

"I need a drink," she said tonelessly. She stood up, her hands absently smoothing the skintight pants over her well-rounded hips. "How about you, Lieutenant?"

"Scotch on the rocks, a little soda," I acknowledged gratefully.

She took the two empty glasses from the small table and carried them out into the kitchen. I stubbed out the cigarette in a fragile ashtray made of delicate bone china, then sat down on the couch. A few seconds later Tania came back into the living room, bringing the drinks with her. I took the glass from her as she sat beside me, a cautious and calculating glint in her cold blue eyes.

"Cheers," I told her, and drank some of the Scotch.

"I don't understand Frank telling you about the club." She raised her glass to her lips and drained the contents smoothly. "He told you everything about it, Lieutenant?"

"Everything," I agreed smugly. "Why don't you call me Al?"

"Why not?" She shrugged her firmly modeled shoulders indifferently. "He told you about Martha being a member?"

"Sure," I said, looking wise while I made a hopeful stab in the dark. "I even got to meet Hal Baker."

"I'll give Frank Corben a large piece of my mind in one-syllable words the next time I see him!" she said. "He must be out of his mind, tell you all—"

"Not all—just most of it," I corrected her. "He never got around to saying if Thorro was a member."

"Are you kidding?" Tania laughed mirthlessly. "A husband-and-wife team being members of Frank's club!"

"Yeah," I said blankly. "It does sound a little stupid at that, now you come to mention it."

"Can't you see Martha staying the weekend with Hal, while Thorro's with Betty?" Her laughter sounded genuine this time. "What do you figure they'd talk about at breakfast, Al?"

I finished the drink and put the glass down beside hers on the small table. A warm length of thigh pressed firmly against mine, and when I leaned back again, Tania had cut down the distance between us so now we were real close. The coldness had gone out of her eyes, replaced by a warm, anticipatory glow.

"You know something, Al?" she asked huskily. "Now you know all about the club, we don't have any secrets between us at all!"

"How long you been a member?" I asked.

She traced the outline of my jaw with one finger while she thought about it. "I guess it must be close to a year now," she said. "A girl friend of mine was a member and she introduced me to Frank Corben—that's how I first met Martha. I'd been a widow for six months then and I was terribly bored—you know how it is?"

"I can imagine," I said sympathetically. "Corben didn't mention the fees—an exclusive club like that would be expensive, I guess?"

"Naturally," she nodded, "but it's only money—and it is a very exclusive club, Al!"

"That figures," I said. "You have any idea of the total membership?"

"I guess only Frank could tell you that," she said idly. "The most people I've ever seen there at the one time would be six, maybe seven."

"It could get embarrassing having too many people there together?" I suggested.

Tania nodded, then snuggled a little closer to me, the warm glow in her eyes getting brighter all the time. "That's one thing I can't figure out, honey," she said in a puzzled voice. "How come Frank told you all about the club, just like that? I mean, you'd think he wanted to keep it confidential."

"I guess he was worried about the murder, and him being associated with Martha Thorro," I said. "This Hal Baker character—is he just a member—or a host the way Betty is a hostess?"

"I never bothered to find out," she said, with a touch of impatience in her voice. "Do we have to talk about the club all the time, Al? Don't you ever take time out to relax once in a while?"

"Sure, I relax," I said indignantly. "There are times I can get so relaxed, you wouldn't know me from a corpse, even! Only the other night, I—"

Her lips clamped against mine suddenly, chopping off my voice in mid-sentence. We stayed locked together in a violent clinch while her pliable body molded itself against mine with slowly increasing excitement.

After what seemed a hell of a long time, she moved her head away and looked searchingly at me—a slow smile widening her mouth as she made a gentle purring sound deep in her throat. The kind of sound that gets a tiger's stripes flashing like neons, and the white hunter reaching for his Magnum.

"Well!" Tania purred approvingly. "There's nothing like getting to know somebody the old-fashioned way, is there, honey?"

Maybe it was the memory of the frustrated truck jockey still fresh in my mind, or maybe I was just sick. Either way, I suddenly realized I had a whole bunch of things on my mind—and the redheaded tigress wasn't one of them. I got up from the couch and smiled at her politely, like the one nondrinking guest at a party of seasoned alcoholics.

"It's been fun," I said sincerely. "I have to be getting along now."

She looked at me with sheer disbelief staring out of her eyes while her mouth dropped open slightly. "You're kidding?" she gasped.

"It's all set out in the Sheriff's handbook of rules," I said regretfully. "Page five, paragraph four, subsection E; I quote—'No officer shall indulge in promiscuous byplay with a suspect, or witness, during working hours.'" I checked my watch. "It's five after four now and I don't quit until after six."

"You—you're going to walk out on me *now?*" The lime-yellow sweater rose and fell with frightening rapidity, giving me a sober appreciation of the brassiere manufacturers' constructional problems.

"But I'll be back, Tania doll," I promised, edging toward the door. "I'll be back."

"Ring the doorbell twice," she snarled. "That way I'll know it's you and won't need to bother opening the front door!"

"It's been that way all afternoon," I said gloomily. "Every dame I meet gives me the brush. It's hard to figure out why. My teeth are okay, the new deodorant works just fine—you think maybe dames find me repulsive because I am?"

"Get the hell out of here, you slob," she said viciously. "You make me sick to my stomach!"

CHAPTER FIVE

With the sun sinking slowly in the west on the drive back to town, I experienced the same sensation in my stomach, so stopped off for a steak sandwich on the way. Doctor Thorro's office didn't answer when I called from the diner's phone, so I tried his home number with more success. He didn't sound exactly enthusiastic when I told him I'd like to talk some more, but he agreed to wait there until I arrived.

When I got there it looked like the right kind of house for a guy like Thorro to live in—situated in one of the blue chip suburbs where the Pine City realtors add another zero to the asking price without even twitching. It was a big, rambling house, with an ornate and slightly fussy façade—like the architect had gotten worried at the last moment that it didn't look as if it had cost all the money the owner was paying.

Sprinklers swished gently over the wide expanse of front lawn as I walked up the flagged path to the front porch. The shades were pulled down on all the windows, giving the house a peculiarly lifeless look, which made good sense when you thought about it. I thumbed the button and heard chimes tinkle delicately somewhere inside, and a little while after that Thorro opened the door.

Maybe the lines on his ascetic face were etched a little deeper than they had been in the morning, or maybe it was my imagination. He looked at me for a moment like I was an unpleasant memory, then shrugged his lean shoulders under the coat of his beautifully tailored blue suit. "Come in, Lieutenant," he said quietly. "There's no one else in the house."

I followed him into the darkened hallway, through a vast living room and out onto the back terrace, which had been half enclosed to form a bar. There was a fresh drink on the bar top, and Thorro gestured toward an impressive array of bottles stacked on the shelves. "Can I make you a drink, Lieutenant?"

"Thanks," I said. "Scotch on the rocks, a little soda."

I sat on one of the stools in front of the bar while he made the drink. When he was finished and the glass stood in front of me, Thorro picked up his own drink and looked at me disinterestedly.

"You wanted to ask some more questions, Lieutenant?"

"Yeah." I tasted the Scotch with the reverence due to Chivas Regal. "Do you know a man called Corben—Frank Corben?"

"I've heard of him," he said. "Why?"

"He's the guy who was a real good friend of your wife's—according to Tania Stroud," I said. "But the way Corben tells it, your wife was just a bore about her domestic problems." He winced at that, and looked away for a moment. "This Corben," I continued, "has an interesting setup at his place—unique almost—the 'Retreat' he calls it."

"Oh?" Thorro grunted, his fingers beating a rapid tattoo on the bar top. "Has this anything to do with Bernice's murder, do you think, Lieutenant?"

"I don't know," I confessed. "How did you come to hear of Corben, Doctor?"

"If you must know, he was a patient of mine," he said coldly.

"I would have figured him for a nut," I said absently.

"Lieutenant!" His slate-gray eyes were cold. "You must know better than to use a stupid word like that! Corben was psychologically disturbed, that's all."

"Sure," I said apologetically. "From what I can make out, he seems to be running a kind of private club out there—a very intimate club."

"I'm not a member, if that's what you're hinting at," he rasped.

"I was wondering," I said, "if your wife was a member. Tania Stroud is, for sure."

Thorro rubbed one hand wearily across his forehead. "It's possible Martha was a member, Lieutenant, quite possible. I told you this morning that we led almost completely separate lives."

"So you did," I agreed. "Did you know Tania Stroud is also convinced your wife's death wasn't accidental? She figures you somehow murdered her."

"I wouldn't be surprised at anything Tania believes where I'm concerned." He laughed shortly. "I don't doubt you can find the coroner's report, Lieutenant, if you're inclined to believe her!"

"I'm not inclined to believe anyone at this time—and that includes you, Doctor," I said pleasantly. "I'm trying to find a murderer."

"All right!" He drained his glass empty, then slammed it down on the bar top. "I fail to see how this endless barrage of stupid questions can help in any way, Lieutenant!"

I sighed. "Sooner or later we professional people always run into that kind of answer, don't we, Doctor? Now why don't you make like you're relaxing on the couch and telling me whatever comes into your head, huh? Take Corben for a start. Tell me about him—as your patient, I mean."

"That's impossible," he snapped. "There's a question of ethics involved—you know that."

"There's a question of murder involved—and you know that," I snapped right back at him. "If it's question of professional ethics or withholding vital evidence—"

"All right!" He shook his head wearily. "What do you want to know about Corben?"

"Take it from the beginning," I suggested. "How he first came to you, what were his problems, anything he told you that could possibly be relevant."

Thorro smiled wanly. "Maybe it would be easier if you had his case history, Lieutenant. That is, presuming you have the time to read three closely written notebooks?"

"I'm hoping you'll give me a condensation," I said mildly.

He lit a cigarette and once his fingers had finished with the match, they ran nervously down the front of the suit onto the bar top and got back in the groove with that tattoo again.

"Corben was introduced by another patient," he said rapidly, "and if your suspicion that my wife was a member of his club is true, Lieutenant, you'll appreciate the irony of the situation. The patient who made the introduction was Tania Stroud!"

I lit a cigarette to keep him company and drank a little more of the Chivas Regal. "It's getting more like Old Home Week all the time," I said. "Go on."

"A very complex man," he said, almost to himself. "A man possessed of many devils—mainly a compulsive urge toward self-destruction. He's like a moth circling a flame, irresistibly drawn toward it—it you'll forgive the cliché. If Corben is not immediately involved in an emotional and dramatic conflict, he'll create one. These days, the accident-prone is generally recognized, and the cause is basically the same—a conscious or unconscious desire for self-punishment. Corben is violence-prone, to coin an awkward phrase."

"Is that why he runs that club of his?" I asked doubtfully.

Thorro shrugged impatiently. "Of course. He also has a very strong sex drive which has been diverted by this basic urge for self-destruction;

now he can only enjoy vicarious stimulation."

"How about breaking that down into words of one syllable for me?" I pleaded. "I'm just a working cop."

"There is no satisfaction for him in direct contact with a female at all," he said patiently. "But if he arranges—through his club as a private meeting place—for the enjoyment of others, then the thought of that will give him satisfaction."

"Cheez!" I said emotionally. "They used to say 'Poor fish!' This guy would swim downstream if he was a salmon, even!"

"Right," Thorro grunted. "You have the essence of his problem, Lieutenant, if that's any help? How it could be, I can't possibly imagine!"

"You said if he wasn't involved in a violent situation, he'd create one?" I queried.

"That's right."

"It's an interesting thought," I said sincerely. "How about Tania Stroud?— What's her problem, Doctor?"

"You've already met her, Lieutenant." A wry grin showed on his face for a moment. "You still need to ask?"

"I guess not," I admitted. "But it surprises me that she was looking for a cure."

"I'm not at all sure she was," he said curtly. "The genuine nymphomaniac is a rarity, in the medical sense, Lieutenant. I'm inclined to think Tania was more interested in having a captive audience to listen to her various exploits than in seeking effective therapy."

"It figures," I said. "Let's get back to a few of the solid facts, Doctor. When was the last time you saw Miss Kains alive?"

He made himself another drink and drank some of it, before answering. "My wife's death came as a dreadful shock, Lieutenant," he said in a low voice. "I'm not being hypocritical about this—we weren't close, as I've told you—but sudden death like a car accident—"

"Sure," I said sympathetically, "I understand."

He held the glass in both hands, staring down at the amber whisky while his fingers spread wide in a mute appeal.

"There was an autopsy—the coroner's court. I asked Bernice if she would arrange the detail for the burial with the Eternal Refuge— I wasn't sure I could stand up to it. She made all the arrangements with Williams out there. The last time I saw her was sometime yesterday afternoon in my office—around four, I think. She told me everything was taken care of with Williams and gave me a quick rundown—then she left."

"And that was the last time you saw her alive?"

"That was the last time," he muttered.

"Did she say where she was going after she left the office?"

Thorro shook his head. "I presumed she was going home to her apartment—since the accident there had been a considerable strain upon both of us, you understand?" he said miserably.

"Yes," I said politely. "Just one other thing, Doctor—do you know a man called Baker, Hal Baker?"

"Baker?" he repeated, his eyebrows knit in a thoughtful frown. "Not that I recall. Is it important?"

"In his mid-twenties," I said, "very good-looking guy—black hair, nice sun tan, around six feet tall and all muscle?"

"Yes," he said, snapping his fingers suddenly. "Now I remember! I did meet him once, about three months back. He came into the office to meet Corben; he was in the waiting room when we came out, and Corben introduced us. Does he have anything to do with—with Bernice's murder?"

"I don't know yet," I said. "He's a member of Corben's club, that's all I do know."

Thorro's mouth tightened with distaste. "I can imagine! He looked the type."

I finished my drink, then slid off the bar stool. "Thanks for your time, Doctor. You've been a real help."

"I certainly hope so," he said bitterly. "We would have been married—after a reasonable lapse of time. But now—" His fingers tightened convulsively and the fragile glass suddenly broke in his hand.

He looked down at the shattered glass, and watched with detached interest as blood from one deeply gashed finger dripped steadily onto the bar top. Then he laughed with a harsh, grating sound, "That's kind of funny, Lieutenant, isn't it? I blame myself for Bernice being murdered—fundamentally the fault is mine—so the hidden guilt complex seeks atonement." He held up the bloodied finger, showing the deep gash. "I try and punish myself! You think I should try analysis, Lieutenant?"

The sun had long set by the time I got back to my own apartment. After I'd left Thorro's house I'd gone back to the office and given Sheriff Lavers a rundown on what I'd found out so far. By the time I'd finished, he was about as confused as I was, and that was no help. We'd snarled at each other a little, then called it quits for the day.

I made myself a drink, and got some audio therapy out of a Peggy Lee record playing on the hi-fi machine. By the time the record had finished, I was all stretched out and relaxed in an armchair with my eyes nearly closed. The harsh, imperative squawk of the buzzer brought me to my feet in a traumatic reaction.

It could be anyone visiting, I figured on my way to the door, from Sheriff Lavers to that scratching Williams—come to sell me an exclusive plot at cut rate because he figured I didn't have too much time left to make my arrangements—and that was a thought to stop me opening the door at all. But the essential courage of the Wheelers broke through, along with the wild hope that it could be a dame calling, even, so I manfully swung the door open wide with a welcoming, if cautious, smile on my face.

The wild hope had suddenly paid off. It was a dame all right who stood there with a faint smile on her pert, wanton face—a dame called Betty. She was a maid who didn't look like a maid, and right now she wasn't even dressed like one. The frilly cap had gone from her tight blonde curls, and the black satin uniform had been replaced by a black crepe top with a scooped-out neckline and a white silk chiffon skirt that whispered luxuriantly around her legs as she moved.

"Surprise!" she said in a bright voice. "I bet you weren't expecting me, huh, Lieutenant?"

"You mind if I just touch you—make sure you're real?" I asked nervously.

"Some guys will find the lousiest excuses!" she exclaimed in mock horror. "Keep your hands to yourself, Lieutenant, puh-lease!"

"I don't remember giving you the address," I said. "But maybe you were just irresistibly drawn here by the force of my magnetic personality?"

"Why don't you ask me in—or is your wife home?" she asked casually.

"I'm not married so it's okay for you to come into my apartment," I told her graciously. "The rest of the harem won't mind, I'm sure."

We got into the living room and Betty sank into an armchair, crossing her legs deliberately with that delightfully intimate sound of swishing silk.

"Can I make you a drink?" I asked.

"Sure—you got two hands," she said amiably. "I'll have whatever you're having."

"That could lead to an interesting situation," I said thoughtfully.

I made the drinks, gave her one, then sat opposite her on the couch. "It would be fun to believe the magnetic personality bit, Betty," I told her. "But somehow I can't."

She smiled ruefully. "That Hal Baker—what a dumb, muscle-bound character he is!"

"He is?" I asked innocently.

"Shooting off his mouth like that, before I had a chance to put him wise you were a cop, even," she said. "By the time he'd finished babbling, you were ahead of him, right?"

"Maybe. You drop around to tell me I was wrong?"

She tasted the drink, then wrinkled her nose appreciatively. "This is good Scotch," she said with genuine enthusiasm. "I don't get to taste it very often. Frank Corben is the kind of crumb who's mean about small things—and always the small things that are most important!" Her smile thinned a little as she studied my face intently. "You know damned well you were absolutely right, Lieutenant, don't you?"

"You sure have a double charge of citizen's public spirit, Betty!" I said admiringly. "Taking all this time and trouble just to confirm my suspicions this way. I would never have figured altruism was one of your strong points."

"It sounds to me like there's a dirty crack wrapped up in there somewhere," she said suspiciously.

"You have to have an angle, honey," I suggested patiently. "I'm waiting for the fast curve."

She drank a little more Scotch while she thought about it. Then she recrossed her legs with even more deliberation so the white silk skirt rode up a couple of inches over her knees—delectable knees with cute little dimples—then sighed heavily.

"I don't want any trouble, Lieutenant—Lieutenant? Don't you have a name?"

"Al," I said. "Please call me Al. It makes everything so homey and all. That way I can look at your knees without pretending I'm not—like we're real good friends."

"Okay." Betty shrugged her shoulders, and for one breathtaking moment the scooped-out neckline was much more so. "I figured maybe we could make a deal, Al."

"What kind of deal?"

"I'll tell you whatever you want to know about the club—and you leave me in the clear whatever happens afterward."

"I'm investigating a murder," I said, "and I'm only interested in Corben's club from that angle. I'll make a deal with you this way, Betty. You tell me what I want to know, and if the murder investigation busts the club wide open, I'll do my best to keep you out of it."

"That sounds all right by me," she said. "What do you want to know?"

"How does the club function?"

"There's a joining fee," she said. "Exactly how much I wouldn't know, but knowing Corben, I'd bet it's plenty! That gives a member the right to use the premises whenever he wants—a night, a weekend. He gets a private room with all the privacy he wants and no questions asked."

"There's more to it than that, honey," I said gently.

"Yeah—I guess there is." She laughed but it didn't sound like she enjoyed it. "If a member's looking for company in the club they can always find it with another member—if you get what I mean? Like, if you're a member and you're available, you're expected to oblige."

"And if a male member can't find another female member available, then there's always the club's hostess ready to oblige?" I prodded.

"Yeah, that's right." A faint tinge of pink showed on her cheeks as she lifted her head defiantly. "I guess you figure that 'hostess' is a pretty fancy name for it, huh?"

"It doesn't worry me either way," I said honestly. "How about Corben? Does he join in the fun and games? Or is he too busy managing the club?"

"Him—join in?" She laughed again, this time in genuine amusement. "That creep! He gets his kicks out of peeping through keyholes!"

"How about Baker? Is he a member—or a host, the way you're a hostess?"

"He's a member," Betty said flatly. "He's stinking rich—needs to be to belong to that club—and he can't find anything better to do with his time, I guess. There are a half-dozen guys like him who belong."

"How about the women? Tania Stroud?"

She shuddered. "Do me a favor, huh, Al? Don't mention that witch in my hearing! Given half a chance, she'd be doing my job for free—just for the kicks!"

"Was Martha Thorro a member?"

"Sure, she was," Betty answered promptly. "Although she wasn't a real enthusiast like her dear friend, Mrs. Stroud!"

"Was her husband—Doctor Thorro—a member?" I asked casually.

"No," she said. "At least, I've never seen him at the club—and I would have if he was a member."

"What's the total membership?"

"Around fifteen, sixteen, I guess. I can give you the names, if you want."

"Not now, anyway," I said. "Thanks, Betty—you've been a big help."

She looked faintly disappointed. "Is that all? Don't you want to hear some more? Some of the things that have happened at the club you wouldn't believe! There was this night when Tania Stroud came in late—after midnight—with a guy on either arm and one in back of her, carrying her bags! And not one of them was a member. Well, you can imagine how mad Corben got! He—"

The phone jangled suddenly, and Betty stopped speaking, a disappointed look on her face. I got up from the couch and went over to answer it.

"Wheeler?" a long-familiar voice barked in my ear.

"Yes, Sheriff?" I said resignedly.

"That Eternal Refuge place—some character just called in from there—sounded like a maniac! I couldn't get too much sense out of him, but it sounds like trouble. You'd better get out there and take a look."

"At night?" I said nervously.

"This Williams out there is screaming murder, fire, arson—the whole crime calendar," Lavers snarled. "You'd better get out there right now, Wheeler, you understand?"

"Why not send Polnik—he's got nerves of steel," I lied glibly. "Graveyards at night are his idea of a summer camp."

"Get—out—there!" the Sheriff said, on the edge of a volcanic eruption. "I'll be waiting in my office to hear from you!" There was a thunking noise in my ear as he hung up.

Betty looked at my face and smiled sympathetically. "Trouble, Al?"

"The call of duty," I said miserably. "My theme song is about to become a haunting refrain. 'Don't go down to the graveyard, Daddy, it's better to stay out of the tomb!' That kind of jazz."

"Al?"—she looked concerned. "Are you feeling all right?"

"Never worse," I assured her. "I'll faint at the first inexplicable sound. Thanks for visiting with me, honey, it's been informative if not fun. See you around, huh?"

"How long will you be?"

"Who knows?" I shrugged helplessly. "An hour—a lifetime. The Eternal Refuge—what a *hell* of a place to go visiting after dark!"

"I hear you, but nothing comes through," she sat doubtfully. "Maybe you're sick or something?"

"I'm sick for sure," I brooded. "There's a great nervous nothing where my stomach used to be!"

"Maybe I should wait until you get back, make sure you're all right?" she suggested.

"Thanks for the thought," I told her. "But I could be gone all night for all I know."

"It doesn't matter—this is my free night of the week." She stretched her arms above her head and yawned sensually, the black crepe top suddenly stretched tight across the swelling curves underneath. "You want I should wait, Al?" she asked softly.

"Why not?" I said hopelessly. "I'll probably need every pallbearer I can get!"

CHAPTER SIX

The entrance to the Eternal Refuge showed up stark and foreboding in the glare of the Healey's headlights, and the bronze gates stood open wide, so I drove on in. There was a sudden chill in the night air, and pockets of white mist writhed above the concrete strip all the way down to the main building.

I stopped the car adjacent to the massive Gothic arch that framed the two bronze doors, and lit a cigarette, getting all the light chatter I needed from the fingers that held the match. Two blue lamps burned dimly above the doors, so I could see that one of them was slightly open. While I watched, the door opened a little wider and I got a momentary glimpse of a white face peeking around the edge. Then a slight, dark figure appeared, and bounded down the wide concrete steps toward me.

"Lieutenant?" a trembling voice squeaked as he came close to the car. "Is that you?"

I recognized the voice and felt a little better—at least he was wearing a suit and not a winding sheet. "Sure," I said, and climbed out of the car. "It's Wheeler, Mr. Williams."

"Thank Heaven you're here at last!" He almost fell into my arms and the thought was so repulsive I sidestepped smartly, just in case. "You don't know what I've been through!" he moaned. "It's been a ghastly experience—like living a nightmare! I feel as if the whole world has suddenly gone mad!"

"What's the trouble?" I asked cautiously.

"You'd better come inside and look for yourself," he said, twitching painfully. "The moment I discovered it, I called the Sheriff's office right away. I don't understand what's happening at all!"

"Me neither," I said irritably. "And frankly, Mr. Williams, you're not being a help. This place may be home to you, but it gives me the feeling I'm starring in the late show—with Bela Lugosi playing the second lead!"

"Come, I'll show you!" He grabbed my arm and pulled me toward the steps. "You'll have to see for yourself to believe it!"

"You're the kind of guy they send to the nursery to comfort the kids when the ship's sinking," I snarled at him. "You've got the touch!"

We went up the steps and into the building, then through the dimly lit reception area with its marble-tiled floor and vast emptiness. Our footsteps sounded hollowly down a long-tiled corridor, past a number of dark, oak-paneled doors which were mercifully closed. Williams stopped suddenly in front of another closed door at the end of the corridor, both hands scratching his chest furiously. "In here, Lieutenant," he said in a sepulchral voice, then pushed the door open wide.

I stepped into the room reluctantly, with the superintendent close behind. It was small and dim and completely bare except for the centerpiece—a casket resting on a small bier surrounded by sweetish-smelling flowers.

"What is this place?" I croaked, then added quickly, "Don't tell me—I don't want to know!"

"The casket, Lieutenant!" Williams hissed frantically, one berserk hand seemingly trying to gouge out his right eye. "Take a look for yourself!"

I tried hard to think of a reasonable alternative—like screaming "Uncle!" and running for my life—but there wasn't any real choice. My feet felt like lead weights as I slowly edged close enough to take a look inside the casket.

It was another of those plush, velvet-lined jobs, and it had an occupant. A little old man, with a shock of gray hair, and a wizened-up, gnarled face. He lay there peacefully with his eyes wide open, staring blankly at the ceiling. There was an ugly, blood-encrusted hole in the center of his forehead.

"He's the one who opened up the gates for us this morning," I said numbly.

"Jordan!" Williams agreed, while the index finger of his right hand deserted his eyeball and probed experimentally at the lobe of his ear. "The janitor."

"How did it happen?" I asked.

"He relieves—relieved—the regular nightwatchman two nights a week," Williams said rapidly. "I was home, doing some paperwork, and I realized I'd left some important papers in my office here so I came back to get them." The index finger had found the itch and gyrated madly around his earlobe, giving a weird impression of a guy with a rundown mind trying hard to wind it up again.

"I came into the reception area and called out a couple of times," he continued. "Then I thought I heard someone moving around in the corridor—when I got there, this door was wide open. It should be locked, you understand Lieutenant, like the rest of them at night, so I came in here to investigate. As soon as I stepped inside the room, I heard a door slam behind me and someone ran through into the reception area. Whoever it was must have hidden in one of the other rooms until I'd gone past." He shuddered. "To think if I'd actually discovered him, he could have killed me the same way!"

"Then you found Jordan's body in the casket?" I checked.

"Well, yes, naturally I looked inside to see what had interested the prowler." There was a rasping sound as long nails raked the back of his neck. "When I saw it was Jordan's body, you can *imagine* how I felt—all alone in this room with a murderer maybe prowling around inside the building!"

"I can imagine, but I'm not going to try," I said nervously. "What time did all this take place?"

"I got here at about quarter past nine."

"You never actually got a look at this prowler—or murderer?"

"No," Williams admitted reluctantly. "I only heard his footsteps."

"Then how do you know it was a him, and not a her?"

"I don't." He blinked at me a couple of times. "But surely, Lieutenant, you couldn't think that a woman—"

"I've given up thinking," I growled. "There's no percentage in it. I'd better call the Sheriff and get things organized."

"You can use the phone in the reception area," Williams said helpfully. "I'll come with you, Lieutenant."

He used both hands to obliterate a new area of sudden itch in back of his head. "I don't know what to think now!" he added in a sudden burst of confidential information. "I was attracted to my profession in the first place by the promise of peace and quiet—no ugly disturbances or arguments—a place where a man could be soothed by an atmosphere of tranquil harmony. And now, in the last twenty-four hours, my whole world has been shattered! It makes a man reconsider, Lieutenant, I can tell you!"

"I can appreciate your problem, Mr. Williams," I said soberly, as we headed back down the corridor toward the phone in the reception area. "If I worked in this place, and then suddenly started thinking, they'd be carrying me out wrapped real tight in a straitjacket within the first hour—on my way to the nearest sanitarium!"

By day, the Sheriff's office is bad enough, even allowing for his secretary—that blonde bundle of Southern dynamite, Annabelle Jackson—being around. At midnight, the office was nothing but gruesome, and almost no improvement on the Eternal Refuge—except maybe the stiffs here were walking and talking.

Lavers sat behind his desk, the cigar in his face burning like a short fuse. Doc Murphy lounged against the wall with his hands thrust deep into his pants pockets, an expectant look of unholy glee lighting his satanic face. I was sitting in an uncomfortable visitor's chair facing the two of them, trying to ignore Murphy and wondering why I hadn't chosen a reputable profession like morgue-minding instead of becoming a cop in the first place.

"All right," Lavers said finally. "Let's get back to the first murder—the girl—Bernice Kains. Leave us stay with the facts instead of your wilder fancies about motivation, Wheeler!"

"Anything you say, sir," I agreed politely.

"We'll start with the time of death." He glared questioningly at Murphy.

"Sometime between ten P.M. and midnight," Murphy said laconically. "She was shot with a thirty-two-caliber bullet which entered her left—"

"Yes, yes," Lavers snorted impatiently. "We can skip the medical details. Her body was discovered out at the cemetery early the next morning by the handyman—Jordan."

"Handyman?" I shivered a little. "You have a macabre choice of words, Sheriff."

The burning end of his cigar glowed a violent red. "When was the girl last seen alive?" he growled.

"Thorro said she left his office around four in the afternoon," I volunteered. "That was the last time he saw her."

"I had Sergeant Polnik do some checking at her apartment house," the Sheriff said tautly. "She didn't go back there that night—at least if she did, none of the other tenants, or the janitor, saw her either come in or go out again."

"Maybe she went straight out to the cemetery and sat and waited at the open grave like a good girl until somebody came along to knock her off?" Doc Murphy suggested blandly.

"That's very funny, Doctor," Lavers said in a murderous voice. "It must be all those indifferent autopsies you perform that give you your keen sense of humor."

"It's hanging around this office mainly, listening to you guys try and solve a murder case," Murphy said, cackling derisively. "Oh, brother!"

The Sheriff's face was shaded a mottled purple with instant outrage. "If I may make a suggestion, Doctor," he said, his voice trembling with repressed emotion.

"You may," Murphy said, with a condescending smile.

"Get the hell out of my office!" Lavers screamed at him.

"I was just going, anyway," the doctor said coldly. "If it's of any interest—which I strongly doubt—the old man, Jordan, hadn't been dead long at all when I examined him. Not more than a couple of hours, I'd say."

"Which would put the time of death around nine tonight," I said. "That figures— Williams said he got back there about nine-fifteen, and the murderer was still there."

"I'll let you know the caliber of the bullet in the morning," Murphy said, on his way to the door. "If you ask me real nice and polite, that is!"

The door closed gently behind him.

Lavers glowered at me for a while. "Let's get back to our facts, Lieutenant—if I'm not boring you with tiresome detail?"

"You're about to bore me—but not with detail, Sheriff," I assured him. "Leave us remember the first body was only found early this morning—and now we've got a second murder within twenty-four hours. It hasn't given us much time to collect a lot of facts, detailed or otherwise."

"Obnoxious!" Lavers suddenly crowed in triumph. "That was the word I wanted to describe Murphy. Come to think of it, it'll fit you nicely, too, Wheeler!"

"Sheriff," I said carefully. "It's later than I care to think about and I've had a long, hard day. So let us not waste any more time trading insults, huh? You had Polnik out looking for facts all day, and I was out looking for suspects. Now we still don't have many facts. We do have some suspects. We do have some motives, and we do have a second murder. Right?"

"Right," he said grudgingly. "Now what?"

"So now we can try and establish some facts about our suspects," I said patiently. "We can find what kind of alibis they can come up with for both murders. We can check out our suspects' suspicions about other suspects, too."

"What?" Lavers goggled at me for a moment. "Take that again slowly, will you? I'll bet it makes no more sense than it did the first time!"

"We can check the reports on Martha Thorro's car accident and see if there's any chance it wasn't an accident, like Tania Stroud suggests," I snarled. "We can check if Frank Corben had any opportunity of creating a violent situation around the time the Kains girl was murdered, like Thorro suggests he could. We can check out Mrs. Stroud herself, and this good-time Baker playboy. In fact, we got a real busy day ahead of us, Sheriff"—I got out of the chair and walked toward the door quickly—"so I'm going home right now to get a good rest!"

"Hey!" His stentorian bellow stopped me halfway out of the office. "Come back here—I'm not through yet!"

"Sheriff!" I looked back at him over my shoulder with a reproachful look. "You're not about to tell me you've got a brand-new fact hidden up your sleeve?"

"Only that the time to call Homicide in on the case is a hell of a lot closer than you think," he snarled. "Now go home and sleep on that, Wheeler!"

I went out of his office into the darkness that shrouded the world outside, got into the Austin Healey, and went back to my apartment—where I'd forgotten I had company waiting.

The company was stretched out comfortably on the couch, her head cradled on a cushion, the white silk skirt hiked up around the tops of her thighs. One look at those long shapely legs and suddenly the last thing I needed was a good rest.

"Hi!" Betty said sleepily, then got up into a sitting position, swinging her legs down from the couch so her feet touched the floor. "What time is it?"

"A quarter after one," I told her. "I didn't figure on you still being here."

"That's nice—real gallant!" She stifled a yawn. "Would you like some coffee or something?"

"No, thanks." I dropped into an armchair and lit a cigarette, and a closer view of her legs only confirmed my first impression of their quality.

"What was so urgent that got you out in the middle of the night?" she asked drowsily.

"An old man named Jordan, the one who found Bernice Kain's body this morning," I said, "was murdered out at the cemetery."

"Murdered!" Suddenly she was wide awake. "That's terrible! Who did it?"

"The same person who murdered the girl, presumably," I said. "And don't ask who that is, because I don't know."

Betty shivered slightly and pulled her skirt down over her legs to a point of respectability. "It gives me goose pimples just thinking about it!"

"It gives me a pain all over," I said tersely. "So let's not think about it for a while, huh? How about I make us a drink instead?"

"That's fine by me," she said, shrugging amiably. "You can skip the soda this time, Al."

"Sure." I moved over to the table and made the drinks, then took them back to the couch and sat beside her.

"Here's looking at you, Al!" She drank some of the Scotch, then giggled suddenly.

"I could use a laugh, honey," I told her. "How about letting me in on the joke?"

"It just struck me as being kind of funny," she gurgled. "I never got cozy with a cop in my whole life before!"

"Cops are well organized for getting cozy," I said frigidly. "Why else do you figure we carry handcuffs all the time?"

"Threat—or promise?" She looked at me steadily for a few moments, then sighed gently. "You want me to go, Al?"

"Maybe I'm a little nervous—disturbed even," I said indignantly. "The way you talk, anybody would figure I was clear out of my ever-loving mind!"

Betty sighed again, but this time it was all languid, and very relaxed. When she had finished the drink I took the empty glass out of her hand and placed it beside mine on the small table fronting the couch. A moment later she slid into my arms like my middle name was "Home." Her lips were cool against mine, hinting at a controlled passion—just below the surface—that could explode into a volcanic eruption anytime. The contrast with Tania Stroud's predatory approach was pleasing—and about ten times more exciting. It had me going in no time at all.

Sometime later she pulled away from me suddenly and moved to the far end of the couch. Her hair was tousled, her lipstick smeared. Somehow she'd lost her black crepe top, and the creamy-whiteness of her shoulders contrasted strongly with the strapless black satin bra that fought a losing battle to contain her thrusting curves. "Abandoned" would have been the right word to describe the way she looked—except her blue eyes had a steady, dispassionate gaze as they held mine.

"It couldn't be something I said," I reasoned out loud. "Was it something I did?"

"Everything's fine, Al honey," she said easily. "Real fine—but let's just get our facts straight before we go any further, huh?"

"You've been talking with Sheriff Lavers!" I said, accusingly.

She was too busy looking around the room to bother answering for a few seconds. Then she raised her right arm and pointed hopefully. "The bedroom's in there, huh, Al?"

"That's right," I agreed coldly. "You want to see the kitchen, too? Maybe we could get real cozy and exchange some hot recipes, or something?"

"Let's go!" she said briskly, jumped to her feet and walked toward the bedroom like she was dedicated.

"Anything you say, Betty," I mumbled confusedly.

By the time she reached the door I was right there behind her. She stepped inside the room, then turned her head and looked at me with a serene smile on her face.

"It's just that I've got this thing about couches, Al," she confided in a honey-sweet voice. "They give me a feeling of insecurity—you know?"

"Sure," I said knowledgeably. "It's no rare thing. Some time back an actress who was an intimate friend of George Bernard Shaw said exactly the same thing in almost the very same words—more or less."

"George Bernard Shaw?" Betty thought hard for a moment as she repeated the name, then shrugged her beautiful shoulders with indifference. "Who the hell is George Bernard Shaw—another sneaky cop, huh?"

I was about to do the playwright justice, but right then the white silk whispered in faint protest as it slid to the floor and the sight of Betty—wearing only the strapless bra and the briefest of panties—as she stepped daintily out of the skirt, paralyzed my vocal cords. But I figured G.B.S. would have understood okay—even if he was a vegetarian.

CHAPTER SEVEN

I got into the office around ten the next morning, having put Betty into a cab a half hour earlier on her way back to the five sylvan acres where Frank Corben was king. Annabelle Jackson looked at me distastefully, like I was something better left out in the rain, as I walked up to her desk.

"I can see it's been another one of those nights, Lieutenant," she said frigidly. "You look like a walking corpse and that isn't decent!"

"Control your maternal feelings, honeychile," I told her in an equally frigid voice. "This haggard face is the result of a nightlong endeavor, above and beyond the call of duty!"

"And what was her name?" she said, smiling acidly.

"You think I'd lie to you, magnolia blossom?" I asked.

"Sure," she said without hesitation. "Compared with you, Benedict Arnold was a man of high integrity!"

"If we only had an electric chair in here, I could make some southern fried chicken," I said to nobody special. "Sheriff Lavers in his office?"

"He's out," Annabelle said briefly, her head bent forward over her typewriter, "but Sergeant Polnik's waiting inside with a coroner's report or something, to give you. He's been waiting an hour already, so I guess he'll be real glad you finally arrived—that is, if you can manage to stay awake long enough to get in there, Lieutenant?"

"I dreamed about you last night, honeychile," I said fondly, watching the top of her blonde head stiffen warily. "That's why I can't stay awake this morning—all I want is to get back into that dream." I sighed audibly. "Just the two of us on the banks of Swanee River under a harvest moon—but you wouldn't sit down because you'd gotten yourself a bad case of sunburn. I did tell you it was a nudist camp?"

Her right hand grabbed for the heavy steel ruler that lay within reach of her desk, so I moved fast into the inner sanctum, closing the door carefully behind me in case she decided to throw something.

Sergeant Polnik looked up at me with an expression of almost unbearable pain etched deep into his face.

"Lieutenant," he said slowly, "I been thinking!"

"I know," I murmured sympathetically, "it hurts."

"Maybe I could get me a job driving a truck?"

"You got fired?" I asked incredulously.

"I'm about to quit," he mumbled sadly. "There was a time when somebody knocked off somebody, they'd pick someplace simple, like inside an apartment, or on the street—but now!" He shook his shaggy head in sorrow.

"Now what?" I asked blankly.

"I heard about that second corpse turning up in a box out there just like the dame did," he said in a shuddering voice. "If this is the kind of homicide the future holds for us, Lieutenant, I don't want no part of it!"

"I wouldn't let it worry you, Sergeant," I said in a soothing voice. "Maybe we'll catch up with whoever knocked them off before they have a chance to make any more corpses. Anyway, you haven't had a chance to meet any of the beautiful dames on this case yet."

"Dames?" A pallid gleam came into his eye. "What dames, Lieutenant?"

"You stick with me today, and maybe we'll meet up with some of them," I said optimistically. "Did the Sheriff leave a coroner's report for me?"

"Sure, Lieutenant." He tossed the folder across the desk toward me. "Right there. Dames, you said?"

"Blondes, brunettes, redheads—" I said idly. "Do something for me while I read through this." I found the note I'd made the previous day of the license plate number of the white Mercedes sports car, and handed it to him. "Check out the owner—should be a guy named Hal Baker. I want the address."

"Right away, Lieutenant!" Polnik grabbed the note from my hand and lumbered toward the door, then came to a sudden stop a couple of feet away from it, "How many dames did you say, Lieutenant, exactly?"

"I lost count after the first half-dozen," I lied nonchalantly. "But I remember the blonde said she was crazy about guys with muscles."

"Yeah?" He flexed his biceps automatically. "How about that?"

Fifteen minutes later I'd finished reading the coroner's report on the death of Martha Thorro, and I wasn't any the wiser. She'd been driving her own car at night, and about three miles from Lakeside Drive had failed to negotiate a tight curve, so the car had gone through the safety fence and rolled two hundred feet down a steep hill until it hit a tree.

The autopsy had shown evidence of alcohol, but not enough to prove she had been intoxicated. Thorro had given evidence saying that his wife had left the house around 7:30 that night to visit her friend, Mrs. Stroud, out on Lakeside Drive. To his knowledge, she had only had one martini before she left. She seemed perfectly normal and was in no way mentally disturbed.

Tania Stroud had done her best with innuendo to alter that picture—dark hints at domestic strife with a cruel, heartless husband who was steadily driving poor Martha out of her mind—but she had no way of substantiating any of it. Judging by the record, the court hadn't been at all impressed by her testimony. So—unless Tania was holding out—there was no logical basis for her insistence that Thorro had been directly, or even indirectly, responsible for his wife's death.

The door crashed open and Polnik's elephantine tread shook the whole office as he came up to the desk.

"I got it, Lieutenant!" he said triumphantly. "The Baker Private Zoo and Menagerie!"

"How many green stamps did that take?" I said, goggling at him.

"The registration number," he said in an injured voice. "You asked me to check it out, remember?"

"And that Mercedes is owned by a private zoo and menagerie?" I said wonderingly. "Come to think of it, that Baker guy could belong in a zoo."

"I know the joint," Polnik said proudly. "It's out in Cascada Canyon. I took my old lady out there one Sunday but she didn't go for it—figured all the wild animals were maybe too wild for her. She likes the kind of animals that'll sit up and beg for peanuts—" His shoulders shook suddenly with helpless mirth. "She tried feeding peanuts to a thing they call a puma, or something, and it goddamn nearly took her arm off at the elbow!"

The glades were about as sylvan as they had been the day before, when we got out there an hour later. Polnik wasn't impressed—for him, Nature was strictly a matter of curves that jiggled a little whenever the owner walked around—but when the front door of the pseudo-Tudor house opened and Betty stood there in that cute maid's uniform, his mouth opened so wide he nearly dislocated his jaw.

"Well!" Betty grinned at me derisively. "If it isn't Lieutenant Whatever-it-is! I haven't seen you in a long time, Lieutenant—not since breakfast, anyway."

"I'd like you to meet Sergeant Polnik, Betty," I said formally. "Give him a couple of minutes to get his chin off his chest and he'll look almost human—you'll be surprised."

"Gee!" Betty took a deep breath which flattened the tight black satin like a second skin over her lithe curves, and looked at Polnik with a significant, melting gaze, "I'm just crazy for the genuine caveman type," she said throatily. "Where you been all my life, Sergeant?"

"Duh—duh—" Polnik strangled helplessly, his eyes moist with emotion.

"Gosh!" Betty closed her eyes rapturously. "A real primitive—he can't even talk yet!"

"He doesn't have to," I explained. "He just stands around and listens to me. Right now he's here to listen to me talking with Corben."

"You'll have to raise your voice, Al baby," she said happily. "Good old Frank is out right now."

"When do you expect him back?"

"When I see him—sometime tonight, I guess. He's gone over to Hal Baker's place. You'll find him there if it's worth your trouble."

"I guess we'll do that," I said. "Thanks, Betty."

"You'd better leave the sergeant here, honey—" she giggled suddenly. "You don't want to lose him, I guess—and you know what kind of a place Baker's got out there?"

"I'll take a chance on it," I said recklessly. "Say goodbye to the lady, Sergeant."

"Duh—duh!" Polnik wrestled frantically with his vocal cords and lost again.

"It was nice meeting you, Sergeant." Betty smiled brilliantly at him, winked deliberately, then turned and walked back inside the house, her hips swaying in an exaggerated rhythm under the tight dress as she went.

We were halfway to Cascada Canyon before Polnik got his voice back.

"Geez!" he exploded suddenly. "What a dame!" A huge paw gripped my arm suddenly, and I winced while I waited to hear the bones crack.

"I got to thank you, Lieutenant," he said emotionally. "You did me one big favor this morning!"

"I did?" I said cautiously.

"Yeah." He gulped. "If it hadn't been for you I could've turned in my badge right then—and I never would've gotten to meet that doll!"

"Ah, well," I said modestly. "You can do me a small favor in return sometime—like if somebody shoots at me you can throw yourself in the way so you get the slug in your chest."

"You hear what she called me?" he asked hoarsely. "Primitive—that's how she had me figured right from the start! My old lady should live so long!" He closed his eyes happily so he could enjoy the memory without any distractions, and stayed that way until we got to Cascada Canyon.

A large billboard just inside the six-foot-tall steel gates proclaimed that the Baker Private Zoo and Menagerie was open to visitors on Sundays only, from ten to five. It also said DANGER, in big red capitals, and unauthorized persons entered at their own risk. I stopped the Healey about a foot from the gates and leaned on the horn until finally somebody appeared on the inside.

There was a bad-tempered look on the guy's face as he snarled and pointed to the billboard, emphasizing that Sunday was visitor's day and obviously this was Thursday.

I got out of the car and showed him my badge. Close-up, he looked bigger and even more bad-tempered than he had from the car. A guy with a build like a pro fighter, his muscles bulging under a stained sweatshirt, he could have been an ex-rodeo rider who quit after his face had been kicked a few times.

"I don't know," he growled uncertainly. "The boss has got company—he's real busy right now."

"Sure," I said. "So am I—so leave us not waste everyone's time. Open up the gates!"

He scratched his ear for a moment, then shrugged his wide shoulders. "I guess you're the law—and if you want in, you're in!"

I got back into the car and waited while he unlocked the gates, then drove through.

"Keep right on going on this road," the muscular character yelled in my ear, "about a quarter of a mile. You got to walk the rest. Take the walk to your right and you'll find the boss down there with the big cats."

The dirt road came to a sudden stop a quarter mile further on, the way he'd predicted. There were three cars and a truck already parked there, so I put the Healey beside the truck and we got out.

"Hey, Lieutenant!" Polnik pointed at the truck. "You see that?"

"Sure—it's a truck," I said patiently. "I saw a truck in Pittsburgh once."

"I mean the bars!" he grunted reproachfully. "This must be what they use to bring in all their wild animals, huh, Lieutenant?"

The back of the truck was loosely covered by a tarpaulin, but when I looked a little closer, I could see the strong bars underneath which converted it into a giant, mobile cage.

"I guess you're right, Sergeant," I admitted. "Let's go find Baker—and Corben, I hope."

A sudden, ferocious roar almost split my eardrums, and I saw the blood drain rapidly from Polnik's face "Geez!" he whispered. "What was that?"

"It's a zoo, ain't it?" I said impatiently. "So that was one of the wild animals."

"What kind of animal makes a noise like that?" he asked dubiously.

"Why don't we go find out?" I suggested, and led the way down the right-hand walk.

Fifty yards further on, a sharp turn brought us onto a wide concrete strip, flanked by huge cages on either side. A dignified lioness yawned hugely as we went past; a puma coughed nastily, then disappeared silently into the gloom at the back of his cage. Three tigers padded up and down, doubt and insecurity showing on their faces—looking for all the world like a crisis in some Madison Avenue executive suite.

Then another concrete strip opened up to our left and I stopped abruptly as I saw the two motionless figures staring into a cage at the far end. As we walked toward them there was a sudden tremendous thud right beside us, followed by a spitting snarl of disappointment.

"Lieutenant!" Polnik's voice was a thin squeak. "What the hell was *that?*"

The massive black shape inside the cage returned my nervous gaze with unblinking, tawny-colored eyes.

"A black panther," I mumbled. "That's what the card says, anyway."

Polnik stared at it for a few seconds, then turned away from the cage in shuddering revulsion. "That thing looks to me like I'm lunch!" he muttered. "I see any more like him, Lieutenant, I'll start figuring that cemetery is a fine place to sleep in!"

The two figures stood motionless, absorbed in whatever went on inside the cage, and didn't even turn their heads to look at us as we came close.

Tania Stroud's magnificent figure was encased in a sweater and tight ranch pants—but the outfit was a deep sapphire blue instead of lime yellow this time. Frank Corben wore another of his tweedy suits, which badly needed pressing and looked like they'd skinned the original shaggy dog to get the raw material. An unlit pipe was clenched between his teeth, and the strong sunlight seemed to pierce the transparent skin stretched tight over the bones of his face, making the screaming skull beneath more noticeable than ever.

There was a look of rapt concentration on Tania's plump face—a peculiar, excited gleam in her normally gelid eyes. I looked to see what made for all this concentration—and right away I was hooked along with them. Behind me I heard Polnik's sudden sharp intake of breath and knew he was hooked, too.

Inside the cage was a few hundred pounds of striped ferocity commonly known as a tiger—and for company he had around 180 pounds of muscular male commonly known as Hal Baker. Not even one shiny black hair was out of place, and there was a cool, confident grin on his sun-tanned face as he watched the tiger. He held a fragile wooden chair in his left hand, and a long, heavily plaited whip with a deadly steel tip in the other.

For maybe thirty seconds they just stood watching each other, with neither man nor beast making any movement at all. Then Baker made a sudden jab with the chair and the tiger backed up instinctively as the chair legs thrust toward its face. It gave a spine-chilling roar and dropped into a crouch, ready to spring at its tormentor.

"Yeah!" Baker grinned coldly. "C'mon—stupid! About time you showed some guts."

His right arm moved swiftly so the whip snaked upward in a graceful arc, then cracked in an explosive sound. The tiger seemed to freeze as it heard the menacing crackle. The threatening crouch changed character and became merely a frightened huddle. Stark terror showed in its amber eyes for a moment before it turned and padded swiftly toward the far end of the cage.

"Aw, hell!" Baker snorted disgustedly. "I figured this cat was chicken the first time I ever saw the mangy—" He cracked the whip again and the tiger answered with a low, growling murmur of fright.

"Hal," Tania Stroud called in a throaty voice. "Why don't you ginger him up a little, huh?"

He stared at her for a couple of seconds, then an evil grin spread slowly across his face. "You mean—like this?" he asked softly.

The next moment, the whip arched through the air again and descended across the tiger's back with a bone-shattering force, wrapping itself tight around the giant cat so the steel tip bit cruelly into its soft underbelly. There was a frenzied roar of mingled pain and fear. Baker then jerked the whip free so that it flailed high into the air with a vicious, singing sound and descended again upon the shivering striped body.

"That's it, Hal!" Tania yelled suddenly, her eyes glistening feverishly. "Give it to him good, boy!"

Five, maybe six, more times the whip flailed through the air; then Baker stepped out of the cage, his face glistening with tiny globules of sweat, a satisfied smirk set firmly on his face.

"You're all man, Hal!" Tania threw her arms around his neck and kissed him noisily, in an excess of emotion. "You sure taught that big cat who's boss around here!"

"It was quite an experience," Corben said, then made that glug-glugging sound deep in his throat. "I've never seen anything like it before, you know? Fascinating!"

At the far end of the cage, a quivering striped mound lay on its side—

the dark blood making small pools of glistening brightness on the dusty concrete.

Baker looked up and saw me for the first time. A look of recognition showed in his alert dark eyes, and he smiled politely.

"Lieutenant Wheeler, isn't it? How did you enjoy the show?"

"Like Corben just said, I found it fascinating," I told him. "That's the first time I've ever seen a fight between two wild animals in a cage in a zoo."

CHAPTER EIGHT

The cold, contemptuous silence lasted until we reached the cage that contained the black panther: then Baker stopped suddenly and glared at me.

"If you don't understand, Lieutenant," he said crisply, "I guess I'm wasting my time trying to explain."

"Try me," I suggested. "Maybe I'm wrong and it's not just sadism after all. Maybe a whipping like that one you just gave that tiger tones up its circulation or something?"

He took a deep breath, then spoke with slow deliberation. "It all depends how you feel about living, Lieutenant. Most people want to hang onto life as long as they possibly can—so they don't take any chances they can avoid. But there are other people who figure life's a gamble anyway, and if you don't take a few risks here and there it can get goddamned dull!"

"Like the guys who race cars, fight bulls, and hunt big game in the African jungles?" I suggested.

"Yeah," he said, nodding earnestly. "With me, it's facing up to something that's big and real dangerous at close quarters—like that big cat just now."

"Maybe I could sympathize a little more with your point of view if the animal got a chance of equaling the score—even once!" I said coldly. "Once in a while a matador gets gored, the big game hunter gets eaten—you know, like *they* take a risk?"

He grinned again, then rolled up his shirtsleeves, exposing the upper arm and the deep, jagged scar that ran from his shoulder down to his elbow. "Like that?" he queried politely.

"Yeah," I had to admit reluctantly, "like that."

"You get that from the tiger, huh?" Polnik asked with sudden interest.

"He wouldn't bite a cream puff!" Baker said contemptuously. "No, sir. That was a present from this baby!" He slammed his hand against the bars of the panther's cage affectionately, and there was a faint stirring noise from the back of the cage, then two liquid amber eyes gleamed in the gloom.

"Satan, I call this baby," Baker said jocularly. "He's the goddamn meanest cat I ever saw! He hates people—can scent a human being within a mile, I figure! But maybe that's because I keep him hungry all the time."

"Why, Hal?" Tania asked, breathing heavily. "Why don't you feed him?"

"I feed him okay," he said. "Just enough to keep him from starving all the time. I'm building him up for a showdown. Around a week from now he'll be at his peak—that's when I'm going in there again." His fingers touched the loose knit scar tissue tenderly in a gesture close to a caress. "But this time I'll win!"

There was an opaque, out-of-focus look in his eyes for a few seconds as he thought about that; then he shrugged his powerful shoulders easily and grinned again. "I guess you didn't come all the way out here to Cascada Canyon just to see the big cats, huh, Lieutenant?"

"I came to see Corben," I told him. "But now I'm here and the three of you are together, it could save a whole lot of time if I talked with all of you together."

"Whatever you say," Baker said casually. "Why don't we go on up to the house? Be a hell of a lot more comfortable up there, and I can use a drink, anyway."

"That's fine by me," I agreed.

"It's a ten-minute drive," he said. "We'll take Frank's car and you can follow us in your own, Lieutenant, okay?"

The house was a big sprawling split-level, built into the side of the hill overlooking the zoo. We sat on the covered veranda admiring the view, while Baker distributed the drinks. The ominous mixture of sounds from the caged animals below drifted leisurely up to the house and formed a continuous uneasy background to any conversation.

Tania and Frank Corben were sitting on a couch facing me, and Baker joined them after he'd finished with the drinks. Polnik sat in an armchair beside mine, a slightly glazed look on his face as he stared at the ripe contours of Tania's body, revealed under her tight-fitting sweater and ranch pants. Every time she took a deep breath, I could almost hear the sergeant's mind turn over with a sharp, rattling noise.

Baker took a long pull on his tall, frosted glass, then grunted appreciatively. "That's better! Now—how about these questions, Lieutenant?"

"Sure," I said. "Bernice Kains was murdered the night before last—sometime between ten and midnight. I'd like to hear some alibis for that time. Let's start with you, Corben."

The screaming skull pursed his lips in an old-maidish reaction, then raised his shaggy eyebrows in obvious surprise. "Me?" He glugged nervously for a few moments. "You want me to establish an alibi, Lieutenant?"

"Yeah—you!" I said with great restraint.

"It seems hardly necessary, since I never even knew the girl," he said coldly. "But if you insist—I was home all evening."

"The club?"

"The Retreat—that's the name of my house!" he said sharply. "I was there from about six that night until the following morning."

"Can anybody substantiate that?"

"Betty, the maid," he snapped. "This is ridiculous!"

"How about you, Tania?" I looked at the redhead.

She took an extra deep breath of indignation, and I swear I heard Polnik moan softly.

"Are you out of your mind!" she gasped. "What possible reason could I have for—"

"Just the alibi, honey," I said wearily. "Save your life story for the confession magazines."

"I was home—in my apartment!" she said frigidly.

"Alone?"

"Well—" She hesitated for a moment. "No, there was someone else there."

"He's got a name?"

Her plump cheeks reddened slightly. "You've met him already, as I remember?"

"The truck jockey?"

Baker laughed with genuine amusement. "I got to hand it to you, doll!" he said admiringly. "You got more energy than a whole circus full of wild cats!"

"Shut up!" she snarled at him. "You're not so lily-white yourself."

"How about you?" I looked at Baker. "Were you home, too?"

His face sobered suddenly. "Sure I was—needed an early night so I took the opportunity. But you'll have to take my word for it, Lieutenant. There was nobody else here."

I drank some of the Scotch, then looked at Corben again without saying anything at all. After a little while he got restive, and shifted uneasily on the couch. "What is this, Lieutenant?" he demanded shrilly. "Some kind of third degree?"

"I'm just curious," I said truthfully. "Let me give you a quick rundown: Thorro told me he never got along with his wife, but he got along with his secretary just fine. She was his mistress, and after his wife's death they planned on getting married, even. So whoever murdered the Kains girl and took all the trouble to leave her body in Mrs. Thorro's grave, must have been motivated out of hatred for Thorro."

"How can you be sure of that?" Corben asked fiercely.

"I'm the guy who asks the questions!" I snarled back at him. "Thorro had no idea who could hate him that much, but he suggested I talk with his wife's best friend. So I asked Tania—and she said I should ask Frank Corben. At your place I met Betty, and the one thing you could never mistake her for would be a maid! On the way out I met Baker, who mistook me for a new member of the club, and made it sound real fascinating—so I went back to Tania and she filled in the detail for me. Somehow she got the impression you'd already told me most of it!"

Corben scowled at Baker, who shrugged his shoulders and grinned apologetically. He turned toward Tania.

"You stupid little bitch!" Corben said in a flat monotone. "I should—"

"But you won't," I said.

"All right!" His teeth bit savagely on the stem of his unlit pipe. "So you found out about the club—but that's no reason for me to murder a girl I'd never even met!"

"It was reason enough to go back and have another chat with the doctor," I said. "He was real surprised to hear about the club—and that his late wife had been a member. Apparently in all those long sessions on his couch, you'd never gotten around to telling him either of those facts, Corben?"

"I would have been crazy to tell him!" he snapped.

"Thorro didn't want to discuss a patient," I said easily, "but murder overrides professional ethics, so he finally opened up. You're a fascinating study in psychosis, Frank, did you know that? The way Thorro puts it, you got an affinity with violence—you have to surround yourself with it the whole time. And if there isn't enough violence, you're the kind of weirdo who'll go out and create some!"

"This is outrageous!" he said in a choked voice. "How dare you make these vile insinuations!— I'll call my lawyers—I'll sue you for—"

"You got to admit it makes for an interesting situation, Frank," I said mildly. "Here I got a violent situation—murder—and suddenly I find a psychotic with a fixation for violence right in the middle of it!"

"Just what the hell is it, exactly, you're trying to say?" he asked hoarsely.

"You never even met the Kains girl, you said—but she was Thorro's secretary—she was right in his office! How the hell could you miss seeing her every time you went to Thorro for your analysis?"

The translucent skin, stretched taut across the bones of his face, was an unhealthy gray pallor, as he stared blankly at me.

"Well, naturally," he gurgled, "I did meet the girl, but I never *knew* her, Lieutenant. She was just a receptionist as far as I was concerned."

"How about last night?" I asked briskly. "Where were you around nine?"

"Home."

"Alone?"

"No—not exactly." The pipe bobbled up and down again. "The maid was there."

"You're lying in your teeth!" I said nastily. "I can tell you for sure where the maid was at nine last night—inside my apartment!"

Baker laughed again, and Corben swung around on him, a murderous expression on his face. "Don't laugh too loud, Hal," he said tautly. "Or I might tell the lieutenant something that'll wipe that grin right off your face!"

"Are you threatening me, Frank?" Baker said in open derision. "You don't have the face for it, boy! More like a gopher than anything I've ever seen—outside a gopher, of course!"

"Damn you!" Corben screeched furiously. "I've had all I can take from you—you posturing crumb!"

He swung back toward me, his face working furiously. "Why don't you ask the fearless lion tamer about Bernice Kains? He knew her real well. Any time she had left over from Thorro—and she had plenty— she used to spend it up here with him. They had what you might call an intimate friendship, Lieutenant!"

"You lousy pimp!" Baker snarled, then jumped up from the couch, grabbed the lapels of Corben's coat, and hauled him onto his feet. "You dirty, lecherous-minded keyhole peeper," he said viciously. "It's goddamn well about time somebody taught you to mind your own business!"

"Let go of me," Corben whimpered pleadingly. "Don't you dare lay your hands on me! Lieutenant—I appeal to you—make him let go!"

"I wouldn't want to soil my hands," Baker sneered contemptuously.

He released his grip on the lapels and Corben staggered backward as the pressure suddenly eased. Then Baker half turned, his arm moving like a piston, and sank his balled fist deep into Corben's stomach so the screaming skull folded over it, jackknifed with pain. Baker grunted, then put the flat of his hand against the gaunt face and pushed. Corben fell back onto the couch and lay there, writhing in agony.

"That's right, Hal!" Tania looked up eagerly, her eyes gleaming with excitement—and something else. "Give it to him good—the lousy creep!"

"Shut up, why don't you?" I snarled at her, over the steady droning sound of Corben's physical anguish. "I'm getting awful sick of hearing you sound off like ladies' night in the gladiators' arena!"

Polnik lumbered onto his feet and walked toward Baker with a heavy, deliberate tread. For a moment the lion tamer stood waiting for him with clenched fists, and I felt almost sorry for him if he was serious about standing up to the sergeant's primeval fury. Then he suddenly changed his mind and slumped into the nearest chair.

"The hell with it," he said in a bored voice. "It gets more like a two-reel slapstick comedy all the time."

Corben managed to straighten up a little on the couch, both hands clasped tight across his middle in ever-loving memory of his solar plexus, a look of vindictive hatred plastered across the thin face.

"Ask him about Bernice Kains, Lieutenant," he shrilled. "Go ahead! Ask him how many times she was up here the last couple of months— how many nights she stayed here alone with him? Ask him, why don't you?"

"Because I won't ever get the chance unless you clam up for a while," I said irritably.

Hal Baker took a pack of cigarettes from his top pocket, selected one with great care, then held it between his teeth while he searched for a match.

"Okay," I said hopelessly. "So how about Bernice Kains, Baker?"

He waited until the match had flared before lighting his cigarette; making a big production out of it, blowing out the flame with a thin stream of smoke.

"I don't know what you're talking about," he said calmly.

"He's lying!" Corben shouted excitedly. "I saw her up here myself a dozen times or more! If you don't believe me, ask his foreman—Kozowsky!"

"That headshrinker knew what he was talking about with that affinity for violence bit, Lieutenant," Baker said easily. "This guy is a nut from way back!"

"You mean you never knew the Kains girl at all?"

"That's exactly what I mean," he grunted. "Frank has rocks in his head!"

"What were you doing last night around nine?" asked him.

"I need another alibi?" He looked mildly surprised.

"For two murders, you need two alibis," I agreed, "Somebody knocked off the watchman at the cemetery last night. It figures to be the same person that killed the Kains girl."

"I was here all evening—all night as far as that goes—from around five on," he said.

"Alone?" I said wearily.

"You called it, Lieutenant."

"Now—you see, Lieutenant?" Corben said eagerly. "He hasn't got an alibi for either one!"

Polnik glared at him coldly for a moment, then looked inquiringly at me. "You want I should clobber him this time?" he asked in his gravelly voice.

"Only if he tries to say anything, Sergeant," I said thoughtfully. "Then let him have it right between the eyes."

"You wouldn't dare—" Corben's voice tailed off in a high-pitched squeak as Polnik took a threatening step toward him.

I figured I wasn't about to get any further with more questions right then—another ten minutes with these psychos and I'd need a headshrinker all to myself—so I stood up and gestured to Polnik.

"Let's go," I told him.

"You want to talk with Kozowsky, you'll find him around on your way out," Baker said confidently.

"I'm sure," I snapped.

We got as far as the doorway, then there was a sudden flurry of limbs, and the screaming skull was right beside us.

"Don't leave me here alone," Corben pleaded fearfully. "That maniac will kill me!"

"I guess there's nothing to stop you walking back to your car with us," I said reluctantly.

"Thank you!" The thought straightened up his spine a little, and he was even brave enough to look back at the other two. "How about you, Tania?" he asked hopefully. "Can I give you a ride back to town?"

"With you?" Tania said scornfully. "I wouldn't ride with you to your own funeral—not even for laughs!"

She got up from the couch in a sensual, undulating movement, and moved across the room until she stood in front of Baker's chair, her hips moving in a primitive, jungle rhythm all their own beneath the tight blue pants.

"I'm staying right here," she said softly, "with a real man who knows how to handle a tigress!"

"Yeah?" Baker came onto his feet, facing her. He reached out leisurely and grabbed a handful of her sweater, pulling her toward him for a moment so that their bodies met in sharp collision—then he pushed her away with a lazy arrogance. She stumbled backward and fell onto the couch, her eyes shining hotly as she looked up at him.

"I guess it's just me that's leaving," Corben glugged maliciously. "I don't think he'll need the whip for this one, do you, Lieutenant?"

"Hey!" Baker said sharply, and started to cross the room toward us. "Hold it a minute, you creep!"

"Don't let him touch me!" Corben squealed frantically and skipped behind the protection of Polnik's massive shape. "I appeal to you as an officer of the law, Lieutenant!"

Halfway toward us, Baker stopped and bent down suddenly to pick up something from the carpet. He straightened up and grinned at Corben, holding out a long-stemmed pipe in his hand. "This is yours, isn't it?" he said.

"Oh!" The screaming skull took a nervous step away from the sergeant's protective bulk. "Yes, it is."

"Don't you want it?" Baker asked amiably.

"Er—thank you," Corben mumbled, and took another step.

He finally stopped a couple of feet away from the lion tamer and held out a twitching hand.

"I always figured this thing was way oversize for one of the mice people like you, Frank," Baker said conversationally. "But maybe we can do something about that." Still smiling pleasantly, he broke the pipe neatly in half with a brittle, snapping sound, then dropped the two pieces into Corben's palsied hand.

"Don't bother tossing me out of the club, Frank," he said happily. "I quit already!"

CHAPTER NINE

Sheriff Lavers glared at me for a moment, then shook his head doubtfully. "You sure this isn't all some drunken fantasy of yours, Wheeler?"

"You can ask Polnik—he was there," I said shortly.

"If it's true," he muttered, "all I can say is that the Kains girl must have been a very athletic character."

"We checked with Baker's foreman on the way out," I said. "Kozowsky is a guy who minds his own business, Kozowsky says, and he don't know nothing from nothing about who the boss has up to his house, et cetera, et cetera!"

"You think there's any truth in Corben's story?" Lavers asked.

"I don't know what truth is anymore," I confessed, "but the one guy who would know is Doctor Thorro."

"He's surely the one man who wouldn't know!" Lavers growled. "If Bernice Kains was two-timing him with somebody else, she'd make damned sure he never knew about it!"

"But there would have to be times and places," I said reasonably. "Times when she wasn't with Thorro, times when she made vague excuses instead of good reasons. If he can remember some recent ones like that, it could help."

"You're an optimist, Wheeler," the Sheriff grunted. "It sounds to me like you'll just get more and more involved, chasing a shadow that maybe doesn't even exist!"

"I got nothing else to chase, sir," I reminded him.

"Ain't that the truth!" He closed his eyes in pain at the thought. "Maybe we should call Homicide now?"

"Maybe we should wait a little, Sheriff," I snarled. "I have a hunch about this Hal Baker. If you'd seen him in that tiger's cage—"

"I'm still trying to make up my mind whether you did," he growled. "More like you dreamed up the whole thing in some downtown bar!"

"Your trouble is you don't trust me, Sheriff," I said brilliantly. "Dames distrusting me I can understand—I don't mind, even—but when my boss—" I put one hand over my heart in an exaggerated gesture. "Well, it hurts—right here!"

"Get out!"

"Yes, sir."

Annabelle's Jackson's cute little nose lifted into the air, sniffing interestedly, as I came out of the Sheriff's office.

"Did I hear raised voices?" she asked eagerly. "Sound of argument? Clash of temperament? Are you fired, I hope?"

"Honeychile,"—I leaned my elbows on her desk in a confidential gesture, designed to allow me a more intimate view of her blouse's neckline—"I need some advice."

"You!" She laughed derisively. "It's the girls who are closer than thirty paces who need the advice—and consoling!"

"Well," I said, shrugging ruefully. "I guess if you don't want to help—"

I was betting on the most powerful, single factor in the whole wide world and I couldn't lose—woman's curiosity.

"Advice about what?" she said sharply.

"Imagine you were going steady with the Sheriff—"

She shuddered gently. "I don't have that good an imagination!"

"You have to try until it hurts, magnolia blossom," I said earnestly. "Imagine this is a real big-time thing with the Sheriff—you're way past the matching pajamas stage, even!"

"Lieutenant Wheeler," she said faintly, "you're disgusting!"

"Then," I continued remorselessly, "a great new lover enters your life—me!"

"Now you're ridiculous!"

"There are reasons why you can't give up the Sheriff for me—and vice versa. The Sheriff expects to get most, if not all, of your time—but you want to spend some of it with me. So what excuses do you make to the Sheriff?"

She thought about it hard for a few moments. "I have to sit up nights with a sick friend?" I shook my head sadly. "No?" she sighed. "Well—I'm studying nights so I can get a sheriff's badge all my own?"

"Annabelle," I said sorrowfully, "you're not trying."

"You don't make it easy," she said tartly. "A girl with two different sets of matching pajamas has got real problems!"

"Check."

"She'd have to be a magnificent liar, with a magnificent memory, to start with," Annabelle said firmly. "I don't think it could be done—not if the relationships were the way you said."

"I guess you're right," I said thoughtfully. "Thanks a whole lot."

She looked at me blankly. "What did I do?"

"I'm not sure yet," I said honestly, "but I think you made sense. And let me congratulate you on that, Miss Jackson—you're the very first one on this case."

"I think it's the heat," she said slowly, "or maybe the humidity? Is the top of your head soft to the touch, Lieutenant?"

"Talking of being soft to the touch," I said evilly. "Tell me—is your—"

"Out!" she said briskly, and reached for the heavy steel rule.

I went out for lunch to the Chicken Inn two blocks down, and chickened out when I saw the menu. They specialized in charcoal-broiled food. There are only two things I point blank refuse to do, and eating food covered with a thin layer of soot is one of them—the other is to wear Bermuda shorts, because they're not. So I settled for a tossed salad and coffee, and the sneer on the waitress's face said what was a big spender like me doing in a humble establishment like this. The service was lousy and I tipped a dime just to show us big spenders haven't lost our sense of values yet.

A replacement for the late Bernice Kains was at the reception desk when I got up into Doctor Thorro's office around three in the afternoon. A fragile-looking dame with pale blonde hair and haunting gray eyes. She looked at me like I was a spectral Simon Legree when I told who I was, and that I wanted to see the doctor.

"Doctor Thorro is with a patient at the moment," she whispered mournfully. "I think he's very brave—trying to lose himself in his work this way, after his tragic loss."

"You mean his wife?"

Her eyes widened even further. "Who else?"

"That's a good question," I admitted. "Would you tell him I'm here?"

She hesitated for a moment, then her mouth set firm with determination. "I realize it's none of my business, Lieutenant, but do you think you should disturb the doctor now? This is only my first day here, but already I can see how deeply he's grieving! Don't you think it would be a nice thing if you left him alone with his work and his grief?"

"Honey," I smiled pleasantly, "if you don't get onto that phone and tell him I'm waiting out here, this is likely to be your last day here as well. Not that I don't think your beautiful sentiments are beautiful—I do—I figure they should be preserved, like in a bottle or something!"

Her lips whitened for a moment as she reached for the phone. A few seconds later she hung up and glared at me. "The doctor will see you in a few minutes, Lieutenant!"

I drifted away from her desk and lit a cigarette. Five minutes later the door of Thorro's office opened, and he ushered out an overweight, overdressed, overaged dame who drooled over him like he was her pet chihuahua. When he'd finally gotten rid of her, he nodded curtly and gestured for me to go into the office.

After we got inside he closed the door and walked around his desk back to his chair. His suit was an olive gabardine this time, and as immaculate as ever. He stared at me for a moment, then ran his hand irritably through his close-cropped gray hair.

"Something more, Lieutenant?" he asked crisply.

"I don't know," I admitted. "I'm hoping you can tell me."

"I might—if you'll stop the double-talk and start making sense!"

I eased down into a comfortable, foam-padded chair and lit another cigarette. "You were very close to Miss Kains, Doctor?"

"I've already told you that."

"Close enough to tell if she was cheating on you?"

The pale, ascetic face darkened slowly, and the lean, sensitive fingers thrummed gently on his desktop. His eyes were colder than an arctic mist as they stared through me.

"Are you mad?" he almost spat the words at me.

"Could be," I shrugged. "Frank Corben claimed this morning that Miss Kains was leading a kind of double life—with you and another guy—at the same time."

"That's absurd!"

"If you say so. I just want to be sure," I said politely.

He put his hand to his mouth and worried the long strip of adhesive tape on one finger with strong, white teeth.

"If it's possible for you to look at it dispassionately, Doctor," I suggested, "can you think back over the last two months? Do you remember any times when Miss Kains made excuses not to be with you for any length of time?"

"Of course not!" he rapped. "It's ridiculous—Bernice never.... You know as well as I do that Corben's a psychotic with a predilection for violence. He'll say anything to ..." His voice trailed away slowly, while his teeth worried the bandage with an increasing intensity.

"She suffered badly from migraines, of course. There were times I'd have to let her go home early so she could lie down and rest. I remember a couple of weekends in succession—but it's absurd even to think this way!"

"Would you know if she was faking the migraines, Doctor?" I prodded gently.

"Not in the early stages," he said bleakly. "At the peak, you'd surely know when someone wasn't faking loss of color, a slight distortion of the pupils—this is nonsense!"

"But there were times—if she was lying about the migraines—when she could have been seeing someone else?"

"If she was lying!" he snarled. "But what possible reason could she have for cheating on me—as you so charmingly put it?"

"I wouldn't know," I said. "Like I told you before, this isn't my idea."

"We loved each other very much," he said quietly. "We were to be married."

"Sure," I nodded politely. "I'm still looking for a murderer, Doctor, that's all."

"I know that," he barked, "but I'm finding it increasingly hard to remember all the time. Do you have any more questions, Lieutenant?"

"I guess not," I said.

"Just who is the man—according to Frank Corben—with whom Bernice is supposed to have led this double life?" he asked sarcastically.

"Hal Baker," I told him.

"Baker?" He laughed harshly. "Anything more improbable than Baker, I couldn't imagine! Bernice could never have found anything to attract her in a man like him!"

"If you say so, Doctor," I shrugged. "So it was just a bum lead."

His fingers beat against the desktop with sudden, increasing violence, while the veins knotted in his forehead.

"Maybe not," he whispered. "I tried so goddamned hard to believe in those migraines, but I never could quite convince myself that they were real." He stared blankly at the wall in back of my head for a few seconds, his mouth twisted into an ugly grimace.

"She acted a little strange those last two months—sometimes she'd be wildly excited, and other times deeply depressed." He tried to smile and didn't make it. "That's the trouble with having the mind of a professional psychiatrist, Lieutenant—it's just naturally suspicious. You can't keep yourself from compiling a mental case history all the time. The irregular pattern of her upswings and downswings was starting to worry me—possibly symptomatic of early schizophrenia, you understand?"

"Vaguely," I said.

"But the emotional conflict and strain involved in leading that kind of double life would undoubtedly produce the same symptoms—could easily, in fact, induce a genuine migraine here and there, giving her the perfect excuse at the same time!"

"But you don't know for sure?" I asked. "You never had any definite proof?"

He shook his head miserably. "None at all, Lieutenant."

"This Baker is a guy given to actual violence," I said. "Maybe that's how Corben came to be associated with him in the first place."

"It sounds logical," he said tonelessly.

"If we could prove an association between him and Bernice Kains—we might then establish his motive for murder," I went on.

"You'd do better than that, Lieutenant," he said ironically. "You'd establish my own motive!"

"I had thought of that," I admitted. "Do you have an alibi for the night Miss Kains was murdered, Doctor?"

"No. It was so short a time after my wife's death. I think I told you Bernice and I agreed not to see each other before the funeral. So I was home alone that night, Lieutenant." His clenched fist suddenly smashed down onto the desktop. "My God! That's another thing now I come to think of it—it was her idea we shouldn't see each other during that time. Do you think she wanted an excuse to see Baker—instead of me?"

"Maybe," I said. "I guess only Baker can tell us for sure, and that isn't likely."

"I wish you luck, Lieutenant!" Thorro said shortly. "Now—if you don't mind—I have a patient waiting outside."

"I don't mind at all, Doctor," I told him, as I got up from the chair. "If things keep on going the way they have so far, it's highly probable I'll wind up right here on your couch, anyway. You think you could maybe shrink my head down to about quarter-size? Something small enough to look real nice, stuffed and mounted, on the Sheriff's desk?"

CHAPTER TEN

Late afternoon sunlight filtered through the high stained-glass windows, casting a diffused golden glow around the reception area of the Eternal Refuge. The heavy silence seemed to gather in the corners and whisper behind the locked doors—fifteen minutes by myself in this place and I figured I'd be scratching, too.

Mr. Williams writhed desperately in front of me, his fingers searching down the back of his shirt collar for a particularly inaccessible itch.

"Poor Mr. Jordan," he said dolefully, his voice full of professional regret.

I waited a few seconds to see if the words *in memoriam* would suddenly appear across his forehead like a flashing neon sign, but they didn't.

"I should have gotten around to this before," I admitted, "but everything's been happening so fast at once."

"I understand, Lieutenant," Williams said generously. "Did you know we've put him to rest in the Meadow of Everlasting Love—at our own expense of course? I think Mr. Jordan would have liked that. The directors felt that was the least they could do for him, he spent so much of his time working there."

"I'm sure he's delighted," I said nervously. "Right now, I'm hoping you'll be able to help me find the murderer."

He looked at me doubtfully, while the heel of his left shoe swiftly massaged the instep of his right foot. "Of course, I'm only too anxious to help anyway I can," he said, "but how, exactly?"

"It was Jordan who found Miss Kains's body in the open grave ready for Mrs. Thorro's funeral later that morning," I reminded him. "The only logical reason for someone to murder him must be because he saw either the murderer, or something that could reveal the murderer's identity, and had to be silenced before he had a chance to talk."

"Yes, yes!" Williams nodded eagerly. "I follow your reasoning, Lieutenant—go on!"

"Right there I come to a complete stop," I said dismally. "From here on out I'm relying on you. Did Jordan say anything to you about it—anything at all that could be a clue?"

He scratched the top of his head with a long index finger, like he was drilling for oil. "Not that I recall—" He frowned alarmingly. "Give me a few moments to think back, Lieutenant."

"Sure," I said. "Take all the time you want."

About five seconds later he scratched the tip of his nose vigorously, then shook his head. "No, I'm sorry, but I can't remember anything at all that could be a clue."

"Think again, Mrs. Williams," I pleaded. "You must have talked with him about finding Bernice Kains's body in that grave. Wasn't there anything unusual he mentioned? Maybe you didn't even notice it at the time."

He scratched some more, he thought some more, and still came up with the same negative answer.

"I'm very sorry, Lieutenant," he apologized. "But I really don't think it likely Jordan did see anything significant. He was a very old man, you know, and he was half-blind."

"Half-blind?" I croaked.

"His senses were failing him rapidly, poor old man." Williams fluttered his hands in the air sympathetically. "Anything more than a few feet away from him was just a blur—and you had to speak very loudly before he was able to hear."

"Then why the hell would anybody need to kill him?" I growled bleakly.

"Maybe they didn't know about his infirmities?" Williams said shrewdly. "I'm sure if Jordan had thought he could solve the mystery of how the wrong body came to be in the open grave, he would have spoken up right away!"

"Yeah," I said dully, "I guess you're right. Thanks for the try, anyway."

"Not at all," Williams said.

His fingers pulled savagely at the short hairs growing around the nape of his neck. "Only too pleased to be of any help I can be, Lieutenant."

Which was none, I reflected, as I went back outside to the car, then drove out of the cemetery. There was just one definite fact clear in my mind—I needed a drink—and about a mile later I found a bar. There was a dark booth in one corner, so I sat there with a drink in front of me on the table and brooded.

From the very beginning, when Jordan discovered the body of Thorro's mistress in the grave being readied to receive his wife, it had been a screwball case. The suspects had proved to be nothing else but a bunch of screwballs who'd kept me running around in tight circles getting no place. All I'd gotten in two days was another murder, just as baffling as the first.

A second drink helped me brood some more. Thirty-six hours I'd been investigating and I didn't have one single fact—not one reasonable clue—toward finding the murderer. And it didn't look like it was about to improve, either. The third drink made me remember something somebody said someplace, sometime—"If you want something that doesn't exist, and you want it real bad, then invent it!" All I needed for a starter, anyway, was one simple little fact—one definite clue; and there was an obviously simple solution—invent one. I had one more drink to celebrate my discovery, then made tracks out of the bar, all ready and eager to test my theory.

The sun was below the rim of Cascada Canyon, and long shadows dappled the entrance to the Baker Private Zoo and Menagerie as I stopped in front of the gates. I beeped the horn a couple of times, loud and long, then waited a little while. Finally an ancient pickup wheezed its way down the dirt road from the zoo and stopped with an impressive series of detonations.

The foreman, Kozowsky, got out and opened up the gates, then looked at me impassively.

"You'll find the boss with the big cats," he growled. "I guess you can find your own way, huh?"

"Sure," I said.

"Been a long day," he said, as he hauled himself back into the truck. "I figure on getting home before dark—if this goddamned heap don't fall apart on me!" He started the motor again: there was another series of thunderous explosions then the pickup took up the clutch in one frantic hop, and squeezed past the Healey out onto the road.

Where the dirt road ran out, a quarter mile into the zoo, Baker's white Mercedes was still parked beside the giant, mobile cage. There was a third car standing in back of them that I hadn't seen before—an immaculate, this year's model Buick, with a gleaming black paint job—

which dwarfed my little Austin Healey when I parked beside it.

Retracing the fifty yards along the right-hand walk brought me out onto the concrete strip again, into another world—remote and savage, where swift and sudden death padded silently on four feet. From both sides, gleaming amber eyes followed my progress as I hurried through the deepening gloom until I reached the first intersection and turned left onto the strip which contained the tiger Baker had nearly beaten to death that morning.

Two figures were standing outside the black panther's cage, talking animatedly, so absorbed they didn't hear my footsteps as I came up to them. Baker still wore the tan open-necked shirt and polished cotton pants he'd worn that morning. His clothes made a sharp contrast to the immaculate olive gabardine suit worn by his companion.

"I don't know what the hell you're talking about," Baker said coldly, as I stopped a couple of feet behind him. "But I do know I'm getting awful tired standing here listening to you sound off! This is private property, Mac, and if you don't walk out right now, I'll throw you out!"

"I'm not going until I learn the truth!" Doctor Thorro said fiercely. "I *have* to know about you and Bernice."

Baker knuckled the side of his nose impatiently. "Look I told you a thousand times—I don't know this Bernice Kains. So for the last time, will you get the hell out of here?"

"Found yourself a new patient, Doctor?" I asked pleasantly, and they both jumped, then spun around to stare at me.

"Glad to see you, Lieutenant," Baker said curtly. "Maybe you can get this creep off my back. Right now he should give himself some analysis and then six months in a nuthouse to see if he can get his mind back!"

"I'm glad you're here, Lieutenant," Thorro said, in a quiet, determined voice. "After you left my office this afternoon, I couldn't get out of my mind what you'd told me about Bernice and this man. The more I thought about it, the more I suspected those migraines of hers were a convenient myth. I have to know the truth one way or the other—or else I will need analysis, or worse! Baker denies it, but I don't believe him."

"The hell with this!" Baker snarled. "I don't have to stand around and take it on my own place. You're a cop, Wheeler, or you're making like one all the time. Take this creep out of here while he can still walk!"

He moved to one side as he finished speaking, leaving me a clear view of the black void behind the heavy steel bars. The next moment there was a bloodcurdling snarl and something thudded heavily against the bars, shaking the whole cage. Two tawny-colored eyes stared malevolently at me for a moment, then the panther turned and padded back into the darkness again.

"You know something, Wheeler?" Baker said, chuckling gleefully. "I don't think Satan likes you somehow!"

"It's strictly mutual," I said. "Maybe we should go someplace else where we can talk."

"Talk?" he said angrily. "What's to talk about? All I want is you should take this—"

"I got a whole heap of stuff to talk about," I said coldly. "You can please yourself, Baker—either we talk here or in the Sheriff's office downtown."

"Okay, okay." He shrugged his shoulders resignedly. "We can go on up to the house. But tell this headshrinker to go worry on his own couch first, will you?"

"I'm staying," Thorro said doggedly. "If this concerns Bernice's death, then I think I have a right to hear it!"

"I guess it won't hurt," I said.

"Goddamn it!" Baker moaned in frustrated fury. "I got a good mind to—"

"It's a debatable point," I said easily. "But if you want, we can still examine your mind in detail down at the Sheriff's office. It won't be comfortable like your own place, but—"

"Yeah!" he said disgustedly. "We can walk up from here—if you guys got the strength?"

Three tiers of stone steps cut into the side of the hill brought us up onto the brightly lit veranda of the sprawling split-level. Somewhere inside the house a radio was playing cool jazz, and strictly in keeping, a flamingo redhead was sprawled lazily on the couch—a glass held loosely between the fingers of the hand which trailed close to the floor.

Tania Stroud looked up as we came across the veranda, her eyes widening with interest.

"Well!" she said throatily. "We got company. Isn't that nice?"

"It's not my idea," Baker said sourly.

"The unlovable lieutenant and the sudden death doctor!" she purred. "What do they want, lover?" she gurgled to the lion tamer. "Another wake?"

She heaved herself into a sitting position, and I noticed there was a contented look in her eyes to match the soft purr of her voice. Her clothes had a crumpled look about them, and a dark flush stained her smooth, plump cheeks. She winced suddenly as her shoulders touched the back of the couch, then sat up stiffly to avoid any further contact. It looked like Baker had made a day of it after the action inside the tiger's cage that morning. Maybe he'd tamed a tigress in the afternoon—only this one would never stay tame for very long.

"So we're here," Baker snapped. "So you want to talk—go ahead and get it finished!"

"There's no hurry," I told him, and took time out to light a cigarette as proof.

Thorro's lean face was set in a wooden mask, but something almost frightening went on in back of his eyes as he stared fixedly at me.

"I only want an answer to one question, Lieutenant," he said quietly. "Is Baker the man that Bernice was seeing—" his lips tightened in distaste for the phrase "—the man with whom she was cheating on me?"

"Take it easy, Doctor," I told him. "Maybe you'll find out."

Tania finished her drink and held out the empty glass toward Baker in a commanding gesture.

"You want another drink, you get it," he said indifferently.

The familiar, arctic quality came back into her blue eyes as she glared at him for a few seconds, then got up from the couch and swung her hips indolently across to the bar. A moment later she turned around suddenly with the whisky bottle in her hand, and looked fixedly at Baker again.

"The party's over now," she said in a brittle voice. "Is that what you mean, lover?"

"You catch on real quick!" he said contemptuously.

"You're a very brave man, Hal." Her lips twisted into the semblance of a smile. "Brave—honest—and stupid! You think I'm like the rest of your wild cats—when you're all through you can shut them up in a cage until the next time? I'm different, lover, you'll find out!"

"What the hell are you talking about?" he snarled.

"You'll find out," she repeated, splashing whisky into the glass until it was full to the brim. "You wait, lover, you could be real surprised!"

Baker looked at her curiously, then shrugged impatiently. "I got enough double-talk from the lieutenant already, without you getting in the act." He transferred his attention to me. "For a guy who wants to talk so bad, you're a long time starting, Wheeler."

"I've been looking for a murderer these last couple of days," I said easily, "and I figure I've found him. It's a good feeling—I was just standing here enjoying it. Maybe it's the same kind of feeling you got this morning, right after you'd whipped that tiger into the ground?"

"You talk," he grunted, "but I still don't hear anything!"

"Okay," I said briskly. "I was looking for a murderer, a guy with an immense capacity for hate—why else would he take the risks involved in putting Bernice Kains's body in that open grave? A guy with tremendous ego—maybe a paranoiac. A guy who couldn't tolerate competition, but demanded complete subjection in any relationship with another human—or animal?"

"You sound like you've been around the headshrinker a little too long, Wheeler!" he said softly. "Your brain has gone soft like his."

"I was looking for a guy with motive," I continued in a conversational voice. "A strong enough motive for murder—and this morning Corben gave me one—your association with Bernice Kains."

"He was lying in his teeth!" Baker snapped. "You couldn't take Frank's word on the time of day."

"I was looking for proof," I said, "and a couple of hours back I got it!"

"Proof?" His eyes narrowed a little. "What proof?"

"Jordan—the watchman out at the cemetery—was also murdered last night," I said. "Obviously because he'd either seen or heard something that could identify the Kains girl's murderer when the body was put into the grave. Williams, the superintendent out there, discovered Jordan's body right after he'd been killed. The killer was still hidden in the main building, and after Williams found the body, he ran out. What he couldn't know was that the superintendent got a real good look at him, and tonight Williams got up enough courage to give me the description."

"Who was it, Lieutenant?" Thorro asked in a thick voice.

"The description was of a man about twenty-five years of age, over six feet tall, husky build, black hair, and a deep sun tan," I lied happily. "You know anybody could fit that description, Doctor?"

"He's lying!" Baker shouted wildly. "This is a frame!"

"Why would he make up the description?" I asked icily. "He's never even met you in his whole life before!"

"I don't know why," Baker growled, "but I know this is a frame. I was right here in this house last night when that watchman was knocked off. I never went outside the front door, even!"

"So prove it," I rapped.

"You know I can't—I told you before." His eyes glittered as he looked at Thorro for a long moment, then back at me. "This is a put-up job between you and the headshrinker, Wheeler!"

"Lieutenant?" Tania's voice, husky and sensual, gently thrust across the room.

"Yeah?" I turned my head.

She leaned back against the bar on her elbows, her breasts thrusting against the tight sweater with an insolent disdain.

"He was the other guy in that Bernice Kains's life okay," she said negligently. "He used to boast about it down at the club. Corben used to lap up all the sordid detail—Frank would, of course!" She wrinkled her nose distastefully. "But after a time, you could see it was bugging Hal. Like you said, he's got to enslave anybody completely—it's the only kind of relationship he knows. And this Kains girl wouldn't give up Thorro—I guess she had a practical mind."

Tania looked at Thorro and smiled nastily. "Poor old Jason wouldn't rate beside Hal Baker in the boudoir, but he was loaded, and he was talking marriage!"

"Why didn't you tell me all this when I was here this morning?" I asked her. "When Corben said it was true, you could have backed him up."

"I guess it just slipped my mind then," she said simply. She arched her back a little further away from the bar, and a slow, lazy smile of triumph spread over her face as she looked at Baker.

"I told you you'd be sorry, lover!" she said sweetly.

"That's all I wanted to know," Thorro said in a harsh voice.

"Are you going to arrest him now, Lieutenant?"

"No," I said slowly, like I was making up my mind. "We'll set up an identification parade tomorrow and put him in the middle of the lineup.

If Williams picks him out as the guy he saw running out of the cemetery building last night, that's it."

"I'd like to be there, if I may," Thorro said stiffly.

"Be my guest," I told him. "I'll call you in the morning and let you know the time."

"Thank you." The muscles around his jaw corded for a moment. "Then there is no need for me to stay here any longer. Good night, Lieutenant." He turned and walked quickly across the veranda, then out to the long, steep descent that would take him back through the zoo to his Buick.

"I'm going to call my lawyer right away!" Baker said wildly. "I'll have your badge, Wheeler! I'll—"

"Stop running off at the mouth for a while!" I grated. "Who's to listen to you any more, Baker? You're strictly past tense. All that's waiting for you is a straight line from that identification parade in the morning to the gas chamber!"

"You're not taking him with you, Al?" Tania said in an eager voice.

"We'll pick him up in the morning," I said. "Don't try leaving in a hurry tonight, Baker, you won't get any place!" I looked at Tania. "You want a ride back to town?"

"No, thanks," she said, smiling warmly. "I'll stay right here."

"Stay right here?" I gaped at her incredulously. "You mean, alone with Baker?—after you just gave him that big push along the line leading straight into the gas chamber? You must be out of your mind!"

"I figured you wouldn't understand, at all, you dull-minded slob," she said complacently. "You got Hal so mad right now, he's about ready to go out and strangle all his big cats to death with his bare hands!" She took a deep, lingering breath. "You think I'd let all that wonderful primitive violence be wasted on a bunch of tigers?"

CHAPTER ELEVEN

I fumbled my way uncertainly down the first steep descent from the house, feeling for each stone step with my foot, and making sure it was firmly planted before I put my weight on it. The night had shut down completely, with no moon, and once I was below the level of the house, its lights were of no further use to me.

By the time I reached the head of the third flight of stone steps I was sweating a little, remembering too late that the well-equipped cop has a flashlight—and a moron like me most likely winds up with a broken neck. One thing about my slow, cautious descent—it gave me plenty of time to think.

The more I thought, the less faith I had in my theory about inventing facts you couldn't come by honestly. The cooked-up story of Williams describing Baker as the fleeing killer from the cemetery—with such startling accuracy yet—hadn't gotten me any place. With a small piece of luck, I'd figured it might bust Baker wide open; but his only reaction had been wild indignation at being framed, and for that I couldn't exactly blame him.

Doctor Thorro had stalked off into the night like a man with a mission. Either he was going home to cry bitter tears for his lost, unfaithful love, or else coming right back with a shotgun to blast Baker's head clean off his shoulders. Whatever he did would be strictly my fault.

Tania Stroud had been goaded into backing Corben's story that Hal Baker had been Bernice Kain's other lover. But there was no guarantee she'd ever testify the same way in court—especially with that jungle spectacular she had planned for tonight as a kind of reprise.

So—look at it any which way it figured that Wheeler had made a king-sized boo-boo. I could foresee a bright future as the horrible example held up to all the rookie cops, and me standing in the gutter, waving my tin cup hopefully while they walked quickly past on the other side of the street.

My right foot hit level ground on the next step, which meant I'd made it down the three flights of steps, anyway. My eyes had gotten accustomed to the darkness and I could make out the denser bulk of the cages on either side of the concrete walk. The noises that filled the dark night with soft menace were enough to kill any desire I'd ever had to make an African jungle safari.

Even worse was the fetid animal stench that enveloped me more closely with each successive step. The acrid smell of mingled fear and thwarted ferocity struck at my senses with an almost physical impact. Then a sudden flurry of movement from somewhere too near for comfort, followed by a horrific thud which shook the bars of a cage, sent me leaping a couple of feet up into the air in sheer terror.

Dimly I realized that harsh, spitting cough was familiar, the way the sound of that vast bulk smashing against the bars of its cage was familiar, but it didn't make me feel any better. That goddamned black panther must have been a hybrid with the brain of an elephant, the way he never forgot Al Wheeler. From then on I walked a hell of a lot faster, until I reached the junction and turned right onto the main concrete walk.

There was an even more ferocious snarl from the panther as if it was leaping toward its prey, then absolute silence. All the softly menacing sounds stopped for a couple of seconds so that I wondered whether my eardrums had been simultaneously punctured. Then I heard a peculiar snicking sound like a steel bolt being withdrawn, or shot home.

My feet got the message even before my brain had time to figure it out, and started walking fast. I'd gone maybe six paces when that grunting cough brought me to an abrupt halt again. Maybe I was going crazy, but I would have sworn it sounded a lot closer this time. I was about to start walking again when there was a new, different sound—a whispering murmur of paws padding down the concrete—which froze me to the spot in stark terror.

Now there was a crystal-clear explanation for that snicking sound—somebody had unlocked the door of the cage and set the black panther free. My heart pounded like it was about to explode, and panic bubbled in my mind, so all I wanted was to run for my life. What stopped me was a memory playback of Hal Baker's jocular comments that morning ... *"Satan, I call him ... he hates people—can scent a human being within a mile radius, I figure! But maybe that's because I keep him hungry all the time?"*

I didn't know how fast a guy would need to run to outdistance a panther, but I did know I couldn't make it. The fingers of my right hand pulled the .38 out of its belt holster without my conscious bidding, as I turned to face the corner of the junction and the invisible wild cat stalking me. My ears strained to pick up the slightest sound, and a few seconds later I thought I heard that deadly whispering murmur again. I squeezed the trigger in an automatic fear reflex, and the sound hammered around the concrete walk in a fury of noise which was topped almost immediately by an ear-splitting scream of rage from the panther.

A momentary silence, then it sounded off again, but this time it was a lot further away, maybe heading in the opposite direction. I wiped the heavy sweat from my forehead, and started running at a fast clip. There was about a quarter mile between me and the parking space where the Austin Healey offered safety. Right then I had no great confidence I'd ever make it. Fifty yards further on, when that eerie, spitting cough sounded again, I had no confidence at all. Pulses in my temples hammered wildly as I came to a sudden stop, listening fearfully to locate the direction of the sound. Satan snarled again and my insides felt hollow as I realized the sound came from up *ahead* of me. Somehow he'd backtracked around the cage area, and now he was right between me and the car, which meant I had to get past him—and that thought was about as attractive a way of committing suicide as any.

The sound of my own harsh, uneven breathing sounded terribly loud; I held my breath in sudden panic, while my ears registered that whispering murmur of paws coming toward me. I fired a second shot and got a repeat sequence of events—the wild cat roared deafeningly and retreated, but not so far this time. The second roar of fury still sounded a lot too close for comfort.

A long minute crawled past, building a stale hiatus where the man waited, panic-stricken, for the beast—and the beast waited patiently for the man. It was the darkness that got me worst of all. I had an illogical feeling that it wouldn't be half so bad if I could only see that damned cat. But the black night seemed implacable, and I might as well wish for wings.

A low, questioning grunt sounded closer again, and my trigger finger stiffened automatically, but I managed to ease off the pressure before the gun fired—there were four slugs left and I couldn't afford to waste one of them. Suddenly, like the answer to a prayer, the lights came on.

The panther was only some thirty feet away from me, its tawny eyes blinking against the light, the tail lashing slowly from side to side as it crouched in the center of the concrete walk—watching and waiting. The sight of that sleek, black shape scared the hell out of me for sure, but it was better than the darkness—at least I could see it now.

It took a little while to make up my mind I had to get closer—two hundred pounds of muscled savagery was going to take a lot of stopping and I figured one mistake was my full allowance. I edged forward maybe six feet and Satan snarled softly, revealing enough teeth to send a dentist into ecstasy—but on me it had a totally different effect.

A new sound made me sure my hearing had been overstrained the last ten minutes, and was now indulging in a few fantasies of its own—like footsteps? I shook my head a couple of times, but the sound persisted, the footsteps growing louder all the time. Then, from a narrow passageway between two cages on the far side of the walk, a man appeared, moving briskly but with no apparent sense of urgency, like he was just out for the exercise.

The passageway brought him out onto the main concrete walk about twenty feet ahead of me, and as he turned and headed in my direction, I saw it was Hal Baker. In his right hand he carried the long, heavily plaited whip with the cruel steel tip. No gun, as far as I could see.

"What's the matter, Wheeler?" He was grinning as he started toward me. "One of the big cats get loose, or something?"

It took a tremendous restraint not to plug him right then. It was enough he'd used to live panther as a murder weapon, but topping it with a little cute conversation was pushing it too hard.

"Baker," I said, my voice sounding in need of a lube job, "you are a—"

I didn't even get to start a detailed description—because behind him, the panther's tail lashed furiously as it tensed its whole body ready to spring. Maybe I was a sentimental slob, but I couldn't let it happen to a guy like Baker even, without giving him warning.

"Behind you!" I yelled desperately. "The panther!"

His eyes widened for a moment, the grin sliding off his face, as he stared at me for a split second before he spun around to face the wild cat.

"Satan?" His voice sounded genuinely surprised. Then he laughed suddenly and the whip crackled as he moved his right arm gently.

"You want to try again, Satan?" There was a jeering, ugly tone to his voice. "You want to feel the whip again, huh, baby? Well—c'mon then!"

The panther snarled its hatred in a spine-chilling low-pitched ripple of sound, its tail lashing the concrete in a series of sharp, staccato explosions. Baker's arm jerked upward and the whip flailed through the air in a soaring arc—and at the same instant the panther sprang. It seemed to move through the air at an incredible speed and crashed into Baker before the whip descended, knocking him to the ground.

Then the rest was nightmare—man and cat locked together in a macabre embrace of death as they rolled over and over across the concrete walk, while from all sides, the inmates of the cages snarled and howled in slavering excitement. I got as close as I could, but there was no chance of a shot at the wild cat without the equal danger of hitting the man; they were locked in that rolling embrace so tight that most times it was almost impossible to distinguish one from the other.

They came to a sudden stop ten feet away from me, and for a moment in time they seemed frozen in a tableau, with the beast triumphantly straddling the man beneath. Then the illusion was shattered by Baker's wild scream of terror which was cut off in mid-cry. It looked like Satan was playfully nuzzling Baker's neck, until the sleek black head was lifted and I saw blood dripping slowly from the savage jaws.

The panther was still looking at me questioningly when I shot it twice—right between those luminous, tawny eyes—and watched the powerful body slump heavily across Baker's body so the sleek head rested peacefully on his shoulder.

I did what I had to, and looked closely to make sure Baker was dead, and lost my stomach right after. Maybe five minutes later I walked slowly away in the direction of the parking space. I had to go back up to the house but this time I'd do it the easy way and drive—I never wanted to see a zoo again for the rest of my life.

When I got there, I left the car on the small concrete strip out front of the house and walked around back, then up the stone steps onto the veranda.

Tania Stroud was sprawled on the couch as she had been earlier, the only difference being she'd worn more clothes then. Somewhere a radio was playing lazy and cool jazz, and the soft light from a shaded table lamp cast rippling shadows across the ivory skin of her naked body.

"That you, Hal?" she asked, without bothering to turn her head. "It's about time! You shouldn't leave a girl the way you left me, lover, it's not fair! What was all the rumpus about?"

"Hal won't be coming back, lover," I said gently. "A black panther just tore his throat out!"

She leaped from the couch onto her feet in one convulsive movement and stared blankly at me in whimpering disbelief.

"It's true," I snarled. "There was nothing I could do about it—even if he did ask for it!"

"He's dead?" Pearl-shaped tears rolled slowly down her plump cheeks, as she folded her arms across her breasts and hugged tightly in a desperate, instinctive search for comfort and reassurance.

"Don't ask me to weep," I said.

The bar looked like an oasis in a dried-out desert of human emotion; and I needed a drink so bad, I hadn't even bothered with a second look at those lush curves Tania unconsciously paraded in front of me. In no time at all I'd made a drink, downed it, and made another.

"Poor Hal!" Tania whispered almost to herself. "He was such a wonderfully violent man. It's hard to believe he's dead—all that vitality.... How did the panther get loose?"

"You're kidding?" I scowled at her. "He let it loose—figured he had a perfect murder weapon to get me off his back—somehow there was an accident and Lieutenant Wheeler got to be dinner for a black panther!"

"Please!" She turned toward me with an imploring look. "For God's sake, don't joke about it!"

"I'm not joking," I rasped. "I had that damned wild cat stalking me in the darkness for about ten minutes before Baker showed up—and I couldn't raise a grin, even!"

"Tell me what really happened?" she repeated.

"You know it!" I said impatiently. "Baker figured he had a perfect setup to get rid of me. Then I guess he got impatient, so he put on the lights and came out onto the walk to see why I wasn't dead yet. It was his bad luck he came out right in front of that wild cat!"

I finished the second drink, feeling the Scotch soothe my insides and build a warm glow where the cold fear had been only a short time before.

"There was a shot," Tania said slowly. "Two shots?"

"Li'l ole me," I said grimly. "Down there in the darkness, trying to keep a respectable distance between us—me and the wild cat, that is!"

"You mean the panther was already out of its cage then?"

"What the hell else would I mean?" I glared coldly at her, "You think I'd start shooting while it was still inside the cage?"

"That's what doesn't make any sense," she said obtusely.

Her clothes were a small, untidy heap at one end of the couch. She walked toward them slowly, then started to get dressed. I took time out to manufacture a fresh drink for myself, then lit a cigarette, wondering if any ad agency would be interested in my personal endorsement (for money) of their client's cigarettes. Something like, "I always smoke ——s. There's nothing to compare with their cool, refreshing taste after being chased by a panther!"

"Al?" Tania's voice intruded on my creative thinking.

"Yeah?" I grunted, then looked at her.

She was standing beside the couch wearing white silk briefs and a matching bra, one leg poised to thrust into the blue ranch pants. "There's something wrong about this," she said in a bewildered voice. "Hal Baker was right here with me when you fired those two shots—that's what made him leave to find out what had happened down there."

"Tania—honey!" I said wearily. "Don't you believe me that he's dead? You can't help him now with a cover-up story. He doesn't have any use for an alibi anymore—all he needs is a good mortician!"

"I'm not trying to cover for him," she yelled furiously. "I'm telling you the truth, you stupid idiot! When you fired those two shots at the panther, Hal was right here with me. So how could he have let it out of its cage? Remote control or something?"

"You're wasting your time," I grunted. "If you don't believe he's dead, go take a look for yourself."

Tania wrestled the ranch pants up over her hips, then glared at me again with her face a mottled color.

"All right!" she panted, waging a losing battle with a zipper. "Hal's dead—I believe it! So what's the point in telling you it couldn't have been him who opened that cage, if it's not the truth?"

"Look!" I muttered desperately. "It figures to be Hal. Who else could—" My voice trailed away as I stared back at her blankly.

"What's the matter, Al?" she finally asked anxiously. "Lost your mind—I wouldn't be surprised?"

"I just thought of a couple of things—or six," I said weakly. "This is the truth? He was with you right up until he heard the shots?"

She sighed hopelessly. "How many times do I have to repeat myself before you'll believe it?"

"Just this one time," I assured her, "and now I'll believe it."

"Well!" She pulled the orlon sweater down over her head impatiently. "It's about time."

I gulped the rest of my drink and put the glass back on the bar top. "Call the Sheriff's office," I said quickly. "Tell them what's happened and for them to get out here with a meat wag—ambulance—right away. If you speak to Sheriff Lavers, tell him I had to leave but I'll call him right back."

"Hey!" Her voice was muffled through the folds of the sweater across her face. "You aren't going to walk out on me now?—leave me all alone here after what's happened?"

"You don't have a thing to worry about, honey," I said cheerfully. "After you call the Sheriff's office, you got nothing to do but sit here and think pretty thoughts about that truck jockey friend of yours. If you get bored, just imagine you're pulling the hairs out of his chest, and start counting!"

CHAPTER TWELVE

I parked the Healey on the brightly lit driveway behind the gleaming black Buick and got out. The sprinklers still swished gently over the wide expanse of front lawn as I went up the flagged path to the front porch. The same delicate chimes tinkled inside the house when I pressed the button, and after a short wait the door opened.

"Lieutenant?" Doctor Thorro looked genuinely surprised to see me. A nervous tic pulsated rapidly just under his right eye, and from the haggard look of his face, maybe he had been shedding bitter tears for his lost, unfaithful love.

"I figured you'd want to know what happened at Baker's place after you left, Doctor," I told him. "I also figured you had a right to know."

"Thank you," he said in a low-pitched voice. "Won't you come in?"

I followed him through the house to the bar on the back terrace, and lit a cigarette while he made me a drink. He listened attentively while

I told him what had happened when I left the house and walked through the zoo—the panther let loose from its cage, then Baker facing it with only a whip in his hand, and finally how he had died.

"A horrible death," Thorro said when I'd finished. "But I can't say I'm sorry, Lieutenant. I can't feel anything for the man who murdered Bernice—I'm glad he's dead!"

"I'm glad, too," I admitted. "I could've been in real trouble if things had worked out differently."

"How's that?" He frowned curiously.

"That story about the cemetery superintendent identifying him as the watchman's killer was strictly my own idea," I explained.

"It wasn't true?"

"Not one word. But I needed something to put the pressure on—and if it hadn't worked, Baker could have fixed my wagon but good!"

"You took an enormous risk, Lieutenant!" He smiled bleakly. "I admire your courage—you're a lot smarter than I gave you credit for, I'm afraid."

"There are still a couple of things I'd like to know," I said carefully. "But you don't have to tell me if you don't want. How come Bernice Kains was playing you and Baker at the same time?"

His face darkened a little and the nervous tic worked overtime while his long, sensitive fingers traced meaningless patterns on the bar top.

"That's a question I'm still asking myself," he said softly. "The obvious answer is unpleasant—that I was too valuable an asset to lose—fairly rich, successful, talking marriage once the way was clear." The corners of his mouth turned down sharply. "But Bernice was a girl with strong, excitable passions, Lieutenant—and the lusty sadism of a man like Baker would have an irresistible appeal for her!"

"Yeah," I said sympathetically.

He shrugged listlessly. "But it doesn't matter anymore—it's finished and done with. I just have to convince myself of that fact, but I'm afraid it will take a long time before I'm successful!"

I finished my drink, then looked at him admiringly. "You sure got a talent, Doc," I said, respectfully. "You almost got me crying into my drink right now!"

His thin, ascetic face looked suddenly blank, and his fingers stopped making their intricate patterns on the bar top, waiting poised ready to continue if the emergency signal was canceled.

"I beg your pardon?" he said coldly.

"How about some analysis—for free, Doc?" I asked politely. "I'll tell you my problems and you tell me where I went wrong."

"Is this your idea of some joke, Lieutenant?" he snapped.

"No, sir!" I said indignantly. "This is for real. I figure you owe me, Doc—in return for me taking the trouble to come over and tell you what happened to Baker tonight."

"All right," he said grimly. "I'll humor you, Wheeler, if you insist."

"Thanks a million," I told him. "It all started right after Bernice

Kains's body was found in your wife's grave, you remember?"

"I remember." The bleak look in his eyes confirmed it.

"I questioned you later that morning, in your office," I said. "You didn't have any ideas who could hate you that much, but maybe if I talked to Tania Stroud, she could help. So I talked to her—and she sent me to Frank Corben, and I met Betty, the maid, and Hal Baker. I heard all about the club and how your wife had been a member, how she'd died in an auto accident that Tania figured wasn't an accident at all—she was sure you'd killed your wife."

"This is part of your problem?" he asked stonily.

"Bear with me, Doc," I pleaded. "It gets worse. Late that afternoon I came here and told you about the club. Then you mentioned Corben had been a patient of yours—and so had Tania Stroud. You got all ethical when I wanted to know about Corben's problems, but you broke down real easy and gave me his case history. Brother!" I shook my head admiringly. "What a build-up you gave old Frankie-boy! Affinity with violence—got his kicks through keyhole peeping—a real nut you made him—and that way you also made him a red-hot suspect."

"I see no point in dragging all through this again, Wheeler," he said wearily. "Is there any point?"

"I asked about Baker," I said, ignoring his question. "You'd never met him. Then I gave you a description, and right away you remembered he'd been in the office once, waiting for Corben, about three months back."

I stared in open admiration. "You sure got a colossal memory for names and faces, Doc!"

"You're either drunk or hysterical," he said tautly. "I think you should go straight home and get some rest—a lot of rest!"

"Then the last time we talked in your office," I continued happily, "I asked was it possible Bernice had been cheating on you—remember? No, it was absolutely impossible, you told me, and five minutes later you had me convinced it wasn't only possible, but highly probable. All that jazz about migraines—how come you always believed her?—but when you came right down to it, you had to admit with great sorrow that maybe you hadn't."

He placed a clean glass beside mine on the bar top, and made fresh drinks with a meticulous attention to detail.

"I guess the crux of my problem when I get right down to basics," I confided in him, "is I'm mad at you because you handled me like a tame rabbit and it took me such a hell of a long time to realize."

His face was expressionless as he placed the fresh drink in front of me. "I don't think I understand what you mean, Lieutenant. Tame rabbit?"

"I guess you're a top analyst—and you can have my vote for the smartest psychotic of the year any time you want! Put it another way, Doc: It was you, not me, who handled the whole investigation. It was you who gave me all the leads—knowing in advance what information

I was likely to get, and filling in any of the gaps if I missed out. You wrote me a ticket that started from Bernice Kains—and with a few stopovers along the way—had to finish up with Hal Baker!"

"Finish your drink, Lieutenant," he said harshly. "Then get out—or I'll throw you out!"

"Doc!" I said pleadingly. "I still got some problems—like did you arrange your wife's auto accident or not?"

His eyes dilated suddenly and for a moment I thought he was about to take a swing at me, but he didn't.

"The watchman out at the cemetery—Jordan," I said softly. "Did you know he was half-blind anyway?"

He raised both hands into the air, then slammed them down hard onto the bar top.

"All right, Lieutenant!" he said acidly. "I presume your clumsily humorous crudeness is a shock tactic, aimed at making your accusations more effective. Let's not waste any more time—for some obscure reason you now believe that I am the murderer, and not Baker. Is that correct?"

"That's correct," I said crisply.

"Then why did Baker set loose that panther in an attempt to have you killed?" He smiled thinly. "I'm surprised you've forgotten it so soon, Lieutenant, it must have been an unpleasant experience?"

"It wasn't Baker who unlocked the cage, Doctor," I said. "He was still in the house—right up until he heard the shots I fired to keep the wild cat away—and Tania Stroud's a witness to prove it."

"Who would believe that bitch?" he snarled.

"Me," I told him. "You left the house first but my guess is you didn't go too far. You hung around outside and listened to the conversation, and got a brilliant inspiration. If you set free the panther while I was on my way out—and the wild cat for sure would make mincemeat of me—it would nicely solve all your problems. You'd tell the police how sure I was of Baker's guilt, and they wouldn't question it was him who let loose the panther. So he'd go to the gas chamber for three killings he didn't commit—and your revenge would be complete."

He sipped his drink appreciatively while his eyes studied my face with absolute concentration. "You couldn't prove a word of it, Lieutenant," he said finally.

"There's an easy way to prove it," I said cheerfully. "A process of elimination, Doctor. We can prove the cage door was opened deliberately and not by accident—we can prove neither Baker nor Tania did it, and I certainly didn't! So who else could have done it but you? Then there's motive. Baker was the guy who stole your mistress—you wanted revenge on both of them so you murdered the girl and framed Baker for the killing."

Thorro lowered his glass gently back onto the bar top, then ran his fingers slowly through his prematurely gray hair. A blank, blurry look came into his eyes for a few moments, then he smiled suddenly. "I guess you're right, Lieutenant. It would all be circumstantial, but that eliminating process would be hard to beat."

"So long as we prove you murdered Baker," I pointed up happily, "we don't need to prove you killed the others, do we?"

"I don't quite follow?" he said with a frown.

"You can only go to the gas chamber once, Doctor," I explained. "And, of course, once is usually enough."

He finished his drink, then inverted the tumbler on the bar top, and somehow managed to stop it becoming a theatrical gesture.

"What difference does it make now?" he asked himself out loud. "I killed Bernice, Lieutenant. From the moment I found out she was cheating on me with Baker, I started planning. My wife's death set the whole scene for me."

"Death—or murder?" I asked.

"It was a genuine accident, I assure you," he said, good-humoredly. "Of course, I did my best that night by starting a vicious row which made her nervy—making sure she was late for her evening with Tania so she'd drive fast to make up time—pumped enough liquor into her to take the edge off her driving. But then I'd done that kind of thing a dozen times before, and she always came home unharmed."

"You figured you had the law of averages working on your side?" I said coldly.

"Let's say I was giving fate a gentle shove from time to time," he nodded. "I'm sorry about that watchman—is it true what you said about him being half-blind?"

"It's true."

"I'd just gotten Bernice's body into the grave when I heard him coming," Thorro remembered out loud. "I scrambled out and ran like hell for cover in the trees—when I looked back he was standing there staring after me. Later on, I felt I couldn't be sure if he'd seen me or not—and I couldn't afford to take the chance he hadn't, either!"

"What was the significance of placing him in that casket?"

"None," he said with a complacent grin. "It happened to be the nearest convenient receptacle, that was all. I believe in making the most of opportunity, Lieutenant, just as that panther did tonight. I released Satan after you'd passed the cage, you know, and naturally the animal sprang out. But when he saw I'd locked myself safely in his cage, he didn't waste his fury on me—he went straight after you as I'd anticipated."

"Okay," I said dully. "We'll go down to the Sheriff's office and you can make a full statement when we get there."

"I'm in your hands, Lieutenant," he said politely. We walked through the house toward the front door, and Thorro hesitated beside a door in the hallway for a moment.

"You really think I'll go to the gas chamber, Lieutenant?" he asked in a patronizing voice.

"I'll make a book on it," I said firmly.

"Make a point of being in court for the trial," he said lightly. "It will be an experience for you, Lieutenant. I will put on a superb performance—even you may be convinced. Don't forget I'm an expert."

"In what?"

"Insanity," he chuckled, and the sound fingered my spine with ice-cold fingers. "You mind if I get my coat?"

"Sure—go ahead," I told him. "You wouldn't do anything stupid like going out the window now, would you?"

"I don't think so." He gave it careful thought for a moment, then shook his head. "It would be too undignified, Lieutenant."

He disappeared into the bedroom and returned quickly with his topcoat over his arm. There was a smug, superior smile on his face when we reached the door, and I didn't go for it much.

"Let's go," I grunted, and opened the door. Thorro took a quick step backward, and the next moment the hard barrel of a gun dug painfully into my kidneys.

"I thought it was psychologically right," he said softly. "Admit guilt, be apparently resigned to one's fate, clutch at frantic straws like an insanity plea. Then who will refuse a reasonable request for permission to get one's topcoat? And who's to know that one has taken the gun out of the bureau drawer at the same time, eh, Lieutenant?"

"Sure," I said bitterly, thinking how stupid can I get? "You're a genius, Doctor. What now?"

"We'll walk out to your car," he said coldly. "You'll drive and I'll sit beside you with this gun in your ribs."

"Where do you figure on running to—New York?" I sneered. "How far do you think we'll get before we're picked up?"

"I'll worry about that later," he snapped. "Let's get into the car first, shall we?" A sharp prod with the gun barrel emphasized his words.

We went out onto the porch, then walked down the path toward the cars parked on the driveway. When we were still ten or twelve feet away, a figure rose suddenly from behind the hood of the Buick, a gun in his hand.

"All right, Doctor!" Lavers said harshly. "Drop that gun!"

Thorro swore viciously and the next moment the gun barrel sliced down across the back of my head with painful force so I stumbled forward onto my hands and knees. I lifted my head and saw a crazily spinning Thorro pull the trigger—heard the loud explosion and the shrill whine a split second later when the slug ricocheted off the Buick's hood.

Then, from way over on the other side of the front lawn, came two more shots in quick succession, and my head cleared a little—enough to realize that the world had stopped spinning, but Thorro hadn't. The gun dropped out of his hand as the slugs spun him sideways. He took two quick, mincing steps trying to regain his balance, then his knees buckled under him and he slumped heavily onto the grass.

The sprinklers whirred softly, spraying the length of his body in a gentle, soaking action, but I figured it would take a little more than that to wash away his sins.

I climbed back painfully onto my feet and felt the back of my head tenderly. It was still there, which was something. A bulky figure materialized out of a rosebush and lumbered across the lawn toward me, waving a .38 in friendly greeting.

"You okay, Lieutenant?" Sergeant Polnik rumbled anxiously.

"Fine—thanks," I told him.

Polnik stopped for a moment beside Thorro's body and stared down at it disgustedly. "What did he take us for?" he asked curiously. "A bunch of amachoors or something?"

"That damned slug nearly clipped my ear off!" Lavers said breathlessly as he joined us. "You were lucky we arrived at the right time, Wheeler!"

"Sure, Sheriff," I agreed. "How come you arrived at all?"

"When that Stroud woman called in about what happened at Baker's private zoo, she had enough sense to work out why you'd left in a hurry," he grunted. "There was only one person left who could have let that wild cat out—and that was Thorro. So we came straight over here—lucky for you!"

"Yes, sir," I agreed, but not so happily this time. "Just one thing bothers me. You saw us come out of the house—right?"

"Of course!"

"Me first—and Thorro with a gun in my back?"

"Naturally."

"I was just curious," I said in a brooding voice. "When you yelled out for him to drop his gun—you couldn't know exactly how he'd react, right?"

"Right," Lavers nodded.

"He could have dropped the gun—or taken a shot at you like he finally did—or he could have put a slug straight through the back of my spine!"

"Right!" he said.

"So how come you were so goddamned sure he *wouldn't* put a slug into me?" I asked nastily.

"Oh, I wasn't at all sure about that," Lavers said blandly. "It was something we had to take a chance on—but I figured, when we got right down to it, Wheeler, you were expendable!"

It was after midnight when I finally got back to my apartment, and thankfully put the key in the door. Before I had a chance to turn it, the door suddenly opened wide, and a welcoming voice said, "Good evening, Lieutenant. Come right on in!"

Facing me was a blonde with a pert, slightly wanton face, and a glorious figure displayed to fantastic advantage in a bikini pajama outfit made from a rich blue satin material. Perched on top of her close-cropped, tight blonde curls, was an honest-to-God frilly maid's cap—and taken in conjunction with the bikini pajama outfit it made for a difference. She didn't look slightly wanton any more—just wanton.

"Betty?" I gurgled. "How the hell did you get in here?"

"I told the janitor I was your sister this time," she said and giggled happily. "He was real sweet—told me how much he admires your folks. He figures they must be real determined people who don't disappoint easily."

"How come?" I asked blankly.

"Well—the way he sees it—you were their first child and they always wanted another boy, but they aren't about to stop trying, no matter how many girls they have first."

"What is this janitor—a kook or something?"

"He's been janitor here for seven months he told me," Betty said innocently, "and I'm the nineteenth sister of yours he's met already. He wanted to know how many there were in the whole family, but I told him Ma never had time to count yet!"

I tottered past her into the living room and sank gratefully into the nearest armchair. Two seconds later a drink was placed gently in my hand.

"Our kind of maid service is personal service," Betty said softly. "You'll be surprised!"

"Forgive me if I ask a personal question—like what the hell are you doing here?"

"I'm a waif in a storm!" she said dramatically. "One of the homeless orphans, tossed out of their homes to brave the bitter snow and—"

"Sure, sure!" I said hastily. "What happened?"

"Corben came back from Baker's place raving like a maniac," she said suspiciously. "Did you tell him anything that I'd told you out there?"

"Me?" I tried to look innocent.

"He was climbing up the wall before he got inside the house even!" There was a note of nostalgic wonder in her voice. "I never knew a guy could get as mad as he was—raving at the top of his voice that I was a traitor and stool pigeon, planted on him by that lousy police lieutenant, and a lot more I won't bother repeating. Then—" her voice was suddenly indignant—"he hauled off and clobbered me!"

"Corben?" I said, disbelievingly.

"Who else? Right in the eye—see?"

She leaned forward across my legs so I could get a closer view of the mouse Corben had plastered onto her right eye—but with that pint-size bikini top fast losing contact with her anatomy, who was to look at a mouse?

"Well, why don't you take a look?" she said impatiently. "Oh—I get it!" She straightened up again quickly. "So there it was—finish!"

"What did you do right after he clobbered you, Betty?" I asked.

"I clobbered him right back," she announced. "Busted all his front teeth—they weren't his own of course—and I figured he maybe swallowed one because he sounded like he was choking to death when I left."

"What did you hit him with?"

"A chair leg," she said absently. "So—here I am!"

She slid easily onto my lap and snuggled up close. "You don't mind me staying with you, Al honey?" she asked in a throaty, wanton voice.

"How long?" I asked cautiously.

"Maybe a week—then I'm going to get me a job in a club or something, but right now I could use a rest."

"Yeah," I said bleakly.

"Yeah!" She bit the lobe of my ear greedily, "I'm not that tired, of course!"

"No?" I said.

"Well, then," I said excitedly. "Why don't we—"

"No!" She placed my hand firmly on her thigh, then dug her nails sharply into the back of it.

"Well, then," I said excitedly. "Why don't we—"

Her lips met mine with that cool, controlled passion—and what I remembered from before about the hint of a volcanic eruption waiting to explode beneath her cool surface was nothing but the truth.

Finally she moved her head away and sighed dreamily. "Like you said, lover," she murmured huskily. "Why don't we?"

I pulled her toward me again, but met up with sharp, determined resistance as she jabbed her elbows into my chest.

"You changed your mind so fast?" I snarled.

"I've got this thing about insecurity, remember?" She pointed imperiously toward the bedroom door.

"Sure—I forgot!" I apologized.

Once on my feet, I slid one arm around her shoulders and the other under her knees and carried her across the living room toward the security she needed so bad.

"Al?" she said softly as I kicked the door shut behind me, "Whatever happened to that pal of yours—you know—the cop?"

"Which one?"

"George something Shore—the one with the actress who hates couches the way I do?"

"Oh—him!" I dropped her onto the bed and she bounced pleasantly. "Did you ever get to see *My Fair Lady?*"

"Did you?" she asked demurely, her fingers busy with the bikini pajama outfit.

Well, I can tell you right now that was the best show I ever saw. Small cast, but they carried the whole thing without any trouble. Straightforward plot with a thunderous climax—and the lyrics were out of this world. You might have trouble in getting tickets—but keep trying—it's worth the trouble!

THE END

The Exotic
- - - -
Carter Brown

CHAPTER ONE

The sudden, strident sound of the phone ringing must have triggered off some guilt complex buried deep in her mind. Anyway, she took one violent leap off the couch, fought a desperate losing battle to keep her balance as her ankles tangled with a small footstool, then fell backward onto the carpet with a horrible, jarring thud.

For a couple of seconds I had a fascinating view of her delectable legs waving frantic semaphore signals for help, then she managed to force herself up into a sitting position. She glared murderously at me, with one silky strand of blonde hair hanging over her eyes, as I moaned with helpless laughter.

"You brute!" she said coldly, wrestling her skirt back down over her thighs. "Why don't you answer the damn thing?"

I realized the phone was still ringing impatiently, and staggered across the room, both hands clasped tightly to my aching sides.

"Wheeler," I gasped into the mouthpiece, then dissolved into maniacal laughter.

"*Lieutenant* Wheeler!" Sheriff Lavers' angry voice grated in my ear. "It sounds like you were expecting me to call. I guess it's just a goddam big joke to you—real funny, eh?"

"It's a riot," I panted. "But how come you know about it? You got my apartment bugged with a TV camera or something?"

"Don't try and change the subject!" he bellowed furiously. "I'll have your badge for this, Wheeler! I'll have you tossed out of the force! I'll— I'll—" There was a momentary silence while he obviously took a deep breath.

It suddenly occurred to me we weren't talking about the same thing, and it was a sobering thought.

"What did I do?" I asked cautiously.

"Do!" His voice exploded in my eardrums so painfully that I knew I'd still be getting the fallout effect fifteen minutes later. "You know damn well what you did—putting that corpse in a cab and having it delivered to my house! I'll see you in San Quentin for this before I'm through! I'll—"

"Shut up!" I yelled brutally.

There was a stunned silence that lasted long enough for me to get a word in edgewise. "I don't know what you're talking about," I told him. "But I'll come right over and find out. Meantime, Sheriff, why don't you take a deep breath and hold it until I get there?"

I hung up on his outraged silence carefully, then looked at the blonde. She'd gotten onto her feet and was busy checking for bruises, her hands moving tenderly over the area where her skirt was tightest.

"It breaks my heart, honey," I said sadly. "But duty calls—and all that jazz. Like I have to go now."

She looked at me bitterly, and her voice was that way too. "Maybe it's just as well," she said, "unless you want to make love standing up. That acrobatic display knocked all the romance out of me just like that!"

"Tough," I said sympathetically. "It's been fun, doll, and maybe some other time?"

She shook her head. "Not on your life! Next time I'm out selling magazine subscriptions, I'll know better, and stay on the other side of the welcome mat."

"Ah, well—" I smiled vaguely and drifted toward the door. "Just shut the door behind you, honey, on your way out, huh?"

"Hey!" Her eyes widened suddenly. "You didn't even buy a subscription yet!"

"Listen, gorgeous," I said over my shoulder as I left the apartment, "how the hell would a guy like me find time to read?"

I picked up my Austin Healey from the all-night parking garage and drove out to Lavers' house. The County Sheriff had sounded real mad on the phone and maybe he had a right—if he wasn't roaring drunk and just imagining the whole thing. But who the hell would bother paying taxi fare to have a corpse delivered to him?

About twenty minutes later I swung the car into the driveway and saw that a real, life-sized cab stood outside the front porch.

As I got out of the Healey I had that nasty, sinking sensation in the pit of my stomach that's mostly reserved for the sight of my bank manager. When I moved closer, a portly figure detached itself from the people clustered behind the cab and hurried toward me.

It was Sheriff Lavers himself, and his temper hadn't improved very much. He growled, "If you hadn't been laughing your fool head off when I called, maybe I wouldn't have jumped to the obvious conclusion that only an irresponsible jerk like Wheeler could have pulled a stupid stunt like this!"

"Well, thank you, Sheriff," I said nastily. "And if that's meant as an expression of confidence I'm overwhelmed—like the girl said when she discovered her boyfriend was triplets. I may also take it up with my lawyers in the morning."

"All right, all right!" he snorted. "I'm prepared to admit that even you wouldn't kill a man just because you needed a corpse as the punch line for a bad joke."

"There is a corpse inside?" I nodded toward the cab. "For real?"

"Go look for yourself," he grunted.

When I opened the rear door of the cab there was a corpse on the back seat, all right. A fat, bald-headed guy pitched sideways onto the seat with two bullet holes just above his left ear. Sometimes they bleed a lot, and sometimes they don't—this guy was a mess.

I closed the cab door quickly and stepped back. "Recognize him?" Lavers asked.

"Not that I remember," I said in surprise. "Why? Is it somebody I should know?"

"I forgot you're only interested in homicides. That is, or was, Dan Lambert. An ex-con by about a week."

"What's his line?" I asked.

"Did three years on a grand larceny rap. Swindled his clients out of close to a hundred thousand dollars, and we never did get to find the money—maybe now we never will," Lavers said.

"How come he got delivered, dead on arrival, to your home?" I asked.

"That's a good question," Lavers said and snorted. "I've been trying to make sense out of the cab driver for the last half hour—see if you can do any better. He's inside the house right now, with Sergeant Polnik keeping an eye on him."

I followed the Sheriff up the walk to the front door, then into the living room. Polnik nodded absently at me, a worried look on his Cro-Magnon face like his old lady wanted him home now, if not sooner. The cab driver, standing beside him, was a small, lean character and if he didn't have ulcers already, he would have any moment now.

"Keno," Lavers barked at him. "This is Lieutenant Wheeler. Tell him your story and we'll see if he can make any sense out of it—which I doubt!"

The cab driver protested.

"What for?" His voice was a high-pitched whine, like maybe his differential needed fixing. "I told you a hunnerd times already—how'm I going to pay off the hack, if I got to stick around here all night making like a record with the needle stuck?"

"So tell it one more time," I suggested, "and you can get your hack back on the road. Maybe we'll take the corpse out of the back seat for you, even."

I wouldn't have figured that his pallid face could lose any more color, but the word *corpse* did it fine.

"Yeah." He expelled his breath slowly. "Well, like I already told the Sheriff maybe a dozen times, I'm cruising past a joint called the Topaz Bar—on Crescent Street—you know it?"

"The Lieutenant knows every bar in downtown Pine City," Lavers said bleakly, "and every bar between here and L.A., I wouldn't be surprised."

"So,"—Keno's shoulders twitched painfully—"these two guys came out, carrying the fat guy between them, and wave me to pull over to the curb. I don't go for drunks in my cab any time, but I don't got a fare in the last two hours and a guy got to live, don't he?"

"You got the Bill of Rights to back you on that point," I assured him. "What then?"

Keno wiped his sweating brow.

"Well, they stagger around the sidewalk for a while, then they manage to shove him into the back seat. One guy shoves a sawbuck and a piece of paper into my hand and says for me to take their pal home—then he and his friend beat it.

"So I do like he says and look what happens!" He smacked his forehead with the palm of his hand. "I should've stayed home all day like my horoscope said already."

"You still got that piece of paper?" I asked.

Lavers grunted and thrust it into my hand. It was a sheet torn out of a cheap notebook, with Lavers' name and home address—but not his official title of Sheriff—printed clumsily with a blunt pencil.

"The easy way to unload a cadaver," the Sheriff said angrily. "All you need is a cab driver too dumb to notice when you dump a stiff in the back seat of his cab."

"Hey!" Keno protested. "How the hell was I to know the guy's dead?"

"What kind of a hackie are you?" I demanded. "Didn't you try talking to him on the way out?"

Keno glowered and gestured impatiently.

"In all that traffic? Look, mister, I don't got the time for light chitchat—not with all them maniacs driving the streets this time of night! One goddam crazy jerk near ran me off the road already on the way out here—scraped the rear fender and door, then beat it before I got a chance to give him a piece of my mind, even."

Lavers gave an impatient growl, like maybe he figured this was no time for light chitchat either.

"Wheeler," he said, "you'd better get over to the Topaz Bar and check there. I got a good mind to book this—this somnambulist—for driving with his eyes shut."

"Now, wait a minute," Keno wailed. "It's like already I tell you guys, I didn't have a chance to notice—"

"Yeah, yeah," I broke in. "The car that scraped your fender. You get his license number?"

He shook his head sorrowfully.

"No time for that, it all happened so fast. It was one of them long, low imported jobs—a sports car. That's all I saw."

"What color was it?" I queried.

"White, I think—yeah, it was white for sure."

"What does it matter?" Lavers snarled. "You get over to that bar, Wheeler, and see what maybe you can dig up. Polnik and I can take care of the detail here."

"Whatever you say, Sheriff," I said politely. But first I had a thought. "I guess Lambert's swindled victims won't be crying into their coffee when they hear he's dead, huh?"

"They just might," Lavers said. "His partner made good all their losses down to the last cent."

"His partner?" I was suddenly interested. "Just who is this Daddy Christmas?"

"Lieutenant Wheeler!" The veins corded in his neck and his face turned a bright crimson. "I told you to go check that bar, do you remember? So get the hell on your way!"

"Sheriff, I'm gone already," I assured him as I edged quickly from the room.

Outside, I took time out to walk around to the far side of the cab and see that the left rear window was open. So I stuck my head inside to take another look.

Coming face to face with the demon king so suddenly had a kind of unnerving effect on me—and it wasn't helped by the corpse that lay slouched between us, either.

"Why don't you knock?" Doc Murphy leered at me from the other side of the cab. "It's more polite."

"I'm glad it's you, and not one of my better nightmares somehow gotten a life of its own," I told him honestly. "What is this? The Old Ghouls' reunion or something?"

"I'm just doing my job, Lieutenant," Murphy said with smug superiority, "and five will get you ten it's more than you can truthfully say."

"Look," I said, "with two slugs in his head the guy's dead. You got to be a doctor to know that?"

"It helps," he grinned.

"Maybe you'd like to tell me how long he's been dead?" I asked.

"No longer than ninety minutes, I'd say."

"How come you're so precise?" I asked skeptically. "He was wearing a miniature watch on his earlobe, maybe?"

"I wonder, Lieutenant," he said carefully, "if you'd consider doing me a big personal favor?"

"And wind up on a slab in the morgue?" I shuddered at the thought. "Not a chance! I made up my mind a long time back, Doc—when I die I'm going to make good and sure I'm in some place outside of your jurisdiction!"

"Fine," he said with an evil smile. "I'll see if I can arrange something for you, Wheeler."

I pulled my head back out of the cab and took a look at the rear left fender. It was scraped the way Keno had said. Then I poked my head inside again, and Murphy grimaced horribly.

"Will you stop doing that, Lieutenant!" he pleaded. "It's not fair to a man with Irish blood in his veins."

"Got to ask you something else," I explained. "Like how close do you figure the gun was?"

"Not very," he muttered, and shrugged. "There are no powder burns or anything. Ask me after the autopsy."

"Could you make a guess?"

"Strictly a guess," he emphasized. "Between ten and twenty feet away, maybe."

"Thanks, Doc," I said. "There are times when you're almost useful, you know."

"I wish I could say the same for you, you trivial troglodyte!" he snarled. "Aren't you supposed to be investigating a murder, or something?"

"What else?" I stared at him coldly for a moment. "Don't you know you're the chief suspect?"

I went back into the house again and Lavers goggled at me for a moment, not believing his eyes.

"Do you remember whether the rear window on the left was open or shut when they put the fat guy into your cab?" I inquired of the driver.

Keno frowned and scratched his head before he answered. Finally he said, "I guess it was open. The last fare before that one was a fresh air fiend—a nut! I don't remember winding it shut again when he got out."

"Thanks," I said gratefully.

"Wheeler!" Lavers roared.

"I'm leaving for the bar right away, sir," I assured him quickly.

CHAPTER TWO

The beautiful blonde head of Annabelle Jackson, the Sheriff's secretary, was bent dutifully over her desk when I got into the office around ten the next morning. Not only her beautiful head, but the beautiful rest of her was also bent over her desk as she fished for a pen that had dropped behind it.

The sight of those curves sharply outlined beneath her tightly stretched dress was irresistible. I slapped her playfully and she straightened up real fast, like she'd just been blasted off a launching pad.

Then she spun around toward me, delivering a roundhouse right at the same time—but I had a whole lifetime's experience of slap and tickle behind me, and I was waiting for it. I caught her slim wrist while it was still maybe twelve inches from my face.

"You!" Annabelle blazed with frustrated fury. "You—you sex maniac!"

"Magnolia blossom," I said, shaking my head sadly, "that's a cotton-pickin' untruth, and you know it! I was only paying my respects to the cutest little—"

"Don't you dare say it!" she panted desperately. "I've got a good mind to complain to the Sheriff about the lecherous lieutenants in this office."

I let her wrist drop and looked at her with pretended misery. "Lieutenants, plural? You mean I'm just one of the boys?"

For a moment she seemed undecided whether to laugh or crown me with her typewriter. She never did get around to making a decision because suddenly a voice boomed my name from the inner office—and when my master used that tone of voice, I answered—or else.

The Sheriff had a cigar jammed in his teeth as usual when I went into his office, and the usual apoplectic expression on his face to go with it.

"I hope you'll pardon me for interrupting your mating games, Lieutenant." He was heavily sarcastic. "I keep forgetting that it's spring—maybe because you act the same all year round, anyway!"

"That's all right, sir," I assured him. "I can understand your—nostalgic interest."

Right then his face disappeared in a dense cloud of cigar smoke, so I never did get to see the reaction.

"Sit down, Wheeler," he said finally in a strangled voice. "That is, if you have the time to discuss something as trivial as that murder last night."

"My time is your time, Sheriff," I told him as I sat in the nearest visitor's chair. "I'm happy to discuss anything with you, however trivial."

"All right, then!" The smoke cleared enough for me to see his beady eyes glaring malevolently at me. "Now just let's cut the comedy, shall we? I seem to remember telling you to check the Topaz Bar last night."

"Right!" I said, striving for that explosive efficiency that cops on television have got without even trying.

"That was the last I saw of you until now," he snapped. "Is it too much to ask what happened?"

"I checked at the bar," I told him. "The bartender remembered Lambert being there, no trouble at all. He was there for three hours or maybe longer, drinking steadily the whole time. And the drunker he got, the more he talked."

"How do you mean, talked?" Lavers wanted to know.

"Well, he kept telling anyone who cared to listen, how he was going to fix that bastard real good with some guy called Lavers. He didn't give the bastard a name, which is our bad luck. But he kept on waving a piece of paper around with your name and address on it."

"And so?" Lavers grunted.

"So the bartender remembers Lambert talking to a couple of guys who were almost as high as he was. Then the bar got busy and the next time he had a chance to look, Lambert and the two guys were gone. The bartender figures it's likely that the other two lushes could've put him in a cab and sent him out to your place—just because they were loaded enough to play good Samaritans."

"Hogwash!" the Sheriff said loudly. "They're the men we want—they obviously set him up inside the bar, killed him when they got him outside, and dumped his body into the cab."

He had it all figured, for sure. I didn't go along with him.

"It doesn't make sense that way, Sheriff. How about the noise—two shots—right outside a bar full of people?"

"You got a better idea?" he demanded.

"I've got quite a few," I told him. "For a start, the piece of paper with your name and address on it—maybe we could check it with a sample of Lambert's handwriting? Then, how about the white sports car that scraped the cab's rear left fender?"

"How about it?" Lavers asked.

"The cab window was down on that side," I reminded him. "And that's the direction the slugs came from, according to how Lambert was sitting and where he was hit."

Lavers got an inkling then of what I was talking about. And he blinked at me incredulously.

"You figure somebody would be crazy enough to run their auto alongside the cab in thick traffic, and start blasting at the cab's passenger?"

"So maybe it sounds crazy," I admitted. "But not as crazy as your theory about the two lushes blasting him on the sidewalk right out in front of the Topaz Bar!"

The Sheriff slid back in his chair and puffed at his cigar furiously, like maybe it was responsible for his problems. I saw that he couldn't think of anything to say, so I jogged him along a little.

"This guy Lambert I know nothing about," I said. "Tell me his story, huh?"

"Nothing much to tell," he grunted. "And what there is of it, is the old, old story—a partnership with one partner honest and the other a crook."

"What kind of business was it?" I asked.

"Lambert and Hamilton, investment counselors," the Sheriff said. "The business built up fine and things seemed to be going well. Then one day Hamilton chanced on something that somehow didn't look right—so he called in an accountant for a spot check of the books. The audit showed a missing total of close to a hundred thousand bucks!"

"It's like you say, Sheriff—an old story," I agreed. "How did Lambert plead?"

"Not guilty. When he was arrested he claimed he'd been framed, and he claimed it again at the trial. Trouble was, his partner had already made good the loss to the firm's customers by then, so that Lambert's story didn't make much sense to the jury. They found him guilty, he drew five years and they paroled him after three."

"What about this Hamilton?" I asked. "Did he carry on the business on his own?"

"No," Lavers shook his head. "He wound it up about a month after the trial. I don't know what he's doing now."

"What about the hundred gees? I take it it never showed up—not in cold cash, or in yachts and swimming pools either?"

"Right," Lavers mumbled through his cigar. "It's a lot of money to have stashed away. A nice motive for murder, wouldn't you say?"

"Maybe as good as you'd need," I admitted. "But how about this unnamed bastard that Lambert was going to fix but good? That guy would have a pretty good motive too, if you ask me—with or without money involved."

Lavers waved his cigar impatiently.

"It gives me no pleasure to agree that you're right, Wheeler," he said. "So we've got a choice of motives but damn little else to go on. You have any bright suggestions as to where we start?"

"We might maybe get Polnik to check the Topaz Bar again and see if he can get a line on Lambert's two loaded friends," I said.

"That's easy enough. What else?"

"A little visit to his relatives, maybe," I suggested. "Did he have any?"

"A daughter, Corinne Lambert," the Sheriff said. "She runs a dress shop out on Pine Tree Boulevard. There's no other relative that I know of."

"I'll go see her," I said. "If Lambert talked to anyone about his plans, she'd be the likely one."

"Maybe so, maybe not." Lavers didn't sound enthusiastic. "I guess it's worth a try. But I can't help feeling that the missing hundred grand is the strongest motive we'll ever get—that kind of money can bring enough hoods around to start an army."

I thought about it for a while, then shrugged.

"I don't see this as a pro job," I said. "If a pro had already gotten the money, there'd be no need to knock off Lambert—and if he hadn't gotten it yet, the last thing he'd want would be Lambert dead. Who knocks off the golden goose, Sheriff?"

He looked at me with distaste.

"I hope you don't expect me to answer that, Lieutenant," he said. "All right—go find an amateur killer. I don't care whether he's pro or amateur as long as you find him."

"Yes, sir," I said, with no eagerness at all.

I'd gotten as far as the door when he called to me. There was the kind of expression on his face that Charlie Chan used to wear—inscrutable, they called it.

"That automobile you've got, Wheeler," he said vaguely.

"The Austin Healey?" I said proudly.

"It's one of those foreign sports jobs, isn't it?" he asked.

"That's right, Sheriff," I assured him. "She can do a hundred and ten—"

"What color is the paint job?"

"White," I said without thinking.

"I thought so," Lavers said in a peculiarly satisfied voice. "Do you have an alibi for the time of Lambert's death, Wheeler?"

I stared at him, first with surprise and then with a grin.

"Sure, I've got an alibi. She's blonde and beautiful. Right now I can't seem to recall her name—but she sells magazine subscriptions."

"Sells mag—" He gaped at me for a moment, then shook his head slowly. "No, I guess I don't have any right to ask."

"That's okay by me, Sheriff," I said generously. "I have lots of confidence in your discretion—you're no blabbermouth—so I'll tell you anyway."

"Thanks, Wheeler." He tried hard not to appear too eager. "You have my word that I'll respect your confidence."

"Well, then—" I looked around hastily, like I was taking care nobody could overhear. "The answer, Sheriff, is no! I didn't buy any magazine subscriptions after all!"

The gorgeous Annabelle Jackson reared back defensively in her chair when I returned to the outer office, her lovely eyes as wary as all get out.

"What seems to be the trouble?" I asked reasonably.

"Just you come within six feet of me and I'll yell for a cop!" she threatened.

"Honey chile," I said reproachfully, "anyone would figure you don't trust me, or something."

"Anyone would be right," she assured me. "I wouldn't trust you around my dear old grandmother, and she's pushing eighty-six!"

"Maybe she's too old to protect herself, but at least she's old enough not to worry," I said. Then I changed the subject. "Do you know a dress shop on Pine Tree Boulevard, run by a dame named Corinne Lambert?"

Annabelle closed her eyes and shuddered faintly.

"Please, Lieutenant!" she said. "Miss Lambert would drop dead with horror if she heard you call her place a dress shop. It's a *boutique!*"

"That's the hip word for it these days?" I asked interestedly, because I always figure that education is real important.

"For her kind of place, yes. It means it's such an exclusive establishment, the price tag is delivered personally—they whisper the message in your ear."

"And then?" I queried.

"Then if you're still on your feet, they add the tax."

"What's this Lambert dame like?" I asked.

"How would I know, on my salary?" Annabelle said bitterly. "In that place I couldn't even afford to buy a pair of—well, I just couldn't."

"You mean, you wouldn't bother wearing—" I saw the steely glint come back into her eyes, and smiled quickly. "Never mind! So the Lambert place is an exclusive clip joint, huh? And they make a lot of money?"

"Millions, I should imagine," Annabelle said wistfully. "And why not? It's the ambition of every Pine City girl to own one of their creations before she dies."

"It sounds fascinating," I said thoughtfully. "I think I'll go over there and see if any of the Lambert creations make me feel the same way."

"You'd look real cute in something fashioned out of heavy canvas, with heavy duty leather accessories," Annabelle said sweetly. "Something that's just right to wear when the big men in their little white coats call for you."

I parked the Healey outside the entrance and read the sign that said *exotic BOUTIQUE*—just like that. In the beautifully draped window there was one plaster model wearing a shimmering fantasy in what looked like spun gold. Then I recalled what Annabelle had told me about their price tags, and figured that maybe it wasn't a fantasy after all.

Inside there was a subtle fragrance of very feminine and very expensive perfume, in keeping with the expensive decor and the white lamb's-wool carpet with its ankle-deep pile. There were half a dozen dressing rooms to one side, and a long plate-glass counter with bright silver trim right ahead of me. More plaster models displayed more shimmering fantasies, and the only thing missing was people.

Then the heavy brocade drapes in back of the counter whispered sibilantly, and a girl appeared. A dark-eyed brunette with the slender grace of a gazelle, who looked at me nervously like she'd never been alone with a man in her whole life before—or maybe it was just that guys didn't browse around the *boutique* as a rule.

"Please?" Her voice had a faint, liquid accent. "Can I help you, sir?"

"You are Corinne Lambert?" I asked.

"Oh, no." She smiled shyly. "I am Carla, her assistant."

"Well, I wonder if I could see her—" I began.

Then the heavy drapes parted a second time, and a silver blonde stepped out beside Carla. The two girls made a striking contrast, Carla with her dark hair styled in a soft pixie, and the blonde with bright clusters of thick, shoulder-length curls. She was brown-eyed too—always startling in a blonde. But with a figure like that, who cared what color her eyes were?

The figure was wrapped in a linen dress with a scalloped neckline and swinging skirt that flared from her fully rounded hips. Her breasts were full and deep, straining against the fabric of her dress in a kind of primitive revolt against being constrained. Frankly, I was on their side—or it could be my imagination was running a fever again.

"I'll handle this, Carla," she said briefly to the dark-eyed, slender girl, then smiled at me with dazzling white teeth. "Maybe I can help you?"

Her voice was throaty with a velvety purr that made you imagine she'd said all kinds of exciting things she hadn't.

"A gift for your wife, perhaps?"

"I don't have a wife," I said.

"Well, then, maybe a gift for somebody special?"

"I don't think I know anyone special." I looked at her thoughtfully. "Do you know anyone special?"

Maybe she had no sense of humor—her smile was still there, but it had gotten a little fixed around the edges. "That's hardly the point, is it?" she said. "I mean, if you could tell me the sort of person you're buying the gift for, then I could—"

"You are Corinne Lambert?" I asked unnecessarily.

"I certainly am." The smile gave out altogether now. "What is this all about?"

"I'm Lieutenant Wheeler from the County Sheriff's office. I'd like to talk to you about your father."

"Why didn't you say so in the first place?" she said coldly, like she resented her time being wasted. "All right, you'd better come into my office. Carla, stay here and look after any clients who come in."

The brunette nodded gracefully. "Yes, Miss Lambert."

"Come through here," the silver blonde said curtly to me, and disappeared through the heavy drapes.

I walked around the counter and pushed my thickish way through the brocade, then stepped into a disappointingly prosaic office at the other side. It was small and cluttered, and dominated by the presence of Corinne Lambert—like most surroundings were, I thought.

She turned to face me, eyeing me keenly and speculatively, and folding her arms under her bosom so that those startling curves became even more so.

"I'll be glad if you can be brief, Lieutenant," she said crisply. "I don't have much time."

"It's about your father, Dan Lambert," I said.

"I've already been told about what happened," she said with an impatient shrug. "A man from the sheriff's office was here last night. I wonder you don't maintain a better liaison down there, Lieutenant."

"You don't quite understand," I said mildly. "Your father was murdered. I'm supposed to find the killer. So I'd like to have a talk with you about your father."

"I see." She didn't sound terribly interested.

"I'm maybe a little surprised," I said curiously. "I rather expected to find you upset over your father's death. You don't—"

"I don't appear to be?" she finished for me. Then her brown eyes studied my face for a few moments, with the remote concentration of a scientist confronted by a new virus under his microscope.

"We are not an emotional family, Lieutenant," she stated. "I'm sorry about my father's death, naturally. But we were never close to each other. In fact, this last week has been the first time I've seen him in more than three years."

"You didn't visit him in jail?" I asked.

"He never expressed any wish to see me while he was there," she said calmly, her voice recording a matter of statistics.

"That seems—unusual," I remarked.

She shrugged and laughed simultaneously, but there was no joy in the laughter.

"My father was a self-sufficient man, Lieutenant." Her tone was brittle. "I thought he made that obvious, seeing that he was caught embezzling but managed to hang onto the profit!"

"It was certainly worth hanging onto," I said. "Almost a hundred thousand dollars, wasn't it? Do you figure somebody killed him for the money?"

"I feel sure of it," she said. "What other reason could there possibly be?"

"At this stage I can't say," I told her, and found myself wishing that she'd relax and maybe act a little more human. I took out my cigarette case and offered her a smoke. She accepted with a stiff little "thank you."

I held a light for both of us, then spoke again.

"Your father was drinking in a downtown bar last night. He kept telling everyone there he was going out to see Sheriff Lavers, and fix somebody real good. Seemed like he figured to pay off a score, maybe. Would you have any idea what he was talking about?"

She thought about it briefly, breathing smoke.

"That sounds just like Big-mouth Dan Lambert when he was drunk," she said brutally. "Always shooting off his mouth, always fixing to cut somebody down to size—anybody, from the manicurist in the hotel barber shop who wouldn't date him, to the elevator boy who let him out at the wrong floor! There you have a pretty good picture of what my father was like, Lieutenant. Liquor was the great equalizer where he was concerned."

It was a lot of contemptuous talk, but it hadn't answered my question. I tried again. "Do you think what your father was saying in the bar had any significance?"

"I don't, really," she said, then shrugged. "But of course I could be wrong. As I've told you, Lieutenant, I didn't have much to do with him. I have my own busy life here—I was never interested in my father's plans."

"Yet you seem pretty sure that the money, the hundred grand, was the motive for his death," I said. "How come?"

Corinne Lambert threw back her exquisite head, and for the first time there was real amusement in her laughter. She said, "Why wouldn't I be sure? And why aren't you? A hundred thousand! What better motive could anyone have?"

Then her face sobered and she looked at me curiously. "Don't tell me you don't know about Lenny Kosto," she said.

"All right!" I snarled. "So I don't know about Lenny Kosto!"

She drew thoughtfully at her cigarette and nodded slowly.

"Then perhaps I'd better tell you," she said. "He was in jail with my father—was released a few weeks before him, I think. The last time I saw Dan alive was a couple of days back, and he was worried. So worried that he mentioned it to me, which was unlike him. It seemed that this Kosto and another man were in town and bothering him about the hundred thousand."

"Bothering him how?" I asked.

"They wanted a cut from it, and wouldn't believe that he didn't have the money. Neither did I, for that matter. But I guess Dan had been denying having the money for so long, he'd almost come to believe it was true himself."

I figured that my visit had been worthwhile.

"Do you know what this Lenny Kosto looks like?" I asked.

"I haven't the faintest idea, Lieutenant," she said flatly. "I've never seen him and Dan didn't describe him. Matter of fact, it wasn't a fond farewell between Dan and me. He wanted some money and I refused to give him any. I told him to use some of his hidden pile and he got mad at me. So we had a fight, as always."

"Did he happen to mention the name of the other guy?" I queried. "The one who was with Kosto?"

"Not that I recall, Lieutenant. But I imagine they'll still be together, and when you find Kosto you'll find the other one," she said casually.

"Looks like you've got a pretty good imagination, Miss Lambert," I said admiringly. "Matched only by your filial devotion to your father, maybe."

"The relationship between my father and me is none of your business!" Her eyes were cold, her voice gone hard. "And I don't have to take such remarks from you! Now I suggest that you get out of here. I've wasted more than enough time as it is."

"I'll go pretty soon," I told her. "But first—do you have any idea why your father came back to Pine City when he was paroled?"

"To pick up the money he'd stashed away some place, obviously," she sneered. "But I guess your brilliant mind couldn't figure that one out for itself, Lieutenant."

"My brilliant mind doesn't need to figure anything out while it's around you," I pointed out mildly. "Seems to me you've got everything figured already."

She stubbed her smoke on an ashtray, wasting a good inch of my cigarette. She said, "Dan Lambert was my father—he was also a bum. Make out of that anything you want, it doesn't bother me. He was the only family I ever had and he gave me nothing. No love, no kindness, not even a casual interest. I'm sorry he's dead, the way I'm sorry to hear about anyone dying—but that's all."

I looked at her thoughtfully.

"So he gave you nothing," I said. "Yet you haven't done real bad, would you say?"

"What are you talking about now?" she demanded wearily, like maybe she didn't know how much longer she could put up with me.

I gestured toward the elaborate setup on the other side of the brocade drapes. I said, "It's quite a business you've got out there, Miss Lambert. I hear tell it's so exclusive you choose your own clients, almost."

"That's just a wild rumor," she said tersely. "But it's a very good business, of course. I built it up myself. The *boutique* owes nothing to Dan Lambert."

"Well, thanks for your time and the information you've given me," I said, real polite.

"I'm sorry I can't say it's been a pleasure, Lieutenant," she said, then flashed her white teeth in a brilliant smile. "But then, talking about my father never was! Sorry I haven't been of much help to you."

"I wouldn't say you haven't," I said.

On the way out, wading through that thick pile of the carpet, I came across the shy and slender brunette. She was busy dressing a plaster model just inside the doorway.

"No clients come in yet?" I said sympathetically. "But I guess Tuesday's a bad day, huh?"

She sighed prettily, with a worried little frown creasing her otherwise flawless skin.

"I'm afraid Tuesday's no different from any other day, Lieutenant. If things don't get better, I really don't know how much longer Miss Lambert will be able to keep the *boutique* open."

After what Corinne had just said, if I looked at Carla in surprise I wasn't kidding.

"That's tough!" I said. "And I thought the place had such an exclusive reputation, and all."

"Maybe that is our trouble," she said with a wan smile. "Too many people are frightened by our reputation for high prices. Actually, we have many lines at very reasonable prices—but people don't come here to find out."

"Miss Lambert doesn't seem to worry," I said. "Not so it shows, anyway."

"I think she worries secretly, all the time," Carla confided. "It must be costing an awful lot of money, just to stay open."

"That so?" I nodded and grinned at her, patting her cheek. And I said, "I got a feeling somebody around here is kidding me, honey, but I don't think it's you."

Out on the sidewalk, I looked back over my shoulder and saw that Carla was still watching me through the plate-glass doors. It was hard to figure the expression in her dark, liquid eyes. Right then I got a nasty feeling I could be wrong, after all, about who was kidding me in the *exotic BOUTIQUE*.

I went into the corner drugstore and used the phone to call the Sheriff. I told him what I'd heard about Lenny Kosto and his unknown buddy.

"There you are!" Lavers said jubilantly. "I'll bet that's the two guys in the bar who put Lambert into the cab. Maybe you'll recall that I said all along it was them who killed him."

"That's what you said, for sure, Sheriff," I agreed. "So what?"

"What do you mean, so what?" he demanded.

"So we still have to prove it," I said. "Before we can do that, we need to get with these characters. What about you getting a run-down on this Lenny Kosto? It could help Polnik when he checks at the Topaz Bar again."

"Do you have to suggest a thing like that?" Lavers raged. "Do you think I'm a moron who wouldn't think of doing it myself?"

"I think you're real smart, Sheriff," I assured him. "And it gives me a lot of pleasure, you being so smart."

"How come?" Lavers demanded.

"Because if you're smart, that makes me a genius," I said, hanging up on him and getting in the last word for once.

CHAPTER THREE

The office was on the fourth floor of an old, unfashionable building on the wrong side of the street. *Hamilton Hamilton, Importer* was stenciled neatly on the frosted glass panel of the door. I figured that importing must be quite a switch from the kind of business which had been carried on by Hamilton and Lambert, Investment Counselors.

Inside, the office was small and had a dusty air to it, like nothing much had happened there since Pearl Harbor. There was a railed-off area which contained a desk and a secretary sitting at it. Behind her, there was a door with *Mr. H. Hamilton* on it in bold black letters.

It was all very businesslike in an old-fashioned, faintly shabby way, and the over-all effect was depressing. Or it would have been, without the happy presence of the secretary.

She was a blonde—not a silver one this time but an orthodox everyday blonde—and her eyes were blue, not brown. She watched me walk toward her, and likely we were both interested in what we saw. She idly rubbed a pencil against the side of her turned-up nose, and on her it was a cute gesture.

"I'd like to see Mr. Hamilton," I said. "Would you tell him I'm here? Lieutenant Wheeler from the county sheriff's office."

"I'd just adore to, Lieutenant," she said with enthusiasm, "but I can't. Mr. Hamilton isn't here today."

"Too bad," I said. "Do you know where I might locate him?"

"At home, I think. You want the address?"

"Thank you," I said, and waited while she wrote it down, tore the sheet off the note pad, and handed it over.

"It's a pleasure, Lieutenant," she said, dazzling a smile at me. "Anything else I might do for you?"

"Well, now ..."—I leered at her—"hardly at this stage. I've only just met you."

I turned away toward the door and she spoke again, excitedly.

"Wait a minute, Lieutenant. I have something I would like to show you."

I swung back inquiringly, and the blonde got up from behind her desk and walked away slowly toward the window.

It was the kind of walk that has kept the movies alive since television, when they ripped up the code of ethics and set about getting an audience the old-fashioned way. And this cute blonde had a real talent for it.

Her walk was a kind of sinuous, undulating, rhythmic motion that was more than fascinating to watch. She had me enthralled before she'd taken half a dozen steps. I stared after her and for once I had no words.

When she reached the window she stopped for a moment with her rounded hips still oscillating gently, like she'd left her motor running and it was in fine tune. Then she turned around and started back toward me.

The front view was as startling as the rear one had been, with the white silk blouse clinging close to the high peaks of her smallish breasts as they impudently thrust against the yielding material. By the time she was sitting down again at the desk, I was staring bug-eyed.

"I sit here all day, five days a week," she explained lightly. "I almost never get to see any nice, virile-looking guys who look at me the way you did when you came in. So when one does come in, I like to make an impression."

"You've made an impression, all right, honey," I said maybe a little hoarsely. "If I was sure you wouldn't scream for help, I'd prove it right now."

She picked up the pencil and tapped her cute nose with it again, and her eyes mocked me with a wicked gleam.

"It's not that I'd scream, Lieutenant," she said demurely, "It's just that I'm a romantic-minded girl and this old office isn't my idea of a suitable background for ecstasy—anyway it's dusty, too."

"Honey," I said thickly, "it so happens my apartment—complete with hi-fi machine and five wall speakers waiting to reproduce sweet and soft music—is exactly the kind of background you've been waiting for."

"Well, I don't know ..." She tapped her nose again, giving the idea careful consideration. "I guess I would have to see your apartment first, Lieutenant, before I could be sure."

"That can be arranged, honey," I said eagerly. "Maybe if we went and had dinner someplace first and then—"

"Dinner first is a nice idea," she agreed, also eagerly. "How about the Hacienda around eight tonight? And please don't be late, Lieutenant."

"I promise not to be," I vowed. "And the name is Al, honey."

"I'm Agnes Green," she said, smiling calmly. "I guess maybe that's why I walk the way I do. A girl has to do something to compensate for a name like Agnes."

"I think you overcompensate, Agnes," I told her, "but it's a good fault."

"Thank you," she said. Then, "I hope you find Mr. Hamilton at home, Al. It's about the Lambert killing, maybe?"

"It's about the Lambert killing for sure," I said.

"He hasn't talked about it—not to me, anyway," Agnes said thoughtfully, "but I sometimes think that Mr. Hamilton still isn't used to the switch from investments to importing."

"What does he import, exactly?" I asked.

"Novelties, mostly." She sniffed. "Tricks—you can be the life of the party for only thirty-five cents—that kind of junk."

"Like the kind of stuff you see in the magic shop windows?" I asked in astonishment.

"Sure," the blonde said, "and in the mail order ads on the back pages of comics."

"How's business?" I inquired, taking another look around the dingy office. "Doesn't look like it's thriving exactly—but then, I fool easily."

"It's never gotten up off its knees since I've been here the last eight months," she said. "But I have a feeling that he just doesn't care—Mr. Hamilton, I mean. It gives him something to do, and that's all he wants."

"If I had a blonde as cute as you walking around my office all day the way you perform," I said truthfully, "that's all I would want, too."

"Mr. Hamilton doesn't get the same kind of walk," she smiled. "I don't mind exercise, Lieutenant Al, but being chased around an office all day isn't my idea of a healthy life."

I grinned down at her.

"Looks like I've got what Mr. Hamilton hasn't," I suggested.

"Oh, he's got it, I guess," Agnes said seriously. "But he's had it a while longer than you have and now it's getting a little yellow around the edges, if you know what I mean."

"No, I don't," I said, fascinated. "I don't quite know what you're talking about."

"Get out of here, Al Wheeler!" she said in mock annoyance. "And don't be late at the Hacienda—the last time I drank three tequilas on my own, I finished up doing a Mexican hat dance at the wrong party and just wearing a hat!"

"I'll be exactly three tequilas late, honey," I promised. "And please—can I be the wrong party this time?"

The Hamilton house was one of those wilder West Coast fantasies that look at first sight like they belong in Disneyland—until you remember that there's some point to the things built in Mr. Disney's domain. If this place had any architectural style at all, I guess you could call it medieval-modern, with a touch of rococo-schizophrenic on the side.

A butler opened the door to me and I told him who I was and he said he would inquire, if I'd kindly wait. I told him if it took very long I'd be less than kind about it, and he gave out with a flash of brilliant repartee like "Very good, sir," without having to think about it, even.

A minute later he returned and graciously inclined his head.

"Mr. Hamilton is out at the moment, sir," he informed me. "But Mrs. Hamilton would like to see you in the drawing room. If you'll follow me?"

"Tell me something, Jeeves," I said, following his stately tread down the wide hallway.

"It's Perkins, sir," he corrected.

"Tell me something, Perkins. What's the difference between a drawing room and a withdrawing room?"

He turned his head slowly, and gave me a deadpan look along with a bland answer. "I would say, sir, that it depends entirely upon the mood one is in and the company one is keeping at the time."

I just about had it figured out by the time we got to the drawing room and Perkins announced me, after which he backed out into the hallway again.

A tall, dark-haired woman in her mid-thirties walked across the room toward me, dressed like maybe she'd just stepped from the cover of *Vogue*.

"I'm Gail Hamilton, Lieutenant," she said in a confident contralto. "I'm sorry Mr. Hamilton isn't here at the moment, but I expect him any time. Sit down, won't you?"

I sat uncomfortably on an antique straight-backed chair that had probably been designed to punish some of the Puritan fathers for wondering how they could be both at the same time. Mrs. Hamilton sat opposite me and crossed her legs. They were as slim and elegant, and as expensively attired, as the rest of her. I looked her over, only from force of habit.

She wore a navy blue linen suit that looked crisp and cool. Her figure was perfectly proportioned without looking sexy, and her face was flawlessly beautiful without being in the least exciting. It added up to a triumph of breeding over natural attributes, I figured.

"You wish to see my husband about Dan Lambert being murdered last night, of course," she said.

"That's right, Mrs. Hamilton," I agreed.

"I'm sure I don't know why that dreadful man had to come back here at all," she said. "You would think he'd have been satisfied with all the worry and shame he caused us in the first place! I never did trust him, you know, Lieutenant."

"You didn't, huh?" I said.

"Not from the first time I met him, at our wedding. But Hamilton wouldn't listen to me until it was too late. He's a fool that way—trusts anybody!"

"I see," I said, smiling vaguely.

"Now, of course," she said bitterly, "the whole dreadful scandal is going to be raked over again. And it couldn't have happened at a worse time—just as the Daughters of the Western Pioneers are about to elect a new president!"

"Oh?" I queried. "I beg your pardon?"

"It so happens that I'm the favorite candidate," she said, smiling modestly. "Or I was! Heaven knows how our members will react to all this vulgar newspaper publicity. And *murder* this time—it's even worse than before!"

"It's tough on Lambert, too, I suppose," I suggested. From this dame's attitude you'd have thought he'd got himself killed to spite her.

My quip went way over her head.

"It's going to lower our prestige," she said. "Hamilton's and mine, I mean. I told him, after he'd dissolved his partnership with Lambert, that he was a fool to keep working when there was really no need. I mean, I have more than enough money for both of us. But he wouldn't listen, and now that silly importing business of his is going to get some of the publicity!"

"And that's bad?" I asked.

"I shudder to think, Lieutenant—" she closed her eyes for a moment at the horror of it "—what some of my friends will say then they read that Hamilton is making a career out of importing jokes!"

"Maybe they'll buy some and help his business along," said, trying to be helpful.

Her face paled slightly at the thought, but before she had a chance to tell me that her friends kept their magic in the bank where it belonged, the door hurtled open forcefully and a man strode into the room.

"Ah, at last!" Gail Hamilton said. "Hamilton, this is Lieutenant Wheeler from the county sheriff's office. Lieutenant, this is my husband."

Hamilton Hamilton was a big big man, about five inches over six feet tall. He had a hefty build to go with it—once muscular but now gone a little to fat, like a pro football player ten years retired. He was almost too strikingly handsome with his artfully brushed iron-gray hair, piercing blue eyes, deeply sun-tanned complexion, and excellent teeth.

He came at me with a large smile and crushed my hand painfully as he pumped it up and down, like the ship was leaking real bad and I was the last hope.

"Glad to know you, Lieutenant," he said and his voice boomed. "It's about poor Dan Lambert, I guess?"

"That's everybody's guess, and so far they're right," I said a little sourly. "I'd certainly like to ask you a few questions, Mr. Hamilton."

"Of course. Always happy to help the police, Lieutenant. Sit down and—what about a drink?"

"Scotch on the rocks with a little soda would be fine," I said.

"Perkins!" The house trembled at the impact of his roar.

"Darling!" Gail Hamilton protested with a shudder. "Do you have to do that? Can't you ring for the butler?"

The door opened and Perkins came in with a stony look on his cherubic face. "You screamed, sir?" he asked coldly.

"Why don't you get some of that starch out of your vest?" Hamilton chuckled. "For what I'm paying you a month, I could get three dancing girls."

"Hamilton!" His wife tottered to the couch and collapsed in it gracefully. Only Perkins remained calm.

"I shall endeavor to master the Scottish Reel, if that is your wish, sir," he said. "Would you prefer me to wear a kilt?"

"Ah, I was only kidding!" Hamilton said good-humoredly. "We want some drinks pronto. I'm having a tall, cold Tom Collins—how about you, honey lamb?"

"Nothing for me, thank you," his wife said frigidly.

"And a Scotch on the rocks with a dash of soda for our friend the Lieutenant," Hamilton continued. "Make it a very special drink for him—served the way I like a guest to be served. Understand?"

"Yes, sir." Perkins nodded and withdrew.

I sank cautiously down onto the stiff-angled chair again and Hamilton sprawled in a huge rocker, maybe built originally for the use of Whistler *and* his mother. We looked at each other and I figured maybe it was time I made with the questions.

"Before he was murdered, did you know that Dan Lambert was out on parole and had come back to Pine City?" I asked.

"Sure." Hamilton grinned wryly. "That kind of news gets around fast. I didn't like it, but there was nothing I could do about it."

"Do you know the circumstances of his death?" I queried.

"Only what I've been told by the police," Hamilton said with a shrug. "About him arriving at the sheriff's home in a cab—dead."

"He'd been drinking heavily in a downtown bar," I said. "The bartender says that he was pretty drunk and threatening to fix somebody real good with the police. We don't know who the somebody was, at this stage."

"Doesn't sound like Dan to act that way," Hamilton said soberly. "But of course I'm thinking of the old Dan Lambert I knew. I guess three years in jail can change a guy, huh?"

"And not for the better, usually," I said.

"He always used to be what people imagine fat men are and most of them aren't—good-humored, easygoing. I just can't see him sounding off drunkenly like that. But then, you did say he was very drunk, Lieutenant?"

"Would that be unlike him?" I asked. "I've been told he always was a heavy drinker."

"Not Dan." He shook his head positively. "He was a social drinker, sure, but I never saw him stoned in my whole life."

Gail Hamilton joined the discussion with a preliminary sniff.

"The way you talk about him, Hamilton, anyone would think he was your best friend," she said. "Not the man who nearly ruined your life and stole a hundred thousand dollars from you—right under your nose!"

Hamilton's tanned cheeks flushed a darker color, and maybe he would have given out with an angry answer if Perkins hadn't arrived with the drinks at that moment. There was an uncomfortable silence until the butler had set down the glasses and left the room, and by then Hamilton was smiling again.

"Well—" he raised his glass "—good luck, Lieutenant."

"Cheers," I said, and lifted my glass to my lips.

I didn't get to taste any Scotch, so I tilted the glass a little further and was rewarded with a thin trickle down the front of my tie instead.

Hamilton laughed, rocking backward and forward on his chair in a delirium of delight.

"Got you that time, Lieutenant!" he roared. "Known in the trade as a dribble glass. Kind of funny, huh?"

I dabbed my tie with a handkerchief, knowing for sure that the light-colored silk would stain. I bared my teeth at him. "Sure! It's a riot."

"Don't worry about your drink," he gurgled. "Perkins will be right back with a fresh one—in a real glass this time."

The butler appeared on cue, relieved me of the trick glass, and offered me a commiserating glance along with the fresh drink.

"You're a good sport, Lieutenant," Hamilton said handsomely. "A lot of people get real mad at a dribble glass for some reason."

"Maybe because it dribbles," I suggested.

"Because it dribbles? Hey—that's a good one!" He collapsed back into his delirium for a few moments.

When he'd sobered again, I got back to the business in hand.

"I'm interested to hear as much as you can tell me about your association with Dan Lambert," I said. "For a start, how did you come to be partners in the first place?"

"We were in the Army together, and got along fine," he said. "Things had been tough with Dan—his wife had died giving birth to a daughter, and he was a lonely guy. I was luckier. When I got out of the service, I settled down on the West Coast and got myself married to the most beautiful girl I ever met."

He made a clumsy, sitting bow in his wife's direction, and Mrs. Hamilton acknowledged it with a small, complacent smile.

"For a while I didn't know what kind of business I wanted to get into," he went on, "until I began to fool around with stock issues for local companies and got interested. I guess I learned quite a lot. Then, about five years back, who should turn up on our doorstep but Dan Lambert?"

"If you'd had any business acumen at all," Gail Hamilton said crossly, "you'd have tossed him right back into the gutter where he came from. But you always were a sentimental fool!"

"Nothing like the little woman to give a guy a great big boost when he needs it real bad," Hamilton said easily. "Anyway, Dan and me got talking and it turned out that he'd been in business for himself back east, as an investment counselor. He said he wouldn't mind starting up again right here in Pine City, and in the end I decided to go along with him as equal partner."

"Did you check his record back East?" I inquired.

Hamilton smiled again but this time the smile lacked confidence.

"No, sir! I figured I knew Dan better than any eastern banker—but boy, was I wrong about that!"

"And how did the business go?" I asked.

"It went fine. In practically no time at all we had it on its feet, and we grew fast."

"And it was mere chance," I asked, "that you discovered he was embezzling funds?"

"Yeah. He was always particular that we service our own clients and that one partner didn't intrude on the other's accounts. It worked pretty well, I thought. But then one day when Dan was gone for the afternoon one of his clients, called me urgently.

"It seemed that this guy had a sudden need for ready cash and wanted to check the amount of his holdings. It was one of those things that wouldn't wait, so I got his file out of Dan's office and when I looked at it—" he shrugged hopelessly "—it didn't look right at all. So I stalled the client for a while, and went right out and hired myself a bunch of public accountants to make a spot audit—and that was it."

"How did Lambert react when he found out?" I asked.

"He was real mad. Like a maniac!" Hamilton grimaced. "He said he'd been framed—what else could he say, anyway? He stuck to his story right through the trial, even after I had refunded all the money embezzled from his clients."

"There's just a small technical point, my dear," his wife said sweetly. "It was my money that repaid the investors—not yours!"

"Oh, sure!" He scowled at her for a moment. Then he dragged his gaze back to me, and spoke earnestly.

"It was my wife's money, like she says. I want you to fully understand that, Lieutenant. And I'd like to make my own position clear while we're about it. For the last fifteen years I've been a legally hired gigolo. I get three meals a day and all the money I want. As long as she doesn't actually catch me tom-catting around with another woman, I'm sweet!"

"Hamilton!" Gail got up from the couch, a stricken look on her face, and walked quickly toward the door. In a muffled voice she said, "How could you! In front of the Lieutenant! I'll just never forgive you!"

Then she burst into harsh, raucous tears and ran from the room.

Hamilton watched her go, then rocked gently on his chair with a look of smug victory on his face.

"I hope you'll excuse my wife, Lieutenant," he said in a perfunctory tone. "She's a highly emotional woman—bruises real easy."

"Anyway, getting back to this Lambert," I said. "Nobody ever found out what he'd done with the stolen money? Which was close to a hundred thousand dollars, I understand?"

"Right on both counts, Lieutenant," he said, nodding. "Wherever he hid it, he sure picked a hell of a good place!"

"Would you figure that's why he came back to Pine City?" I asked. "To pick up the money?"

"Who knows?" Hamilton shrugged again. "There could be another reason. His daughter's right here in town, you know. Or did you?"

"I did," I assured him. "I always figured a *boutique* was something unmentionable said in French until I saw one for the first time this morning."

"Her prices are unmentionable," he said, chuckling delightedly. "So they tell me."

I stood up and stretched my legs, and Hamilton hauled himself from the chair with a grunting effort. He said, "You're going now, Lieutenant?

I'll have Perkins show you out."

"No need to bother him," I said. "I can find my way." He crossed the room with me, then took my elbow as we stopped near a big, ornate fireplace.

"Gail's a collector," he said in the kind of reverent voice everybody uses when they don't know what they're talking about. "Those two vases—" he pointed at what appeared to be two ugly, painted earthenware pots "—you wouldn't believe it, but they're supposed to be three thousand years old!"

"Must have cost a bundle," I said, not greatly interested.

"Gail paid ten grand for the pair, and figured it was a steal," he assured me.

He moved over to pick up the nearest vase, turning it in his hands for a moment and then—without warning—suddenly tossed it to me.

"Catch!" he said casually.

I made a frantic, twisting effort that nearly dislocated my hips, but his airy toss had been careless and the vase didn't come to within three feet of me. I shut my eyes and waited for the crash, listening for the sound of five grand smashing itself into small pieces—but nothing happened. When I opened my eyes again, the goddamned vase was bouncing gently across the carpet.

"Rubber, you see?" Hamilton was off again, holding his sides and shaking with helpless laughter while the tears rolled down his cheeks. "Your face when you fumbled it! Oh, boy!"

He moaned helplessly. If he kept going that way he would have a heart attack—I hoped.

I went out of the drawing room into the hall, closing the door on the sound of his obscene mirth and heading along the hallway to the front door.

I hadn't quite made it when a door opened quietly right beside me and Gail Hamilton peeked out at me nervously. She held a finger to her lips in a warning of silence, then beckoned me inside.

I shrugged. Maybe her husband was a practical joker and she was a practical seducer and they were both happy with their hobbies? There was one easy way to find out, so I stepped into the room. She shut the door quickly and quietly behind me, then spoke in a nervous voice that was hardly more than a whisper.

"Lieutenant—I have something to tell you and I don't wish my husband to hear."

"Well," I said feebly, "we all got our problems, Mrs. Hamilton, and I guess—"

"Don't be absurd," she snapped. "I want to give you some confidential information which I think may help you in your murder investigation. Do I appear the kind of woman who would seek advice on personal matters from a stranger?"

"Sorry," I mumbled. "Your husband's practical jokes have gotten me kind of confused, I guess."

"Oh, my goodness!" She closed her suffering eyes for a moment. "Did you get the rubber vase, too?"

I nodded miserably.

"And the chair with the collapsible legs?" she asked.

"No," I said, sweating. "I missed out on that one."

She looked at me and shook her head sadly—yet when she spoke there was a maternal kind of fondness in her voice.

"He's just an overgrown boy at times, Lieutenant. But in many ways he is also a wonderful man. Sometimes I'm cruel to him about things that happen because he's so honest himself, he always believes everyone else is the same. But I guess he can't help his honest and generous nature—any more than I can help being the way I am."

"Mrs. Hamilton," I said gently but wearily, "did you bring me in here to tell me that?"

"Of course not!" She snapped back into the attitude suitable for the coming president of the Daughters of the Western Pioneers. She said, "When I first heard that ghastly man was back in town, I was worried that he might attack Hamilton. That he might try and do him some injury—after all, Lambert had cheated him and lied about him before, so who knew what he might do a second time!"

"I see your point," I encouraged her. "So?"

"So I secretly hired a private detective to keep an eye on Lambert the whole time he was in Pine City," she confided. "But Hamilton must never know about this, Lieutenant. He'd be furious—take it as a personal insult to his courage or something silly like that."

I was glad she'd called me into the room. I said, "When did you hire this detective?"

"Seven days ago—right after I heard about Lambert being in town," she said promptly. "He might have some information which could prove useful to you, Lieutenant."

"He might, at that," I agreed.

"When you see him, you may tell him he has my permission to speak freely," she said generously.

"Thank you, Mrs. Hamilton," I said solemnly. "There's just one little point—who is this private eye?"

"Oh, how stupid of me!" She almost blushed. "I forgot. His name is Mervyn Starke, and his office is on Fairfield Drive."

"Mervyn Starke?" I looked at her suspiciously. "You sure this isn't another of your husband's practical jokes?"

CHAPTER FOUR

For sure, the private eye with his feet on the desk in a shabby backroom and a bottle of bourbon clamped between his teeth is a well-worn cliché. But I figured Starke was maybe carrying the modern trend a little too far, when I opened his door and saw the IBM machines purring away contentedly at some kind of electronic investigation.

They weren't all there was to see, though there was nothing any more exciting. A cerebral-looking blonde with lank, straight hair that hung down on either side of her face, sneaked up on me while I wasn't looking.

"Something you wanted?" Her voice was as thin as her legs, with the built-in sneer you mostly find among art dealers and successful pimps. Though what she had to be superior about, was something I didn't understand.

She wore a loose, shapeless dress, and underneath it I guessed that her figure was as flat as a can of stale beer. The frames of her glasses were light blue and they combined with her mud-stained eyes to give a kind of eerie effect.

"I'd like to see Mr. Mervyn Starke," I told her.

"Do you have an appointment?" she asked, and there was a natural sharp edge to her voice.

"Yeah," I said, pointing to the nearest IBM machine. "Your boss told me any time I want to play with one of them, to come right over. Right now I feel like taking in a little wild computation."

Her muddy eyes opened wide, revealing more mud. She said, "Are you out of your mind?"

"Stark, raving mad," I agreed. "Stark—with an E."

"Oh." Her thin lips pursed in a straight line. "Now I understand. You're a humorist!"

"I'm a police lieutenant." I flashed my badge under her nose to prove it. "I want to talk with Merv—if he's not out having his hairdo fixed or anything?"

She thought of about ten things to say, then changed her mind and walked off quickly. I noticed that even her rear view was straight up and down.

I lit myself a cigarette and wondered if it was straight-up-and-down dames that brought out the worst in Wheeler, or if I was just using her as a substitute for Hamilton and his unspeakable practical jokes. Either way it made me a slob, so I quit worrying.

When the blue-tinted frames flashed under my nose, I knew that the dame had sneaked up on me again. Maybe they had secret tunnels and trap doors in this place.

"Mr. Starke can give you ten minutes," she said.

"That's real big of him," I said.

"Come this way," she sneered.

I followed her through a general office until we reached a teak-paneled door which was completely blank.

Merve, baby! I thought admiringly, *this is real class—like chic, yet.*

Miss Leftovers, 1961, knocked gently and an even gentler voice inside bade us enter. I went in and the girl closed the door behind me, leaving herself on the other side of it, which was a relief.

The desk was big enough to plan a war of the planets on. Down in one corner, where the owner could reach without straining himself, was a whole battery of push buttons big enough to make a Pentagon colonel blush.

Seated behind all this was a sharp-faced character with thinning brown hair brushed carefully across his head to hide the bald patches, an impressive domed forehead, and a sharp, pointed nose.

He lifted his gaze from a neatly typed document in front of him and looked at me with serene gray eyes.

"I am Mervyn Starke," he said simply. "State your business briefly, please."

I pointed at the push buttons, very interested.

"What happens if you push them all at one time?" I inquired. "No more world?"

"Please!" He blinked with astonishment and impatience. "I don't have time for levity."

I grinned at him, and wondered out loud—"What's with the electronics outside? You got them wired to the guilty parties in your divorce cases, maybe?"

"It so happens that most of my work is on behalf of insurance companies," he said in a bored voice. "In cases concerning possible fraudulent claims, statistics can play a vital part. The machines keep our statistics up to date—they also keep the companies up to date."

"How fascinating," I said.

"I pay for the use of the machines, the companies pay a little more for the results. Everyone is happy. I trust that is a full and satisfactory answer to your question, Lieutenant Wheeler. And now perhaps we can get down to the business that brought you here?"

"Thank you," I said. "How did you know my name?"

"You have a certain reputation in Pine City for—" he smiled thinly "—shall we say, eccentricity?"

"Well, now—" I smiled at him gratefully "—I thought it was for woman-chasing!"

"That, too," he said with chaste disapproval. But he was still anxious to get down to my business like the busy guy he was, and he tapped the impressive-looking document on the desk in front of him.

"You want to know about the Dan Lambert assignment, I take it. I have all the detail right here."

"Mrs. Hamilton told me you were working for her," I said. "Do you read the newspapers, Merv?"

He winced and said, "Mr. Starke, if you don't mind! Of course I read the newspapers."

"Then you'll know that Dan Lambert was murdered last night, huh?" I queried.

"Naturally, I know." He made another impatient gesture. "But I do wish you'd—"

"All in good time," I said easily. "There's a little question I'd just like to ask you first. Why didn't you inform the sheriff's office that you had vital information concerning the killing?"

"I needed the authorization of my client before I could do such a thing," he said coldly, "and in any case I'm not sure I have any vital information."

"I'll be the judge of that, real fast, once you've read your report to me, Merv," I told him. "You can start on it just as soon as you like."

"Perhaps we can save time if I cover the salient points from memory, Lieutenant." He cleared his throat, put his elbows on the desktop, and tapped the tops of his fingers together a couple of times, like a hot-gospeler warming up for his spiel.

"That'll be all right," I agreed, "as long as your memory is accurate."

He nodded, and said his piece.

"Lambert was paroled from San Quentin eight days back." Starke's voice was a flat monotone. "He arrived in Pine City the following day and booked a room at the Emperor Hotel—which is a fleabag on Bay Road. He saw his daughter Corinne Lambert on three occasions, each time at her dress shop—"

"It's a *boutique*," I corrected.

"—on Pine Tree Boulevard. He made no attempt to contact either Mr. or Mrs. Hamilton in all that time."

"Now tell me something I don't know," I suggested.

"The day after his arrival," Starke went on, ignoring my remark, "two men came to the same hotel and booked a room right next to his. From then on, wherever he went, one of the men followed him."

"Their names?" I asked.

"One was a Lenny Kosto, who was Lambert's cellmate for a long period in prison. He was released three weeks before Lambert was paroled. The other man was Mike Soulos—a hoodlum formerly associated with Kosto in various criminal activities. Apparently they are a team again.

"Last night," Starke continued, "Lambert entered the Topaz Bar at approximately eight-fifteen. Kosto and Soulos joined him an hour later. They drank together for an hour, then the three of them left. Kosto hailed a cab and, with the help of Soulos, managed to get the intoxicated Lambert into the back seat. The cab left the scene at ten-eleven precisely."

He paused, and I didn't know why. I encouraged him.

"Get on with it, Merv. Your man tailed the cab—did he see the white sports car that scraped the cab's fender?"

"No," Starke said quietly.

"What's the matter with this guy, he's blind or something?" I yelped. "Surely he must have seen—"

"I'm sorry. My man didn't tail the cab," Starke said sorrowfully.

I stared at him, and his face was miserable, embarrassed.

"He didn't tail the cab?" I cried. "Why the hell not? It was his dinner break, maybe?"

Starke's smooth face had a pinkish tinge.

"Well, he was going to tail the cab, naturally," he muttered. "But something prevented him. Actually, when he got back to his own car he found an officer waiting for him. He—he was parked beside a hydrant."

"It isn't true!" I cried emotionally. "And for this you need electronic computers yet?"

He was real ashamed about it, for sure. He handed me the operative's report, then bowed his head in submission.

"Let's see you press all your push buttons at once, Merv," I snarled at him. "Maybe that way you could get a cup of hot coffee delivered, even."

Mervyn Starke had been right about one thing, anyway. The Emperor Hotel was a fleabag for sure, its foyer a trash can of abandoned hopes and desires.

Like the blonde who watched me walk in there, maybe.

She was hard and brassy, with a cheap cotton dress that was too tight about her sagging curves. She was slumped wearily on a derelict couch, which was almost symbolic. Her eyes, sunk far into puffy flesh, tried to catch mine as I neared the hotel desk, and she crossed her legs hopefully, hitching her skirt way up above her knees.

The desk clerk was an overall dirty gray color with eyes like a ferret. I figured that if he was to shrink a bit, somebody might just step on him automatically, then maybe complain to the sanitation department.

"You want a room, mister?" he asked in a whining voice. "It's two-fifty in advance." Then he glanced at the blonde for a moment, and leered suggestively. "Or I can let you have a double for three seventy-five."

"I wouldn't give you two bits for the whole lousy fleabag," I told him cheerfully. "Information's what I want. You got two guys here called Kosto and Soulos. What's their room number?"

"So who wants to know?" the clerk said cautiously.

I dropped my badge onto the register in front of him, and maybe he was impressed.

"Sure, Lieutenant, anything you say!" He smiled and I wished he hadn't. "Kosto and Soulos, huh?" He ran his hand along the rack, searching. And finding only an empty pigeonhole. "Room two-one-six. I guess they're up there right now."

"I'll go take a look," I said. "You don't need to call them that I'm coming up, either."

"Whatever you say, sir," the guy whined.

"If they're waiting for me when I get up there," I promised him, "I'll come back here and break every bone in your body—one at a time."

"Yes, sir, Lieutenant," he said rapidly. "Don't you worry. From me they hear but nothing!"

The old elevator wheezed its way up to the second floor. Room 216 was at the end of a dark corridor that smelled of dampness and meals cooked on hotplates from 1911 on down.

I rapped at the closed door and a voice growled from inside, "Who is it?"

"A real good friend of Dan Lambert's," I growled right back. "Open up—we got to talk."

I eased my thirty-eight from its belt holster as I listened to the inside bolt slide back. Then the door opened maybe a foot, and an unshaven gorilla glared out at me. I pressed the barrel of the thirty-eight firmly against the bridge of his large nose and smiled pleasantly.

"Open up real slow, friend," I said, "or you'll be wearing a hole on both sides of your head."

For just a moment he looked like maybe he wanted to argue. Then he thought better of it, and did like he was told, backing into the room with me following.

"What's with you, Mike?" another voice asked impatiently. "Who the hell—"

By that time I was far enough into the room for the owner of the other voice to see both me and the gun. He came off the bed real fast, one hand diving for the nearest pocket of his coat which was draped over the foot of it.

"I wouldn't do that, Lenny," I advised him. "Not while I've got this gun at Mike's nose. One squeeze of the trigger, and Mike kind of disintegrates."

His hand stopped its movement, and slowly he lowered himself back in a sitting position on the bed. He would be Kosto, and he was the brain of this outfit for sure—a guy of about my own size, with a lean, intelligent face and bleak blue eyes.

The eyes stared at me calmly.

"So what's the beef?" He clasped his hands behind his head now, and lay back full-length on the bed. "If this is a stickup, pal, you've got the wrong room. I doubt if we could scrape up ten bucks between us. Right, Mike?"

"Yeah, that's right," Mike growled, watching me through slitted, animal eyes. "Only thing is, this is no stickup! This close I can smell a cop."

"A cop? Hey, is that right?" Kosto grinned at me curiously.

I frisked Soulos and found that he wasn't heeled. Then I moved over to the foot of the bed and checked the pockets of Kosto's draped coat, where I found a snub-nosed thirty-two.

"I bet you don't have a license for this, Lenny," I said.

"I never saw that gun in my whole life before," he said. "I've been framed!"

I dropped the thirty-two into my pocket, then put my own gun back in its holster.

"You sure it isn't the gun that killed Dan Lambert?" I asked.

"You're right, Lenny, this *is* a frame!" Mike Soulos snarled. "Cops!" He spat on the floor in disgust. "What chance does a guy got with dirty, lousy cops!"

"You got no chance with this one, pal," I told him coldly. "It's sewn up real tight."

"Looks kind of like you got the advantage of us, copper," Lenny said, staring up at the ceiling over his bed. "Looks like you know us, but good. But we don't know you from nothing! Where you from? Homicide?"

"County sheriff's office," I said. "Lieutenant Wheeler, if you want a formal introduction."

"Yeah?" Lenny laughed, and there was open derision in the sound—and in his eyes when he looked at me. "You're *that* kind of a cop, huh? The little guy with the big badge, from Nowheresville. You're out of your league, Lieutenant—way out!"

"Stop it before you frighten me to death!" I said mildly. "And now let me say a few words for a change, huh? I got big news for you two guys."

"Big news like what?" Lenny wanted to know.

I grinned at him pleasantly, and obliged.

"Like when Lambert came back into town, his ex-partner Hamilton heard about it but didn't worry. But his wife got plenty worried and did something about it. This'll fracture you guys! Know what she did? Hired a private eye outfit to keep tabs on Lambert the whole time. They tailed him everywhere, checked on everything he did, noted the people he met and talked to—the whole works!"

The two hoods stared at me for long moments, like maybe they were letting what I'd said soak into their minds. Then Lenny stiffened on the bed and broke the silence.

"What's that got to do with us, Lieutenant?"

"Plenty," I assured him. "So the private eye's got a whole book yet on Lambert's movements. Like last night, for instance."

"Tell us what happened last night, huh?" Lenny suggested.

"Lambert went into the Topaz Bar at eight-fifteen," I said. "An hour later he was joined by two guys named Kosto and Soulos. They all drank together for the next hour, then the three of them left at precisely ten-eleven.

"Outside the bar, Kosto called a cab. With Soulos helping, they got the drunken Lambert into the back seat but stayed behind when the car left. It's a very efficient private eye outfit, you see. They got the whole story."

"So we put Lambert into a cab," Lenny said calmly. "Somewhere along the way he gets knocked off. It's our fault?"

"The Sheriff doesn't figure it happened that way at all," I said. "He figures Lambert was already dead when you put him into the cab. And the Sheriff's real mad about the deal.

"The trouble with the Sheriff is that he's got no sense of humor at all," I went on. "He didn't even grin when the cab delivered Lambert's corpse to his house."

"The guy was alive when we put him in the cab," Mike growled.

"So you say," I said. "Trouble is, the hackie can't back you up on that.

He says he doesn't know if Lambert was put into the cab alive or not. He was too busy driving to notice, he says."

"It's a frame!" Soulos was raging, his huge hairy hands clenching and unclenching slowly. "A stinking frame!"

"Why do you figure we would want to knock Lambert off?" Lenny Kosto asked. "It don't even begin to make sense!"

"I hear tell you were his cellmate at San Quentin," I told him. "I figure that might explain it."

"Explain it how?" the hood demanded.

"All right, then, if you want me to draw pictures," I said. "You must have learned about the hundred grand that Lambert had embezzled and which was not recovered. So maybe you figured Lambert had it hid away someplace. You trailed him here to Pine City because you wanted to muscle in on a cut of the dough."

"What an imagination you got!" Kosto said.

"In Pine City you stuck closer to him than a mother the whole time," I went on. "You waited for him to lead you to the jackpot. But he didn't and you got impatient, then real mad at him. So in the finish you put a couple of slugs into his head, to make you feel a whole lot better about all that wasted time you'd spent. That's the way it adds up—but good!"

"You're out of your ever-loving mind!" Kosto sat up on the bed and swung his feet to the floor. He stared at me. "You figure a couple of poor working pros like me and Mike can afford the luxury of knocking a guy off just for kicks? Oh, brother! I think you must be nuts!"

"It don't matter what I figure, Lenny," I said, shrugging easily. "It is what the Sheriff thinks that's important. And what a jury thinks, is real important also. Right now the Sheriff thinks he's got enough to send both you and Mike to the gas chamber."

Kosto rubbed his forehead thoughtfully with the back of his hand.

"O.K.—so that's what the Sheriff thinks," he said. "But you've got something else on your mind, Lieutenant. Or you wouldn't bother giving us this big spiel. You'd have us both in bracelets and on our way downtown by now. So what's the pitch?"

"Play along with me," I suggested. "Play on the level and maybe I can give you boys a break."

"A break from a cop?" Mike Soulos rumbled with laughter. "Hey, Lenny, this guy's a comic!"

"Shut up, will you?" Kosto said evenly. "What's on your mind, Lieutenant?"

"You trailed Lambert to Pine City," I said. "It was his hundred grand you were after. Right?"

"What else?" Lenny grinned. "He was lousy company!"

"Then tell me what happened between you in the Topaz Bar last night," I said.

"Like what?" Kosto wanted to know.

"Like why was Lambert yelling he was going to fix some bastard real good with Sheriff Lavers? And why did you and Mike actually help him on his way?"

"The hell with this cop!" Soulos growled. "Play it smart, Lenny, I'm warning you. Tell him anything, he'll twist it around and make it come out worse for both of us. He's a stinking cop—and don't forget it!"

"Lay off for a while!" Kosto said impatiently. "This is for me, Mike—big stuff—thinking." He tapped the side of his head with one finger, grinning at the gorilla. "I got to use the brain real good—right?"

"Just so's you use it right," Mike said worriedly.

Kosto got onto his feet with his hands thrust deep into his pants pockets. He walked up and down the room slowly, thinking real hard with that brain of his.

"Like it was this way, Lieutenant," he said carefully. "All the time in stir, Lambert keeps beefing he was framed—you know?—the song every guy sings until he gets tired of hearing the echo? But Lambert never did get tired. We figured for sure he had that hundred grand stashed away someplace nice and safe, so like you said, we tailed him to Pine City. We figured he would have to go pick up the dough sooner or later, and when he did we'd be right there in back of him."

He shook his head dismally. "It didn't work out that way. We tried real hard to persuade him to get the dough—even told him we'd be satisfied with ten grand each and he could keep the rest."

"That was real big of you!" I said sarcastically.

"But it was no use," Kosto said with a shrug. "We just couldn't get through to him."

"No matter how hard you tried, huh?" I said, watching Soulos' apelike hands opening and clutching savagely.

"We sure tried everything we knew," Lenny said casually. "Then—out of the blue—last night he calls and says to meet him over at the Topaz Bar. When we get there he's been drinking already, but it's the excitement, not the liquor, that's got him real steamed up about something."

"About what?" I asked.

"He claims he's finally gotten the proof that he was framed, and he says he's going right out there to give it to the country sheriff. For a while Mike and me figure he's flipped or something, but he kind of keeps right on about it and it gets so we're both believing him, even."

Lenny grinned and took a crumpled cigarette from his shirt pocket. He stuck it between his lips. "You got a match, copper?"

I tossed him a folder and he lit the cigarette slowly, his eyes remembering how Lambert had sounded the night before. "He had it all figured out, for sure!"

"Tell me about it," I said.

"He said that the guy who framed him must still have the hundred grand, or most of it, and he would get it. Lambert figured he would then be publicly cleared—but most of all he wanted revenge, to make sure that the guy got what was coming to him."

"And so?" I prompted.

"So that's where we came into the picture," Kosto said with a shrug. "Right after Lambert had seen the sheriff like he planned to do, he wanted us to go with him and see this guy—wanted him roughed up a little—wanted it fixed so the guy couldn't run any place until the cops came for him. For this, Lambert promised us two grand apiece."

"You believed the guy?" I asked.

"Yeah, I guess I did, at the end. I sure hadn't believed him in the beginning. But then I figured no guy could put on an act like that—and where was the percentage, anyway, if he was kidding?"

"Where did he say he got this proof he'd been framed?" I asked.

"He didn't say at all."

"Well—what kind of proof was it?" I wanted to know. "A letter, a confession? Written evidence, or what?"

"I wouldn't know," Kosto said. "The guy wouldn't go into any details. He said he had it, and I believed him. So we helped him into the cab to go to the sheriff's office—and that's all we ever got to know."

Mike Soulos looked at me and somehow managed to twist his face into a kind of eager smile.

"So now you get it—all wrapped up nice and neat for you, huh, Lieutenant? So now you make like you promised and give Lenny and me a break, huh?"

"Just what have I got from you?" I snarled. "Nothing I didn't know already from the bartender and the private eye!"

"So! I told you already!" Soulos lost his smile real fast, and swung around to Kosto with a murderous gleam in his black little eyes. "What kind of a deal you make with a stinking, lousy cop, huh? You should maybe get your head examined! A brain!" He tapped the side of his head in a burlesque of Kosto's gesture, and mimicked his voice. "I'm thinking, I'm thinking!"

"Mike, cool it, will you!" Lenny said tautly. "I got mind to—"

"Lenny Kosto, the smart operator!" Soulos bellowed with harsh laughter. "All the time making big deals. Big deals like the hundred grand we don't got from Lambert, huh? Big deals like the one that just laid an egg with this lousy copper—right, Lenny? I wonder you lived so long, you're so damn smart!"

"Cool it, I told you!" Kosto snarled and threw himself at the big guy, his fists flailing.

"All right, you guys!" I yelled. "Break it up!"

If they heard me it didn't seem to make any difference—by now they had grabbed each other and were busy wrestling around the room. Soulos had Kosto where I figured I wouldn't want to be—clutched in a giant bear-hug that seemed to bend him backward with bone-smashing force.

In exchange, Lenny had his hands locked about Soulos' throat, making an awkward but enthusiastic effort to squeeze the air out of his windpipe.

I figured that because I was a cop, maybe I should do something before Lenny's back snapped clean in half. So I joined the party.

I slammed forward straight into the two of them, hoping the impact of my weight might force them apart. But they came apart even before my weight hit them! They just seemed to melt away as I hurtled.

It was too late for me to realize that I'd been tricked, when Soulos' booming laugh hit my ears and his massive paw snatched my wrist and twisted it high into the small of my back. It was a savage grip and he wasn't fooling. He gave me a choice—bend over double or have my arm broken!

"See how he walked right into that one?" he said to Kosto.

"Like a sucker!" Kosto said, enjoying my predicament. Then to me he said, "It's like I told you, Lieutenant. This is the big league where you don't belong, slob! O.K., Mike, fix him!"

"A stinking cop!" Soulos said blissfully. "A dirty, stinking cop like I said!"

Next moment the back of my head exploded in a mushrooming cloud of pain, and all that was left were the vast, brittle chunks of throbbing darkness.

CHAPTER FIVE

They were gone, of course, when I came to. And so was the gun I had taken from Kosto's coat—but they'd left my own thirty-eight in its belt holster. I shook my aching head. The back of it hurt like hell, but there was no cut there.

I figured that Soulos must have hit me with his fist and not a gun. It was a sobering thought I didn't need, because I had too many already.

I went out of the room and down the stairs and into the hotel lobby, moving slowly to try and stop the red-hot needles from jabbing into my brain. The clerk was sprawled out on the derelict couch where the brassy blonde had been when I came in. There was nobody else in sight. I figured to kick him awake, then I thought about it a second time and bent low to get a closer look at his face.

He was breathing raggedly through his open mouth, and they'd done a real good job on him. Both eyes were closed tight and almost invisible, lost in the raw and swollen flesh. His nose had been smashed, and if he'd had any teeth before they started on him, he didn't have any now.

I went to the desk and called an ambulance, then Sheriff Lavers' office. It didn't take me long to tell the Sheriff what had happened—a minute or two, I guess. Then it was his turn, and he was in no hurry to get finished.

The ambulance arrived—they picked up the desk clerk and took him away—and still Lavers kept right on talking. I hung on another few minutes because I figured maybe I had it coming. Then I put the phone down very gently and walked away.

My watch said the time was six-thirty, and I'd had a long day. I needed things like a drink, some aspirin, a shower—and I had a date at eight o'clock.

The way I was feeling right then, I didn't care a damn if there were four more homicides within the county's jurisdiction and they all happened in the next ten minutes. Lavers could have them—Homicide could have them—I just didn't want any part of them.

By the time I'd gotten back to my apartment, had the drink, aspirin, and shower, I felt better. I was halfway toward my door, and thinking of Agnes' remarkably attractive talents as a walker, when my phone rang.

For a while I debated in my mind whether to answer it, then the thought that it could be Agnes maybe about to cancel the date or something made up my mind for me. It was my mistake.

"Wheeler,"—Sheriff Lavers' voice was ominously gentle—"as a matter of interest, just how long was I talking to myself the last time?"

"How do I know, Sheriff?" I asked innocently. "I wasn't there. When did you finally run down?"

I held the phone expectantly away from my ear, but instead of the explosion, there was about a twenty-second silence—deadly, like the eye of a hurricane. Finally, I figured, he'd find the words so I kept the phone at arm's length—but when he spoke again I had to pull in the phone fast.

"I've got some news for you, Lieutenant," he said, almost genially. "That white sports car you've been so hot for—it's been found."

"So?" I said cautiously.

"So it belongs to a guy named Swanson," he told me. "And here's a twist. He reported it stolen last night, an hour before Lambert was shot."

"Maybe he was being cute," I suggested.

"Could be," Lavers said placidly. "Or maybe somebody else was being cute—like your friends, Kosto and Soulos."

"Don't!" I pleaded. "Every time you mention their names, the back of my head twinges."

"Small wonder," he growled. "Anyway, listen to this. Swanson's car was found about fifteen miles out of town by the Highway Patrol, around four o'clock this morning. Abandoned, of course. I just happened to check with the Patrol a while ago, on the chance. You should have thought of it last night, of course."

"Is there a scrape on the fender?" I asked, ignoring the Sheriff's typically generous buck-passing.

"There's a scrape, all right," Lavers said. "Swanson got his car back about midday, I hear. You want to go talk with him?"

"That depends, Sheriff," I said anxiously, "whether I'm still working for you."

"I thought about it afterward," he said easily. "I got to realizing Kosto and Soulos would be a couple of tough babies to handle on your own,

Wheeler. I guess I can't blame you for making a stinking mess out of it!"

"Thanks very much," I said between my clenched teeth. "You figure it's all right if I go out alone on a dark night, Sheriff?"

"Don't get sore at me, Lieutenant," he said practically. "It wasn't me who gave you that headache!"

"All right!" I surrendered. "But this Swanson—I've got a date around twenty minutes from now."

"Maybe you aren't working for me after all?" he said coldly.

"So give me the address!" I said patiently, but only just.

He gave it to me and I wrote it down. "I'll go right along there and talk to him," I said. "Any word on Kosto and his playmate yet?"

"Nothing yet," Lavers said. "There's an all-points out on them and I don't think they'll get far."

"I hope you're right," I said. "What about that desk clerk? You get a report on his condition?"

"He'll live, but he'll be hospitalized for a long time," Lavers said soberly. "Looks like they've got to start over and build him a new face. You were damned lucky, Wheeler, they didn't give you the same treatment!"

"It figures," I pointed out. "Like Lenny Kosto said, they're a couple of pros, Sheriff. They can't afford to kill a cop just for kicks—or to beat up a cop for kicks, either. They figure it this way—they beat up a cop, they got it coming back with interest the next time they get booked. But a little nobody guy like that desk clerk—who's to worry about what happens to him?"

"I don't like your philosophy," Lavers growled, "but I'll admit it has a certain macabre logic in it. And now if you can spare the time from that woman-chasing date of yours, go see Swanson and then let me know how you got on."

"Will do," I said. "But first, how about the autopsy on Lambert? Did Doc Murphy find anything interesting?"

"I feel sure he did," Lavers assured me. "I figure he always does. But from our point of view the only interesting thing is that both slugs were thirty-two's."

"Is that so?" I said, remembering. "It was a thirty-two I took from Kosto."

"And it was a thirty-two he took right back from you," Lavers said, remembering also. "You'd better watch out for this Swanson guy, Wheeler. You never know. He might have a friend with him, too, huh?"

"You're real cute," I told him. "But don't break a leg laughing, will you?"

He was still laughing when I hung up.

I got to the Hacienda at ten after eight, and padded around the dimly lit bar like a frustrated puma who doesn't know the mating season's finished because nobody bothered to tell him. Then I saw the blonde sitting alone at a corner table, and I headed toward her like a homing puma.

"You're late," Agnes said coolly.

"You're magnificent," I said rather hoarsely, and sank onto a chair opposite her.

I wasn't kidding. Her blonde hair had been tweaked and curled so that it kind of floated around her head like a lost cloud. She wore a black crepe sheath with two diagonally cut straps that plunged from each shoulder deep into the warm intimacy between her small, taut breasts.

It was a pleasure to look her over. And judging by the laughter in her face, she found it a pleasure to be looked at the way I was looking.

"You like this little number?" she asked.

"It serves its purpose, honey," I said. "And how!"

She looked real pleased.

"I figure it was a steal at a week's salary," she said. "I sort of gave up eating, but it's worth it if that gleam in your eyes means anything other than you're hungry."

A waiter hovered at my elbow like a myopic vampire in search of my jugular. I ordered my usual Scotch on the rocks with a little soda, then looked dubiously at the clear glass in front of Agnes.

"Tequila?" I ventured.

"What else?" she demanded, with an elegant shrug of her satin-smooth shoulders. Then she figured maybe she'd put my mind at rest, or something. "This will only make two, Al."

"And one more makes a hat dance?" I reminded her.

"Tonight, I dance for you alone," she said warmly. "I shall weave a veil of shrouded mist around my beautiful, whirling body that will cast an enchanted spell—gosh, I'm starved, Al lover! When do we eat?"

"Right away, honey," I assured her. "You figure to lift that veil for some chili con carne?"

When we had finished dinner, I broached the delicate subject.

"Agnes, honey—there's something I have to ask you." A dreamy, tequila-shining look came into her eyes.

"If you want to ask me a big favor, Al," she said huskily, "now's the time."

"You mean you don't mind if I have to go and work a little, tonight?" I said thankfully.

"Work?" She stared at me.

"Just visit with a guy for a few minutes, is all," I assured her. "No reason you can't come along with me."

"Oh, fine!" she said coldly. "That's just great! You can call me 'Sergeant Green' and I'll kiss you. Right in front of the county sheriff, if you like."

"Honest, honey, this thing will take only a few minutes," I said quickly. "All I have to do is ask the guy a few questions about his car that was stolen last night."

Pouting, she shrugged.

"Well, all right," she said sullenly. "I guess I don't have any choice.

But I'll tell you one thing. I'm not moving from here until I've had another drink!"

"Fine," I said hopefully. "Scotch?"

"Tequila." Her mouth set determinedly.

"But that will be the third," I reminded her.

"The third, sure," she agreed. "But I don't care."

"Baby, in just a hat?" I pleaded. "It's cold outside!"

A slow, wicked smile parted her lips in a tantalizing O. Lazily she said, "I don't need to worry, do I, lover? You'll keep me warm?"

Ten minutes later when we'd finished the drinks, I finally talked her into leaving. Outside, we climbed into the Austin Healey.

Agnes settled into the seat beside me and looked around with interest and approval.

"I like this," she announced. "It's so snug—with only a gearshift between us. Why do they have it on the floor?"

"To shift gears with," I told her, as I pulled out from the curb. "It's one of the new things, honey."

"I think some of the older things are best." She leaned her head against my shoulder. "Don't you, Al?"

"I wonder whatever happened to the old-fashioned girls?" I said out loud. "The death-before-dishonor brigade—the dames who'd tremble and faint at the thought of being alone with a man in the same room?"

"Well," Agnes said calmly. "That way they could be alone with two men in the same room and the fun lasted—"

"It was just a thought," I said sourly.

Swanson lived in a tenth-floor apartment on Tower Heights, which put him automatically into an upper-income bracket. I restrained Agnes from trying to force the elevator door shut before we could get out, just so we could have another private ride together. Then when we finally found the right apartment I pressed the buzzer and waited.

It wasn't a long wait. The door opened and a magnificent redhead stood there, looking at me as if I was something that should be fumigated fast. I looked at her more kindly. She had the looks and the figure—everything a dame needs to make anyone look at her with interest.

She wore a black lace dress with the neckline scooped low across her deep, fully rounded breasts. There was something vaguely familiar about her, I thought. Maybe it was the sparkling white teeth when she spoke—or maybe the brown eyes.

"Lieutenant Wheeler!" she said icily. "Why on earth are you hounding me like this?"

"Hounding you?" I said. "Huh?"

"You heard what the girl said!" Agnes crooned accusingly. "What about that, Al?"

"I don't know what about it!" I said, and stared at the lovely redhead. "What do you mean, baby? We've met some place before?"

"Are you drunk, Lieutenant?" she asked stonily. "We met this morning when you came to see me at my *boutique*."

"Corinne Lambert!" I goggled at her, understanding at last why she'd seemed familiar. "But, hey—you were a silver blonde then. How come you changed into a redhead so fast?"

"Why, Al!" Agnes giggled playfully. "You naïve little policeman! Don't you know that these days, any girl who's really chic, has a set of different-colored wigs—one for each day of the week, just about?"

"You're kidding!" I said.

"No, I'm not. It saves so many trips to the beauty parlor, and a girl can change her color every day, if she likes, to suit her mood." Agnes smiled sweetly at Corinne. "How long is it since you wore the green one, darling?"

There was a sudden blaze of fire in Corinne's eyes, and I stepped in quickly to stop a possible war.

"I came here to see a guy named Swanson," I said. "I guess we must have the wrong apartment."

"Not at all," Corinne said calmly. "This is Tony Swanson's apartment. He happens to be my fiancé—he's busy making us a drink so I answered the door."

"A drink, for real?" Agnes said dreamily. "Thank goodness we're in time!"

Corinne raised her eyebrows superciliously, looking at the blonde but speaking to me. "Is this a new policewoman you're breaking in, Lieutenant?"

"No, no—this is a kind of business-pleasure combination," I said vaguely. "Could I talk with Mr. Swanson now?"

"I guess so," she said grudgingly. "I hope it isn't going to take very long."

"That's what I hope, too," Agnes said.

"No more than a few minutes," I said hopefully.

"Then you'd better come in," Corinne suggested, and led the way.

We went into the apartment living room, which was spacious and expensively furnished. A tall, athletic-looking character was standing in back of the bar at the far end of the room.

He was something less than thirty, I figured, with brown curly hair, and a neat mustache gracing his upper lip. I'm waiting for some individualist to start a fad for mustaches worn on the lower lip.

He looked at us with polite interest. "Corinne, honey, you found some company, huh?"

"I wouldn't know about that," Corinne said curtly. "This is Lieutenant Wheeler from the Sheriff's office, and this"—she glanced disdainfully at Agnes— "is his assistant, or something."

Swanson looked at Agnes with frank interest.

"Well, if only I'd known that law enforcement offered opportunities like this!" he said in a wondering voice.

"I'm Agnes Green," the blonde told him solemnly, "and my hair's my own."

"That's obvious," Corinne said tightly.

"What do you have under that wig, honey?" Agnes inquired. "A crew-cut toupee?"

Swanson did some fast footwork now.

"What was it you wanted to talk to me about, Lieutenant?"

"Your car," I said.

"But it's all finished with," he smiled. "The Highway Patrol found it for me early this morning."

"I know all about that," I said patiently, "but I still need to ask you a few questions."

"Sorry." He grimaced, but brightened up again almost immediately. "How about I make you a drink while we talk?"

"You got any tequila, handsome?" Agnes asked eagerly.

"Afraid not." Swanson looked chagrined at the omission. "Could I fix you something else?"

"No, thanks." Agnes shook her golden head. "I'd hate for this feeling to wear off."

I named my drink and Swanson busied himself with the glasses. Five minutes later I had some facts from him.

His car was a white Jaguar sports model, and he'd left it parked outside Corinne's *boutique* about a quarter after nine the night before. When he came out of the *boutique* about twenty minutes later it was gone.

"What did you do then?" I asked, and he shrugged.

"Naturally I reported the theft to the police right away. And I got the car back this morning, I'm happy to say."

"With a brand-new scrape on the right fender?" I said. "Which didn't make you happy at all?"

"You can say that again," he said angrily. "The lousy so-and-so who stole it! He just didn't have any basic appreciation of fine machinery!"

"Tough," I sympathized. "When you left the car parked, did you leave the keys in the ignition?"

"I'm not that stupid, Lieutenant!" he protested. "But it's an odd thing, now you mention it. There was no sign of anyone having fooled with the car to get it started. They must have had a duplicate key that fitted perfectly!"

"You figure that somebody carefully planned to steal your car?" I asked him.

"It sounds kind of stupid, doesn't it?" he said and grinned apologetically. "I guess maybe I'm letting my imagination run away with me!"

"Maybe not," I said, thinking out loud.

"Why do you say that?" Swanson asked keenly.

"Well, look at it this way," I said slowly. "Whoever stole your car used it to get alongside the cab carrying Dan Lambert out to Sheriff Lavers' house, and blast a couple of bullets into the side of his head."

"They used *my* car for that?" Swanson stared at me with a kind of shocked horror.

"So if somebody planned to commit murder," I pointed out, "it would be logical for them to spend a little time getting a duplicate key made somehow to fit the car they intended to use."

"Yeah," Swanson nodded slowly. "I see what you mean."

"But Lambert's murder didn't happen like that," I said, and now Swanson obviously didn't know what I meant at all. "It couldn't have been planned—not more than a couple of hours ahead, at the most. Because nobody could know for sure what Lambert intended to do before he began shooting off his mouth in the Topaz Bar around nine."

Corinne Lambert looked at me quickly.

"You're building up to something nasty, Lieutenant," she said coolly. "I can tell. So let's have it."

"Sure," I obliged. "Let's kick it around a little, just for laughs. Say we nominate Mr. Swanson as the murderer—and see how it all works out."

"What?" Swanson said feebly.

"Please go on, Lieutenant," Corinne encouraged. "This should be most interesting."

"All right," I said. "He figures on driving the five blocks from the *boutique* to the bar where he knows your father will be—killing him—then driving straight back. He plans to establish an alibi with your help, Miss Lambert—that he never even left the *boutique*."

"You know, Al, with your kind of mind," Agnes said seriously, "you should have been a murderer. You're just wasted material as a cop!"

"I'll go along with that," Corinne said—and probably she meant it in a different way.

"But then Mr. Swanson has second thoughts about his plan," I persisted. "He figures the chances are too great against him. Someone who knows him—or the car—might see him driving those five blocks either coming or going. So he figures it's good insurance to make liars of them—he calls the police and reports his car stolen, and immediately afterward drives it to the bar, intending to stick to his original plan."

"And does he stick to it?" Corinne asked tartly.

"No. He strikes trouble. Before he has a chance to get close enough to his victim, Dan Lambert is bundled into a cab by two guys with whom he's been drinking. Mr. Swanson follows—he has no choice. After a while he manages to run the Jaguar alongside the cab and shoot Lambert through the open window. He scrapes the side of the cab in doing it. After which he drives fifteen miles out of town along the highway, dumps his car, phones his accomplice to come pick him up in her car and take him back to town."

There was a silence during which I figured maybe I'd impressed everybody with my theory. Until Corinne broke it with an angry protest.

"I don't think I ever heard anything so thoroughly stupid in my whole life!"

I shrugged and stayed right with it.

"It explains a few things, you must admit," I said. "How come the thief could fit a duplicate key without any trouble? The answer is: If it was actually the original key. And it certainly would be a smart move to report the car stolen before he used it. Even if the law didn't believe, later, that the car had been stolen, they'd have had a tough job proving it."

Swanson nodded soberly. He said, "I see your point, of course, Lieutenant. It's kind of frightening when you think of it that way. Makes you wonder how many innocent people have been trapped in similar circumstances."

"I'm beginning to wonder if that's the Lieutenant's little specialty," Corinne said grimly. "Trapping innocent people!"

"I hope you're right, honey," Agnes said eagerly, "even if I'm not innocent, exactly."

The sound of the door buzzer chopped off Corinne's ready retort, which was probably a good thing. I saw her look at Swanson kind of uncertainly for a moment, then she shrugged. "I'll get it."

"Thanks, darling," he said, and looked almost relieved.

She trotted away on her smart high heels. I heard the door open, then the sound of Corinne's voice in the entrance hall.

Her voice was joined by a booming bass—and a moment later she came back into the living room followed by the impressive bulk of Hamilton Hamilton.

"Well, well!" Hamilton gaped at us for a moment, like a guy who'd realized he'd forgotten to put on his pants before he left home. But he recovered quickly, acting true to form. "How about this! Looks like you've got the nucleus of a party here, Corinne! How are you, Swanson? Nice to see you again, Lieutenant—and Agnes! What a pleasant surprise!"

He beamed at us all in turn.

"Good evening, Mr. Hamilton." Agnes giggled suddenly, then a sharp hiccup made her stop in horror. "Excuse me!" she said with dignity. "It's the tequila—you know?" She gazed around the room vaguely. "Would somebody care to lend me a sombrero?"

"Steady, honey," I pleaded. "This is the wrong party yet."

"I'll try to remember," Agnes promised.

Now Hamilton was booming his voice at Corinne, patting her hand as he spoke. "I thought about it, my dear, then I made up my mind to call on you and see how things were. When nobody answered the doorbell of your little apartment in back of the *boutique*"—he beamed at Swanson—"I figured there was only one other place you could be."

"It was nice of you to visit me, Mr. Hamilton," Corinne said evenly. "But please don't waste your breath with condolences—my father never did mean anything to me."

There was a moment or two of embarrassed silence.

"Oh, well," Hamilton said uncomfortably, "of course, I—" Then he clutched at the first straw that came into his mind. "I know! Let's have a party—at my place! You're all invited here and now!"

"A party!" Agnes clapped her hands together excitedly. "What a wonderful idea! Let's go, Al, huh?"

"Sounds fine," I agreed.

"Great!" Hamilton boomed. "You see, Swanson? Neither you nor Corinne have any choice—it's definitely a party."

"Fine," Swanson said in a hollow voice. "But look—are you sure your wife won't object?"

Hamilton thundered his laughter.

"Sure, I'm sure!" he said with a big wink. "This is her big night to be elected president of the Daughters of the Western Pioneers. She won't be home for hours! Let's go, friends."

CHAPTER SIX

"This is it!" Hamilton said proudly, and flicked a switch so the whole spacious basement was brilliantly lit. "My own little kingdom under the house. You like it?"

It was one huge room, about fifty by forty, with benches lining three walls, and littered with every conceivable novelty that had ever appeared in a magic shop window. And a lot more that never had, most likely. I glanced at the whole fantastic scene and didn't feel too happy about it all.

Remembering the last time I was in the house, when Hamilton was limited by time, gimmicks, and his wife, I shuddered to think what might happen once we were all trapped inside his workshop, so to speak.

"Well, in we go," he said happily. He dropped his hand onto Agnes' shoulder and urged her forward gently but firmly. "You lead the way, my dear."

She stepped forward obediently, while Hamilton burlesqued a wink at the rest of us. Then he pushed a button on the wall near the doorway.

There was a piercing shriek from Agnes as a draft of warm air suddenly blasted up through a fine mesh grating under her feet. It sent her skirts flying overhead—lifting them high enough to reveal a pair of well-shaped, slender legs, and a cute pair of black lace panties above them.

Hamilton dissolved into near-helpless laughter, which had about the same volume of sound you hear when you're real close to the bottom of Niagara Falls. Blindfolded by her up-swirling skirts, Agnes twisted around crazily but finally managed to stumble clear of the blast, to shake her clothes down around her and smooth her disheveled hair.

"Turn it off!" Corinne Lambert said sourly. "You won't catch me walking over that silly thing!"

"Wouldn't want you to, old girl," Hamilton chuckled, pressing the switch again. "Never play the same trick twice—it loses its effect, I always say."

Corinne didn't trust him, and walked gingerly over the grating, but with no ill effect. I followed Hamilton and Swanson into the big basement room.

There was a handsome, well-stocked bar tucked away in one corner, and there Hamilton played host, mixing the drinks with generous proportions. After that we stood in a group and watched for maybe twenty minutes while he demonstrated, with high glee, some of the mechanical novelties in his collection.

There was a perfect replica of a human skull with two rotating eyeballs that told the time, one eye denoting the minutes and the other the hours. There was a rectangular metal box with an imposing ON-OFF switch making the impulse to switch ON almost irresistible, and when you did the lid rose slowly, a mechanical hand appeared, carefully moved the switch to the OFF position, then vanished back inside the lid.

"How fascinating!" Corinne said in a bored voice. But no amount of sarcasm was likely to stop Hamilton on his favorite pastime.

Two drinks later he was demonstrating an aerosol bomb that sprayed lifelike cobwebs any place you wanted; a realistic shrunken head, made of rubber, which he contrived to drop down the scooped-out neckline of Corinne's dress—and which gave him another prolonged spasm of laughter while he watched her frantic and immodest efforts to retrieve it. I watched, too, of course.

When Corinne had finally gotten rid of the thing, she looked about her and shook her lovely head. "You know, all this stuff must have cost you a fortune, Hamilton," she said.

He stopped laughing then, and a wariness came into his eyes as he looked at her. "No more than your *boutique* cost you, I imagine, my dear." A rasping, angry tone had come to his voice, though he quickly rebuilt his smile and looked at her pleasantly enough.

"At least the *boutique* is designed to be of some use, to sell something," Corinne told him disdainfully. "All this is just—just childish indulgence!"

Hamilton shrugged, like he couldn't care less what she thought, but I figured that maybe he did care a little, and was having some trouble keeping that smile on his face.

"I indulge my childishness, you indulge your vanity," he said. "What's the difference, Corinne?"

"Oh, forget it!" she said impatiently. "I need another drink."

"Please?" Agnes said brightly. "Which way is the little girl's room?"

"Straight through that door there," Hamilton said, pointing helpfully to send her on her way.

The door closed behind her, and Hamilton frantically made signs for everybody to be quiet and listen. Ten seconds later there was a piercing shriek. The door flew open, and Agnes dashed across the intervening space into my arms.

"Hey, what's the matter?" I asked.

"It's terrible, Al!" she sobbed hysterically. "There's a man—a woman—somebody in there! It's dreadful, they must have slipped or something—but you've got to help them quickly!"

"What on earth—" I said, then saw that Hamilton was gleeful again.

He motioned for us all to follow him into the room. A few moments later we stared down at the pathetic hand which protruded from between the closed lid and seat, looking for all the world the way Agnes had interpreted it.

"Plastic, of course," Hamilton explained amid his laughter. "It's a magnificently lifelike imitation of a human hand, though, don't you think?"

"Mr. Hamilton!" Agnes dabbed at her eyes with a dainty silk postage stamp. "I think you're absolutely dreadful! Frightening a girl that way. From now on I'll always be scared I might slip—"

"Never mind, honey," I soothed her. "I'll protect you."

"Protect me?" she said stiffly. "Listen, Al Wheeler, there are places where that just isn't a practical proposition!"

For a girl who likes to wind up her tequilas with hat dances, this practical approach was out of character. There are some things that are practical anywhere, anyway, and I was trying to put across that point when a shrill trumpeting sound from a mechanical elephant announced that Hamilton, back at the bar, had the next batch of whiskies ready and waiting.

"I'm not sure what I want most," Agnes confided in a whisper. "A drink—or to fly around the room like an eagle. You decide for me, huh?"

"A drink would be best," I said, taking her arm and steering her to the bar. "You won't have so far to fall."

When we got there, Corinne and Hamilton were engaged in a fierce argument, watched by the embarrassed Swanson who obviously wanted to break it up but didn't quite know how.

"I never had any time for my father," Corinne said harshly, "you know that. But he was the brains of the outfit, all right."

"What do you mean, the brains!" Hamilton demanded angrily.

"He was a lot damn smarter than you, anyway!" She threw back her head and laughed loudly. "Look how easily he chiseled you out of a hundred grand, for a start!"

"Any cheapskate can steal, there's nothing clever about that," Hamilton roared furiously. "But let me tell you that Dan Lambert wouldn't have gotten anywhere without me! I had the local know-how, the connections right here in this town, while he was just a stranger from back East! Before you can sell people investment in stocks and bonds, you have to sell yourself first. If you don't have folks' confidence, you just don't get their business. It's as simple as that!"

Corinne smiled condescendingly, which must have really bugged him. Lazily she persisted, "I still say Dan was the brains of the outfit. What have you done since, in the last three years without him?"

She answered the question herself, a contemptuous wave of her arm embracing the whole room. "This is all you've done—indulged yourself in a second childhood which must have cost you a fortune, while your crummy little importing business went downhill so fast, it was like falling over a precipice!"

"Goddammit!" Hamilton roared, the veins cording in his forehead. "Who the hell are you to talk this way? You've sunk fifty thousand dollars into that dress shop and I'll bet you haven't sold twenty damn dresses yet, since the first day you opened!"

Maybe that stung Corinne, whose smile switched to a sneer.

"If I haven't done very well, at least you'll admit I've never had any trouble getting more financial backing to keep me going, have I?"

Hamilton stared wildly at her and his face was purple. "You—you insufferable little bitch!" he said thickly. "I ought to strangle you with my bare hands!"

"Hey!" Swanson was finally roused into action. "Take it easy, Hamilton. You don't know what you're saying!"

"Sure I know what I'm saying!" Hamilton snarled. "I'm saying what I mean—the truth—she's just a lousy little—"

"I'm warning you, Hamilton!" Awkwardly Swanson managed to get some determination into his tone, maybe just for effect. "If you don't shut up I'm going to smash your face in!"

"Don't worry," Corinne said airily. "Let him talk. I'll bet the Lieutenant is lapping up every word."

The color faded from Hamilton's tanned cheeks as he quickly glanced in my direction, then closed his eyes for a moment while he forced a lousy imitation of his old smile back to his face.

"Take no notice of us, Lieutenant," he said in a strained voice. "Corinne and me—we have our own ideas of fun. We like to bawl each other out sometimes—just for practice."

"You figure you still need practice?" I asked mildly.

"With you around, Lieutenant," Corinne interjected, "maybe we do need practice. For our own good and protection."

"Exactly what do you mean by that, honey?" I wanted to know.

She told me frankly.

"I never met anyone quite like you for twisting the words out of a person's mouth—so the way you repeat it, it sounds different altogether."

"Well, what do you think of that!" I said dismally. "And I was trying so hard to be a social success!"

"You're wasting your time," she said coldly. "You'll never make it, Lieutenant."

"If this is a party," Agnes said drowsily, "I'm going home. Except that I'm too tired to go anywhere."

She tottered away toward a comfortable-looking armchair, turned around, and sank into it. Then there was a flash of movement about the chair and she screamed.

Wide metal bands had sprung swiftly from behind each side of the armchair to encircle the blonde's arms and body and clamp her tightly to the chair's back. It was the one thing needed to restore Hamilton's good humor.

"Trapped!" he roared. "You're in my power, my proud beauty!" He pranced about her, twirling imaginary mustaches, miming the antics of the old-time villains of melodrama—until Agnes' frantic but useless efforts to free herself were too much for him and he melted into the mad laughter again.

"Well, I'm glad everyone's having a good time with your little jokes, Mr. Hamilton," Agnes said resignedly. "But why do all your gadgets pick on me all the time?"

Hamilton got control of himself at last and unlocked the metal bands, which promptly sprang back out of sight behind the chair.

"You're a good sport, Agnes," he said. "Not like some sour types of dames I could name. Let's all have another drink—"

"Well, I don't know," I said hastily. "I figure maybe we'll be getting along."

Agnes was at my side, looking up at me eagerly.

"Getting along where, Al?" she asked hopefully.

Hamilton spoke to Swanson and Corinne again, and I took advantage of their chatter to murmur intimately with Agnes.

"In my apartment there's all that hi-fi waiting for us," I said, "untouched even."

"Hi-fi?" Agnes blinked her eyes thoughtfully. "Isn't that a kind of game they play in South America?"

I didn't bother to tell her that the game I had in mind could be played anyplace.

Footsteps sounded crisply on the concrete walk outside the basement, and a moment later Gail Hamilton came into the room. She looked almost regal in a rich, full-length gown of delicate blue silk and a dazzling, red satin cloak, its high collar secured primly by a blazing, diamond-encrusted pin.

She stared in surprise at the five of us grouped around the bar. Her husband was just as surprised, maybe.

"Meeting over already?" he asked. "Well—I didn't realize it was so late, my pet. Are you the new president of the Daughters of the Western Pyrenees?"

"Pioneers," she said quietly. "You're drunk, Hamilton."

"Nonsense!" He couldn't prevent himself working a "sh" sound into it. "I'm as sober as a—" he looked around for inspiration and his eyes lit up when he saw me "—a lieutenant. That's right, Lieutenant Wheeler, huh? You're sober?"

"Maybe," I said, then looked at Gail. "Is it in order to offer congratulations, Mrs. Hamilton?"

"Thank you, Lieutenant." Her lips smiled politely but her eyes were still worried. Then she looked at Corinne Lambert and her chin lifted an inch higher.

"I'm sorry, Miss Lambert," she said icily. "I feel that my husband owes us both an apology—but the fact is that you're not welcome in my house!"

Corinne laughed bitterly. "Don't worry, honey, it wasn't my idea to come here. But Hamilton insisted we should all come—he used a brilliant new phrase, I seem to remember." She turned to Swanson for moral support but all he did was gulp nervously, then pretend he was home in bed just dreaming the whole thing.

"I remember now!" Corinne snapped her fingers. "It was something about 'when the cat's away.'"

Gail Hamilton's lower lip trembled for a moment or two, but she quickly regained her composure. Evenly she said, "Thank you, Hamilton. I am to be insulted in my own house with ammunition supplied by you, it seems!"

He shrugged angrily and snarled, "I didn't say anything like that. Can't you see what her game is, Gail? It's a talent she inherited from her late unlamented father, I guess."

"Shut your filthy mouth!" Corinne screamed, then picked up her glass from the bar top and hurled its contents at his face.

"Corinne, darling," Swanson said nervously, "I think maybe we'd better go now?"

"You go!" she blazed. "I'll go when I'm good and ready!"

"Al," Agnes asked quietly with her head on my shoulder, "are we going someplace to play that game now?"

"Anytime now, honey," I agreed.

"That's nice," she said contentedly. "Exercise is good for the figure, I always figure, and if you figure to have a good figure you must figure on—"

"Shut your sweet big mouth," I suggested politely.

Hamilton finished wiping his face with his handkerchief, then glared at Corinne. Softly he said, "I'm going to fix your wagon for you, kid. But good!"

"Hamilton," his wife said in a slow, distinct voice, "if this person is going to stay in my house, I'm leaving as of now. Just make up your mind as to which you prefer."

Hamilton glared savagely at Swanson. "Get out of here, will you, and take Corinne with you!"

"She won't go," Swanson said helplessly. "I tried before."

"Why should she go?" A new voice sounded suddenly in back of Gail Hamilton. "A cute chick like her? She can stay right here for as long as she wants. Ain't that right, Lenny?"

Gail turned her head and recoiled instinctively at sight of an unshaven, vicious giant who stood so close to her.

He was Mike Soulos, of course. Beside him, Lenny Kosto held the thirty-two carelessly in his right hand and smiled at the frozen tableau in front of him.

"We saw by the lights that you folks were still up," he said conversationally, "so we thought we'd drop by for a nightcap."

Then he pointed at Hamilton. "You—make us a drink each."

For a long moment Hamilton glared dully at him, but then the gun twitched in Lenny's hand, and Hamilton nearly broke a glass setting them up fast.

"Hey, there!" Lenny gave me a smiling nod of recognition. "It must be old home week, Mike. Look who's here—the bush league cop!"

"The cop?" Soulos's voice was thick with anticipation. "You mean that dirty, stinking cop, Lenny?"

"None other," said Lenny happily.

"Yeah, so it is!" Soulos glittered his savage gaze at me. "How is that fat head doing, cop? You got a dirty, stinking headache to go along with your dirty, stinking self?"

Gail Hamilton shuddered and turned her head away, then screamed thinly when Lenny took her arm and forced her toward the bar where Hamilton had the drinks ready.

"Just you stay with the rest of 'em, lady." Lenny nudged her with his shoulder so that Gail stumbled and would have fallen if Swanson hadn't caught her. Then Lenny said, "Nobody gets hurt if they behave. All we want is a couple of drinks and"—he nodded at Hamilton—"a nice quiet talk with red-nosed Rudolf, here."

"And maybe the cop, huh, Lenny?" Soulos said in his thick, slap-happy voice. "We have a little easy talk with the dirty, stinking cop, too, huh?"

"Maybe," Lenny said. "But he's not important right now. Never was, for that matter." He picked up the nearest glass and drained it in one giant gulp, then threw the glass back onto the bar top. He said, "They got a lousy bar service here—a guy has to wait all the time."

Hamilton took up the glass with fumbling fingers and dropped it with a splintering crash to the floor.

"Clumsy!" Lenny said—then there was a sound like a pistol shot as the back of his hand slammed across Hamilton's face with brutal force. "Better get another glass—and make sure you don't drop this one, huh?"

"The trouble with this guy—" Soulos chuckled delightedly "—is he ain't nothing but a slob—right, Lenny?"

"Right," Kosto said. "You make that drink yet, slob?"

Hamilton pushed the new drink along the bar top toward him, and watched as Lenny drained it dry in one long gulp.

"That was a little better," the hoodlum said, wiping his mouth with the back of his hand. "You're learning, Fatso."

"Hey, Lenny," Soulos said, his face darkening, "so maybe this is fun, but how about we get down to business, huh?"

"You're right," Kosto agreed. He gestured with the gun. "Come on, Fatso—out!"

"What—what are you going to do with my husband?" Gail demanded in a tense, high-pitched voice. "If you dare harm him in any way, I'll see that you're—"

"Shut up, lady," Lenny said indifferently. "Or maybe we'll rip that fancy gown off you just for the laughs. Might be an idea, at that. How would you like to dance for us, huh?"

Gail shivered, and bit down on her lower lip. She said nothing more as her husband moved out slowly from behind the bar.

"You got the right idea, Fatso," Lenny told him. "Just keep on walking, right outside. We want a long talk with you, someplace where it's nice and private."

Hamilton's face was gray under the suntan.

"What—what do you want with me?" he asked shakily.

"It's a private deal," Lenny said. "You'll find out."

Soulos gave Hamilton a vicious shove that sent him staggering toward the door. "On your way, Fatso!" He lumbered along behind Hamilton until they'd both disappeared outside.

Lenny looked at the rest of us. He said easily, "Everybody gets to sit right here, nice and quiet. That way, no one gets hurt."

Then his eyes singled me out.

"You got a gun, maybe, Lieutenant? I want it."

"You think I carry a gun on my night off?" I said. "Who'd think of meeting up with you and your gorilla friend in a house like this one?"

He took a pace toward me, then stopped, his eyes narrowed.

"I think you have got a gun, cop," he said softly. "I want it. So you take it out real slow, nice and easy, and two fingers is plenty."

"I don't have a gun," I repeated patiently. "How many times have I got to tell you, Lenny? I know you're maybe a little slow on the uptake, but this is getting ridiculous."

"Hey, Lenny?" Soulos called from outside. "What's keeping you?"

"You figure I got a gun," I said angrily, "you might just as well figure that Agnes here has got one—tucked into a garter, maybe?" I looked at her beside me, catching her gaze and holding it for a moment. "Honey, show the man you don't have a gun hidden in your garter or someplace, huh!"

She stared at me blankly for a split second, then caught on.

"Well, all right," she shrugged. "If he really wants to know."

Lenny was about to growl an impatient word or two—but he held them back and looked in surprise as Agnes bent and caught hold of the hem of her dress, and slowly lifted it.

She straightened with the lifting motion, raising her hem inch by inch above her nyloned knees and slowly revealing her rounded thighs in a kind of slow-motion strip tease.

Her skirt reached the tops of her stockings and she glanced at me appealingly, but I pretended not to see or understand, so she kept the skirt going higher and higher. Her pretty, black lace panties came into view, and still the dress moved higher. It was a show put on to attract Lenny's attention, but I got so interested myself I almost let my attention wander along with his.

But in time I dragged my mind back to the job on hand. Lenny was watching Agnes with a devoted concentration now, a faint film of sweat glistening across his forehead. It was one of those now-or-never situations and I figured if I didn't make the move now, it would be never in another couple of seconds.

I made a standing jump for the end of the bar—throwing myself forward almost horizontal to the floor. I heard Lenny's gun blast with a terrifying sound—then I landed on my hands and knees and skidded into the corner, hard up against the bar.

It put the solid wood structure between Lenny and me for the three, maybe four seconds it would take him to move to where he could get an unobstructed view of me. Then I came up on my knees, my fingers scrabbling frantically for the thirty-eight and finally dragging it from the holster. Lenny fired a second time and the slug plowed a thin furrow along the bar top maybe six inches above my head.

Then all hell seemed to break loose. The women were screaming like crazy—but above their noise, even, came the thunderous inquiring bellow from Soulos outside. Then there was the thump of his feet as he came charging back into the basement room. I edged forward a couple of feet, moving toward the near end of the bar where Lenny was standing just around the other side.

I peeked carefully, giving myself every chance to use the gun when I saw an enemy. But all I saw at first was Agnes, standing frozen to the spot with her eyes shut tight, her mouth open wide in a scream, and her hands still obediently holding the hem of her dress up around her waist.

Then two more shots sounded in quick succession, the blasts hammering the confining walls—rebounding from one to another with an almost unbearable thunder. One slug smashed at a wall high above me, and the other thudded into the thick teak paneling between me and Lenny.

It figured that with Soulos back in the room, their strategy was for Lenny to keep me pinned down and busy, while Mike edged around the end of the bar until he'd widened the angle enough to get a shot to me. My equally obvious strategy was not to worry about Lenny—*not to worry!*—but wait and see if I could get a glimpse of Soulos a split moment before he saw me.

I eased along another couple of feet, and that brought me nearly to the end of the bar but back from it, closer to the liquor cabinets behind. Then Lenny fired another couple of blind shots and I heard Mike's clumsy movement across the floor. He was moving around in a wide radius like I'd hoped he would—and moving fast for his bulk, figuring on that vital moment of indecision when I would be taken by surprise.

Too bad! He didn't get that vital moment. He didn't get it because I was ready and waiting for him, and I figured that I needed the moment a hell of a lot more than he did.

He had the gun in his fist pointed at me when he came into view, but

I was already squeezing the trigger of my thirty-eight and the slug took him high in the chest. He faltered for a moment, then kept coming. I fired a second time, quickly aiming lower so that the bullet got him in the belly. They've got to be really good to keep coming at you when they're shot in the belly.

Mike's gun exploded—maybe it was a reflex action as he was hit that second time, and there was a great shattering of glass as the slug hit among bottles in back of the bar.

Then Mike Soulos sank down to his knees, his lips pinched back from his gums in a soundless scream of agony. The gun spilled out of his hand, and the giant torso flopped downward with a thud as he stretched out on the floor and lay still.

I jumped the last two feet of distance which would bring me around the end of the bar. Lenny Kosto was standing maybe fifteen feet away, staring across at Soulos' body. Thin rivulets of sweat coursed down his face, and his mouth worked nervously. At that split second I had him cold—but then I had to go and do something downright stupid!

"Drop the gun, Lenny," I called. "Now!"

He moved faster than I'd have figured it possible for any guy to move. The gun leaped in his hand as it blasted, the slug tearing along the bar just inches away from me. Then he made a leap sideways—my shots missed him by a mile—and spun in mid-air so he was facing the doorway. He was running almost before his feet hit the ground.

By the time I'd scrambled to my feet and was running too, Lenny had vanished into the outside darkness. I had no choice but to just keep after him—though it isn't a smart thing to go chase an armed guy into the darkness.

Out there I paused for a moment. I heard Lenny's running footsteps on the concrete walk ahead of me someplace. But only for a moment or two.

Then suddenly he got real smart, and there were no more footsteps to be heard. I stayed right where I was, listening hard, and with a nasty sinking sensation in my insides. Could be, Lenny had just stepped off the path and was waiting for me to come close enough so he could get a shot at me from the garden foliage.

The garden stuff loomed blackly in the darkness, and at places it grew right up close to the edges of the path. In that kind of cover, Lenny could maybe stick a gun right into my ribs as I went past and squeeze the trigger before I knew what time of day it was.

I strained to catch the slightest sound—and heard a couple of dozen sounds of the night that had nothing to do with Lenny. Not all of them, anyway. But how was I to know which was which?

I ventured maybe six feet further along the walk, then paused to listen again. I heard a slight rustle in a clump of bushes about twenty feet ahead of me, as near as I could tell in the dark. I listened hard and heard it again—followed this time by a hushed and muffled sneeze!

I grinned and figured that Lenny was up there, for sure. But I didn't know quite where, yet. It was very dark, with only a few gleams of light from distant places and the sheltered shaft from the opened doorway of Hamilton's basement. My eyes had become a little more accustomed to the night. But I had to take care not to make a black target out of myself by putting my frame between the lit doorway and Lenny's hidden position up front.

I sank back flat against bushes along the path and moved slowly. I heard that rustle of sound again, very softly and closer now.

I came to a silent stop maybe ten feet from a clump of tall garden foliage, and I figured that Lenny was in there. It was tall enough for him to stand upright in it. I listened and waited for a rustle of sound again.

It came at last—maybe he was straining to see along the path and make out what had become of me. I grinned, and moved very carefully to slip a bullet from inside my belt carrier without making a sound. I hefted the bullet in my hand for a moment, then tossed it so it landed with a little rolling clatter near the clump of tall bush.

Instantly there were two shots from within the clump—they came in quick succession and I saw the two gun flashes in there. Obviously Lenny had fired toward the sounds so near to him on the path. With a grin I lifted my gun and fired at where I'd seen his gun flashes.

There was a yelp from Lenny and I crouched low, waiting for the return fire I expected. But instead there was only a quick and urgent call from the guy.

"Hold it, Lieutenant! Don't shoot anymore! I quit! You hear me, Lieutenant? I quit!"

"Prove it," I called. "Toss your gun onto the path."

There was a rustle of movement and the sound of a heavy gun thudding on the concrete. I moved quickly toward it, found the gun and picked it up.

A quick examination of the weapon showed why Lenny had quit. He had no more bullets left in the chamber.

I slid it into my coat pocket, but kept my own gun in my hand as I watched Lenny step onto the path. I went up close to him, quickly frisking him to make sure he didn't have another weapon of some kind. I trusted this guy like I'd trust a rattlesnake holed up in a cave, maybe.

He was moaning softly—it was almost a whimper. I saw that he was holding his left shoulder. I felt real sorry for Lenny. The way you'd feel sorry for a guy that fell and broke a leg running off with junior's piggy bank.

"So you got me," he said. "I quit, it's all over. You got my gun and everything. Right, Lieutenant?"

He was more than a little anxious about this interesting situation, I figured. And I knew why. Lenny Kosto trusted me about as much as I trusted him.

"You quit, sure," I said softly. "You know it, and I know it. But who else knows it, Lenny?"

That's exactly what he'd been afraid of. He licked his lips.

"Hey—you wouldn't do that, would you? Not a lousy thing like that, huh, Lieutenant?"

"Why wouldn't I, Lenny?" I asked.

"Where—where's the percentage?" he asked, real nervous.

"It's all the percentage I need, you slob!" I growled. "Soulos is dead—I knock you off now and everybody's happy."

"Now, wait a minute, Lieutenant—" His voice had gone frantic, the words falling over each other in their hurry to get out. "You got to treat me right—it'll pay you to treat me right, see?"

"Maybe so, maybe not," I told him. "I don't feel like taking your word for anything, you punk!"

"Look," he said desperately. "I treated you right, in that hotel room, didn't I?"

"You call being slugged over the head a nice way to be treated right?" I asked.

"Mike wanted to do more than that," Lenny assured me. "He wanted to give you the kind of treatment he gave the desk clerk, afterward. It was only me that stopped him, Lieutenant. You owe me something for that, huh?"

"Not a bent nickel!" I told him in disgust. "And that's the way we play it in the bush leagues, Lenny. The easiest way, because it's the best and surest way. If I blow a hole in your head right now, you slob, you'll be out of my hair forever."

"*Wait!*" He didn't doubt that I meant it, and his voice had become a thin wail of terror. "I can tell you all about Lambert. Things you want to know. Real important things, Lieutenant. How about we make a deal, huh?"

I just stared at him in the darkness, figuring it was good to let him sweat it out a little. He spoke again.

"What you got to lose? You got me cold, anyway, you can still throw the book at me when you get me before a judge. So we make it a deal, huh?"

"You've told me about Lambert already," I said coldly. "It didn't amount to a row of beans."

"I didn't tell you everything yet," he said quickly. "There's a whole heap of stuff that Dan told us that night in the bar—you ain't even heard the half of it!"

"So try and convince me, Lenny," I suggested. "You got all of ten seconds."

"That ain't enough!"

"You got nine seconds," I said, waving the gun in his face.

"But for Pete's sake, I can't tell you everything in that little time. Lieutenant—"

"Seven seconds," I said.

"All right, all right!" The words fell over each other again, tumbling out in a frantic stream. "Lambert told us he got tipped off that his partner—that fat slob Hamilton—was the guy who made the big deal with the hundred grand out of the cash register. And that Hamilton was the guy that framed Lambert."

"For crying out loud!" I said in disgust. "Lambert was saying that for three years, to anybody who'd listen. You got two seconds left, Lenny!"

"Hold it!" he said. "There's more. You want to know who tipped Lambert off? His own daughter."

"How would she know?" I asked wearily.

"How would I know how would she know?" Lenny groaned. "All I know is that Lambert told us about it in the bar. His daughter's tip had given him enough, he figured, so he could tip off the Sheriff and convince him it was true!"

"Is that all you got to tell me?" I asked.

He was beaten now. With his hand still pressed tight against his hit shoulder and some blood oozing through his fingers, he said, "Yeah, that's all I give you because it's all I've got. So now you let me have it, huh? All right—cop!"

He was scared but finished, and because he was finished he'd managed to put all of his venom into that last word. I grinned at him and lifted my gun again.

"You want to see something real interesting?" I asked. Then I triggered the thirty-eight three times—there were three empty clicks and that was all.

"You—you—" Lenny glared at me in the darkness. "So your rod was empty, too, huh? Here you got me going off my head and all the time—"

"That's maybe the trouble with us dirty, stinking cops," I said. "We're nothing but a bunch of dirty, stinking sadists. Just the same, I guess we'd better get you to a doctor so he can do something about your dirty, stinking shoulder. All right, Lenny—let's get going."

He grunted with pain as he walked. I herded him back along the concrete path toward the basement entrance of the house.

"So that was why you came here tonight?" I asked him. "Because you figured Hamilton still had the hundred grand, and you were going to cut yourself a piece of it?"

"That's right," he admitted unhappily. "You got to figure the percentages, Lieutenant."

"How do you mean?" I asked.

"All the time I wasted on that poor slob Lambert! The trouble I went to, just getting into the same cell with him! All those months in stir when I'm trying to get under his guard and find out where he's got the hundred grand holed up!"

"Tough, huh?" I said.

"Tough, for sure," Lenny growled. "Then when we're out of stir we tried again, all kinds of ways. We beat him up a little. We pleaded with him for just a small cut and we wouldn't bother him anymore. And all the time he didn't have a hundred bucks, let alone a hundred grand!"

"So you figured to keep following it up, after so much trouble, huh?" I said. "What made you think that Hamilton would be any easier, even if he did have the money?"

"Because he's yellow," Lenny snarled. "It sticks out a mile. He's just a natural con man, that guy—and you know what they are! You only got to stick your little finger in their eye and they fall down dead."

We came into the basement room where Hamilton had returned long ago. Gail was in tears, but she cheered up a little at sight of me, for some reason.

"Thank God you're all right, Lieutenant!" she said.

"Somebody call up Sheriff Lavers' office," I said, "and then somebody call a doctor."

"I'll do it," Swanson said, and hurried from the basement.

Corinne Lambert smiled at me coolly and spoke lazily. "Would you like a drink now, Lieutenant?"

"Nice idea," I agreed. "Thanks. Make one for Lenny, too, if you like."

"Him?" Hamilton snarled viciously. "That two-bit hoodlum? He and his friend were going to kill me, Lieutenant! For no reason at all, the bums!"

"Like I said, Lieutenant," Kosto sneered. "Just a natural con man. Now he's real brave, huh?"

"Are you going to stand there and let him insult me, Lieutenant? Or do I have to stop him myself?" Hamilton demanded. "It's a fine thing when a pair of scum can come into a man's home and—"

"Ah, shut up!" I said wearily.

"What? What did you say?" He shook with rage. "I'll report you for this—"

"For Pete's sake, will you stop making a damn fool of yourself?" Corinne Lambert broke in. "Who cares about whether you're insulted or not!"

"I've got a good mind—" Hamilton began.

"That's the biggest laugh of the week," Corinne said as she stepped toward Lenny and me with two drinks. "I doubt if you've got any kind of a mind."

While Lenny and I took our drinks, Corinne spoke to me.

"I see your girlfriend's in trouble again. What do you keep her around you for—other than the obvious? For laughs?"

I had forgotten all about Agnes. Now I looked around to see what had become of her. Last I'd seen of her she'd been standing with legs and panties on display and screaming her pretty head off.

Now the nylon and black lace were still exposed to the public view and there was nothing she could do about it. Her skirts were twisted high around her—but she was back there in the trick armchair with the wide bands circling so they clamped her arms to her sides and her body to the chair.

"So much excitement!" she exclaimed. "After you'd chased Lenny outside, Al, I just looked for the nearest chair to flop into. All right, so I forgot! Everything always happens to me!"

I had the scowling Hamilton go over and release her.

She got to her feet and untwisted her dress to let it drop back over her legs.

"It's certainly been an exciting night!" she sighed. "But it wasn't exactly the kind of excitement I bargained for—darn it!"

CHAPTER SEVEN

I got into the office around ten-thirty, which I figured wasn't bad considering I hadn't gotten home until around three A.M. And alone, at that. Agnes had figured that probably she'd had enough adventure for one night—and the effect of the tequila had worn off, anyway.

"Good morning to you, Lieutenant," Annabelle Jackson said almost pleasantly when she saw me. "I hear you had lots of fun and frolic last night."

I stopped and stared at her in wide-eyed admiration, but for a different reason from the usual.

"Fun and frolic yet!" I stood there starry-eyed, like I was a television fan maybe. "Oh, you professional law-enforcers! So very brave, so nonchalant! How typical—fun and frolic!"

"All right, already!" Annabelle said in an aggrieved voice. "So it was a silly phrase to use. But do you have to make a Federal rap out of it?"

"I guess not," I admitted. "Sorry, honey chile. It's just that it's a lousy morning and my liver aches—you know?"

"I've never had my liver ache," she said interestedly. "But I remember once I had my—no, never mind."

"Is Sheriff Lavers in his lair?" I asked. "You know what, magnolia blossom? One of these days when I don't care about my pension any more, I'm going to bring a bow and arrow into this office and do a Robin Hood on him."

"He's inside," Annabelle said. "He's got somebody with him, but he told me to send you straight in there when you arrived."

"The somebody," I said. "A she?"

"A he," she told me complacently. "Be glad about that, huh? Think of your liver."

I knocked, then went into the office. I saw the visitor out of the corner of my eye as he sat facing Lavers' desk.

Lavers nodded casually, then concentrated his attention on the visitor. I stood aside and waited politely for an opportunity to cut into the conversation.

"I believe there's only one successful way to practice detection," the visitor said—and I knew that voice from the last time I'd heard it.

"And that is?" Sheriff Lavers asked politely.

"By the intelligent application of trusted and orthodox methods of procedure," the familiar voice said smugly.

"I absolutely agree!" Lavers was real enthusiastic. "I only wish that some of my staff would appreciate the truth of that." Then he glared pointedly at me. "Instead of continually flying off at tangents all the time and getting nowhere!"

I watched, fascinated, as Mervyn Starke's slim fingertips tapped slowly together; the domed forehead shone warmly with reflected sunlight.

"I find it most heartening, Sheriff," Starke said smoothly, "to meet a man of your keen discernment occupying such a high office. It is not always the case, I'm afraid."

"Well, now—" Lavers almost blushed with pleasure. "I can only say that I do my very best at all times, using the most scientific, the most tried and trusted methods at my disposal."

"Like lieutenants?" I suggested brightly. "But that's wrong, sir, isn't it? I mean on your graduated scale, it's sergeants who are disposable and lieutenants expendable?"

Lavers favored me with a scowl, then spoke to Starke.

"Here's a classic example of the tangent-flier school. He is Lieutenant Wheeler. Have you two met before?"

"Yes, sir," I said enthusiastically. "Mr. Starke is a leading exponent of the park-near-a-hydrant school."

Starke put a hand to his mouth and coughed gently, while Lavers stared at me until he decided to quit worrying about what I meant.

"You were saying, Mr. Starke?" he asked.

"As you know, Sheriff Lavers, my agency was hired by Mrs. Gail Hamilton to watch every move Lambert made," the private eye said. "We have therefore been in a unique position to draw conclusions from our close observation, which started the first day Lambert returned to Pine City—and continued virtually uninterrupted until barely an hour before his death."

"True," Lavers said, and it took me a few seconds to realize that he wasn't ribbing Starke. "What are your conclusions?"

"Firstly,"—the private eye held up a long, spatulate finger to emphasize the point—"Lambert was convicted of embezzling a large sum of money which remains unrecovered. So it is assumed Lambert came back for one of two reasons—either to recoup the hundred thousand dollars he'd hidden away somewhere, or to revenge himself against the man who exposed him—his former partner, Hamilton Hamilton."

"Are you going to sit around for the next three days talking like that?" I exploded. "Quote 'either Lambert wanted revenge or the hundred grand he'd stashed away' unquote?"

"Wheeler!" Lavers said ominously. "You should be listening hard to this. You might learn something of value from Mr. Starke's application of tried and trusted methods of procedure."

"There are so many, sir?" I inquired. "The rope, the electric chair, the Inquisition, the Star Chamber, the whip, the Chinese water torture—"

"Shut up!" Lavers snarled. "Please continue, Mr. Starke."

"During the week we had Lambert under observation," Starke said, "he made no attempts to recover any sums of money. We can vouch for that. And the only person he spoke to, apart from the two hoodlums who were hounding him, was his daughter Corinne Lambert."

"And so?" Lavers said intelligently.

"Yet on the night of the murder he appeared at the Topaz Bar, triumphantly claiming to have evidence which would prove that he'd been framed. He was so confident about it that he set out to put the evidence before you, sir—and as we know, he was doomed never to arrive."

"Sheriff," I said brightly, "I'm getting to love these tried and trusty procedures—it gets real exciting when you start to use words like 'doomed.' It's kind of jazzy, don't you think?"

"Either keep quiet or get the hell out of my office," Lavers said harshly.

"So I'm a clam," I said, and sank into a chair.

Starke humored me with a faint smile, then concentrated on the Sheriff again.

"Dan Lambert was never close to his daughter—in fact she almost hated him. If she knew that he was innocent—if she knew the identity of the real embezzler three years back—and kept silent then, why would she suddenly volunteer the information now?"

Lavers frowned in deep thought for a while, then shrugged. After which Starke spoke again with deep significance toning his voice.

"Sheriff, I think that Lambert got the information from his daughter, all right—but accidentally. He just stumbled onto it, in other words."

"Could I have a little say?" I asked Lavers.

"So long as it makes sense," he warned me.

"Leave us not be coy about this," I said to Starke. "If Lambert didn't swindle his clients out of a hundred grand, there's no doubt at all about who did. It could only have been his former partner, Hamilton Hamilton. Right?"

"Exactly, Lieutenant," Starke said, nodding pleasantly, like I was the only boy in the school who got his arithmetic right.

"Let us presume," he went on calmly, "that the premise is correct. Hamilton stole the money and framed Lambert. Supposing by some means Lambert's daughter had proof of this. What would she be likely to do?"

"I figure she'd blackmail Hamilton—bleed him white," I said with conviction. "And I somehow think that's what happened!"

"I doubt very much whether she's bled him white—not yet at least," Starke said coldly. "So if her father stumbled on some proof she had of his innocence, his first thought was to rush out and clear himself. But her first thought would be to protect her blackmail income—and that might presuppose protecting the blackmail victim himself."

"Are you saying that Corinne Lambert murdered her own father?" Lavers said in horror. "But how?"

Starke shook his head.

"She couldn't have done it alone, naturally," he said. "She needed an accomplice. Now, let's look at the thing carefully. The car in which the murderer drew up alongside the cab to shoot Lambert through the window, was reported stolen by a man named Tony Swanson, who by some remarkable—"

"—coincidence is Corinne's fiancé," I finished for him.

"Correct." Starke smiled, but it was a forced smile and his teeth were slightly clenched.

"And let's just skip the one we all know, about reporting a car stolen when it's not and using that as an alibi, shall we?" I said reasonably.

"Certainly," Starke agreed, but his smile was almost a snarl now. Then he went on calmly. "So now we have Corinne Lambert and Tony Swanson in partnership to murder her father. They had the time, the opportunity, and the motive—to prevent her father from ruining their profitable blackmailing setup. Beyond all doubt, that *boutique* of hers is losing money hand over fist. It could not have survived for this long without new money being pumped into it at regular intervals."

Lavers rubbed his chin thoughtfully, then reached for a cigar. Doubtfully he said, "I don't know. There is still no real sign of evidence. What do you think, Wheeler?"

"If I can keep clear of 'doom' and all that jazz," I told him, "I'd like to tell how last night I had Lenny Kosto at the wrong end of a gun, and convinced that I was going to kill him. That's the only time I'll believe that Lenny was telling the truth."

"So what did he say?" Lavers asked.

"He swore that Dan Lambert told him, at the Topaz Bar, that Corinne had tipped him off about Hamilton."

"Lieutenant—really!" Starke tittered politely behind the back of his hand. "The word of an ex-convict like Lenny Kosto, given at gunpoint? I'll bet he'd have told you he knew the inside story on the Lincoln caper, and who framed John Wilkes Booth—if he'd thought it might help."

"I certainly agree with that," Lavers said firmly. "I think maybe Wheeler has a psychological block where Kosto is concerned." He grinned nastily. "Any man who can take the Lieutenant the way Kosto took him in that hotel room, Wheeler feels must be kind of something special. Right, Lieutenant?"

"Oh, sure," I said politely. "But there comes a time when a man is prepared to back his own judgment, too. My judgment tells me that Lenny was speaking the truth at that particular moment." I grinned at Lavers. "So, as I'm a fair-minded cop and a guy who likes to keep an open mind about these things—I say to hell with your judgment because you must be wrong!"

I addressed the last part of my speech to Starke, who now sat staring intently at me, like he was studying me closely for some very serious reason. I stood it for as long as I could, then prompted him with a growl of inquiry.

"My girdle's sagged or something?"

"I'm sorry," he apologized. "I was thinking. I am very, very interested in your line of reasoning, Lieutenant."

"I'm quite, quite happy to hear it," I sneered.

"You believe that Corinne Lambert volunteered the information to her father concerning Hamilton?" he asked.

"For sure," I assured him.

"Why are you sure?" he demanded.

"Because it's my guess that the golden goose is fresh out of eggs—that Hamilton is broke, in other words," I replied. "He's gone through that hundred grand in one way and another. He's had three years to do it, mind you. That basement room of his, and his importing business, must have cost a hell of a lot of money—not counting the blackmail payments!"

"So, because he couldn't pay any more, Corinne sold him out to the father she never cared about?" Starke queried. "Why?"

"Why not?" I said. "Hamilton had outlived his usefulness to her once he was broke. After seeing them together last night I'm quite convinced they hate each other's guts. But maybe it wasn't always like that."

"You're implying some emotional involvement at some stage?" Starke asked thoughtfully. "A sexual relationship, perhaps?"

"I figure it's possible," I said seriously. "It could explain the obvious hatred that exists between them now."

"Yes," he said slowly, nodding. "At the same time, of course, one must not overlook the man with the strongest possible motive for Lambert's murder—and that's Hamilton himself."

"Sure," I agreed. "One must not overlook him under any circumstances."

Starke's chin slowly lowered onto his chest and he was obviously thinking deeply. Or maybe he was sleeping with his eyes open. Either way it was a gift.

"I'll be on my way, Sheriff," I said politely.

"What?" Lavers was immersed in cigar smoke. "Oh, sure—by the way, Ballistics checked Kosto's thirty-two. It wasn't the gun that killed Lambert."

"Thanks for the information," I said, getting onto my feet. "I'll see you around, Merv?"

Merv was still too busy thinking even to hear me.

Annabelle was waiting for me when I got back to the outer office. Her feminine curiosity, along with other noticeable assets, was straining at the seams.

"Al, please," she asked, "who *is* that guy in there?"

"That," I told her, "is Mervyn Starke, celebrated private investigator, man of genius, iron will, and courtly manners—so he says. What do you care?"

"There's just something about the way he looks at you," she said slowly. "It does something to me—inside."

"Like suddenly something snaps?" I suggested.

"That's it," she said vehemently. "That's it exactly."

"Then watch out, honey, when you stand up," I warned her quietly. "That kind of thing can lead to embarrassment."

"Al Wheeler, what on earth are you talking about?"

"Elastic," I said. "Aren't we all?"

Right then, if I couldn't hear the clarion call, I could at least sense that it was time for Wheeler to wheel on—but fast.

I went out of the office, into the car, and out to the dingy street where the building stood that housed the dingy office of *Hamilton Hamilton, Importer.*

It would be nice to say that a joyous ray of sunshine named Agnes Green greeted me as I entered—but it wouldn't be true. Instead, a rather cold-faced blonde named Agnes Green greeted me with no warmth at all.

I looked at her anxiously for a moment, then said, "It wasn't me, honey, I swear it!"

"What wasn't you?" she snapped.

"Whatever it is you're brooding over, lover-doll," I explained carefully. "It was some other guy—it was all his fault and I'll beat his brains out!"

"It's you!" she said. "How about a date, he says. Dinner at the Hacienda, he says. Great. Sounds like real romantic stuff. So a girl blows seventy bucks on a stunning dress, a hairdo to go with it—not to mention some chic French underwear—"

"Well, that wasn't wasted, anyway," I soothed her.

"Please!" she said coldly. "I can't stand innuendo regarding sex in casual conversation—it's in the worst possible taste, I always think."

"Pardon my mania," I said faintly.

Then she returned to her original theme, undaunted, chattering like all get out!

"So I say 'yes' to the date. And what happens? A couple of drinks—food—then he says he has to go work a little—so next thing I know I'm in an apartment being insulted by that Lambert bitch while he talks sports cars with some other guy.

"But the night hadn't started yet, hardly. We go to another place that's run by a lunatic and I get my clothes blown over my head and I'm manacled to a chair a couple of times just for laughs. Not to mention having to lift up my skirts to the waist for a hoodlum to leer at—and me in that Paris underwear that wasn't built to stop the draughts!

"On top of all of that I'm exposed to gunfire on all sides and I suffer more frights than a maiden aunt who comes home and finds burglars in the house—male burglars, of course. And when it's all over at last, what happens? He gets a police car to drive me home because he's got to go back to the office! My golly, it's enough to make a poor girl swear off guys for life—and I'd do it if I was just a little older—fifty years or so, say."

"Pardon me, Miss Green," I said. "Is Mr. Hamilton in his office today?"

"Yes, he is." She looked at me blankly for a moment. "Is that why you came here? To see *him?*"

"Who else?" I asked lightly.

She opened her lovely mouth to make a suitable remark but for once she couldn't think of anything. I grinned at her from my superior height and she made a face. Then I went into Hamilton's office.

I found him standing over by the window, peering intently through a toy telescope. After I'd cleared my throat a couple of times, he lowered it and turned around.

"Ah, Lieutenant," he said with a flash of white teeth, and they set off the handsomeness of his tanned face with its crinkly iron gray hair above. Lenny Kosto had been right about him, I figured. He was a con man, born and bred. He had everything a con man needed, from looks to personality.

"I must congratulate you on your bravery last night," he said heartily. "Of course, one has a right to expect that sort of thing from the police who are paid to protect us. But it's very gratifying to see it in action."

He lifted the telescope to his eyes again and once more became absorbed. I inquired about it politely.

"Are you planning a voyage to the moon, or something?"

"Not likely," he chuckled, then thrust the telescope into my hands. "Here—take a look for yourself."

I took a look for myself and became just as absorbed. Each click of the iris as I turned it produced a different picture, and the versatility was amazing. An education, you might say.

You learn something new every day, I've been told, and in three minutes flat I'd learned enough new things to tide me over the next couple of weeks. I was sorry when Hamilton finally wrenched it out of my hands.

"Not bad, huh?" he chuckled hugely. "Japanese—strictly under-the-counter stuff, of course. The Portuguese used to be rather good at that kind of thing, but they seem to have faded out the last few years or so." He sat heavily onto his well-upholstered chair, shifted around until he was comfortable, then looked at me vaguely.

"Anything I can do for you, Lieutenant?" he asked politely.

"Yeah, thanks," I said. "A couple of things, Mr. Hamilton."

"Name them," he invited.

"You can tell me what it was that Corinne Lambert had that would prove you embezzled the hundred grand and framed her father for the rap," I said. "And you can tell me what she's done with the dough now that you're broke."

His mouth dropped open and he stared up at me, bug-eyed, like a guy who wondered if he'd heard it right.

"You can see we've got most of it figured out good, can't you?" I said reasonably. "It's just the last few little details we haven't got around to yet. This is where you can be a big help, Mr. Hamilton. And that reminds me of another point you could maybe clear up for us, while I'm here. How long ago did you stop sleeping with Corinne Lambert?"

I watched the changing expressions chase each other across his outraged face, with a succession of emotional colors that clicked on and off like a neon sign. Then—it had to happen sooner or later—he got his voice back. Man! You can say that again!

The windows rattled, the floors bent, the walls shook, the furniture cringed. This guy was wasted in an office dealing in pornographic novelties—he should have been in grand opera!

Eventually there came a time, however, when even his magnificent basso profundo started to come apart at the edges. There was the usual small crack, then a couple more—a nasty moment in full throat when his voice jumped a couple of octaves and he sounded like Little Red Riding Hood. It was the beginning of the end. There were squeaks and rattles while the veins corded desperately in his throat—and the ever-increasing periods of silence when his mouth opened and closed vigorously, giving him a remarkable resemblance to a goldfish. And sadly, in the end, there was absolute silence, punctuated occasionally by a slight wheezing sound.

"Do you mean, Mr. Hamilton," I said politely, "that you'd like me to go?"

He shook his head in helpless fury and started looking around for a weapon. I had no intention of bringing him in right then and I decided it was time I got out. In the smaller office, a warm ray of sunshine was unexpectedly beaming on me.

"Al, lover," Agnes purred, "I've been mean to you!"

"It happens," I said resignedly. "But then—I guess you figured you had a reason."

"Reason!" Her laugh said straight out that she spat on reasons. "I think I must've been out of my mind!"

"It happens," I said easily.

"So I'm forgiven?" she wanted to know.

"Not yet," I said amiably. "It needs a little more E for effort. Give it the old college try, huh?"

"Well, I've said I'm sorry, Al baby."

"Try O for original approach," I said. "Think big."

"Nothing comes," she said plaintively.

"Well," I prompted, "try W for—"

"That's it!" Agnes cried in triumph. "All right—you just stand there and watch, Al."

She walked away from me toward the window, in that sinuous undulating, rhythmic motion that made for an infinite variety of patterns beneath her tight skirt. She stopped when she reached the window, her hips oscillating gently at first, then working up speed until it began to look like a final warm-up at Indianapolis. She held peak revs for maybe ten seconds, then slowed down to normal.

My appreciation of the show was interrupted by the click of a telephone in Hamilton's office, like he'd lifted his receiver to make a call. I went to the switchboard near Agnes' desk and very carefully lifted another receiver to listen in.

I heard Corinne Lambert's voice answer the buzz-buzz at the other end. And I heard Hamilton speak to her, briefly and gruffly.

"I want to see you, kid. When?"

"I've no wish to see you ever, Hamilton!" Corinne snapped.

"I don't care what you wish, you bitch!" Hamilton snarled. "I'm coming to the *boutique* to ask you a few straight questions. I'll be there late this afternoon."

He hung up; and so did I. Then I said to Agnes, "Let's have some lunch, huh? No need to ask your boss. His voice has gone weak and needs a rest."

"How silly!" she said. "He has a very powerful voice!"

"That was early this morning, honey. Everything is in a state of constant flux or change, they say—so why should Hamilton's voice be any exception?"

"Well ..." she said doubtfully, "if you're sure it'll be all right, Al?"

"I guarantee it," I said confidently. "On this one, I'm happy to stamp the Wheeler seal."

"What's that?" she asked brightly.

"A walrus balancing a rubber ball on the end— Hey, if we don't hurry we'll be late for lunch. Come on, gorgeous." I grabbed her elbow and steered her out of the office.

It was a pleasant enough lunch—a long lunch—and by the time I had walked Agnes back to her office it was around three-thirty. The sun shone, I had a date with Agnes for nine that night—it was a peaceful world where only a homicide intruded.

Something nagged at the back of my mind when I wheeled the Healey away from the curb. A couple of miles later I remembered what the something was—a remark Starke had made about Hamilton being the most likely suspect because he had the most to lose if Lambert could prove his own innocence.

But according to Starke's own agency report, the only contact Lambert had, outside the two hoodlums, was with his own daughter. So how in hell could Hamilton have guessed she would tip off Lambert about him? And how could he guess that Lambert would go to the Topaz Bar and spend two hours getting stupid drunk before heading for Sheriff Lavers?

The more I thought about it the more it bothered me, until I felt there was one easy way to find out for sure—and that was to go talk with the wonder boy, Starke, himself.

When I reached his office the cerebral-looking blonde came toward me unhurriedly—she was an unpleasant sight and my spine started in to twitch so I couldn't stop it. How unattractive can a dame get, would you say?

This time she wore a tight but shapeless dress that proved a point—tight or loose clothing regardless, she still had no woman shape. The light blue frames of her glasses cast flickering shades across the neutral muddy tones of her eyes, as she looked at me in silence. Any time now, I figured, she would strike a gong in back of her some place and I'd be turned into something unspeakably slimy, writhing around on the floor.

"Lieutenant Wheeler, is it not?" she said in a voice as flat as her figure.

"Lieutenant Wheeler it is," I said determinedly. "I wish to see Mr. Starke."

"You can't." I was sure I detected a note of triumph in her voice. "He's out!"

"He would be," I said, and thought about it for a moment. Then I said, "Well, one of the other guys will do."

Her eyebrows peeked over the top frame of her glasses.

"What other guys?" she inquired coldly.

"One of Starke's operatives, of course," I said. "Anyone will do, just so long as I can ask a question or two—"

"What do you mean, operatives?" she broke in.

"One of his legmen," I said patiently. "One of the guys who work at private detecting for Starke."

"You seem to be laboring under a misapprehension, Lieutenant," she said with a sneer. "There're no guys connected with this place, no one except Mr. Starke and myself."

I looked at her and shook my head.

"I don't understand," I told her. "I'm confused."

"That's obvious from where I stand," she said in a neutral voice. "Have you thought of analysis, Lieutenant? I'm told that much is being done in that direction. The interpretation of dreams, for instance, can sometimes produce startling results—"

"Yeah, I'll bet," I growled. "Wait a minute, dream girl. You're not ribbing me about this? About there being only you and Starke in this whole setup?"

Ribbing me? It was a needless question. Another look at her muddy eyes reminded me that this dame hadn't joked with anyone in her whole life!

"Would you care to sit down for a while?" she asked. "I'll get you a glass of water—"

"Just so I got it straight," I said harshly. "There never has been anyone but you and Starke in this—this so-called detective agency?"

"Mr. Starke and me and the IBM machines," she said patiently. "That's all, ever."

By then she exhausted her patience as she gazed at me and asked, "Is there anything else I can do for you, Lieutenant?"

"I can't think of a thing," I said, and backed away quickly in case she could.

There was a bar right across the street, and I rested my head and my feet as I sank a couple of badly needed drinks. Then at five-thirty I remembered the point of my going to see Hamilton in his office.

I had made the obvious play—if nothing's happening, then start something—hoping Hamilton would be convinced that somebody had shot off their mouth to me in confidence, and that he would go leaping around to find out who.

I had been ready to tail him when he left—but then I'd listened into his phone call to Corinne Lambert and found there was no need to watch him as yet. He was going to see her late in the afternoon. Well, was this late enough?

I had one more drink and figured that now was the time to go see. If Hamilton went to call on Corinne at the *boutique* like he'd said he would, likely he would wait until closing time so he could get talking with her without any interruption.

I had just enough time to make it in the Healey by then, I figured. Barring traffic jams.

CHAPTER EIGHT

There was a traffic jam, and it was close to six-thirty when I parked outside the *boutique*. It looked like it had been closed for some little time—the shades were drawn and the place had that lonely look a store seems to take on outside of business hours when the whole world passes it by.

I recalled Hamilton at that crazy party saying in his badgering tone of voice how he'd tried to call on Corinne at the apartment she had in back of the *boutique,* only she hadn't been there and he'd figured there was only one other place she'd be.

I wondered whether there would be a separate entrance to the apartment. A short walk up and down the sidewalk showed that there was. On the down side, a narrow passage with its own small gate, no more than three feet wide, passed along one side of the store building. I saw that at the far end of the passage there was a closed door.

Walking down that narrow passage was like leaving the world way behind. Brick walls towered high to each side and the only sounds were those that floated in from traffic passing along the street out front.

There in the shadow of the *boutique* building I could have been on Mars, for all the contact with humanity I enjoyed. The thought stayed with me, sobering me if I needed any sobering, as I reached the shut door.

I banged the old-fashioned knocker a couple of times and waited. There was no sound inside, no movement. I wondered whether Hamilton was still in there with Corinne. If he was, I figured to join the party and force things along a little more. If he'd gone already,

Corinne might be angry after the interview and ready to tell me some more.

There was one tiny window nearby, neatly curtained. Along with the door it seemed to suggest that it was a very small apartment in there. Two rooms and a bath at most, I figured. I banged the knocker a second time, much harder than before. To my surprise the door swung open slowly.

"Hey, I'm sorry!" I called apologetically. "You know how it is, huh? You always want to be sure there's nobody—"

I quit right there, because there was no point in talking to an empty room.

Maybe the door hadn't been shut properly, the lock not clicked in place, so that my harder banging at the knocker had opened it, I thought.

Or maybe a dematerialized demon was silently screeching its head off while it waited for me in there. Mentally I took hold of myself and told myself I was a big boy now. I stepped inside.

I took a couple of steps gingerly, cleared my throat nervously, and called, "Miss Lambert? Corinne? Are you home?"

Even to me, it sounded kind of stupid.

I went through the two rooms and the bathroom, calling out her name now and then but wasting my breath. Obviously the little apartment was empty.

A wide outer door was thrown open from the second room, and I investigated it. Facing it across a distance of just a few feet was the rear door of the *boutique*. That one, too, was open.

Here, of course, was a logical explanation staring me in the face. Corinne was in the *boutique*. Likely she was working in there, setting up a new display—doing one of a score of things that have to be done around a shop.

I walked across to the second door and went inside. There was a narrow hallway about fifteen feet long, and it led me into the small office where I'd first met Corinne. A lot of junk was heaped about the desk and strewn across the carpet—papers and books connected with the running of the business—so it was impossible to tell whether Corinne had left the room five minutes or years ago. I called her name again, but there was only the empty echo of my voice to make an answer.

The heavy brocade drapes parted with an indignant murmur as I shouldered through them into the *boutique* proper. Outside the night was building up fast, but inside it was faster.

Long shadows splayed across the luxurious carpet, making a fantasy of patterns to an ever-changing theme. The shimmering, spun-gold effect of the dress worn by the nearest plaster model was muted in the fading light, but it still sparkled dimly and played tricks on my eyes, so once or twice I almost imagined that the model itself moved instead of the light that played around it.

THE EXOTIC

I was more than a little uncomfortable. I am a guy who rates a waxwork show as one of the most horrifying experiences available—and even if these models were of plaster, what was the significant difference?

"Corinne!" I called. "Where are you?"

My voice floated away lazily to be absorbed by the carpets and drapes, after which complete silence ruled again. The hell with it, Wheeler, I thought—you could hang around here all night while she is sitting out a movie or something.

But I had come all this way and there was no point in leaving again until I'd made good and sure. I went quickly to the front part of the establishment, my feet making no sound on the thick and plushy pile.

I followed this pleasant lamb's-wool trail until I reached the big display window in front. It was backed by a frosted glass panel, to stop people outside looking past the goods displayed there and straight into the shop.

The shadowy bulk of two plaster models loomed large, but badly defined through that frosted glass panel. And I knew that this was the curse of the Wheelers working and I couldn't just turn and go away. I had to make sure—and that meant if I had to rip up the carpet, even.

The frosted glass panel was secured by a catch. I slipped it easily and then pushed sideways at the panel. It didn't budge, which was not exactly a surprise to me—all sliding doors act this way; I've never seen one that worked perfectly yet. Finally I got both hands flat against the glass and heaved. Something had to give, and it did. There was a harsh grinding sound and the panel suddenly whooshed along the track.

It was too sudden, of course, and I overbalanced, stumbling forward onto the slightly raised display platform on my hands and knees.

There was a gentle swooshing sound from somewhere beside me, as one of the fantasy-wrapped plaster models toppled forward from the side wall to hit the floor. I got partly tangled up in the fantasy and there seemed to be yards and yards of it, as I clawed the shimmering material from about my head. I came up for air at last.

I guessed that I would look slightly haywire to anyone on the street outside, flopped forward on the floor of the window with a plaster model beside me and tangled up in a lady's gown. All I needed now was the cop on the beat to come along and start getting interested in what went on.

I struggled to my feet, softly cursing. I moved to a better position from where I might set the model upright again, hoping that my clumsiness hadn't severed the head from the body or some such unpleasant thing.

As I stooped to get a grip of the shoulders, something happened to make me pause. I noticed that the wig which had slid from the model's head was—a silver blonde one. It gave me a queer feeling, just looking at it. The hair was long—it had been about shoulder-length on the model—and the ends were clustered in tight curls.

It looked horribly familiar. I remained where I was, kind of frozen in an uncomfortable, half-crouching position. One half of my brain tried to reason something out, and the other half just sat there among the crazy surroundings and jibbered.

But somehow I managed to silence the jibbering half and made an attempt to get things straight.

It seemed a simple enough exercise in logic, I told myself, when you got right down to it. I'd knocked the model over and the wig had slid from its head, and if the wig looked familiar—so what? Silver blonde was a fashionable color and wigs were the latest fad. I picked up the wig and in the now-faded light I felt among the ruffled heap of gown for the model's head.

I found it for sure—but it wasn't bald like you would expect a model's head to be when it's just lost its wig. There was a lot of short but thickish brown hair, I saw, when I cleared away the yards of gown to look at it closely.

Right then I needed a stiff brandy or something. Gently I rolled the model by its shoulders and saw the eyes and face come into view. Likely, I had a kind of fatal inkling of what I would find, even before the liquid brown eyes of Corinne Lambert stared up at me in blank amazement.

"Too bad, honey," I sympathized. "But maybe you went around asking for this, huh?"

And I meant it. Ever since the first time I'd met Corinne, I had realized that she didn't have what it takes to win friends and influence people.

Now I turned her head gently from one side to the other and there, on the right side—just above her ear—the hair was slightly matted with a dark, viscous fluid. She had taken two slugs pretty close together—it was the way her father had been killed before her.

I left the window and found a telephone on the glass showcase nearby. I called in, and told the sergeant on duty to get somebody out here. I also told him that I wouldn't wait because I had business elsewhere, and he was to report to Sheriff Lavers what had happened.

After which I would have liked nothing better than to totter off to the nearest bar and maybe recuperate. But I was too busy to do that, either.

I left the premises the way I had gone in, closing the doors gently behind me without clicking them locked. I made my way to the parked Healey and sat in it for maybe half a minute before starting out. There were a few things I wanted to straighten out in my mind, and when finally I got going I figured that I'd gotten them as straight as I needed.

Then I pushed the Healey along as fast as the traffic would allow—anxious to reach the end of the trail and wind things up.

The Hamilton house was a blaze of light when I wheeled the Healey up the pebbled driveway. Somehow it all looked unreal, something straight from a fantasy, in a way that had never struck me about it before. Maybe it was a "sign" of something or other, I thought as I climbed from the car. I'm a guy who's always strong for signs.

I buzzed at the front door and the butler took his time about answering. Then when he answered he still took his time.

He had opened the door just enough inches so I might see his cracked smile of recognition when he looked at me, and hear his unruffled greeting in the voice he imagined was equal to every occasion.

"Good evening, Lieutenant, sir."

"Hi, Perkins," I said impatiently. "Mr. Hamilton, Importer—is he home?"

"I'm sorry, sir, no." He shook his head sympathetically, like he wouldn't have had this happen for the world "The master hasn't returned since this morning."

"Then how about Mr. Hamilton of Hamilton and Lambert, Investment Counselors—is he home?"

His professional smile was sagging at the corners.

"Is this some kind of joke, Lieutenant?" he inquired

"I wouldn't try to burden you with another joke, Perkins," I told him. "I somehow think you've had your fill of jokes in this grand old establishment."

"You can say that again—I mean, how very true, sir," he said.

"But the point is, I still want to see Mr. Hamilton or somebody," I pointed out. "Why don't we start all over again, Perkins?"

"As you wish, sir," he agreed—like a father humoring a child, maybe.

"Good evening, Perkins," I said bleakly. "Is *anyone* home?"

"Ah, yes, sir, I'm happy to say. Mrs. Hamilton, you know. She's in the drawing room. Shall I announce you, sir?"

"Let me do it all by myself, Perkins," I suggested brightly. "Just this once, so I can tell the folks back home?"

"I rather think not, sir—" he tried to say, but I pushed past him into the hallway and headed along it.

I had taken maybe just half a dozen paces when he caught up with me. His voice tugged at my sleeve nervously.

"Wait, please, Lieutenant. I should have told you—she isn't alone—Mrs. Hamilton, I mean. There is a gentleman with her and they're talking—"

"Talking, huh?" I raised my eyebrow at him. "Well, if her husband is broadminded about it, why should I beef? And why should you for that matter?"

"I don't quite understand you, sir," he said worriedly.

"I'm talking about something that concerns you and me and all of us, Perkins," I told him sternly. "Where, may I ask, do you stand on the broader moral issues that confront all thinking people today?"

"Lieutenant, sir!" he almost pleaded now, half-running to keep up with me along the hallway as I headed for where I recalled the drawing room to be.

"*Sir*, indeed!" I said severely. "Are we to reinstate the old rights of the feudal Sir—which included all the wenches who lived on the estate? Or are we to be all modern and sophisticated—throw your wives into the center of the table every Saturday night and keep on changing—"

He clutched politely if frantically at my arm.

"You can't go in there!" he almost screamed. "Mrs. Hamilton gave me express instructions that she must not be disturbed under any circumstances—"

"Disturbed?" I said excitedly. "I should think we must all be disturbed at the modern trends, the falling away of old values, Perkins! Shuffle and cut, deal out a hand of seven wives to each player, one for each night of the week—"

He hadn't stopped me from reaching the door of the drawing room—which was closed—but there I paused with my hand on the knob to glare at him.

"Is this what family television has brought us to? The ultimate in modern parlor games, fun for young and old, infinite variety played on a constant well-established theme?"

"But, sir—"

"Audience participation every Wednesday night with huge jackpot prizes," I admonished him. "Only last week one lucky man ran his winnings up from one old discarded mistress to a year's supply totaling three hundred and sixty brand new wives—"

"Please, Lieutenant!" The poor guy was nearly in tears. "This could mean my job!"

"I'm sure it will not," I told him sincerely. "I won't need you any further, Perkins."

"No, sir?" The old mask slipped back over his face and he clamped it tight. "Thank you, sir."

I didn't bother to knock, because I'm a guy who likes to see the effect of a surprise entry when surprise is a possibility.

I went into the drawing room and it didn't look any different at all. Even the trick rubber vases were still there, waiting for the next sucker to happen along. And Gail Hamilton was there.

She sat on the couch, and she swung her gaze at me in blank astonishment as I moved toward her. She wore a beautiful gown made of luxurious pearl-colored silk, and I hated to think what it must have cost.

On Agnes, I took time out to reflect, it would have looked real stunning—sexy—a wow! On Gail Hamilton it was impeccable—modest—right.

"Lieutenant Wheeler—" She tried to play the perfect hostess even under these unexpected circumstances, but she couldn't quite manage the smile. She asked, "Didn't Perkins answer the door?"

"He certainly did," I assured her. "Don't blame him for my bursting in on you like this, Mrs. Hamilton. He tried everything to stop me—but my business just won't wait, I'm afraid."

"It must be very urgent business indeed!" a calm but resonant voice said from nearby.

I grinned across at him. He was sitting in an armchair turned away from me, which was why I hadn't noticed him before. At the oblique angle I had a glimpse of his half-turned face, with its domed forehead and the sharp, pointed nose.

"Hi, Mr. Starke," I greeted him as he completed his turning movement to smile at me politely. "I'm so glad you're here."

He raised his eyebrows.

"Glad?" he queried.

"I called at your office this afternoon to see you," I told him, "but you were out."

"I frequently am," he said calmly and I fought off an impulse to slug his superior mug right then and there.

"I called on your husband today also, Mrs. Hamilton," I said. "Just before lunch, at his office."

"Oh?" she said. She was polite, but maybe a little impatient.

"We had a little talk," I said. "He was very rude to me. But then, I guess I was rude to him first."

"How interesting," Starke remarked in a bored voice.

The armchair squeaked as he shifted position wearily, like he wondered how much longer I was likely to stick around and block whatever had been going on between him and Gail. Still he retained the look of resigned acceptance which was a subtle insult in its own right.

"What is it all about, Wheeler?" he asked. "Are you trying out some new wrinkle in your busy—and if I may say so—inept game of investigation?"

"You do like to hear yourself speak, don't you, Merv?" I grinned at him. "For once, you'd better quit. I'll do all the speaking and I guarantee you won't be bored if you just sit there and listen."

"I haven't heard anything to interest me yet," he said.

We sneered at each other and I turned to speak to Gail again. Her face was tautly strung, I thought.

"Your husband got mad at me, Mrs. Hamilton, because I asked him a few questions in the line of duty. I figured maybe he could help me clear up a few points about the Lambert murder, you see?"

She nodded rather vaguely, her serious eyes searching my face for a clue as to what this was about. Or maybe to make sure I was not out of my mind already.

"I asked him what it was that Corinne had in her possession that would prove it was Hamilton and not her father who'd got away with that hundred thousand dollars. And I asked him when did he stop sleeping with her—just one or two harmless little questions like that."

For a moment, the absolute despair showed in her face—then it was wiped away in one quick sweep, and replaced by a conventional mixture of shock and disgust.

"I think you must be insane, Lieutenant!" she gasped. "To even consider for a moment that Hamilton would do such outrageous, terrible things—why—" Words failed her.

"I trust Hamilton threw you right out on your ear, Lieutenant," Starke asked amusedly.

"Verbally, anyway," I agreed. "He was very overwrought in his language and so on. But that was the one idea, you see, to make him good and mad so he would do something."

"Do what?" Starke asked in surprise.

"Make some move," I said. "So I might watch for the effect and get a lead. It wasn't a very subtle approach, but I was anxious for action—you know?"

"No, Lieutenant," he said smugly, "I do not. To me sounds like a very crude method—"

"Let's not go into your opinions right now, huh?" I suggested. "Let's wait till a little later when they might be worth a second thought."

"Please yourself," he said generously.

"Well, I lingered in the outer office after I'd left Hamilton," I went on, "on account of his cute secretary had something she wanted to show me and anyway I wanted to see whether Hamilton left his office. If he was going anyplace, I figured to tail him. But it didn't happen that way."

"The plans of mice and men—" Starke began, but I cut in.

"Instead, Hamilton made a phone call. I listened in, like the busybody I am, and heard him speak to Corinne Lambert. He was good and mad at her—said he was coming to see her at the *boutique* late in the afternoon."

"Why was he mad at her?" Starke had to ask.

"Maybe he figured, from the questions I'd asked him, that she'd been shooting off her mouth about his private life," I said, grinning. "Maybe he figured to scold her, you know?"

"So what happened?" Starke demanded. "You followed him when he went to the *boutique?*"

"Actually, no," I told him. "I spent some time trying to see you at your office and doing one or two other things. Then late this afternoon I headed for the *boutique* to see what went on and hoping to join the party."

"And—did you find my husband there?" Gail asked nervously.

"No, Mrs. Hamilton, I didn't. But I found Corinne Lambert, for sure. She was modeling in her big front window."

"Modeling?" Gail queried in surprise.

"With the latest in bullet holes adorning her head," I told her. "She'd been shot twice, just above her right ear. She was quite dead, naturally."

There was a silence in the room, so all I could hear was the quickened breath of the woman who stared at me in so stricken a manner. Until she forced herself to speak at last.

"Oh, no! How horrible—how very horrible—" It was little more than a whisper.

Starke got to his feet, his face almost jumping its muscles with excitement.

"Is this true, Wheeler?" he demanded. "It isn't some damn fool joke?"

"Not to Corinne Lambert, it isn't," I assured him. "You know, if you tried real hard, Merv, maybe you could quit sounding even more stupid than you look!"

He was about to make a suitable retort, no doubt, but Gail broke it up by touching my sleeve and asking gently, "Lieutenant—after you found that poor girl's body, you came straight here?"

"Straight here," I said.

"May I ask why?" she inquired with a tremble in her voice.

"To see your husband, Mrs. Hamilton," I said. "What else?"

She moaned, and looked at me with those stricken eyes.

"But—you can't seriously think that he killed her!" she almost begged.

"I'm very sorry, Mrs. Hamilton," I said with a shrug. "You'd have to know sooner or later, anyway. Your husband is a liar, a swindler, and a murderer."

She came straight up out of her couch and the palm of her right hand met the side of my face in a stinging slap. It was right out of character—and painful as hell. I stared at her with smarting eyes.

"How dare you!" she hissed. "How dare you besmirch the character of a fine man like Hamilton! Why, I'll—"

"Gail!" Starke said softly, restrainingly. "My dear, I know that this terrible thing is almost impossible to believe. But I'm afraid Wheeler is right. And as he says, you'd have to face up to it sooner or later. Let's look at it calmly, shall we? Who else but Hamilton could have killed Corinne?"

"I don't know," she said weakly. "I—I really don't know!"

She swayed slightly. Starke came forward, caught her by the arm, and helped her back to the couch. She thanked him with a silent nod of her head, then rummaged in her purse until she found the inevitable handkerchief.

Starke watched her for a moment, then turned back to me. When he spoke he kept his voice low, almost in a whisper.

"Do you think Hamilton will come back here?"

"Sure, he'll come back to his home," I answered confidently. "Why wouldn't he?"

"You don't think he's more likely to make a run for it?" the guy asked in a troubled, softly excited tone.

"At this stage, and from his own point of view," I said, "why should he run?"

"Well—he just might start wondering what your objective was in attacking him today the way you did. And he might suddenly realize your reason for having done it. In which case—"

"I don't figure Hamilton thinks that way," I said with a shrug. "Like Lenny Kosto said, he's a con man. And they're always too busy figuring out their own schemes to worry about anyone else's."

He sighed doubtfully.

"I hope you're right, Lieutenant," he said. "It's going to be a bad error on your part if he doesn't come back."

"I'll take my chances," I said.

"I know one thing," Starke said. "This is all too terribly ghastly for Gail, here. She absolutely worships the ground her husband walks on."

"Because she owns it?" I asked.

"You're impossible, Wheeler!" he said, and swung away.

But he didn't swing far. There was a resounding crash as both drawing room doors were flung wide open and Hamilton Hamilton came into the room. He headed straight for me, with fiery lights in his eyes.

"What the hell are *you* doing here?" he demanded.

"Paying a courtesy call," I said politely.

"Get the hell out!" His voice had come back fine, I noticed. "Get out of my house, you insulting—"

"For crying out loud!" I clutched at imaginary air. "There's more acting around this place today than you'd find in ten Broadway productions!"

"I'm warning you, Wheeler!" Hamilton thundered. "I'll give you exactly ten seconds to leave—"

"Knock it off!" I snarled at him. "Behave yourself—or I'll handcuff you to one of your own chairs!"

I'd already learned he was an easy guy to stop, and that stopped him. His eyes widened and he took a pace backward from me. But he still played along with his rumbling voice—or did it have an undertone of nervousness now?

"What—what is the meaning of this outrage to which I and my wife have been subjected!"

"Be quiet, Hamilton," Gail said brokenly. "Corinne Lambert's dead, and the Lieutenant seems to think that you did it—that you murdered her."

"Me?" I felt I could have written the dialogue for him. "Me, a murderer? Why I'll—"

"Do shut up!" I said wearily. "And listen. That means all three of you. I'm so goddamned sick of hearing people trying to sound and look the way they figure they ought to sound and look under the circumstances!"

"I'm sure I've never met a more boorish man in my life!" Gail said stuffy. "He comes into our house and insults everybody—"

"Leave us not go through that jazz again," I said coldly. "Given half a chance, I can wind up the Lambert murders in the next ten minutes, if you'll maybe let me get a word in edgewise. All right?"

They settled into a hostile silence.

"I'll tell you how it all worked," I said, "without any interruption from anyone, including you, Mrs. Hamilton."

"Me?" she sniffed disdainfully. "At least I hope I'm one person who does not forget her breeding under the strain of sudden crisis!"

"Bully for you," I said. "Now let's go—"

They listened intently at last, while I laid it out basically, the way it had been laid out in Sheriff Laver's office with Starke present. How Lambert was the innocent and Hamilton the real swindler who had framed him. How Corinne Lambert had somehow discovered this and got proof of it, and used it to blackmail Hamilton until his money ran out.

When Lambert came back to Pine City on parole, he'd wanted to prove his innocence. Hamilton was afraid he wanted revenge. His wife was even more worried, to the point where she hired Starke to keep an eye on Lambert and protect her husband. Then Lambert was murdered on the same night that he'd jubilantly declared he had enough proof to clear himself, and intended to go to the sheriff's office.

I went over it all step by step, and my listeners were now following the story with immense interest. As well they might, I thought to myself. Each in their different way, they were all involved in the puzzle sufficiently to be anxious about the answer.

Next I hashed through the possible motives—talked about the different suspects—then took it right up to where Corinne had been murdered a few hours ago.

"You know, Wheeler," Starke ventured in a bored voice that didn't ring true with his eager listening, "you haven't recounted one single new fact."

"Because I'm saving them up," I told him. "I wanted everybody to get the background exactly right, so later we don't have to go over it again."

"I'll bet you're just loving this!" he said nastily.

"I know of better ways to spend my time," I said, with a passing thought for Agnes. And for just a moment I nearly got lost in the memory of her cute walk, its rhythm floating unbidden before my mind's eye.

I dragged my mind back to the business on hand, mentally slapping Agnes's cute bottom and sending her on her way. And I grinned at Starke.

"New facts, huh?" I said. "I have some, maybe. Not new to you, perhaps, but new to the other two people here."

"You do like to sound off, don't you?" he sneered. "That's one thing I'll give you full credit for, Lieutenant. You can always talk at least, even if your actual work doesn't amount to a row of beans."

"Look who's talking!" I grinned.

Next I related the story of Starke's detailed agency report on the movements of Dan Lambert right up until the time he'd left the Topaz Bar and was poured into the cab. And I enjoyed telling the boffo line, about the story of Starke's operative being unable to chase the cab on account of he was getting a ticket for parking near a fire hydrant.

Neither of the Hamiltons thought it was all that funny, and I'd now come to agree with them because I'd found it out the hard way.

"That kind of thing happens to everyone at some time or other," Starke growled. "Does it really matter now?"

"It matters a hell of a lot now," I told him cheerfully. "Like I told you, I went to your office to see you today but you were out. Maybe that was real lucky for me. About the luckiest thing that's happened to me in this case so far!"

"How do you mean?" he asked.

"I asked your girl—is she human, by the way?—if I could maybe see one of the other guys in the office instead of you, one of the operatives. And what did I find?"

He stared at me in wary silence.

"Let's not fool around with it, Merv," I suggested. "There are no other guys in your office. No operatives, no legmen. The whole remarkable organization consists of you, the girl, and the IBM machines."

"So it's some kind of crime to run a one-man organization?" he inquired.

"Not at all," I said with a grin. "But the trouble is, you've been too modest, Merv. Hiding your light, and all that jazz."

"Explain that," he suggested, while Hamilton and his wife watched and listened with puzzled frowns.

"Did you think I wouldn't?" I said. Then I continued.

"You should have told me in the first place that the dossier on Dan Lambert was all your own work. You presented it to me like it was a report from an employee—but actually, you were the guy who did all the tailing, all the watching. *You* were the guy who was parking next to a hydrant—only it never happened. It was just your humiliating but rather neat excuse for why your man wasn't tailing the cab when somebody shot Lambert."

"This is absurd!" Starke cried, and I saw that there was a faint film of perspiration glistening on his high forehead. "I don't know why I stay here listening to you, Wheeler!"

"You really must," I begged. "The story gets much more exciting very soon now."

"Get on with it then," he grated.

"You knew the whole setup, Merv," I pointed out. "You had lots of time to plan—to have a copy made of the key to Swanson's Jaguar, for instance—no problem at all for a man of your talents.

"When you'd finished the job and Lambert was dead, you drove out of town and dumped the car. Who would think of checking *your* alibi, anyway? Stop me if I'm wrong."

Gail Hamilton could stay out of it no longer. For a woman, she'd done a good job of remaining silent anyway.

"Lieutenant,"—she seemed to be choosing her words carefully, speaking slowly—"what possible motive could Mr. Starke have for killing Lambert? Your theory doesn't make sense to me. I just can't see how—"

"You will," I assured her gently. "Starke, you know, had the best motive in the world. A client prepared to pay big money to have the job done."

"A—a client?"

"How much did it set you back, Mrs. Hamilton?" I asked politely. "Five thousand? Ten? Fifteen, perhaps?"

"Lieutenant Wheeler! You must be—"

"Not insane!" I begged. "I resent that—it's a cliché! Why don't you try some word like allergic or something, for a change?"

Hamilton moved back into the tight circle again, feeling the urge to break his silence. His face was haggard, and his voice almost humble.

"Tell me one thing, Lieutenant. Why did my wife want Lambert dead?"

"To protect you, Hamilton," I said. "Like Starke said, she worships the ground you walk on—as long as she owns it. She had made good the hundred thousand dollars you swindled out of your clients. And why? Because most likely she half-suspected it was you and not Lambert who'd taken the money. She didn't really want to know for sure, I guess—but if it made you happy and she still had full ownership—all right!"

Hamilton gestured with a baffled movement of hands. Then Gail Hamilton sank backward onto the couch and burst into loud and fierce tears.

"The thing that had me stumped at first," I went on, "was that she herself put me in touch with Starke—why would she do that? My guess is that she figured it would cut down the risk, not add to it. If she herself told me about Starke, then I couldn't find out later and wonder why she hadn't."

"Have you forgotten something, Wheeler?" Hamilton asked. "What about Corinne?"

"What about her?" I countered.

"Well—why was she murdered?"

"I guess it's just that everybody has their own idea of what's right for them," I said with a shrug. "You take Mr. Starke here. An intelligent man, with a driving ambition for success—monetary success, I mean.

"So one day the golden opportunity arrives—in the shape of your wife. How long it took her to get to the real point—that she wanted Lambert not followed but dead—we'll probably never know. But maybe it didn't take all that long. Old Merv here would have been way ahead of her!"

"You still haven't explained about Corinne," Hamilton said.

"Can't you see?" I said. "A joint conspiracy to murder wedded Starke and your wife in an unholy alliance for life. But the way he saw it, he'd been paid off the fee for killing Lambert, but now what? He could blackmail her for small sums here and there—as long as he didn't get too greedy and raise the ante too much."

"I think maybe I'm beginning to understand," Hamilton said, and his voice was suddenly ugly.

There was an ugliness of a different kind in Starke's face, but I didn't let it bother me. I went on with my talk.

"From the way Starke saw it," I said, "this wealthy woman—wealthy beyond his dreams—was stupid enough to worship her dear husband. The husband was a fool but Starke couldn't kill him—he just didn't dare. Because that would end any possible hope of a future in security with the widow."

I took a deep breath and hoped that it would last long enough for me to finish.

"Starke figured he had to get rid of the husband in a way so the wife would never suspect he had anything to do with it. Merv being a bright boy and having those electronic computers and all, it didn't take him long to work out a way.

"The answer was," I went on, "to murder somebody else and frame the husband for it. That would get rid of the said husband, but permanently—and leave the way open, eventually, for a life of wedded bliss with all the monetary trimmings so dear to Starke's loving heart!"

"So that's why Corinne is dead?" Hamilton muttered, almost like he was asking himself and knew the answer anyway.

"Try asking Merv," I suggested. "He's the bright boy who knows for sure."

Hamilton straightened his flabby shoulders and walked with a heavy tread toward Starke. His movements were kind of slow, but purposeful. I watched him with interest. And so did Starke who was tending to shrink back.

Hamilton came to a stop a few feet away from him and stared at him for a moment before speaking tiredly, softly.

"I want to tell you something. I loved Corinne. I don't expect you to believe it—and I don't care if you do or not! I always tolerated my wife because of her money—but let me tell you about her. She's an iron-willed snob. She's sexless and dull. No guy on earth could live with her and be satisfied for long.

"Still, her money brought me comfort in other ways, and I stayed with her. But it was Corinne I loved. And there was a short time—maybe six months back—when I think she loved me. And now she's finished—dead."

He took another pace forward. Starke tried to move away but Hamilton crowded him into a corner.

"She's dead!" Hamilton said. "And you killed her!"

His hands, with hooked fingers, reached for the soft, white throat of Starke. The private eye screamed at him.

"Keep away from me—I'll kill you. I'll kill you!"

They closed in on each other then, because that was what Hamilton wanted and Starke couldn't get out of it. They wrestled with ineffective violence at close quarters, grunting for savage breath, spitting and hissing with exertion.

They stayed locked together for a few moments and then Starke got a hand free and cupped it under Hamilton's chin, levering it up and away. They broke apart, gasping hugely. Then, as Hamilton plowed in to get at him again, Starke yanked a gun from his back pocket and fired three times at Hamilton's chest from point-blank range.

Gail Hamilton screamed just once, but remained where she was, twisting away on the couch so she could no longer see the tragedy, and her voice dying to a whimper.

Her husband coughed once or twice with a gurgling sound and fell to his knees, then in a continuing collapse he subsided gently to the carpet with his life-blood welling out from under him.

Starke pushed himself away from the wall and came toward me, whimpering a little the way Gail was doing but for a different reason. His eyes stared and blazed with a maniacal fury.

"It was you!" he hissed. "All your goddamned fault, Wheeler! If you hadn't stuck your interfering nose into things, everything would have gone fine—like clockwork!"

"You've been bugged by those computers of yours, Merv," I said. "You got to remember people are different. Ever heard of a machine having a honeymoon, for instance?"

He snarled, and he kept right on coming, and I noticed that I was looking straight down the barrel of his gun. It gave me a slightly nervous feeling—like sheer terror.

"Well, I'll get *some* satisfaction out of this mess!" Starke said softly, fiercely. "At least you will not be around to see it when I go to the gas chamber, Wheeler!"

"Mervyn!" Gail Hamilton's voice was suddenly back with us, its tone almost normal. "Mervyn—I want you to come here for a moment, please."

"When I'm all through with this," Starke said, waving the gun at me, his fingers clutching it tightly enough to make me sweat.

"Now!" Gail insisted, her voice tinged with annoyance. "I want you here at my side *now!* It's important!"

He hesitated a moment longer, then sidled toward the couch, not taking his eyes off me for a moment, and keeping me covered with his gun.

When he stopped beside Gail he looked down at her briefly, then swung his gaze back at me.

"What is it, for God's sake?" he asked with a snarl.

"I have something for you here, Mervyn, in my purse," she said quietly. "Here it is."

He turned his head quickly once more to look, and that was the moment I figured that I'd better move, but fast. I plunged a hand to my gun holster under my coat—but it wasn't needed.

Gail Hamilton lifted the pretty little pearl-handled twenty-two from her purse with a smile, and shot Starke twice in the face.

She moved across the couch in desperate haste to avoid being soiled by his body when it sprawled across the couch. Her face registered involuntary distaste when she realized she was still holding the little gun—she threw it from her quickly.

"Guess I'd better call Sheriff Lavers," I said.

"Of course, Lieutenant," she said calmly. "Or would you prefer to call Perkins and have him do it for you?"

"Perkins has probably fainted clean away by now," I said.

I used the telephone, meanwhile figuring that I might yet make it for my date with Agnes. The time was eight-fifteen. It had been a long day—but the night could have its rewards.

I went back into the drawing room, where Gail Hamilton was sitting with her head high and her hands folded serenely on her lap.

But there was a wistful smile on her face.

"My goodness, Lieutenant," she said softly. "What will the Daughters of the Western Pioneers think of me now!"

THE END

Angel!
Carter Brown

CHAPTER ONE

It was a nice open road and I held the Austin Healey at a legal sixty-five, because it's always embarrassing for a cop when he picks up a speeding ticket. Then, one second later, my life was changed abruptly from carefree to full of trouble.

The guy headed straight toward me came out of nowhere, traveling at around three times the speed I was, and driving on both sides of the road at the same time. I didn't know where the hell he'd gotten his license, but you'd figure *somebody* would have told him the highway is no place for a light plane.

My foot automatically tramped on the brake, while the airplane hurtled toward me so close to the ground that its undercarriage filled my windshield. Beside me was a wide shallow ditch that didn't look exactly inviting, but was a hell of a lot preferable to the imminent threat of decapitation, so I swung the car off the road with my foot still clamped hard on the brake.

At the last moment the plane roared upward, its wheels clearing the top of my windshield by no more than six inches, I'd swear. The Healey came to a painful stop with its front wheels nestling gently in the ditch. By the time I'd gotten out to check if there was any damage to the front end of the car, the airplane had soared brightly into the dull blue yonder. If ever a guy wished for lightning to strike, it was Al Wheeler at that moment.

It took ten minutes to coax the Healey out of the ditch back onto the road, and a further fifteen minutes to find that mailbox that said "Kramer" in large white letters. I followed the rough track that led toward the house for maybe a quarter-mile, then turned off onto an even rougher track which led straight toward the landing strip about a mile from the house itself.

There was a tight knot of around six people at the end of the strip watching the light plane about to make its landing. I left the Healey in back of a tree around a hundred yards away from the strip figuring that goddamned pilot was capable of anything, but if he wanted my car bad enough he'd have to get through the tree first. By the time I'd walked across to the group watching the plane set down, I was gently seething inside, feeling like an inactive volcano about to change its mind. When the County Sheriff first said for me to investigate some complaints about stunt flying I had been mortified—me a homicide lieutenant attached to his office and all—but after that nerve-twitching experience on the road I was a truly dedicated cop.

"Kramer?" I said in a voice loud enough to be heard over the noise of the approaching airplane.

A tall guy, with an athletic build only just beginning to fatten, turned around and looked at me with an expression of annoyance on his handsome face. "I'm busy right now," he said curtly. "Save it for some other time."

"I'm Lieutenant Wheeler from the County Sheriff's office," I said formally, "and what I've got saved up for you won't wait for another time."

"Police?" He grinned contemptuously. "What is it? — a parking ticket?"

"You can tell me the name of the maniac who's flying that plane for a start," I suggested coldly.

"What for?"

"Because I'm a cop and I asked you. Because I'm about to book him as a public menace, get his license taken from him, have him spend sixty days in the county jail, I hope," I said, all in one breath. "You want to play this cute, maybe I can arrange for you to keep him company."

The airplane was now rolling down the strip toward us, and the rest of the group suddenly decided my conversation with Kramer was of greater interest. Besides Kramer, there were two other men, and two women; right then I only caught a glimpse out of the corner of my eye but even at that, the two women looked startlingly beautiful.

My threat seemed to have sobered Kramer a little. "It's Stu MacGregor flying the kite," he said in a placating voice. "One of the best damned pilots who ever flew Mig Alley. What do you mean, he's a maniac?"

I told him how I'd been buzzed by the plane and forced off the road, using brief, pithy words. A broad grin creased his face when I'd finished. "Hell!" he said jovially. "You don't want to take it so hard, Lieutenant. Stu was only kidding."

"Sure, where's your sense of humor?" a slightly drunken voice boomed at me. It didn't seem to fit its owner, a small, wiry guy with a face like a chihuahua and a fast-receding hairline. "What's the matter, Lieutenant? Can't take a joke, huh?"

I looked at Kramer inquiringly, and jerked my thumb in the little guy's direction. "What's that?" I grated.

"That's Sam Forde," he said uneasily. "It's a kind of jet jockey's reunion we're having. We all flew together in Korea—"

"And Europe before that!" Forde interjected. "While the Lieutenant was out checking gas coupons, I bet!"

"Take it easy, Sam," Kramer said tightly. "This guy is the law and you're not helping any."

"Not unless he wants a Purple Heart to add to the rest of his decorations," I snarled. "And if this MacGregor's had as much to drink as the pint-sized hero here, he's in worse trouble."

"Let's be a little civilized here," a studious-looking character said in an easy voice. "And keep your big mouth shut, Sam, for a moment." He ignored the murderous glare from the little guy standing beside him. "I'm Hoffner, Lieutenant, Red Hoffner. You know, Mitch Kramer and Sam Forde, the four of us—including Stu MacGregor—all flew together during the Korean War like Mitch told you. This is a reunion of old buddies and I guess maybe Stu did get a little overexuberant. And you're right—I'd be hopping mad if I'd been forced off the road like that, too. I'm sure Stu will apologize in a minute and—" He got a good look at the expression on my face and his voice wavered as he said, "Well, you don't want to make a Federal case out of it, do you?"

"Yes," I said simply.

There was an uncomfortable silence that lasted a few seconds, until one of the women spoke. "Lieutenant"—her voice was polished, and faintly amused—"I'm Sally Kramer." She brushed her long red hair away from her face in a feminine gesture so natural, it must have taken her a hell of a long time to perfect it. "Right now this man of mine and his playmates look like a bunch of overgrown college kids, and I know it. But the rest of the time they are sober, industrious citizens, believe me!"

"Including this MacGregor?" I asked irritably.

"Of course!" Her smile was definitely an appeal this time. "Don't you think—after Stu's apologized—we should have a drink and forget the whole thing, Lieutenant?"

"I'm prepared to forget the whole thing after I've hauled that fly-baby in front of a sober, industrious judge," I said bleakly, and the smile faded from her face faster than a sponsor from a low-rated television program.

The sound of the airplane's motor stopped abruptly and I watched the massively built guy climb out and walk toward us. He was big enough for two normal guys, and the muscles bulged and rippled under his tight sweatshirt as he came closer.

"Hey, you guys!" he yelled in a bull-like roar. "There was some punk driving one of those itsy-bitsy foreign sports cars on the road about fifteen miles back like he owned the goddamned county. So I buzzed him!" He threw back his head and roared with laughter. "Came straight at him with my wheels just a couple of feet off the deck—you should have seen him press the panic button!" Helpless laughter reduced him almost to incoherency for a few moments. "One minute, there he is big-dealing himself down the road," he gurgled, "then in comes MacGregor, shouting wild Scottish war chants, and the next minute the punk's in the ditch!"

It took a while for the conspicuous absence of any other laughter than his own to penetrate his consciousness. Finally he stopped gurgling and glared nastily at the stony-faced group.

"What the hell's the matter with you guys?" he asked thickly. "Is this a funeral or something?"

"Mr. MacGregor," I said very politely indeed, "allow me to introduce myself. I am Lieutenant Wheeler of the County Sheriff's office, and also the punk you forced off the road a little while back."

If quick-frozen horror was salable, MacGregor had a potential fortune plastered all over his face right then. His mouth opened and closed a couple of times, giving him a remarkable resemblance to a stranded dogfish, but no words came out.

"Stu!" Kramer said in a strangled voice. "You want us to enroll you with the Dale Carnegie course for when you get out of the county jail—if ever? Oh, brother! You and your cotton-pickin' big mouth!"

MacGregor's face was brick-red in color by then. "Lieutenant," he said weakly, "how was I to know the punk—I mean, driver—was a cop?"

"You would have preferred it was some little old lady with a weak heart, maybe?" I asked acidly.

His face went a couple of shades darker while he tried desperately to think up an answer. The hiatus was finally broken by the blonde, who stood beside the redheaded Sally Kramer, clearing her throat gently. I took a good look at her for the first time and realized my mistake—I should have looked sooner, a hell of a lot sooner.

Her wheat-colored hair was wind-blown into a tousled frame for the most exciting feminine face I'd ever seen in my whole life before. She wasn't beautiful—there was too much vitality for that. Taken separately, her dark blue eyes were too big, her lips too full, her cheekbones too hollow; but when they came together, they formed a face that was hauntingly provocative.

She wore a tight black sweater that shamelessly shaped the contours of her full deep breasts, and a pair of harlequin stretch pants, patterned in multicolored dots, that did equal service in revealing the full feminine curves of her rounded hips and firmly tapering thighs. At a conservative estimate, I figured she was around 105 per cent woman, and reflected happily that was exactly my kind of woman.

"Stu's put his big foot right into his mouth," she said easily, her voice husky with a pleasant-sounding rasping quality underneath. "I have a suggestion, Lieutenant. Supposing Stu stands still and lets you punch him in the nose—would that make you feel any better?"

"Hey, Angel!" MacGregor protested indignantly. "You want to get me a busted nose?"

"Better than sixty days in the county jail, flyboy!" she said lightly. Then she looked at me, her dark, lapis lazuli eyes glittering with amusement. "What do you say, Lieutenant? I appeal to your sporting instincts."

"Sporting instincts!" MacGregor nearly choked. "Sounds more like a variation of the old Roman game, the martyrs versus the lions!"

"This is Stu's problem," the studious-looking Red Hoffner said impatiently. "It's up to him to figure it out." He talked to Kramer, ignoring the rest of us. "Meantime we've got an aerobatics contest going, remember? Come on, Mitch, it's your turn."

Kramer looked embarrassed. "It's my property and my plane," he mumbled, "and all you bums are my guests, too, unfortunately. I can't walk out on Stu right now, Red."

"So what do we do?" Sam Forde, the pint-sized hero, said belligerently. "Stand around here the rest of the morning while the Lieutenant plays footsy with Stu? Come on, Mitch, it's your turn next."

"Don't be a piker, Mitch," MacGregor grunted. "Red's right—it's your turn to show us something new!"

"Can it, you guys," Kramer growled at both of them. "We got enough troubles right here on the ground already."

"Then the hell with you," Hoffner snapped. "It's my turn, Sam—Mitch has just chickened out!" He turned on his heel and strode purposefully toward the airplane.

The wheat-colored blonde looked at me steadily, the smile deepening across her face. "How about it, Lieutenant?" Then she saw Hoffner suddenly returning and a resigned expression chased the smile from her face. "Oh, hell!" she said dismally. "This lucky-mascot jazz can get to be too much of a good thing."

"Bend over like a good girl, darling," Sally Kramer told her in a faintly malicious voice. "And don't try to tell us you don't enjoy it!"

"Angel!" Hoffner said in a peremptory voice.

With a deep sigh, the blond turned her back on Hoffner and bent forward obediently, placing her hands on her knees. The studious look suddenly vanished from his face as he contemplated her uptilted, deliciously proportioned curves so snugly encased by the multicolored dots. He waited a few moments, then raised his right hand and gave her a resounding slap right where the stretch pants were stretched the tightest.

"Luck, Angel," he said solemnly.

"Ouch!" The blonde straightened up, gently massaging the area of assault. "Luck, Red."

Hoffner spun around and marched, back toward the airplane again, while I stared at the blonde, opened-mouthed.

"What the hell is this?" I gurgled. "A remake of *Hell's Angels*?"

"It's gotten to be a kind of tradition," Kramer said coldly. "Angel is our mascot—good luck charm—whatever you want to call it. If it's any of your damned business?"

"Now, now, Mitch," his wife said reprovingly. "Losing your temper will get you no place with the Lieutenant, I'm sure." She gave me what I guess passes for a sunny smile in a redhead's circle. "It's kind of involved, I admit, Lieutenant. The boys fly up into the big blue sky where the angels live, so what better mascot could they have than a real live angel right here on the ground? And, though I hate to say it, they'd have to go a long way to find a better excuse for slapping a beautifully shaped derriere!"

"There you got me," I admitted gloomily. "But—angel? Angel who?—like Angel Tingkbottom?"

"She's just—Angel." Sally Kramer shrugged, then looked at the blonde who was still rubbing tenderly. "Right, Angel?"

"Right," the blonde said nonchalantly. "And you still haven't answered my question. Do you want to punch Stu on the nose now, Lieutenant? You have my solemn promise he'll stand real still for you and not hit back."

MacGregor's impassioned mumblings were drowned by the sudden roar of the airplane motor starting up. There was no percentage in trying to talk to Angel over that horrific racket, so I watched with the rest of them as Hoffner taxied the light plane down to the end of the strip, then turned the nose into the wind ready for takeoff.

Thirty seconds later the light plane thundered over our heads, its downdraft scattering Angel's hairdo into an even more tousled disarray. When I figured I could be heard at a normal voice level again, I answered Angel's question.

"I have no ambition to punch MacGregor in the nose," I told her patiently. "Not while he just stands still, anyway. In a fair fight he'd murder me—not that I ever do fight fair and— Ah, the hell with it!"

I glared at the knowing smile that had spread across her full, curved lips again, and felt an odd need to justify my attitude to her.

"That was a damn-fool stunt he pulled on me," I snarled, "and he's old enough and big enough to know better. For all he knew or cared, it could've been a little old lady driving the car—or some green kid who might have panicked completely, wrecked the car, and incinerated himself. So I figure on doing my very best to put him where he'll have plenty of time to meditate on his sins. I hope I make myself absolutely clear?"

"Transparently," Angel said lightly.

"In spades!" MacGregor said violently. "I picked this bum for a sniveling do-gooder from the first moment I had the misfortune of looking at him, even. You sure tried, Angel, but this isn't a man you're dealing with—only a goddamned lousy imitation, hiding behind a badge and—"

I punched him on the nose. Right up until then I'd been a real good cop, like the Sheriff would be proud of, but every guy has his limit and MacGregor had just flown past mine.

He staggered back a couple of paces, blood flowing freely from his injured nasal organ, and blinked in surprise. Like I had already told him, he could murder me in a fair fight and I wasn't about to be murdered, not even for the Marquess of Queensberry yet. I swung the edge of my right hand hard into the side of his neck, putting a lot of weight behind the blow. He didn't even stagger, just bent a little, then came at me in a shambling trot with his eyes gleaming redly, full of murderous intent.

At the last moment I sidestepped and jabbed an elbow savagely into his kidney as he went past. The pain bent him into a crouching position like I'd devoutly hoped it would, while the momentum of his run carried him a couple of paces past me. I raised both hands over my head, with the fingers tightly interlaced, then jumped into the air and drove downward toward the nape of his neck. At the moment my interlocked hands actually hit him, I had both feet off the ground so my whole weight was behind the driving force.

This time MacGregor staggered all right; he lurched forward another three woozy steps, then suddenly pitched onto his face and lay sprawled face down on the grass. I unlocked my fingers painfully, walked over and knelt down beside him, levering him onto his back. He was breathing just fine and I felt a strong sense of relief when I saw it. The flow of blood from his nose had reduced to a trickle, so after I'd used my pocket handkerchief to clean up his face as best I could, I got back onto my feet again.

"Don't worry about Stu, Lieutenant," Kramer said, with something that sounded almost like respect in his voice. "That guy is indestructible."

"That's what I was hoping," I admitted, then fumbled awkwardly for a cigarette.

The mocking gleam in Angel's eyes stopped me just as I was about to strike a match.

"Lieutenant?" The rasp in her voice had an openly mocking sound to it.

"I was framed!" I gurgled. "You had this all figured out right from the start?"

"Are you still about to arrest Stu?" she asked calmly. "Because if you do—"

"—he's got four witnesses to say he was the victim of a brutal and unprovoked assault by a cop," I finished for her. "Don't worry, Angel, I know when I'm licked."

"Well, I'm damn glad that's all over with," Kramer said in a relieved voice. "One thing's for sure, Lieutenant—I guess none of us, including Stu, will ever pull a real stupid stunt like that again."

"Yeah," the pint-sized Sam Forde agreed reluctantly. "But I would have liked to see the Lieutenant get a couple of lumps for himself, all the same." There was a genuine wistful yearning in his voice that almost made me feel sympathetic toward him for a moment.

"Men are fundamentally such animals," Sally Kramer said in a disdainful voice. "Don't you agree, Angel?"

"Why, sure." The wheat-colored blonde gave her a look of wide-eyed innocence. "Why else would they have such a strong appeal for us women?"

The sudden returning thunder of the airplane's motor obliterated any answer Sally Kramer might have given. I looked up instinctively as the plane swooped down over our heads in a steep angle of descent. Steely fingers gripped my arm, and I turned to see an eager, almost dedicated look on Kramer's face.

"Watch this!" he yelled, close to my ear. "This is one of old Red's specialties."

The airplane continued its drive, gradually flattening its angle of descent until it was no more than thirty feet above the ground. Then it banked and began to climb steeply. I figured Hoffner was about to execute a loop—but right at the top of the loop, the plane straightened out effortlessly so it was climbing in an almost complete reversal of its original angle.

"You see that?" Kramer's grip on my arm tightened. "Brother! That's a perfect *chandelle* done the hard way. Did you see how close to the ground he was when he started the bank? You need perfect coordination right from the start in a *chandelle*, or you've goofed already. If Red had goofed at that height—"

"I get the picture," I assured him.

The airplane had circled around and now came back over our heads again, making a series of 180 degree turns in opposite directions, crossing and recrossing the airstrip, entering one turn from the other with a symmetrical climb and dive performed in each turn.

"Lazy eights!" Kramer yelled enthusiastically. "If you could measure his loops either side of the strip, I'd bet a million there wouldn't be a foot difference between them. I tell you, Lieutenant, this guy flew exactly the same precision stuff when he had three Migs on his tail, and—"

The sudden explosion hit the whole bunch of us with stunning impact, and it was followed by another, more ear-shattering, as I looked stupidly in the direction of the plane. A low ball of fire hung momentarily in the sky, and flaming hunks of fuselage fell rapidly toward the ground. Bits and pieces of lighter debris scattered in all directions. The silence that followed was almost unbearable.

"Oh, my God," Sally Kramer said in a thin voice, "what happened?"

"What about Red?" Angel asked in a rasping snarl. "We've got to do something, he's—"

"There's nothing we can do for Red," Forde said brutally. "He's with the real angels right now."

"How could a dreadful accident like this happen?" Sally Kramer babbled hysterically. "Cliff checked over the plane this morning, Mitch! There couldn't possibly have been anything wrong with—"

"Accident, hell!" Kramer said violently. "That goddamn plane was *blown* to bits! What I want to know is, was it intended for Red Hoffner—or me?"

CHAPTER TWO

Sheriff Lavers glared at me balefully. "I should have known better," he said in a mournful voice. "I should have figured sending you out there was a bad mistake right from the start. Ordering you to check on a complaint about stunt flying obviously injured your ego, Wheeler—so you had to find a murder for the sake of your pride—a kind of status symbol, right?"

"I'm flattered you have such a high opinion of my organizing capabilities, sir," I said politely, "but it wasn't me who planted that bomb in the airplane."

He crammed a cigar into his fat face, lit it with a small gesture of despair—and a match—then scowled at me. "No doubt at all that it was a bomb?"

"We have the word of the City's bomb squad, kindly loaned by Captain Parker," I reminded him. "MacDonald, their explosives expert, figures it had to be something with a timing device attached, planted in the fuselage of the airplane."

"But Hoffner was the second one to fly the plane," Lavers objected. "MacGregor had flown first. How could whoever planted the bomb know—"

"I guess they had a prearranged order of flying," I said. "I remember Hoffner told Kramer it was his turn next, then got impatient when Kramer said he had to talk to me first. That's why Kramer's question, whether the bomb was intended for Hoffner or himself, is a good one."

"Maybe you're right," the Sheriff grunted. "What did Doc Murphy say, after he'd seen the corpse?"

"Which piece?" I asked delicately.

His jowls paled a little at the thought. "What time did it happen?"

"Near enough to eleven-thirty this morning."

"It's four in the afternoon now," he grated. "What the hell are you doing in my office, Wheeler, when you should be out questioning suspects?"

"I had to wait for the bomb squad to tell me I had a murder, first," I said wearily. "After Sergeant Polnik got out to the Kramer house, I left him to keep an eye on the whole bunch of them. I hate to drag this up, Sheriff, but it's only twenty minutes since MacDonald gave me the official opinion of the bomb squad."

"All right," he snarled. "So you've been in my office twenty minutes too long, already!"

There was a brisk tap on the door, then his secretary came into the office. Like always, Annabelle Jackson was a sight for any man's eyes, sore or otherwise—the original Southern belle who never told, to coin a brand-new phrase.

"If lieutenants could have girl Fridays, I wouldn't need to run against you next election, Sheriff," I said wistfully.

Annabelle gave me a look that would have fractured a steel pylon, then concentrated on her boss.

"There's a Mr. Phillip Irving outside," she said evenly. "He says it's urgent he see you right away."

"Tell him I'm busy," Lavers snorted. "Tell him I've got a brand-new murder on my mind!"

"But that's what he wants to see you about, he says," Annabelle continued in an unruffled voice. "He said to tell you he's Mr. Kramer's attorney, and he has some very important information."

Lavers looked at me for a moment like he held me personally responsible for the whole thing, then shrugged his massive shoulders resignedly. "All right—show him in."

The guy who walked into the office a few seconds later was of medium height and slim build; an impeccable-looking man, dressed in an impeccable Brooks Brothers suit with matching accessories. His light brown hair was nicely brushed into an inconspicuous neatness, and the square-cut lenses in front of his eyes were half-framed in a pale tortoise shell.

"Sheriff Lavers—" he held out an impeccably manicured hand— "I am Phillip Irving, Mr. Kramer's attorney."

Lavers nodded and shook hands briefly, introduced me as the lieutenant handling the case, then invited Phillip Irving to sit down. The attorney sat down, crossed his legs at a precise angle, and rested his elbows on the arms of the chair, his fingertips pressed together in a steeple like angle.

"I need hardly say how distressed I was to learn of the terrible tragedy that happened this morning," he said in a dry, colorless voice. "As it happened, I only left the Kramer house an hour before it happened, myself."

"It was more than a tragedy, Mr. Irving," Lavers growled, "it was murder. Somebody planted a time bomb in that airplane."

Irving didn't look surprised. "As I suspected." He tapped his fingertips together briskly. "It is well that I came straight to you, Sheriff. Mitch Kramer—I regret to say this of a client—is an impetuous and foolhardy man. It's my opinion that he's been asking to be murdered for some time now."

"He didn't look like a man exactly tired of living when I saw him this morning," I said mildly.

After he'd given me a lengthy reflective look, Irving pursed his lips and closed his eyes apparently in meditation. I mentally counted off seven seconds before he spoke. "I shall have to give you the full background," he said solemnly, like I was his one chance for a hung jury. "It may take a little time, Lieutenant, but I think it vital you understand this."

"We've got all the time in the world, Counselor," I assured him, carefully avoiding the Sheriff's bloodshot eyes.

"As a young man, Kramer was born and brought up in a small town named Canyon Bluffs—it's roughly a hundred miles from here."

"I hope you'll spare us the details of his childhood sweethearts," Lavers said in a choked voice.

"In 1942, at the age of nineteen, Kramer joined the Army Air Force," Irving continued, blandly ignoring the Sheriff's comment. "In 1945, he was a hero—an ace, I think they called them—a fighter pilot with nineteen enemy planes shot down. When he returned home, he was given the typical small town's welcome for the returning hero. A client of ours, who also lived in Canyon Bluffs, was so emotionally overcome by all this that she decided this was one hero who should receive some practical reward from a grateful country.

"This woman was an extremely wealthy, eccentric, and elderly spinster—almost a recluse. She set up a trust for the young Kramer that would give him an assured income of around four thousand dollars a year for life. A week later, as a good luck gesture, she added half of the stock she'd bought—in a moment of weakness she freely admitted—in a new company that had just started operations in a backyard of some neighboring town. The real reason she bought the stock, she told my father who was handling her legal affairs at the time, was because she was so amused by the fancy-sounding name they'd given themselves."

Irving closed his eyes again momentarily. "This story still appalls me even after all these years. The fancy-sounding name was Allied and General Electronics Incorporated! Need I tell you, gentlemen, that Kramer's income is now somewhere in the region of seventy thousand dollars a year, and his total assets probably exceed a million by this time? I haven't actually checked lately."

"So now he's a very wealthy man," I said. "You mean this is the motive for an attempt to murder him?"

"I do indeed, Lieutenant," he said, nodding gravely. "When the Korean War came, Kramer went back to the Air Force and covered himself with glory all over again. When that was finished, he settled in Pine City, married a charming girl, and I really thought he'd come of age at long last. I was sadly wrong, gentlemen! He's nothing more than an aging Peter Pan, lamenting his former glories, perpetually reliving his heroic achievements in a world that has long ago forgotten them. He has no respect for money, even." There was a tone of genuine horror in his voice. "He will not face up to his responsibilities. Instead he surrounds himself with a bunch of former cronies as dissolute as himself, and seems determined to either drink himself to death, or court an abrupt and fatal accident!"

"This is all fascinating background, I'm sure," I said, with the politeness wearing somewhat thin. "But it doesn't explain that crack you made about him asking to be murdered. What we'd like to know is the name of the guy he was asking."

"I think you'll find that out for yourself, Lieutenant," he said stiffly, "when you investigate the shabby bunch of hangers-on he now surrounds himself with!"

"You mean one of them inherits his money after he's dead?" Lavers asked.

"What a ridiculous suggestion!" Irving nearly snorted. "His wife inherits the whole estate, naturally."

"Then that gives her a hell of a lot more motive than his flying buddies," I said reasonably.

"Sally Kramer is one of the finest women it has ever been my privilege to meet," he said stonily. "She is devoted to her husband. I am certain in my own mind that some of these so-called friends of his are deeply indebted to him—they've sponged on him and borrowed money from him for years! There are surely other factors in this, too, Lieutenant.

What about jealousy?—his wealth?—his beautiful wife? None of these men are adults emotionally, any more than Kramer himself is adult in this sense. For men who have a brutal disregard for the sanctity of human life—who spend their days boasting of the planes they shot down and the men they killed—any imagined slight or drunken envy is more than enough motivation!"

"Mr. Irving," I said soberly, "can I ask you a personal question?"

"Certainly!"

"What did you do during the war?"

"I worked hard for my degree at law school," he said frostily.

"It figures!" Lavers growled savagely. "Do you have any proof that any of these men planted that bomb in the airplane in an attempt on Kramer's life?"

"Of course not!"

"Do you have any proof of definite motive in any of these men for wanting to murder Kramer?"

"I would think their motivation was obvious, as I've already explained," the attorney said icily.

"But you don't have any proof?"

"Well—in the literal sense of the word, I suppose I don't, but—"

"Then do me a favor, Mr. Irving!" Lavers yelled. "Get the hell out of my office!"

"What?" Irving jumped to his feet, an expression of blank disbelief on his face. "You can't talk to me like this!"

"I can—I am!" Lavers bellowed at him. "My stomach's turning over just listening to you! If you're not outside in the next five seconds I'll have the Lieutenant throw you out!"

The color drained from Irving's face and for a moment I figured he was about to argue, but then he apparently changed his mind and walked, with a few tattered remnants of dignity, toward the door. There was a short silence after the door closed behind him. The Sheriff glared at me, his face a violent scarlet.

"I'm glad I didn't have to throw him out, Sheriff," I said mildly. "You can never tell with those kind—sometimes they bite."

Lavers took a deep breath, and consciously relaxed a little. "I am not given to flag-waving," he said in a measured voice, "but that little runt dug right under my skin. The way he tells it, you'd figure 'hero' was a dirty word—and while these guys were risking their necks for him, he was busy working his way through college, or something!"

"There's nothing wrong in that—only his attitude," I said cautiously. "But there were a couple of interesting details in all that elegant syntax, all the same."

"Oh, sure!" Lavers snarled impatiently. "The background stuff on Kramer—but the way he told it, you'd figure he was dictating a book or something."

"I wasn't thinking of that," I said. "Kramer's not interested in money, Irving said, and he's the guy who should know because he's the guy that handles Kramer's money. Mitch Kramer is a bum, but his wife is a beautiful girl who inherits all the estate if Kramer dies. Then, coincidentally, Irving himself only left the Kramer house an hour before the airplane blew apart."

The sheriff stared at me, his jowls quivering with excitement.

"You're right, Wheeler," he said, nodding emphatically. "All that could add up to a very interesting picture. Maybe a double motive involving both Kramer's money and his wife—and Irving also obviously had the opportunity. I bet that's why he left so carefully an hour before it happened. If he'd planted the time bomb in the airplane he'd know exactly when it would blow—so he figured if he was then well away from the house it would point up his innocence. Right?"

"Whoa there, Sheriff!" I said hastily. "It was just a thought. But it wouldn't do any harm to check his books and see if he's siphoned off any of the Kramer dough—and we might check on whether there's anything between him and Sally Kramer. Then, depending on what we find, we might look into the angle of the bomb—whether or not Irving might have the know-how to make one. Although I suppose anyone who's read the Mad Bomber news stories could improvise well enough. We gotta take it step by step, don't we?"

"This isn't like you, Wheeler," he said gloomily, "baffling me with logic. But I guess you're right. I can organize an investigation of his books with no trouble at all—but the wife angle is your department."

"Your logic isn't so bad either, Sheriff," I said with a leer. "I figure I'd better get on back to the Kramer house and get to work."

"Sure, you do that." There was an almost friendly warmth in Lavers' voice that was so unexpected, it unnerved me completely.

"You know something?" he added dreamily. "If there's any justice in the world—and while you're a police lieutenant I'm inclined to doubt it—Phillip Irving will be the guy we're looking for."

"I can see it now, Sheriff," I said admiringly. "Your figure, cast in bronze, mounted on the courthouse roof and delicately poised on the ball of one foot. Both eyes wide open—bloodshot, and gleaming vindictively—while the scale held in your right hand will be tilted at a right angle."

He opened his mouth to blast me, but I quickly held up my hand in a restraining gesture. "I know," I said humbly. "Out!"

Annabelle Jackson watched me curiously as I came out of Lavers' office, her honey-blonde hair gleaming with dangerous vitality.

"Another murder, Lieutenant?" Her voice was slightly barbed. "And another cat-prowling caper for lecherous Al, I'll bet!"

"How can you say things like that, little corn pone?" I said reproachfully. "Only this morning I met an angel yet."

"I bet the experience scorched her wings with one sizzling sheet of flame," she said scornfully. "I hope she didn't have too much altitude at the time?"

"She had both feet on the ground, head down and tail up," I said vaguely, "the way any self-respecting good luck mascot should be."

"Huh?" Annabelle's delectable body quivered with sudden shock.

"I can demonstrate how the good luck operates," I said hopefully.

"You take one step closer toward me and I'll scream for the Sheriff!" she said nastily.

Like Samson said, you can't win 'em all, I told myself bravely, and walked outside to where the Healey stood, mute and lonesome, yearning for a hard foot on the loud pedal.

It was a little after five when for the second time that day I drove up the rough track that led toward the Kramers' house. I parked the car beside a mud-splattered Corvette and got out in time to see a thin little guy walking slowly toward the car, limping badly as he dragged his left leg.

"Heard you coming up the drive," he said brusquely when he reached me, then stared at the Healey with a peculiar expression on his face, almost like that of a castoff lover regarding his former mistress.

"Pistons need a little adjustment," he pronounced in the hushed voice that's obligatory for all members of the College of Surgeons. "I don't mind fixing it for you, if you're staying awhile?"

"Thanks—but no thanks," I told him. "Who are you, anyway?"

"I'm a mechanic"—his dark eyes glared at me balefully—"the best!"

"You work for Kramer?"

"Sure, if it's any of your business."

"It is," I said curtly, then told him who I was.

His thick black hair was badly in need of a cut, and he hadn't shaved the last couple of days by the look of his beard. His dark blue coveralls were covered with grease and dirt, and right then he looked like something that comes out of the cellar in the second reel of the late late show. There was a strong feeling of naked hostility about him, so strong, I felt I could almost reach out and touch it.

"There was nothing wrong with that airplane," he said harshly. "I checked it over first thing this morning—not one goddamned thing wrong with it! You hear me good, Lieutenant?"

"I hear you," I said mildly. "I remember Mrs. Kramer said something about Cliff having checked the plane over, just after it blew up this morning."

"That's right. I'm Cliff White," he said flatly. "That airplane was in perfect condition when they started flying it this morning! You want to check on my engineering record, you can—"

"I'm happy to take your word for it, Cliff," I assured him.

"You are!" For a long moment his eyes didn't believe me. "Listen!" he said thickly. "I know cops better than that—find a fall guy. Pick the easiest one, the little guy who can't fight back, that's the way you lousy cops operate!"

"That plane was fine," I snarled at him, "right up to the moment somebody put a time bomb into it."

"Time bomb?" His mouth sagged open for a moment. "So that's how it happened?"

"According to all the experts and I got no reason to argue with them," I said. "They figure it was hidden inside the fuselage—you think that's possible?"

White nodded, after thinking about it for a moment. "Sure, I guess so. Maybe somebody went out to the hangar last night and did it—they'd be safe in figuring nobody was going to check the inside of the fuselage. What a dirty, lousy trick to play on the guy flying the kite!"

"There's a word for it—murder," I said obviously. "I'm hoping you can help me find the person who did it, Cliff."

"Not much chance of that," he muttered. "I don't rate socially in the Kramer house—strictly a hired employee. So, apart from all the noise, I don't know what the hell goes on in there most of the time."

"How long have you been working for Kramer?"

"Since '53. Right after I came out of the hospital, he offered me the job. I've been here ever since."

"You knew Kramer before then?"

"Sure." His mouth twisted into an ugly grin. "Knew him real well—went right through Korea with him, almost." He paused for a long moment while he stared down at his twisted left leg.

"Major Mitch Kramer, the ace of the squadron, and Cliff White, his ever-faithful mechanic—that was us. Right up until one lousy morning when maybe the major was a little more hungover than usual, and it made him careless."

He scraped his left foot across the ground in a sudden spasm of fury.

"You know what he said afterward? 'You stupid bastard, White,' he said. 'Why the hell didn't you get out of the way?' A great guy, the major!" He spat angrily into the dirt. "Yeah, a great guy! After I got out of the service he found a specialist who figured maybe he could do something for my leg—so I had nearly a year in the hospital while this guy tried grafting bones that didn't take—and the major paid all my expenses. When the doc finally quit trying, the major gives me a swell job looking after his airplane. So"—his face was more twisted than his leg right then—"he's been such a swell guy to me, now anybody calls me a gimp, I smile! You can figure out how easy it is for a gimp to smile, Lieutenant—right?"

If there was anything to say to that, I didn't know what it was, or how to say it, either. I lit a cigarette for something to do, then looked at my watch like I was suddenly surprised how late it had gotten.

"Well, I guess I'd better get on into the house," I said, striving for an easy, nonchalant voice. "Nice talking to you, Cliff. See you around."

"You bet, Lieutenant." There was that wistful eagerness back in his voice. "How about I fix those pistons for you, huh?"

"Not just now," I said a little too quickly, "but thanks for the offer, anyway."

I walked on toward the front of the house, feeling his cold venomous gaze boring holes right between my shoulder blades.

CHAPTER THREE

Sergeant Polnik stared at me for a long moment after he'd opened the door, his monolithic face contorting into a painful spasm. It didn't disturb me any—I knew he was thinking, and any cerebral activity caused him a great deal of physical anguish.

"Lieutenant?" he said dubiously. "You want to come into the house, huh?"

"Right!" I said admiringly. "That's why I knocked."

"That's what I figured," he said, his voice gloomy. "I knew this was too good to last."

This was going to take a little time, I guessed, and short of clobbering him with an iron bar, I couldn't see any other way around it. "What?" I asked patiently.

"Me handling the case out here while you was busy in the Sheriff's office," he said in a brooding voice. "First time I ever worked a case with you, Lieutenant, when I got two beautiful broads to watch over all the time. I figured it couldn't last."

"Every sergeant has his day," I said sympathetically. "The case has only just started anyway, Sergeant. So who knows how many more beautiful broads there are, just waiting to be interrogated?"

"Interrogated!" he repeated happily. "That's a classy word for the one my old lady doesn't like me using around the house."

"It is?" I croaked.

"Yeah." His repulsive face was suddenly wreathed in an even more repulsive smile. "Like you say, Lieutenant, who knows how many more broads are waiting to be interrogated? I never thought of that before. If you want to talk to 'em now, Lieutenant, they're out the back, drinking on the terrace."

"Just the broads?"

"No," he said sourly. "Them three crazy fliers are with 'em, too. Whatever happened to the big guy, MacGregor? Looks like he was run over by a truck or something?"

"He does?" I said happily.

"Sure. His nose is one big mess—like the rest of him," Polnik grunted. "You want me to come with you, Lieutenant?"

"I don't see why not," I said judiciously. "Whenever there's more than one broad involved in a case, it's my policy to be fair and share the fruits of benevolent fortune."

"I gotta say one thing about you, Lieutenant," the Sergeant said, beaming at me, "you're all heart."

"That's what keeps me worrying about my blood pressure all the time," I snarled as I started down the wide hallway.

A sledge-like elbow dug painfully into my ribs. "A little less interrogation, Lieutenant," Polnik wheezed confidentially, "and you got no problem at all, right?"

When we reached the terrace, which splayed out from the back of the house in a confused splendor of plate glass and terrazzo, I stood for a moment in the doorway and studied the tight group of people seated around a low, circular table. Sally Kramer was a picture of feminine elegance, dressed in a lace-frosted white blouse, banana-colored tapered pants, with a burgundy cummerbund separating the two. On one side of her was her husband, Mitch Kramer, with a dark contemplative look on his handsome face, and on the other side was MacGregor, looking exactly the way Polnik had described—to my intense satisfaction.

The beautiful and provocative Angel was sitting between MacGregor and Sam Forde, wearing a tight-knit shirt and pants that had metallic gold thread through them, so she sparkled like a sunny day at Fort Knox. In sharp contrast to the chic appearance of the two girls, the three men were still dressed in the same clothes they had been wearing that morning.

I stepped out onto the terrace, and as my footsteps sounded loud and clear, the whole group turned and watched stonily.

"Good evening, Lieutenant," Sally Kramer said in a cool voice. Her right hand brushed her long red hair back from her face in that practiced gesture. "Come to join the wake?"

"Shut up, Sally!" Kramer said tightly. "It should have been me in that kite this morning, and I'm not about to forget it."

"Darling!" She placed her hand lightly on his forearm for a moment. "You can't possibly blame yourself for Red's death—it would be ridiculous."

MacGregor stared at me out of red-tinted eyes. "Looking for another fight, Lieutenant?" His voice was liquor thickened and ugly. "The next time it'll be different—a hell of a lot different!"

"Right now I'm looking for a murderer, old buddy," I said pleasantly. "Maybe you fit the requirements?"

Angel smiled suddenly, her dark blue eyes laughing at me—at the rest of them—at the whole damn world, for all I knew.

"You mustn't spoil the wake, Lieutenant," she said in that husky voice, while the rasping undertones kinked my spine with a sudden spasm of desire. "We're all just sitting around, getting good and drunk, grieving the loss of a flyboy supreme. We're right in the middle of the 'Good old Red! You remember that time—there we were, at twenty thousand feet, and then ten of 'em came straight out of the sun' bit. If you—"

"It's not funny, Angel," Sam Forde said murderously. "Red was our buddy—don't you ever forget that! —and we don't have a sense of humor about him getting it this way."

"Neither do I," I agreed. "And I didn't come to join a wake, either, but to ask questions."

"Pull up a chair, Lieutenant," Angel said easily. "Be Mitch's guest."

Her eyes still mocked me with something between derision and challenge. "Can I make you a drink?"

"Not right now, thanks," I said solemnly. "I'm particular about the company I keep when I'm drinking."

"So are we," MacGregor snarled. "I wouldn't drink with a bum like you if—"

"Can it, Stu," Kramer said icily. "Can't you see the Lieutenant is deliberately trying to needle all of us?"

"For God's sake," Sally Kramer said wearily. "Won't you all try and behave like adults for once in your lives—instead of always playing overgrown adolescents? Ask your questions, Lieutenant, and I'll try and answer them if none of these middle-aged ex-heroes will."

"I'd like some detail about the fun and frolic organized for this morning," I told her. "Does this kind of thing happen often?"

"I already told you this morning," Kramer snapped. "It was a reunion—we flew together in the war, and in Korea, too. We like to get together and do a little flying—and a lot of drinking and talking afterwards. I didn't know there was a law against it."

"How often do these get-togethers happen?"

"Whenever we feel—felt—like it," he said stiffly. "The last one was around two months back, I guess."

"And the one before two months before that," Sally Kramer said in the same tired voice, "and the one before was maybe a month before that and the one—"

"I told you to shut up!" Kramer said explosively.

"Was everyone here last night?—or did they arrive bright and early this morning?" I asked.

"They all arrived yesterday afternoon," Sally Kramer said, "and stayed here overnight. There was a party last night that went on into the wee small hours, as you'd imagine."

"Was this morning's activity planned last night, or decided on this morning?"

"We knew we were going to fly this morning," Sam Forde said impatiently. "That was the whole point of the reunion, always."

"How about the detail?" I prodded. "Was that taken care of last night?"

Forde shrugged irritably. "Of course—what else?"

"Hold it," Kramer grated. "I see what the Lieutenant's driving at. Sure, the detail was taken care of last night. We always had a contest—an aerobatics contest—the winner to be decided by popular vote. So the detail was strictly worked out, Lieutenant. Each man to have exactly thirty minutes in the air—no more, no less."

"And the order of flying?"

"Sure." His right eyelid twitched suddenly. "That was figured out, too. Stu first, then me, Red, and Sam was the last man. We tossed for it early last night, like we always did."

"How much of a pause on the ground—between flight turns, I mean?"

"No longer than it took to switch pilots," Kramer said firmly.

"So if somebody decided to get rid of you by planting a time bomb in the fuselage of the plane," I said evenly, "he'd have had no problem in figuring out a time when he'd be sure you were actually flying the plane?"

"I guess not," Kramer whispered softly. "That's what you figure it was, a time bomb?"

"That's what the experts figure," I said.

"And there's no mistake about it being meant for me, and not Red?" He breathed the question.

"I don't see how there can be," I said reasonably. "Who could know I'd arrive when I did so you got it involved in the argument about MacGregor buzzing me on the road? Who could be sure Hoffner would get impatient and take your place in the plane?"

"That's the way I had it figured," he said. "But who hates me so much they'd want to murder me?"

"It's a good question," I said obviously, "and that was my line. Don't you have any ideas on the subject?"

Kramer shook his head hopelessly. "None," he said heavily. "It's like a nightmare and I keep thinking I'll wake up out of it any minute."

"Whoever planted the bomb in the plane probably had some familiarity with airplanes, as well as with explosives," I pointed out. "The most likely people I can think of are a bunch of ex-fliers."

"Are you saying that it was either Sam or me that murdered Red?" MacGregor bellowed angrily. "I'll knock your teeth back into your dirty, lying mouth!" He pushed his chair back violently and lumbered onto his feet, took a couple of quick steps toward me, then stopped suddenly.

"A great big heap of garbage like you," Polnik's voice grated from in back of me, "I couldn't miss at twice the distance!"

I looked over my shoulder and saw the .38 held solidly in the sergeant's massive hand, its barrel pointing at MacGregor unwaveringly. The bull-like face changed color three or four times, then MacGregor reluctantly subsided back into his chair.

"If you wanted a time bomb, I wonder how you'd go about getting one," I said to the group in general. "Would you get someone to make it for you? Would you do it yourself? Probably any one of you men would have a rough idea of how to put one together—what with the knowledge of explosives that you could hardly have avoided picking up during the war."

Sally Kramer stiffened suddenly and grasped her husband's forearm again. "Mitch—the museum!"

"*Shut up!*" He closed his eyes painfully for a long moment. "Every time you open your damned mouth, Sally, you put one your shapely feet right into it!"

"The museum?" I echoed.

"Where else could it have come from?" Sally Kramer turned toward her husband, her eyes blazing ferociously. "Don't be a fool, Mitch! Saving the museum isn't important anymore, but saving your own life is! Somebody tried to murder you this morning and killed Red Hoffner by mistake. What's to stop them trying again and being successful the next time, if they aren't caught before they get a second chance?"

"The museum?" I repeated, louder this time.

"Yeah," Kramer muttered reluctantly. "I guess you're right, honey."

"*What* museum?" I screamed.

"My own private war museum," Kramer grated. "I keep it down in the cellar, and up until now I've always kept it strictly private."

The way he told it, it tied in uncomfortably closely with the impression I'd gotten when I saw Cliff White, the mechanic, for the first time. That late late movie bit where the monster's always kept in the basement—something that shrieks and slobbers fitfully, and makes a nasty, slithering sound whenever it moves. For a moment there, I was tempted to pull rank and send Polnik down to take a first look, but then I remembered if the war museum contained anything at all lethal, the Sergeant would be sure to blow himself up.

"So let's take a look at the basement," I said abruptly to Kramer.

"Why not, Mitch?" Sam Forde said nastily. "Give the Lieutenant some idea what a real war was like."

"Don't be so belligerent, Sam," Angel said in an amused voice. "The Lieutenant fought a pretty good war of his own with Stu this morning, remember?"

"He doesn't worry me," I said, giving the pint-sized flyer a benevolent smile. "I realize he has to compensate some way for walking around on his knees all the time." I followed Kramer back into the house while Forde was still trying to think of an adequate comeback.

We went down the half-dozen steps that led to the basement. Kramer pushed the door open, then stepped inside and switched on the lights. There wasn't any tame monster that I could see when I followed him into the large room, but there was plenty to hold my interest all the same. It was more like a private arsenal than a museum—a collection of weapons, ranging from a Colt .45 to a bazooka, and big enough to arm a private army.

"What the hell?" I goggled at Kramer for a long moment. "You figure on fighting World War Three all by yourself?"

He grinned a little sheepishly. "Kind of a hobby with me, Lieutenant," he said. "This is just a bunch of junk I picked up from all over."

"All over is right," I grated. "For the first time I can make sense out of the UN forces stopping at the 38th parallel—you'd cleaned them out of equipment."

I walked maybe four steps, then stopped and picked up a Garand rifle.

"Take it easy, Lieutenant," Kramer said quickly. "It's loaded."

"You expecting the Martians any day now?" I asked coldly, as I gently put the rifle back into the wall rack.

"It's the one thing I figure makes my museum unique," he muttered. "It's all live stuff."

It took a little time to absorb the impact of what he'd just said, as I looked around at the lethal collection, figuring what would have happened if I'd pulled the pin from one of the grenades just for laughs. I opened my mouth to blast Kramer again, then thought better of it. What was the use of trying to explain to an overgrown kid the dangers of his collection? He could have outfitted a dozen new Murder Incorporated syndicates, and still had enough left over to take Pine City with a frontal assault.

"Just take a good look around and see if anything's missing, will you?" I asked in a choked voice.

"Sure," he said indifferently, then drifted leisurely down toward the far end of the basement, both hands thrust deep into his pants pockets.

I lit a cigarette while I waited, and got absorbed in study of a variation on a Bangalore torpedo—usually a piece of gas pipe filled with explosives and used in both World Wars to clear away barbed wire; this one substituted a bamboo shoot for the pipe. Some little time later a sharp ejaculation from Kramer snapped me out of the reverie.

"You found something missing?" I asked eagerly.

"Yeah, Lieutenant." His voice was subdued. "One of the S-2's. Should be three of them right here on this bench, and now there's only two."

"S-2?" I repeated. "That's an antipersonnel mine?"

"Right. The old 'Daisy Cutter.'"

"You leave the door unlocked the whole time?" I snarled.

"Sure." He looked up at me in genuine surprise. "Why not? Most times there's only me and Sally in the house—the cook and maid wouldn't come down here in a million years!—and Sally hates the sight of a cap gun, even."

"How about your flying buddies—and your mechanic? They all hate the sight of guns, too?"

Kramer's face flushed. "All right, so maybe I was a little stupid!"

"In a kind of off-beat way, pal," I said emotionally, "I have to admire you. You weren't just a little stupid, you were so fantastically stupid that, in its own kookie way, it's some kind of achievement."

"But whoever it was stole that S-2, they still had to fix it up with some kind of timing device, didn't they?" he protested.

"Right," I agreed. "Anybody who knew what they were doing would only need an old alarm clock and some wire. Getting the explosive would have been the tough bit, but you sure made that easy for them."

His face reddened some more. "But how the hell could I know that some maniac would suddenly decide to murder me?"

"If it is a maniac," I grunted. "Is anything missing, except for the antipersonnel mine?"

"No," he said, shaking his head decisively. "What else would they need?"

"Having killed the wrong guy the first time," I snapped, "I figured maybe they'd come back for something to help them out in the second attempt."

The color drained from his face as he absorbed the thought slowly. "Hey!" he muttered weakly, "I never thought about that. Maybe I should double-check, huh?"

"It could be a great idea."

Another ten minutes dragged slowly while he carefully checked his whole museum, piece by piece. Finally he was satisfied, and a look of strong relief showed his face. "No, sir," he said, almost beaming at me, "that S-2 is the only thing missing."

"So we might as well get back to the others," I said. "You got a key for this door?"

"Sure." He pulled an impressive bunch from his pocket, selected one key, and eased it off the ring. "This is it."

"Thanks." I took the key from him. "From here on out, this door is locked and stays that way."

"You mean you're not going to take the collection away from me?" he asked hopefully.

"Are you kidding?" I said sourly. "This is just until I can get the bomb squad down here to delouse all this stuff and truck it away. If they figure on separate indictments for each weapon you've got here, I wouldn't figure on getting out of jail this side off the twenty-first century, if I were you, Kramer."

After I had carefully locked the door to the basement, we made our way back through the house and out on the terrace again. The group around the circular table looked up expectantly as we approached.

"Was it something from the museum?" Sally Kramer asked in a tight voice.

"Sure," Kramer nodded. "You were right as usual, honey. One of the antipersonnel mines is missing."

"An S-2?" Forde whistled softly. "No wonder it made such a helluva bang!"

"Must you?" Sally Kramer snapped at him, closing her eyes for a moment as if in pain.

"So what does the genius lieutenant figure now?" MacGregor asked in a slurred voice. "You find any fingerprints lying around the place?"

"I haven't looked yet," I said politely. "But so far, we seem to be doing pretty damned good without checking for fingerprints. You want to check over the facts so far? The killer had to be someone who knew the order of flying you'd worked out between you last night, and someone who'd seen the museum and had enough working knowledge of explosives to wire a timing device to that mine. Also, someone who had good reason for wanting Mitch Kramer dead."

MacGregor stared at me sullenly, then shrugged his massive shoulders. "How the hell would I know?"

"You must have some kind of a brain," I said in a kindly voice, "not too much, I'll go along with that, but there has to be something inside that bullet head. So figure it out for yourself. Who do you know who'd fit on all those counts—except yourself, buddy boy?"

"Don't blow your stack, Stu, honey," Angel said quickly in a warning voice. "The Lieutenant has a point there—the easiest way to prove you didn't plant that mine in the plane is to help him find out who did."

"Okay," Sam Forde snarled, before his hulking friend had a chance to get to grips with the basic problem. "Let's figure it out from your angle, Lieutenant. There's Stu MacGregor for one, and me for another. Cliff White is another hot suspect—red hot for my money. He never has forgiven you, Mitch, for that leg of his!"

"You're letting your imagination run riot, Sam," Kramer said brusquely. "Cliff is one sweet guy." He didn't sound like he believed it himself even.

"I hate to point this up," Angel said lightly, "but if you agree that somebody real interested in getting rid of Mitch would also be interested enough to learn a little about explosives—then you got to include us girls in the lineup of suspects, too."

Sally Kramer stared at her coldly. "Are you out of your sex-ridden mind, darling?" she asked icily.

"Honey," Angel said, smiling sweetly back at her, "we check out with top marks on the other counts. We knew the order of flying the boys figured out last night, and for sure we both knew all about the museum and its lethal exhibits, too."

"Everybody's got in the act," I said miserably. "Now we got five suspects already. Any more?"

The group sat in moody silence for maybe ten seconds, until I tried the Sheriff's favorite theory on for size. "Aren't you forgetting someone?" I asked gently. "How about Phillip Irving?"

"Irving?" Kramer looked at me blankly. "Why him?"

"He was here this morning," I reminded him. "The way I hear it, he only left an hour before you all started flying."

They all looked at each other blindly for a moment like I'd suddenly given them the answer to the whole thing.

"Hey!" MacGregor said hoarsely. "That's right. And he was right here last night when we fixed it all up who was going to fly first!"

"He was here last night?" I parroted interestedly.

"Sure," Kramer nodded. "Stayed overnight, as a matter of fact. Wanted to talk business with me but we never did get around to it. But Irving wiring that S-2?" He shook his head slowly. "The whole idea's ridiculous. He's the kind of guy who passes out from sheer terror when he cuts himself shaving."

"Don't exaggerate, Mitch!" his wife said coldly. "I agree that Phillip's not the type of stuff that heroes are made of!" There was an obvious sarcasm in the use the word *heroes*. "But he's not really a nervous type."

"Only around redheaded women," Angel purred softly.

Sally Kramer's head jerked around toward the blonde, as if a puppeteer had suddenly pulled the strings taut. "Just what do you mean by that crack?" she grated.

"Darling—" Angel shrugged her elegant shoulders "—I was just thinking of last night when the boys we flying blind around midnight and I went out looking for some air. You and Irving were so engrossed in each other out here in the dark, I hated to disturb you. But he sounded nervous to me, all right, worrying all the time that Mitch might come out onto the terrace and find you. I could have saved him the worry—right then Mitch wasn't about to walk anyplace, not without help, anyway—but I guessed you wouldn't appreciate my breaking up a cozy scene."

A split second later everybody started talking at once.

"You dirty, lying little—" Sally Kramer shrieked.

"Just what the hell went on anyway?" Kramer said thickly.

"Angel," MacGregor bellowed, "why can't you ever keep your big mouth—"

"Oh, boy!" Forde said to nobody special. "Here comes the dirt—by the ton—and at today's cut-rate special it's—"

The door onto the terrace opened with a drawn-out, agonized squeak and they all stopped talking—the way they'd started, at the same time. Then the silence made an almost painful contrast to the bedlam of a moment before.

Cliff White stepped out onto the terrazzo, dragging his left leg audibly as he limped past Polnik and headed toward me.

"Lieutenant," he said in a harsh monotone, "a couple of things I figured you should know."

"Like what?" I asked cautiously.

"Like last night, sometime around two, I couldn't sleep because of the racket they was kicking up in here," he said, keeping his gaze fixed steadily on my face and ostentatiously ignoring the others, who watched him intently.

"So I figured on getting me a little fresh air," he continued in the same monotone, "and just when I got outside I saw a couple of people coming out of the hangar—a man and a woman—and this morning I found this on the hangar floor."

White handed me a small gold brooch in the shape of a flying goose. I flipped it over a couple of times in the palm of my hand, sensing that the malevolence in his eyes wasn't directed at me personally.

"Why didn't you tell me this before, Cliff?" I asked him. "An hour back when I first arrived and we talked outside?"

"I figured on saving it then," he said simply. "If you turned out to be the usual lousy cop who'd pick on me because the little guy is always the easiest mark to take a rap—then I could've made you look real stupid later when you started to get tough and lean on me hard. Right?"

"What made you change your mind?"

He shrugged slowly. "You didn't start leaning on me right away like I expected. So I got to thinking maybe I owed you something, Lieutenant. Not much—but something."

"Did you recognize the man and woman?"

"Too dark." He shook his head slowly. "They were just silhouettes when I saw 'em, that's all."

I flipped the golden goose onto the low circular table and the rest of them stared at it blankly, as if they expected it to deliver a formal indictment any moment.

"Anybody recognize that?" I asked.

"Why, sure," Angel said throatily. "It's mine. The boys, with their unique but corny sense of humor gave it me a few weeks back—the nearest I'll get to a real angel's wings, they said."

"How come Cliff found it on the hangar floor this morning?" I queried.

"Because I guess that's where I dropped it last night," she said indifferently.

"You were the feminine half of the couple he saw coming out of the hangar around two this morning?"

"Right." She smiled insolently at me. "But don't get excited, Lieutenant, I have a perfect alibi."

"Like what?"

"Like I visited the hangar with the intended victim and we were—well—close enough the whole time, for him to make damn sure I didn't drop a little ole time bomb into that plane!"

There was a greenish tinge to Kramer's face and he obviously wished he was to hell and gone, up into the wide blue yonder even—any place but where he was right then, sitting next to his wife. In sharp contrast, Sally Kramer's face was a dull puce in color as she stared murderously across the table at the unworried Angel.

"How about that?" I said to Kramer. "Is it true?"

"Sure, I guess so," he mumbled in an uneasy voice. "There was nothing to it, we just went out for some air, you know? Took a look at the plane, that was all. We weren't inside the hangar that long, not more than—"

"Thirty minutes?" Angel prompted in a mock innocent voice.

That did it up in a nice tight package for Sally Kramer. She came to her feet in one swift movement, leaned forward across the table, and swung her right arm in a wide arc. There was a sound like the proverbial pistol shot as her open palm connected with Angel's cheek.

"You cheap, conniving little tramp!" Sally Kramer shouted hysterically. "Get the hell out of my house and don't ever dare to show your dirty face—"

"Take it easy!" Kramer yelled in anguish, then grabbed his wife's shoulders and forced her back into her chair. "What's got into you?" he snarled at her. "You losing your mind, or something?"

"Or something," Angel said steadily in an ice-cold voice. Cliff White cleared his throat loudly. "You want me in here anymore, Lieutenant?"

"No, not right now," I said absently. "And thanks for your information, Cliff."

"I figured you should know," he said woodenly. For a moment he looked at Kramer with a gleam of pure malice showing in his eyes.

Then he turned away and dragged his leg back across the terrace and disappeared inside the house.

Angel rubbed the side of her face gently, where the imprint of Sally Kramer's hand still showed. "The fun seems to have gone out of the party, somehow," she said in an even voice. "I think I'd like you to take me home, Stu, right now."

"Sure," MacGregor said, a bewildered look on his face. "I guess maybe that's the best thing, huh?"

"It most certainly is," Sally Kramer hissed at him. "Get that cheap—"

"Shut your stupid mouth!" Her husband told her with sudden, and brutal, objectivity. "You can sit down, Stu, you're not going anyplace! The idea was we were about to drink to the memory of an old buddy, and one of the finest goddamned pilots of all time—right?"

"Well, sure," MacGregor said uneasily. "But I don't—"

"But nothing!" Kramer snapped. "You're staying."

MacGregor slumped back into his chair, his swollen face a bright crimson, and concentrated blankly on the ceiling.

"Stu?" Angel's eyebrows lifted slightly. "Are you taking me home or not?"

"Hell!" he said miserably. "I'm sorry, Angel, but like Mitch says, this is a wake and I can't walk out on the memory—"

"—of an old buddy," she finished for him. "My problem is, another old buddy's wife doesn't want me to stay and share in the wake for this old buddy. So take me home, old buddy—now!"

"Sorry, Angel," MacGregor muttered. "No can do."

She shrugged gracefully, then pushed her chair back and stood up in a lissome movement. "So I'll walk," she rasped. "I guess it's good for a girl to know where she stands—even when she finds it's only on her own two feet."

"I was about to leave," I said politely. "I'd be happy to drive you back to town, Angel."

"Well!" The dark blue eyes momentarily reflected her surprise. "This is a switch. I thought you were a lot of things, Lieutenant, but a gentleman wasn't one of them."

"Finished your investigation already, Lieutenant?" Forde's voice crackled with malice. "You sure had me fooled. I figured you were right in the middle of asking a whole heap of awkward questions."

"I never like to interrupt a wake," I told him easily. "And I've got enough intriguing answers to last me until the morning already."

I turned my back on him and caught the reproachful gleam in Polnik's eye, and carefully ignored it. "I want you to stay here, Sergeant," I said briskly. "Call the Sheriff's office and arrange for a relief later on—but I want somebody here the whole time. It's my sober opinion that Mr. Kramer is still in danger."

"From his old lady, mostly," Polnik muttered savagely.

"Nobody leaves the house tonight either," I said.

A loud exclamation from MacGregor brought me about face again.

"What the hell!" he said loudly. "What do you mean, nobody leaves the house?"

"You all stayed here last night, you can stay tonight," I said patiently. "If you don't want to do that, you can come downtown with me and I'll hold you overnight as a material witness."

He mouthed something I preferred not to lip-read, and slumped back into his chair again.

"Nobody leaves—except Angel," Forde sneered.

"And she's in my custody," I told him happily. "You ready, Angel?"

"Absolutely, Lieutenant," she said. "In fact, I don't even have the time to say thanks for a wonderful time to my hostess."

"Don't worry—just get out!" Sally Kramer snarled. "The air will be a hell of a lot cleaner when you're gone!"

"It should provide a delightful contrast with your mouth, darling," Angel said pleasantly. "Coming, Lieutenant?"

CHAPTER FOUR

The wheat-colored blonde didn't say much at all during the drive back to town. I didn't try to push any conversation because I figured there was plenty of time for it, and what better place than inside her apartment?—if she had an apartment. I fervently hoped she didn't live with her dear old white-haired mother in a motor court. Taking another side glance at that provocative profile, I figured a duo was impossible—no mother could stand that kind of competition.

"Have you eaten yet, Lieutenant?" she asked suddenly as we came into the city limits.

"Not since lunch."

"Neither have I." Her voice was casual. "Why don't you come up to the apartment with me and I'll put together some bacon and eggs, or something?"

"It sounds just fine to me," I said happily. "I don't want to make like a cop the whole time but—Angel? You got to have a real name somewhere, and I have to put it into the record."

"You just don't have any of the finer feelings, Lieutenant," she said in a resigned voice. "I was christened Amy Krater and if you think that's romantic, you're sick, but sick!"

"Amy Krater for the record," I said hastily, "and Angel for me. It goes real good with Al, right?"

"*Al* Wheeler?" There was that mocking, rasping note back in her voice again. "We're going to get real cozy, is that it, Lieutenant? I wouldn't parlay those bacon and eggs into a big fantasy deal, Al, if I were you!"

"Who?—me?" I said, striving for outraged innocence and missing by a couple of miles.

Fifteen minutes later I parked the Healey outside her apartment house, which had seen better days and had a hell of a lot worse days ahead of it. The neighborhood was the kind you needed money to live in but not too much, and once you'd made a reasonable amount you'd get out fast. The apartment itself was a third-floor walk-up, and when we got inside I saw the furnishings were about par for a furnished apartment—you had a place to sit and et cetera—but the atmosphere was strictly negative. Somehow I felt disappointed; I had expected more from Angel, something a little more exotic like a tiger-skin rug, maybe.

"I call it home," she said cheerfully, as she shut the front door behind us. "It's kind of stinking but the rent is reasonable, and what more can a poor working girl ask?"

"You—work?" I asked incredulously.

"Does that sound so strange?" She quirked her eyebrows at me. "I'm a photographer's model."

"I always thought they were lousy with loot—dripping penthouses and mink every place."

"In New York or Beverly Hills maybe," she said casually, "but not in Pine City, friend. I'm one of the unmentionables who models the same."

"Underwear?" I said, catching on quick.

"Bras, panties, girdles, slips—you name it, I model it." There was a gleam in her eyes as she pirouetted in front of me. "I have the figure for it, Al—or maybe you hadn't noticed?"

"I noticed," I said huskily.

"It's considered to be not quite respectable," she went on, "but it pays." She found a pack of cigarettes in her purse, extracted one, and lit it. "I have some vodka and some Scotch—make your own choice."

"Scotch on the rocks, a little soda, thanks," I told her. "You want me to make the drinks?"

"Fine," she said. "I'll have vodka on the rocks." Then she disappeared into the kitchen and returned a few seconds later with soda and ice.

I made the drinks, gave her the vodka, then sat down cautiously on the nervous-looking couch which only sagged maybe because it had a built-in inferiority complex—from that time it was with an analyst—I hoped. Angel sat in a beat-up armchair opposite, watching me with a carefully blank look in her dark blue eyes.

"I'm sure you're an absolute gentleman, Al," she said easily, "but rescuing me from Sally Kramer's clutches wasn't purely quixotic—right? My bet is you figured it would be a good opportunity to ask a lot more questions."

"I figured it was a good opportunity—period," I said sadly. "But then you killed my fantasy almost before it had gotten started, so I guess questions is all I have left."

"Along with the bacon and eggs," she said and smiled. "Maybe we should eat first? You can keep amused in here, drinking yourself to death, while I go work in the kitchen."

In what seemed no time at all, she had transformed the bacon and eggs into a king-sized omelet—which, if it wasn't a fantasy, hardly needed a launching pad to take it right out of this world. When we had finished eating, I made some fresh drinks and hopefully took them with me toward the couch. Angel neatly lifted her glass out of my hand as I went past her armchair and smiled sweetly at me.

"It was a nice try, buddy boy," she said tolerantly, "but you'd better keep your mind on your work. Men—both individually and collectively—are not exactly popular with me right at this moment."

I relaxed my weight onto the uneasy springs of the couch, gave one long sigh for the things that might have been—looking at Angel's hauntingly provocative face, and the way her gold-knit shirt hugged the ripe contours of her full breasts—then tried to focus my mind on fact instead of fantasy.

"If you don't have any questions, Al," she said finally, "we could have a wake like they're having out at Mitch Kramer's house, and I bet at this very moment it's gotten to be a real riot."

"What's with those guys?" I said, more wondering out loud than asking a question. "Didn't anybody ever tell them the war's over? Even Korea's ten years out of date."

"The drums go bang and the cymbals clang," she quoted with a faint smile on her face, "but the dreams they fade away."

"Huh?" I gurgled.

"That's all they have left now—The dreams of glory. Don't you understand that?" she asked impatiently. "There was a time when all of them were handsome young men wearing uniforms they covered with medals. The heroes of the bright blue yonder, like gods yet! Ten times larger than life and they loved every moment of it. Now what have they got?"

Her eyes held an almost compassionate gaze as she paused for a moment; then she shrugged delicately.

"With each passing year the dreams fade a little," she continued in a soft voice. "They all get a little older, a little heavier, a little balder, maybe? There was a time when they used to face sudden and unpleasant death as just an occupational hazard; but now they have to face up to something even more unpleasant, something their training never provided for—the slow, creeping death of advancing age that all of us have to face. They don't have the stomach for it, Al, and that's why they're so hot for the nostalgic bit—they had their brief moment of immortality and they never want to let it go."

Angel stopped talking and drank some of her vodka, while I stared at her in open-mouthed admiration.

"A poet yet," I said in an awed voice. "I figured you for a lot of things I've been wrong about already, but never a poet."

"From that furtive gleam in your beady eyes, you've still got a hell of a lot of adjusting to do yet," she said, with that rasp creeping back into her voice fast. "I've known that danger signal since I was around fourteen, buddy boy, and it doesn't do anything for my peace of mind."

"Neither does that Midas outfit you're wearing do anything for my peace of mind, either," I said frankly. "But I promise I'll try and stay with the questions. Your masterly summation of the ex-heroes' psychological problems I'll go along with. It still doesn't explain why somebody should want to kill one of them."

"If I knew who it was, I'd probably tell you," she said evenly, "but I don't."

"It wasn't you?"

Her eyes widened in make-believe terror. "Why, Al, baby, you never told me I was a suspect?"

"Maybe you enticed Kramer out into the hangar in the middle of the night so you could plant that time bomb in his plane," I said happily. "Told him to close his eyes and keep them shut real tight, while he counted up to a hundred, and you guaranteed him a real big surprise this morning."

Angel laughed suddenly, on a raucous note. "That's kind of cute," she gurgled, "but it just ain't true, buddy boy."

"I've only got your word on that."

"You can try Mitch—I'm sure he'll back me up."

"That whole bit with Kramer in the hangar kind of left me surprised," I admitted. "I had you figured as MacGregor's girl."

"I am." There was a mocking downward twist to her mouth. "In a peculiar kind of a way, Al. Stu thought it would be a nice idea if I made myself available to Mitch while we were staying out at his house."

"MacGregor has the most original ideas about thanking people for their hospitality," I said. "You didn't raise any objections?"

"It wasn't so much I needed to do Stu a favor," she said idly, "but more that Sally Kramer's the kind of bitch who ruffles my feathers on sight. Anyway, she's so busy two-timing her husband with that milk-and-water lawyer, I thought it might be amusing."

"What kind of guy is MacGregor, pandering to Kramer and using his own girlfriend to do it?" I wondered out loud.

"Now maybe you've got some idea why I was so eager for you to bloody his nose, Al, honey," she said sweetly. "It wasn't to save him spending sixty days in the county jail, that's for sure."

"You're sweet," I said sourly, "like cyanide."

"Us girls have our own tactics," she continued in a good-humored voice. "There's more to unarmed combat than the backs of our hands, buddy boy!"

"I'm beginning to dig your philosophy, honey," I snarled. "If ever anybody goofed, it was those flyboys when they coined the name 'Angel.' You should have melted with a bright blue flame when they dreamed that up."

"Don't get mad at me, buddy boy," she said, grinning impishly. "Or I'll have to start in calling you 'Lieutenant' again."

"Okay," I shrugged, more mad at her for being able to make me feel mad at her than mad at her for using me—if you see what I mean?—I doubt I did at the time. "Let's talk some more about the pride of the YMCA. How long have you known him?"

"The pride of the key clubs, you mean?" She laughed contemptuously. "Stu MacGregor is about the biggest bum I've ever known, and I've known plenty in my reasonably short life to date."

"Why would he want you to play house with Kramer? What is he? A voyeur, or something?" I asked irritably.

For once, Angel took a question seriously. "I don't know," she said after a few seconds' hesitation. "I think that maybe Mitch has got some kind of hold over Stu. When I think about it I can't figure out any logical reason—but whenever Kramer tells him to do something, he jumps!"

"Like just before we left?" I asked. "When you asked him to take you home, and Kramer told him they had an unfinished wake on their hands and that came first?"

"Sure," she said, nodding. "Things like that, although it doesn't add up to anything I can see. Stu is a sales executive with a big engineering corporation and he doesn't need money. He's not married, he's not an alcoholic, he doesn't take dope—so I just don't get it."

Angel emptied her glass, then held it out toward me, "You could do something useful for a change, like making me a fresh drink, Al. You didn't think you were about to get the story of my life just for free, did you?"

"I figured that was all I was about to get," I said regretfully. I got up from the couch and lifted the empty glass from her hand on the way past the armchair. On the way back, after I'd given her the new drink, I sat on the arm of her chair and looked at her hopefully.

"All these questions," I said gently. "It seems like an awful waste of an evening. Now, in my apartment, I have a hi-fi with five speakers, the most out-of-this-world collection of records you ever did see and—"

"Lenny Bruce?" she asked eagerly.

"And—and—what?" I'd fumbled the ball and I knew it.

"Lenny Bruce," she said enthusiastically. "He is the funniest man I ever—"

"My collection is all superb music like Ellington, and magnificent vocals like Sinatra, Peggy Lee, and all," I said in dignified voice.

"What else?" Her voice was bland. "I bet your passion pad just couldn't stand the sound of healthy laughter. It would rape the mood of seduction—right?"

Before I even had a chance to try and refute her irrefutable logic, her elbow suddenly struck my hip in a sharp, malicious, and accurately placed blow that knocked me off the arm of the chair, so the base of my spine jarred painfully as it hit the floor. A moment later she peered down at me over the arm of her chair, her face a perfect parody of the ever-anxious, ever-thoughtful hostess.

"Why don't you go sit on the couch again, Al?" she inquired sympathetically. "You look like an idiot sitting on the floor."

I dragged myself to my feet and limped back to the couch, mustering what little was left of my dignity, then did like I was told and sat down again, gingerly. If this was the new breed of woman, I wasn't too sure I wanted to be around when they got to be a majority. About the only thing left to me when they took over would be knitting—my mind screamed in sheer terror at the thought.

"Did you have any more questions, buddy boy?" Angel asked in that repulsive, rasping voice which boomed out from a large hole in the hideous mask of her face. I had to condition my thinking, ready for the new breed, I figured.

"Sure," I grated from between clenched teeth. "You don't happen to keep a spinal brace around the apartment by any chance?"

"I have an old leather dog muzzle, if that would help?" she said innocently.

"Never mind," I groaned. "So let's get back with the questions. How long have you known MacGregor?"

"Around six, seven months," she said. "I met him at a photographer's party—it was one of those things that looked like it was going to out-*vita La Dolce Vita*—if you know what I mean? So when Stu suggested we cut out, I figured it was a great idea."

"And that was how the great romance blossomed?"

"I wouldn't call it a great romance," she said cheerfully. "It got to be a habit, and after a month or so, Stu took me out to Mitch Kramer's place where I met the other guys, and darling Sally, of course. The guys christened me 'Angel' and made me their mascot, and it was fun in a juvenile kind of way. I got a kick out of it—up until what happened to Red Hoffner this morning!"

"When MacGregor passed you on to Kramer, you got a kick out of that, too?" I said icily. "That's right, you told me—it was the look on Sally Kramer's face that made everything worthwhile, right?"

"You're trying real hard, Al, but you don't faze me!" There was an underlying tautness to her voice that cast a doubt on the words. "I didn't like any part of the situation very much—but Sally Kramer being the creep she is, I figured I didn't have to worry too much about her feelings. Like I already told you, a girl knows all kinds of unarmed combat. There are more ways of killing a cat than kidding it into thinking it'll outshine a mink when its coat is sewn up. I've been playing Kramer just so far and no further all the time, and last night in the hangar I figured he was so eager, he was about to burst a blood vessel. I wanted him to learn the hard way that some women don't come easy, even when they're supplied by one of your best friends!"

"Why don't you be truthful, Angel, honey?" I said, using the mock-sympathetic voice she'd used on me earlier. "Leave us face it—you're just a tease at heart. To be a little more accurate, you're all ice from head to toe—and you'll wind up a frigid old maid who won't even be able to get a job modeling outerwear for the octogenarian set."

"Well, I wouldn't let it throw you, buddy boy," she said evenly. "At least I'll survive you by about thirty years."

"What makes you so sure?" I asked indignantly.

"You'll be all worn out before you're fifty," she said in the dispassionate tones of a diagnostician. "Nothing but skin and bones in another ten years. After that you'll hang on for a while but then—*pffift!*" She made a rude sound of my demise.

"Can I help it if I'm not only attractive but virile?" I asked modestly.

"You're neither, Al, honey," she assured me. "Just frustrated. And the way you're going—like I say—you're about to frustrate yourself to death at a comparatively early age."

"So if MacGregor is the solid company executive with not even a shady divorce in his background, how come Kramer has a hold on him?" I asked, desperately retreating back into the question routine again.

"It's a good question," Angel said happily. "I just don't have an answer."

"Maybe it's a good enough question to hide a motive for murder?"

"Why don't you ask Stu about that?"

"I guess I will," I snapped. "You aren't being very helpful, you damned curvaceous ice cube, you!"

"I'm so sorry, darling," she purred, smiling sweetly. "I didn't realize you wanted me to be helpful. Can I take some fingerprints or something?"

"Only mine," I grunted. "and you've refused that opportunity already."

"But so frustrated!" She shook her head sadly. "Have you ever thought of a hobby, Al, honey? I mean a *different* hobby."

"Like murder?" I snarled.

She twirled her glass gently, so the ice tinkled against the sides. "Seriously, I don't have any idea why somebody should try to murder Mitch Kramer. For me, he isn't worth it."

I got to my feet and left my empty glass on the small table at one end of the couch. "Thanks for dinner. It was wonderful—in sharp contrast to the rest of the evening," I told her.

"I'll walk you to the door," she said casually, and came out of the beat-up armchair in one electrifying movement.

When we reached the front door, she paused for a moment with her hand on the doorknob and looked at me curiously. "Do you really think you'll catch whoever murdered Hoffner, Al?"

"Sure, I do," I said without much conviction. "How can I think anything else—without cutting my throat?"

"Well," she said, turning away from me in a decisive gesture, "I wish you luck."

"Thanks a whole heap," I said bitterly, and opened the door.

"Hey!" she said indignantly as I stepped out into the corridor. "Don't you want any luck?"

I turned my head and froze in mid-stride an instant later. Angel was turned away from me, bent over obediently, her hands hugging her knees so I was confronted by a pair of uptilted curves which strained the gold-knit right down to the last carat. It was a view calculated to send me soaring off into the bright blue yonder without the aid of an airplane even, and it was also an opportunity that was exquisitely irresistible.

"Good luck, Al," Angel said solemnly, in a slightly muffled voice.

"And lots of luck to you, ice-cold Angel," I said happily.

I swung my right arm high, high into the air and let it descend like a minor avalanche. There was a sound like the climactic moment in the "1812 Overture" when they used a real cannon. Angel gave a piercing shriek—then the impact of my hand across her well-rounded bottom sent her skidding wildly along the floor on all fours.

"Let's hope that didn't leave any 'kraters,' Amy?" I chuckled evilly, then closed the door in back of me gently so the noise wouldn't disturb her nervous system.

The trouble was, I reflected on my way down to the car, that the one thing I like about a virtuous girl is always virtually unobtainable. I have a natural gift for this kind of profound thinking—a kind of instant understanding, an insight which few are given.

CHAPTER FIVE

There are mostly only two kinds of lawyers' offices. The first is the dusty and semi-derelict, where taped and bound documents litter the shelves in dusty profusion. This is the reassuring approach—the guy must be a good lawyer, you figure, because he's obviously been in business a long, long time. Yet by the look of the place, his fees must be reasonable, or else he'd have a better-looking office. The second approach is the modern decor, all glass, polished wood, and freestanding stenographers, which just glitters with efficiency. Your first reaction is sheer terror—how much does this guy have to charge to afford this setup? Then the second reassuring thought that he must be a hell of a good, and successful, lawyer to get away with it.

Phillip Irving's office, I saw when I arrived there around ten-thirty the next morning, was about in the middle of the two schools of thought—and from what I'd already seen of Irving himself, it figured. He was a guy to sit on the fence if I'd ever seen one. But the one thing he did go for was the freestanding stenographer bit, and I appreciated it.

The girl who looked up from her desk as I approached had her glossy black hair cut short in a kind of careless cut, like she'd absent-mindedly taken a few stabs at it with a pair of blunt scissors one coffee break when she had nothing better to do. On her it looked good—stunning, in fact—accentuating the firm, healthy, rounded cheeks, and the full curve of her arrogant, yet vulnerable, lower lip. She wore a neat blue shirtdress, which I was sure the magazines said was exactly right for the office, only as they hadn't seen her figure how they could tell was a mystery. But when I took a second look at her figure I realized that for her there was nothing exactly right for the office—nothing short of a suit made out of chain-mail armor could disguise those magnificent curves.

Her limpid hazel eyes looked right back at me with what I would have confidently figured was equal interest once—but since I'd met Angel I wasn't sure about anything concerning women anymore. She took a deep breath against the front of the shirtdress and I began to wonder if even chain mail would have been adequate.

"Can I help you?" Her voice was straight out of that fantasy where I'm marooned in an Eskimo igloo for the long arctic winter, with only ten Hollywood starlets for company.

"Maybe you could give me my confidence back?" I said wistfully. "I'm a very nervous type."

"If you're looking for Doctor Krull—the analyst—he's two floors down," she said briskly. She studied me carefully for a few more moments. "You don't look like the nervous type to me."

"It's only ever happened once before in my whole life," I confided. "In fact, it only happens when I'm suddenly confronted by an absolute in sheer feminine beauty like yourself."

"I can see by the way you're quivering that you really are nervous." She smiled slowly and it was like a sudden gleam of sunshine spreading across a sultry sky. "I'm sure Doctor Krull could take care of it for you."

"I was hoping you could," I said earnestly. "Given the chance to familiarize myself with an absolute like yourself would cure me, I'm sure."

"I'd have to think about it," she said slowly. "Doctor Krull charges fifty dollars an hour, and if you have more confidence in me than in him—"

"I was hoping you might consider the installment plan," I said gravely. "A small down payment and lots of loving interest?"

That slow smile broadened her lips again, and her very white teeth nibbled that luscious lower lip tentatively for a moment.

"I have a strict rule to check the credit rating of any prospective—associate?—but in your case I might be prepared to make an exception," she said, with equal gravity.

"You're very kind," I told her, "and that's something you don't find often in an absolute beauty, Miss—?"

"Johanna Jones," she said. "My friends call me Johnny, Mr.—?"

"Wheeler—Al Wheeler," I supplied the detail eagerly. "My enemies call me Lieutenant."

"You're a reservist, perhaps?" She shook her head. "No, you somehow don't look to me like the type to spend your vacation every summer in a camp with a lot of *men!*" she said with a smile.

"Police," I said, striving to make it sound a friendly, romantic word. "From the County Sheriff's office."

"A cop?" The lower lip dropped in genuine surprise. "You sure don't talk like one."

"Fine," I said vaguely, not wanting to get sidetracked into an abstract conversation. "Johnny—I know this is a ridiculous question—but your absolute beauty dazzles my reason: Are you doing anything tonight?"

"I was," she said thoughtfully. "I think I'm about to change my mind."

"That's great," I said happily. "Can I pick you up around eight?"

She ignored the question completely and slid a Phillip Irving letterhead into her typewriter, then began pounding the keys briskly. I'd just started in being miserable, figuring the curse of an Angel was working against me and she'd changed her mind, when she stopped typing and pulled the letterhead out of the machine, folded it neatly and handed it to me.

"That's my address and phone number," she said softly. "Don't lose it, Al. I hate to be stood up!"

"I'll lose my mind first!" I declared passionately, and carefully put the folded sheet into my wallet. "I'll see you tonight, Johnny, on the pinhead of eight."

I was about halfway toward the outer door when her voice stopped me in my tracks. "Yes?" I turned back toward her attentively.

Her eyes held a puzzled look as she beckoned me back to her desk with one delicately shaped little pinky. To be summoned by an absolute beauty was to obey—I made it back to the desk in double-quick time.

"Tell me something, Al," she said in a strangled voice. "Did you ever see me before?"

"Are you out of your mind?" I said in a horrified voice. "How many absolute beauties are there in Pine City?"

"Then," she said in an awed voice, "you mean you just walked into this office on the off chance it might contain an absolute beauty, and if so, you'd make a date with her then walk out again?"

"Huh?" I stared at her blankly for a long moment, then finally remembered. "Cheez! Thanks for reminding me, Johnny. I wanted to see Phillip Irving."

"Ah!" She sighed heavily with relief. "For a moment there, you had me really going! Mr. Irving's in, but I think he's busy right now. You want me to buzz him?"

"Give him a Bronx cheer if you want, honey," I said with great consideration.

"I don't think Mr. Irving would approve of that," Johnny said in a brooding voice. "Come to think of it, I haven't found anything he does approve of yet, but then I've only been here eight months."

She depressed a key on the intercom beside her, and a tinny voice answered. "Lieutenant Wheeler is out here, Mr. Irving," she said briskly. "He—"

"Send him right in," the tinny voice snapped.

Johnny flicked the key back to the off position, then looked at me with raised eyebrows. "I guess you must give him a guilt complex, or something, Al. Most times he doesn't bother seeing people even when they have an appointment."

"Last night somebody wished me luck and this must be my day for it," I said reverently. "First I get to date an absolute beauty, then I get to see Irving without an appointment even. Who knows? —before the day is through I may get a kindly word from the County Sheriff."

"It's that door there, to your right," she said, pointing to it. "If you get any reactions from him at all, yell out so I can come and see it will you?"

"Huh?"

"In eight months I've never seen him react to anything yet," she said out of an immense frustration. "A couple of times I've toyed with the idea of taking off all my clothes, then walking into his office with just a pad and pencil—to see what he'd do. But I already know the answer to that. He'd say, 'Don't sit in a draft, Miss Jones,' then go right on dictating."

"You should try it on me sometime, honey," I said excitedly. "I have a whole stack of unanswered correspondence at home in my apartment, so maybe tonight?"

The flecks of hazel in her eyes swam closer together while she considered the proposition. "There's just one little thing that worries me about that," she said finally. "Do I have to bring my own pad and pencil?"

I waded through rose-colored clouds toward Irving's office, and was abruptly jerked out of my ecstatic delirium by the sight of his prim face watching me from in back of his desk. Johnny was right, I guessed. Nobody could feel ecstatic around Phillip Irving—with the possible exception of Sally Kramer? I wondered.

He hadn't changed any from the previous day; he still he blended neatly and inconspicuously into the landscape—but here in his natural habitat the effect was even more noticeable. His eyes behind the square-cut lenses matched the color of their pale tortoiseshell half-frames and reminded me of a couple of amoeba swimming in thick mud.

"It was good of you to come so promptly, Lieutenant," he said in that dry, colorless voice. "Please sit down."

I sat in a visitor's chair facing him and lit a cigarette, trying to make sense out of what he'd just said.

"I told the girl in the Sheriff's office that it was most urgent," he continued. "But I must say it's most gratifying that you came in person, Lieutenant," he glanced at the elegant, slim gold watch strapped on his wrist, "only thirty minutes after I called."

"We're only the servants of the people after all, Mr. Irving," I said, stealing the line straight from television. "It's you who pay our lousy salaries."

He placed his elbows on the desk and carefully pyramided his fingertips. "I am not a man to hold a grudge, you understand?" he said briskly. "But after our meeting yesterday I reached some obvious conclusions. One: Sheriff Lavers is not only a man of short and uncertain temper, but he is also a fool. Two: You, Lieutenant, are a law enforcement officer who at least believes in reason. Therefore, I naturally called you this morning instead of the County Sheriff. Further, it is not my intention to even speak with Lavers in the future whenever I can possibly avoid doing same." He took a slightly deeper breath than usual. "I trust I make myself clear?"

"Like crystal," I agreed. "What was it that's so important it brought me running straight over here to your office right after I got your urgent message?"

"During yesterday's unfortunate meeting"—he closed his eyes momentarily to blot out the painful memory—"motives for the attempted murder of Mitchell Kramer that resulted in the homicide of Haffner were discussed. I offered the suggestion that among the bunch of shabby hangers-on Kramer surrounds himself with almost continuously, a strong motive shouldn't be hard to find."

"You did," I agreed solemnly.

His fingertips tapped together briskly. "For this opinion, and because I could offer no immediate proof of my theory, I was abused and humiliated by the County Sheriff. I have here some definite proof of motive, Lieutenant!" He tapped the thin folder on the desk in front of him for emphasis. "Definite proof, Lieutenant," he repeated. "I thought you would be interested?" He pushed the folder across the desk toward me. "You may read for yourself."

"Thanks, anyway," I said easily, "but for now I'd rather have you tell me about it. I'll get around to reading whatever it is later."

"As you wish." He steepled his fingers again, making me wonder if he'd ever been frightened by a cathedral in his youth.

"Samuel Forde is one of the ex-flyers and longtime associates of Mitchell Kramer's," Irving said pedantically. "Approximately two years back he started an air taxi service operating from the Pine City field. He didn't have any capital, naturally." The lawyer almost sniffed. "But of course he did have a very good and wealthy friend in Kramer, who loaned him the trifling sum of fifty thousand dollars to get started."

I whistled softly. "That's what I'd call a good friend."

"At the time it happened, I remember remonstrating with him," Irving said stiffly, "pointing up the obvious facts—that the whole venture was foolhardy and Forde was an incredibly bad financial risk."

His thin lips curled slightly. "I can even quote Kramer's words from memory: 'Sam and me, we're old buddies, flew together all through the war and then again in Korea—I just can't let an old buddy down.' Logic has no chance against this type of sentimental twaddle, Lieutenant, none at all. So in the end Forde got his fifty thousand for his air taxi service."

"And this is a motive for murder?"

A pallid gleam showed in back of the square-cut lenses for a brief moment. "This morning, on my way to the office, I suddenly remembered that loan," he said, his voice quickening a fraction. "There was a nagging persistence in back of my mind that there was something else connected with the loan, too—something important I should remember. So the first thing I did this morning was pull the file on Forde's Air Taxi, Incorporated. There most certainly was something else—a vital detail I would say, Lieutenant—a glaring motive for murder!"

I was fast beginning to understand the way Lavers had felt toward this long-winded glass of carrot juice the previous day.

"Like what?" I grunted.

"At the time the loan was made and the legal papers signed," Irving said triumphantly, "Forde was understandably nervous about what would happen to his air taxi if Kramer should meet an unexpected demise anytime in the reasonably near future. I understood his anxiety only too well—he knew if Kramer died, I would handle the estate and he could expect short shrift from me. So he proposed that both he and Kramer should take out insurance policies on their lives, to the value of fifty thousand dollars, each making out his own policy in the other's favor."

"If it had been Kramer who was blown to bits in that plane yesterday, it would have put Forde fifty thousand dollars ahead?" I said, grateful he'd at last made his point.

"Precisely." He patted the crown of his head gently with the palm of his hand, searching for the impossible, a hair out of place.

"Forde hasn't been doing at all well with this idiotic air taxi—and I have the figures to prove it. I most certainly would say he's in desperate straits right at this moment." Irving leaned back in his chair and regarded me with an air of complete complacency. I figured any time now he would start twiddling his thumbs.

"If it's motive you're looking for, Lieutenant," he said in a patronizing voice, "I don't think you need look any further than Forde, do you?"

"I'm sorry you didn't remember this yesterday in the Sheriff's office, Mr. Irving," I said regretfully.

"So am I." His voice was extremely tolerant of his own foibles. "I think I was possibly too emotionally disturbed to think clearly at the time."

"I was thinking maybe you were too busy defending Sally Kramer's good name and reputation at the time, so you never had a chance to think about anyone else?" I suggested in a mild voice.

He blinked a couple of times, then leaned forward in the chair and replanted his elbows on the desk. "I beg your pardon, Lieutenant?"

"The way I hear it, Sally Kramer is a lot more to you than just the wife of a client," I said lazily. "A hell of a lot more, especially when the two of you get together on the back terrace of Kramer's house."

The color of his face changed rapidly from a pasty white to a bright pink, as he stared at me blankly. "What?" he gurgled in a choked voice. "Are you daring to suggest—"

"I'm not suggesting," I said coldly. "There was an eyewitness, the flyboys' good luck charm—Angel. You must remember her because any man would, even you. She told me, and she'll testify if necessary, that she saw more than enough to convince her that you and Sally Kramer had a relationship which couldn't be classified as platonic, even in the broadest sense of the word."

After I'd finished, the words seemed to be still hanging around a few inches away from my mouth. The hell with it, I thought sourly, Irving had me talking the same as he did already. If I wasn't careful, I'd find myself still working up to the point of the proposition a couple of hours after the girl had given up in despair and gone home.

"But—but—" he mouthed hopelessly, trying real hard to come up with something constructive and never getting within sight of first base.

"Talking of motives," I continued in a harsh voice, "and we were—if fifty thousand dollars is a strong motive for Forde to kill Mitch Kramer, just how strong a motive is all of Kramer's money for his wife to try and kill him?"

The steeple crumpled suddenly like it was hit by an earth tremor, as his shaking fingertips lost contact with each other.

"You can't seriously believe it was Sally who killed Hoffner while trying to kill her husband?" he whispered.

"Why not?" I said reasonably. "She had a double incentive—she'd get all his money and she'd be free to marry you afterward." I paused for a moment before the throwaway line—"If marriage is what you have in mind, of course?"

"Lieutenant!" He pulled a virginal white handkerchief from his top pocket and dabbed his forehead with it be carefully. "I'm prepared to admit I was, well, indiscreet out on the terrace with Sally but—you must believe me—I was only momentarily carried away by my emotions."

"I wish I'd been there to see it," I said wistfully. "I bet seeing you carried away by your emotions would be like tossing a stone into a pool and not getting one single ripple."

"I repeat"—his voice sharpened a little so maybe my needling was jabbing under the skin a little—"that the thought of Sally Kramer trying to kill her husband is completely absurd!"

"Okay," I said easily, conceding the point. "There's the other alternative."

"Other alternative?" he said in a careful enunciation, like I was teaching him a whole new language.

"Sure—you," I snarled at him. "All these years you've been handling Kramer's money for him, making him richer all the time, and hating his guts every moment of it. Then to top that, you have this big thing going for his wife. What a beautiful twin incentive you have, too! With Kramer dead, his wife inherits all his estate—then you marry his widow and you get a beautiful doll along with a million bucks or even more. The more I think about it, Irving, the more I'm convinced you're the hottest suspect I've got so far."

His whole body shook like he had a sudden attack of palsy. "Get out of my office, you stupid idiot!" he stammered wildly. "I won't waste another word on you, you hear me? Get out!"

"As you say," I told him courteously.

I lifted the folder off his desk as I stood up, then remembered I needed an exit line before I exited from his office.

"Mr. Irving"—I figured he had a right to know his rights—"if you want to call a lawyer," I said gravely, "that's just fine by me."

CHAPTER SIX

The Sheriff's bushy eyebrows knotted together suddenly like they'd just been sprayed with a super fertilizer, as I walked into his office.

"You'll have to control this sudden wild enthusiasm, Lieutenant," he snarled. "Keep this up and you could start doing a full day's work before you know it! I mean, it's only twelve noon now—and here you are in the office already!"

I sat down facing him and lit a cigarette, shaking my head regretfully. "The subtleties of your humor always escaped me, sir," I said despondently. "I only wish I had the same razor-sharp wit you have, Sheriff. The lunge and riposte of rapier-keen verbal fencing—the lightning speed which dodges from quote to quip and back again before poor, slow-witted average guys like me can—"

His face had that bright crimson angina look again. "Wheeler! What the hell are you talking about?" he bellowed.

"I don't know," I admitted. "I figured maybe you did?"

"Sometimes I'm convinced we should send you up to that sanitarium in Hilldale and have a psychiatrist run a tape over you," he muttered. "It would be County money well spent!"

"I have been working," I said coldly. "Most of last night I was working—"

"Hah!" he interjected savagely.

"—and also all morning," I went on, ignoring his unmannerly interruption. "I now have a homicide case which is lousy with suspects and motives, and not one single piece of evidence, not one single clue even. I would like to tender my resignation."

"I'll accept it," he said eagerly.

"Oh?" I shrugged disdainfully. "Well, in that case, I withdraw it immediately."

"Tell me about it, Wheeler," he said, biting off the end of a fresh cigar with such savagery you could have figured it was the hand that fed him. "When you've finished, I'll probably fire you anyway."

I told him all the detail of the previous night, and the visit with Irving just before I arrived in the office. He listened attentively, his face getting longer and longer as I went on. By the time I'd finished, he was so listless he didn't even bother to open the folder on Forde's air taxi service that I dropped on the desk in front of him.

"So the angle I figured right from the start about Irving and Kramer's wife adds up?" The thought didn't brighten his face. "But now you've gone and found all these other damned motives for the rest of them, Wheeler. The mechanic's got a psycho hatred because of the accident to his leg that he blames Kramer for. Forde stands to gain fifty thousand dollars once Kramer's dead. And Kramer, according to this Angel girl, has something over MacGregor which for all we know may be just as strong a motive as the rest of them have, right?"

"Right," I nodded glumly.

"Oh, great!" he exploded. "That's all we need! Maybe it's a conspiracy and the whole damned bunch of them helped put the time bomb together—you ever think of that?"

"No," I said with a shudder, "and I'm not going to either. I've got enough problems already yet. Is Sergeant Polnik still out at the house?"

"Even Polnik needs to sleep sometime," Lavers grunted. "I sent a couple of uniformed men out there at midnight—Polnik's due back there at one this afternoon."

I suddenly remembered, dug my hand into my pants pocket, and pulled out the key to Kramer's private arsenal. I dropped it onto Lavers' desk.

"What's that?" He looked at it like it could explode any moment.

"The key to Kramer's war museum," I said apologetically. "I forgot I took it with me last night."

"And this is what Homicide gave me in lieu of a police lieutenant!" He raised his eyes toward the ceiling in desperate appeal. "What did I do?" he demanded passionately. "How can I expiate the sin that brought this visitation upon me?" He lowered his head and glared at me with a sudden ray of hope shining in his beady eyes "I wonder if I could have you exorcised?" he said gleefully.

"So I forgot about the key," I grated. "So what?"

"It's not that key I'm interested in," he snorted. "Kramer had a duplicate."

"He what?" I yelped. "He never damned well told me!"

"Did you ask him?"

"So I'll get the next train to Siberia," I confessed. "How the hell did you find out he had another key, anyway?"

"Because I went out there first thing this morning," he grunted. "I borrowed the efficiency boys from Homicide and we were all set to break down the door when Kramer came up with the second key. MacDonald might be the explosives expert around here, but when he saw what was inside that basement he looked real nervous like the rest of us." There was a grudging satisfaction in the Sheriff's voice as he remembered. "He won't touch it until he's got an explosives truck and another couple of experts, one on either side of him. So we locked it up again. I told Kramer if we found out he's got a third key, I'd have the sergeant shoot him out of hand on the grounds of justifiable homicide. I don't think he does have a third key."

"What else did the crime lab experts come up with, apart from MacDonald's green face?" I asked sourly.

"Fingerprints in the basement," he said bitterly. "Any time you want fingerprints, go down into that damned basement and help yourself. It's got prints the way you got suspects—it's lousy with them!"

"Whose?"

He moved his Kodiak bear shoulders impatiently. "You name it, we got it. Kramer's for a start—his wife's—MacGregor and Forde are well represented—so is White, the mechanic!"

"How about Irving?"

"No," he said. "But even that doesn't prove much—Kramer's wife could have taken the mine out of the basement and given it to Irving, couldn't she?"

"I guess she could," I agreed. "So we still don't have any evidence, Sheriff."

"I'm aware of that fact," he yelled angrily. "Don't damned well keep reminding me, Wheeler!"

"Yes, sir—I mean, no, sir," I said dutifully. "Do you have any suggestions, Sheriff?"

"Why don't you go and—ah, never mind!" He puffed heavily on his cigar and a huge cloud of foul-smelling smoke obliterated his face for a merciful few seconds.

"How about Hoffner?" I asked. "It's not possible he was the intended victim?"

"Not a chance," Lavers said briefly. "I checked and double-checked his background. Blameless—a moderately successful public accountant, unmarried, not even interested in women. He loved to fly but couldn't afford it now—and that was the only attraction Kramer's weekend parties had for him. It gave him a chance to fly an airplane for free."

"So that takes care of that," I said. "I guess I might as well drive out to the Kramer house and ask the whole bunch of them some more questions. I can't think of anything better to do right now."

"You can't do that," he said abruptly. "I let them go this morning—MacGregor and Forde, that is. Once they called their lawyers it would be hard for us to hold them out there anyway. More important, I figured it put Kramer into too much danger, having them all out there at the house, under the one roof. Too tempting an opportunity for a second try."

I looked at him murderously for the overweight Brutus he was. "Could I ask you a question, Sheriff?" I said politely. "Why the hell do you think I left them under the one roof last night? I figured even then about the one chance we had was if the murderer tried again. Now you've balled up even that!"

"You mean you figured to risk Kramer's life again—deliberately—in the wild hope you might catch the murderer when he tried a second time?" Lavers goggled me wildly, with the bright crimson rapidly staining his cheeks again.

"Polnik was there to protect Kramer," I grated.

"Polnik!" His lips writhed in agony. *"Polnik!"*

"Well," I admitted, "I didn't think the killer would have the nerve to try again last night, so soon after his first failure. But the longer they stayed together, the more they'd rub each other's nerve ends raw—so whoever it was would be driven to a second attempt pretty soon, maybe tonight, and I figured on being out there."

"Of all the stupid, cretinous, idiotic ideas—" He stopped suddenly as that ray of hope suddenly reappeared in his bloodshot eyes. "You think it could work?"

"It's pretty wild," I admitted. "But what else have we got? A bunch of suspects all with good motives and all with equally good opportunity—and a weapon that disintegrated right at the time of the murder."

"You're right," he said heavily. "We don't have any evidence at all—not even a clue—and we're not about to find one, either. So, wild, improper, and downright dangerous as your idea is, I guess we're stuck with it."

"Now you're making me nervous, Sheriff," I said truthfully. "Why don't I get around and ask some more questions—see if I can't put some pressure on here and there—squeeze them a little? If that won't work, we can always dream up some excuse to put all of them back together under Kramer's roof."

"Okay," he said finally. "But my guess is you'll be wasting your valuable time."

"Maybe you're right," I admitted. "You still keeping a twenty-four-hour guard over Kramer?"

"What else?" he grunted. "If I didn't and he got himself murdered for real this time, the papers would crucify me after what's happened already."

"Sure," I said. "So I'll be on my way."

"Hold it!" he barked. "There's something else. Only one of them without a strong motive—that Angel girl?"

"I can't find any strong motive there," I agreed. "You think I should make a closer investigation?"

"Would it be humanly possible to get any closer to her than you did last night?" he snarled.

"Yes, but I don't care to admit it," I said coldly. "I'm to make one more try, if you want, Sheriff. Strictly in the line of duty, of course."

"Go away—get lost—please?" he almost pleaded. "If I want to shorten my life there must be more pleasant ways of doing it than by listening to your babble. Don't bother me again, Wheeler, until you've got something worth bothering me with!"

"You're the boss," I said politely, "for some peculiar reason. Do you have addresses where I can find MacGregor and Forde?"

"Miss Jackson has them on file," he growled. "Get them from her. And don't go bothering her, either—she's a nice girl!"

"There are times, Sheriff," I said reproachfully, "when I feel your faith in me leaves something to be desired."

"There are times, Lieutenant," he grated, "when I feel I could happily strangle you to death with my own hands—and this is one of them. So get out!"

Annabelle Jackson was sitting in the outer office, and for once her head wasn't bent over her typewriter. She was thoughtfully munching on a stick of celery and there was a carton of chocolate-flavored skimmed milk on her desk, giving mute testimony to her eloquent curves. Her white silk shirt draped itself around a couple of her more eloquent curves in sheer pride, and her tight gabardine skirt had hiked a couple more inches than it should have, displaying her delightfully dimpled knees with loving abandon.

"Please don't stay around the office, Lieutenant," she said between munches, "not while I'm eating!"

"Enough of this love-talk," I said sternly. "I'm here on official business yet."

"What's official to you is monkey business to anyone else," she observed darkly, "and you're wasting your time leaning across my desk like that—you won't get to see any more of my knees than you already have!"

"The Sheriff said you had the addresses where I could find MacGregor and Forde," I said, hastily regaining an upright posture.

"There!" She pointed at the top typewritten page in her "Out" basket. "Wear it in good health."

I picked up the carton of skimmed milk and made a pantomime of first studying it intently, then transferring my concentration to her.

"Sure, you're putting on weight," I said encouragingly, "but it's all going to the right places."

"I'm just not hungry today," she snarled. "Most days I go to the drugstore and eat a whole stack of sandwiches smothered in mayonnaise!"

I took one of the carbon copies that listed the addresses I wanted, and tucked it into my wallet. "To think," I said in a voice just tingling with nostalgia, "I can remember the days when you didn't wear a girdle, magnolia blossom."

"I still don't," she snarled. "Not that it's any of your nasty-minded business, Al Wheeler."

"I have a sixth sense about these things," I told her. "You want to get up out of that chair and walk around the office a couple of times to prove you're telling me the truth?"

A fresh, sturdy stick of celery suddenly cracked across the bridge of my nose with painful force. "Take off!" Annabelle said vulgarly. "For you, I wouldn't get off this chair—not even to cheer when your hearse rolled by on the way to the cemetery!"

"What kind of foreverness is this?" I said indignantly, rubbing my nose gently at the same time. "Whatever happened to the Old World courtesy and charm of the South?"

"It went West," she said promptly, "met up with a native Angelino barbarian called Wheeler, then shriveled up and died right there!"

"Retribution," I said darkly as I headed toward the door, "that's what it is. You're going to be so fat you'll need two chairs any time now, one for each—" I heard the ominous scraping sound as she lifted a steel rule from the desktop, and leaped the remaining six feet between me and the safety of the outside corridor.

I had a quick hamburger down the street in the Hamburger King's palace, and from the way it tasted the king must have abdicated a long time back, or more likely been assassinated if there was any justice left in the world. After the second cup of coffee, which still didn't kill the dubious taste in my mouth, I collected the Healey and drove out to the airport.

It was around a quarter after two when I got there, and it took another twenty minutes of various directions and misdirection before I finally found my way to the far side of the field and the semi-derelict hangar that bore the legend "Forde Air Taxi Service, Inc." in fading blue paint.

Inside, the hangar was empty except for the pint-sized figure, wearing oil-stained white coveralls and sitting on an upturned empty gasoline can. As I got closer I saw he was busy with a battered-looking logbook and a pencil. There was no welcoming smile on the chihuahua-like face when he looked up and saw me coming.

"You're out of luck, Lieutenant," he said shortly. "My copilot's out on an all-day charter and won't be back until after six tonight—so you'll have to find yourself another air taxi—or walk!"

"That's very funny, Sam," I said mildly. "It's also that kind of lousy wisecrack that probably accounts for you losing your hair so fast."

"So maybe you've gotten yourself some new questions," he snapped, "but I've only got the same old answers. If you want me to run through 'em again, it doesn't bother me. Right now I don't have anything better to do."

"Fine," I said easily. "How is the air taxi business these days?"

"It could be worse—although I'm not real sure how," he grunted. "You thinking of running some competition?"

"I'm thinking of an insurance policy," I said, "one which gives you fifty thousand good reasons for wanting to see Kramer dead. How about that, Sam?"

He tossed the logbook onto the floor in a gesture of disgust, then dug a crumpled pack of cigarettes out of his pocket. "Did Mitch tell you about that?" he asked indifferently.

"No," I said truthfully, "his lawyer did."

"Got a match?"

I struck one for him and he leaned forward to light his cigarette. "Thanks." He inhaled deeply. "Sure we both took out policies to cover the loan I made from Mitch to get this business started. Nothing unusual about that, Lieutenant, it's done every day of the week!"

"It gets to be unusual when somebody tries to murder one of the policyholders," I reminded him. "You had equal chance along with the others to lift that antipersonnel mine out of Kramer's museum, wire a timing device onto it, and put it into the plane. But you stood to gain fifty grand out of Mitch's death where nobody else did, and that makes you kind of unique, Sam."

He rubbed the back of his hand across his forehead irritably. "There was a time I used to kill for free, so fifty grand instead of a medal sounds like a real big league return to me. The way you put it, Lieutenant, you make it sound tempting, even." He blew a thin jet of blue smoke across the hangar and watched it for a moment, then shook his head. "You've got the wrong guy, pal. It wasn't me who tried to kill Mitch and blew up Red Hoffner by mistake. Me and Mitch are old buddies from way back—the time he lent me that fifty grand to get started I didn't have enough collateral to finance a transistor radio! You think I could plan on murdering a guy who did that for me?"

"You make it sound real good, Sam," I said coldly. "I'd like it better if you could come up with a little proof, too—something like an alibi maybe? Even a small one would help."

"Mitch had all the dough, the airplane, and the house," he said, almost as if he hadn't heard my last question at all. "So we started going out to his place once in a while, and it got to be a regular thing the way some guys play golf all the time. The four of us had known each other for a hell of a long time, Lieutenant, and it was good to get together and do some flying for fun instead of work the whole time. I was grateful to Mitch for making it possible—I figured I owed him something for that—I still do. So when it became damned obvious that things were coming apart at the seams, I tried to ignore it—stay out of trouble and not take sides. Mitch was entitled to my loyalty and a hell of a lot more besides."

"It sounds great when you say it," I said blankly. "There's just one thing wrong—it doesn't make any sense."

"I guess about everybody knew Sally didn't exactly approve of Mitch getting together with his old buddies and cutting up capers all the time," he went on. "But I figure she would have gotten over it if that cream puff of a lawyer hadn't stuck his nose in where it didn't belong!"

"The episode on the terrace that Angel told us about?" I queried.

"That—and a lot more before that, as far as I can figure out," he said. "Mitch isn't the kind of a guy to cry on anybody's shoulder. But, boy! After the way Sally's been giving him the runaround, I could sure sympathize with him making passes at Angel!"

"This is where I get confused with the old buddy routine," I told him. "I had Angel figured as MacGregor's girlfriend."

"She was—in the beginning," he said casually. "I don't know exactly what happened, but next thing everybody knew she was only using Stu as a front, and the big romance in her life was Mitch Kramer."

"I've only known MacGregor since yesterday," I said, "but he's sure had me fooled. About the last thing I ever figured him for was an easygoing guy who'd let somebody steal his girlfriend from under his nose without ever squawking."

"Stu likes dames, sure," Forde shrugged, "but they don't worry him any. So if Angel wanted Mitch more than she did Stu, I guess he just thought what the hell."

"I hear it another way, Sam," I murmured. "That Kramer has something on MacGregor—something bad enough to make him do exactly as he's told—like when Kramer wants a new girl he tells MacGregor to go find him one. When Kramer wants MacGregor's girl he takes her and all MacGregor can do is smile."

Forde stared at me for a few seconds in what seemed to be genuine astonishment. "That's the craziest thing I ever heard! You mean Mitch is blackmailing Stu into being his panderer, with the threat of revealing some deep dark secret if Stu doesn't do as he's told?"

"Something like that," I agreed.

"Whoever told you that is sick, Lieutenant!" He tapped the side of his head with one finger. "Sick up here, like out of their mind!"

"Maybe you're right," I acknowledged. "Who would you pick as the mostly likely candidate for a murderer, Sam?"

An expression of deep disgust showed on his face as he glared up at me belligerently. "What the hell else have I been doing all this time but telling you!" he snorted. "That creep of a lawyer! He wants Sally Kramer and he wants to get his hands on Mitch's dough—and he wants both of them real bad!"

"But you don't have any proof it was Irving?"

"Would I be standing here batting the breeze with you now if I did?" he said in a frustrated snarl.

"I guess not," I admitted.

"I don't know how the hell you can miss it when it's staring you right in the face," he growled. "With Mitch dead, that would make Sally a widow, right? So all Irving would need to do then is wait for a decent interval after the death and then marry her, and he'd be marrying all of Mitch's dough at the same time!"

"You know something, Sam?" I asked him in a solemn tone. "You aren't as dumb as you look."

"Thanks," he sneered right in my face. "I wish I could say the same for you, Lieutenant!"

CHAPTER SEVEN

MacGregor had an impressive office all to himself on the top floor of the engineering corporation's main office building. His girl Friday came all the way down to the front reception desk to show me the way, but following her back offered nothing to look forward to. She was built like a board, and if she hadn't worn glasses, it would have been impossible to tell the back from the front. Her glasses were tinted a pale blue—to match the worried look on her face, I figured. When we finally arrived at the right office on the top floor, she opened the door for me and whispered I should go right on in, Mr. MacGregor was expecting me. The tone of voice she used when she mentioned his name was the vital clue to her underweight problem—obviously he was the substance of her nightmares that kept her from sleeping nights.

Like I said, the office was impressive, and somehow in these surroundings, some of it rubbed off on MacGregor. Maybe it was the difference between a dirty sweatshirt and an immaculate raw silk suit. When Angel had told me he was a big-shot sales executive the whole idea had sounded stupid—but once you saw him against the right background it was hard to imagine him as anything else.

He lifted his bulk out of the chair behind half an acre of desk, and held out his hand as I came into the office.

"Lieutenant." His grip was a modified version of the bone-crusher. "Sit down, won't you. How about a drink?"

"That sounds fine by me," I said thankfully. "Scotch on the rocks, a little soda?"

Half of one paneled wall swung open to reveal a lavishly stocked bar complete with a glistening chromed refrigerator. He made the drinks with casual efficiency, gave me mine, then took his own around in back of his desk again.

"I can use this," he said good-humoredly. "Cheers, Lieutenant!"

"Cheers," I said politely, and let some of the ice-cold Scotch slide down the back of my parched throat.

"I guess I owe you an apology for yesterday morning," he said suddenly in a wry voice. "It was a goddamned stupid thing for me to do—buzzing your car like that. Maybe I even deserved the fat lip you gave me for my trouble."

"That's okay," I said easily, "and maybe I'm lucky it wasn't me who got the fat lip."

"You know something, Lieutenant?" he said seriously. "The psychology of the whole thing scares the hell out of me—it really does. Around this place I'm a reasonably sober citizen, responsible for the sales division of the whole outfit. Once I get into an airplane behind the controls something happens—suddenly I'm a twenty-year-old kid again with all the bravado, and a big, wide chip on my shoulder a mile high!" He shook his head slowly. "I know this—but it still happens."

"I'd guess the choice is simple," I said politely. "Either give up flying, or give up the sales division."

"That's a hell of a choice to offer a man," he said, grinning bleakly. "I think I'll get myself a new head shrinker if you don't mind, Lieutenant."

"That would be just fine by, me," I told him. "Right now we can talk about a murder instead."

His face sobered rapidly. "Of course. I'm sorry—go ahead and tell me how I can help."

I drank some more Scotch which gave me a little time to think, and time right then was what I needed. It was getting me confused—how come the bad guys were suddenly acting like nice guys? A half-hour back, Sam Forde had suddenly changed from a snarling, snapping, pint-sized pain in the neck into a guy who valued loyalty to a friend above his own safety, and had acquired dignity in the process. Now MacGregor was pulling the same kind of switch on me; from an ugly-tempered, bird-brained bull, he'd suddenly changed into a warm, civilized, and friendly guy. Maybe I was just losing my mind, I thought without any real hope. Whatever it was, it made what I had to do to him that much harder.

"You can help by being honest, MacGregor," I said finally.

The look of polite and friendly attention on his face stayed right where it was, only his eyes showed a baffled reaction. "How's that again, Lieutenant?"

"Something Angel told me last night," I said stiffly, "about how—"

"Oh, yes!" He grinned widely. "That's something else again, I forgot to thank you for. It was decent of you to run her home, Lieutenant—the way things were it could have been awkward for her if she'd stayed on."

"It didn't seem to worry you at the time," I snapped. "She asked you to take her home first, then Kramer told you to stay, so you stayed."

"Mitch was right," he said evenly. "Red had been an old buddy of ours for a hell of a long time. It was something that only concerned the three of us—the feeling we had for him. I just couldn't walk out on Mitch and Sam Forde right then."

"Not even for your girl?" I queried. "At least, Angel is your girl, isn't she?"

"I guess you could call her that."

"It didn't worry you any when she admitted she was in the hangar in the middle of the night with Kramer?" The friendliness had vanished from his face, and any moment now the politeness would follow. "Angel's a big girl now," he said flatly. "She does what she wants."

"Or what you want—where Kramer's concerned?" I prodded.

His face darkened. "Just what the hell do you mean by that?"

"I'm just curious why a guy in your position has to act as Kramer's panderer," I said brutally. "How many other girls did you get for him, before Angel?"

I was braced, ready to leap out of the chair the moment he started to move his bulk around the desk toward me. That, I would have understood completely, but he got me all confused again instead.

"Are you out of your mind?" he asked blankly, without even moving a muscle.

"I've got this straight from the Angel's mouth," I said coldly. "You encouraged her to be nice to Kramer from the first time you ever took her out to the house. The way she has it figured, Kramer must have something goddamned good on you, because when you're around him you're not a man anymore, just a mouse."

For a couple of seconds he just looked at me with his mouth wide open, then his massive shoulders suddenly heaved as he shook with helpless laughter.

"Angel told you all this?" he managed to say between wild guffaws. "She must have been ribbing you, Lieutenant!"

"She was dead serious!" I snarled.

"Then she must have flipped." Slowly the guffaws died away to an occasional hysterical gurgle, and he dabbed his eyes with a pocket handkerchief. "That's the wildest thing I ever heard," he said finally. "Mitch Kramer blackmailing me into becoming his personal white-slaver! I have enough trouble getting girls for myself, believe me, without doubling-up as a talent scout for him."

I finished my drink without tasting the rest of the liquor—it just couldn't shift the taste of hot ashes in my mouth. MacGregor watched me with almost a compassionate look in his eyes, and that came close to the ultimate indignity.

"Are you sure Angel wasn't pulling your leg, Lieutenant?" he asked soberly. "That's the wildest thing I've ever heard! Sure, Mitch has probably got a million dollars more in the bank than I have, but I make around twenty-five thousand a year here, with bonuses. I have no responsibilities except my own enjoyment—I don't need any of Mitch Kramer's money, Lieutenant. I was born right here in Pine City and you can check my record all the way through if you want. Sure, you'll find a lot of damned stupid things I've done, from drag racing on a highway, to buzzing your car yesterday morning—but some dreadful secret that allows Mitch to blackmail me into pimping for him? Oh, brother!" He dissolved into hysterical laughter again.

It looked like high time I went and found someplace to wipe the egg off my face in privacy. "Maybe you're right," I said as I got to my feet. "Maybe Angel was ribbing me." I grinned at him frostily and the effort involved nearly cost me my whole nervous system. "Anyway, I'll check on it."

"Sure." He made a big effort and managed to straighten out his face. "It was nice to see you. Stop by whenever you have the time to spare, Lieutenant."

"The next time I've got a new funny story for you, I'll make a point of it," I grated. "Thanks for the drink."

On the way out, I caught his girl Friday watching me through her tinted glasses and felt a sudden bond of sympathy. Now we had something in common—we were both about to have nightmares about the same man.

My watch said four twenty-five as I barreled the Healey out of the engineering plant back onto the highway. I figured there was time enough to have a talk with Kramer and still get back to town in plenty of time to keep my date. The long straight road was completely deserted and it gave me a chance to throw off a little of my frustration by letting out the Healey; at 108 mph there was a nasty clattering sound under the hood. Cliff White was dead right, I realized—the pistons did need adjusting. Five minutes later I bounced along the rough track that led toward the Kramers' house, and parked beside the mud-splattered Corvette, which looked as if it hadn't been moved from the day before.

There was a faint sound from behind me as I climbed out of the car, and I turned around to see Sally Kramer running toward me, her red hair streaming behind her. She wore a thin silk robe that the wind flattened tight against the delicate curves of her body, making it obvious she had nothing on underneath.

"Lieutenant," she said breathlessly when she got close, "I'm so glad you're here. I wanted to talk with you privately if I could?" She panted for breath a few moments, then tried to smile. "I was just out of the shower when I heard your little sports car coming up the drive. You'll have to excuse my appearance but I had to see you before—"

There was a scraping sound, and again the noise came from behind, making me wonder for a split second if this was my day to be haunted. Then I turned my head and saw Cliff White standing there in his greasy coveralls, with that same sly, furtive gleam of malice in his eyes that I'd seen the previous night.

"Excuse me," he said brusquely. "Them pistons is getting worse, Lieutenant. If you're staying awhile, I'd be glad to fix them for you."

"No—thanks all the same," I said curtly, and turned away from him, back to Sally Kramer. "You were saying?" I prompted her gently.

"Just how nice it is to see you again," she said dully. "Oh, here's Mitch now. He'll look after you, Lieutenant, while I go and make myself respectable. See you later."

She walked quickly back toward the house, passing her husband on the way without stopping or exchanging words. I lit a cigarette while I waited for Kramer to come up.

"You don't figure I'm good enough to handle your lousy car?" White's sullen voice demanded.

"It's not that, Cliff," I said patiently. "I just don't know if I'll be staying long enough to give you time for the job. Otherwise I'd be grateful for the chance."

"You're a lousy liar, Lieutenant," he said thickly. "I was a fool to think any stinking cop could be trusted!" He headed back toward the hangar, dragging his left leg painfully as he hurried.

"Lieutenant?" Kramer's eyes were curious as they watched the mechanic's retreating back. "What did Cliff want?"

"To fix my pistons," I said. "I told him I didn't have the time right now but I don't think he believed me."

Kramer laughed shortly. "The hell with Cliff—he's overly sensitive. Look at him now—he always does make a production of that game leg of his. If you didn't already know, you'd think the damn thing was wooden or something!"

"Maybe it gets to feeling it is, if you drag it around long enough," I said curtly.

Kramer shrugged his shoulders. "He's making a grandstand play for sympathy the whole time—once in a while it gets under my skin. But come on into the house and let me fix you a drink. I'm being a lousy host!"

We went through the house onto the back terrace again. Polnik was sprawled in a comfortable chair, tall frosted glass on the table in front of him.

"Lieutenant?" He gulped a couple of times as he reared up onto his feet. "I was just—"

"Relax, Sergeant," I told him, "so am I."

"Oh, fine!" He plunked back into the chair with blissful smile on his face. "You know something, Lieutenant? This case is turning out better than I figured it would."

"I'm glad somebody's happy," I snarled.

Kramer was busy at the bar fixing the drinks. I lit a cigarette while I studied the almost cheerful expression on his face, wondering if he was about to pull a sudden switch on me the same way the other two flyboys already had.

"How's the investigation coming, Lieutenant?" he asked, as he handed me the glass. "Making any progress?"

"Some," I said vaguely. "I think, with your help, I can make some more."

"Well, that's great," he said eagerly. "What do you want me to do?"

"Let's go someplace we can talk in private," I suggested.

"This is the kind of house that has a den." He grimaced savagely. "Seeing we don't breed any wildlife indoors, I use it. It's kind of crummy but at least we won't be disturbed."

I followed him back into the house and we finished up in a smallish room on the far side of the house. There were some hunting prints on the wall, a thick rug on the floor, two immense leather armchairs, and a small, well-stocked bar.

"Sit down, Lieutenant," Kramer said. "We can talk in here without being interrupted."

"Fine," I said, and found myself practically engulfed by one of the monster chairs as I sat in it. Kramer sat facing me, a look of rapt attention on his handsome face. "I'm not going to pull any punches, for your sake and mine," I told him curtly. "The way I see it, you're a very lucky man to still be alive right now, and you'll be an even luckier man to stay alive for much longer!"

His eyes narrowed a little. "I guess I can appreciate that in general, Lieutenant—but maybe you've got something specific on your mind?"

"Keeping you alive," I said, "and the only way we can ensure that is by catching the killer before he tries a second time."

"That sounds reasonable." He smiled bleakly. "But now we come to the hard part, eh?"

"You can make it a hell of a lot easier for me by being honest, Kramer," I said tersely, "and this means being honest until it hurts."

"Let's have the rest of it," he snapped.

"I'll give you a quote— 'Who hates me so much they'd want to murder me?' —that's what you said late yesterday afternoon when I was here, right?"

He grinned with embarrassment. "I guess it was me all right—only it sounds a little corny now."

"It was a reasonable question," I said, "I can give you a couple of answers. If you're honest you'll give me some more. Sam Forde, for one—his air taxi business is falling apart and he's into you for fifty thousand dollars. When you die, he'll collect the exact amount he owes you from the insurance company."

"I know that," he said and shook his head uncomfortably, "but of all people, I can't believe that San Forde would—"

"People have been murdered for ten bucks, and don't ever forget it," I said, a little ponderously. "Cliff White—he's a psychopath if I ever saw one—blames you for his bad leg."

He flushed and looked away suddenly. "It was an accident," he muttered, "not really my fault. If the god damned fool had only been paying attention—"

"The truth isn't important, only what Cliff thinks of as the truth is important," I snapped. "He had the best opportunity of all to hide the bomb in your airplane. Everybody would have gotten so used to seeing him around the plane, it would be a perfect cover, almost as if he was in visible."

"All right," he said, shrugging irritably. "Who else?"

"It's about here I need your help," I said evenly. "I want you to fill in some of the detail."

"If I can."

"There's a relationship between your wife and Phillip Irving?"

Kramer's face darkened again. "My God!" he exploded. "Is it so damned obvious that you can spot it inside twenty-four hours?"

"I had some help," I admitted, "but, yes, I'd say it's obvious."

"It's not Sally's fault—not really," he said, talking as much to himself as he was to me. "She comes from a good family, and she's got social ambitions. I guess she didn't realize what she was taking on when she married me—a fly-bum with just the one interest, to keep right on flying. Then my friends were the same as me, so we never did get to make the social set. She figures I'm spineless—no ambition, no proper respect for money. I guess I'm all the things Phillip Irving isn't!"

"Maybe it isn't exactly pleasant," I said, "but you have to face up to it. With you dead, your wife inherits your entire estate, and is free to marry anyone she likes, including Phillip Irving, after a little time. From his point of view, with you dead, he can always marry your widow after a little time—and when he does, he'll get your entire estate along with her."

"My God!" Kramer stared at me fixedly, the blood slowly draining from his face. "You don't honestly think they formed a *partnership* to murder me?"

"I don't know," I growled, "but for sure it's a distinct possibility."

He slumped back into the depths of his chair and stared blindly up at the beamed ceiling for a while. I gave him the time it took me to finish my drink to get used to the idea.

"Then there's something else again," I said briskly.

"Huh?" He slowly struggled back from whatever limbo he'd stranded himself in and blinked at me vaguely. "Did you say something just then?"

"There's the good luck charm," I said firmly. "The nonflying Angel, and she's real mad at you right now."

"Mad at me?" He forced himself to sit upright, shaking his head a couple of times as if to clear it. "What the hell for?"

"The way she tells it, she was MacGregor's girl the first time she visited here, but then he pleaded with her to be nice to you. Any time he's around you, he acts like a dog that's scared out of its wits—Angel says. She's curious to know just what it is you have over MacGregor to make him act this way—and so am I!"

"That two-timing little bitch!" he said, almost out of admiration. "She's had me coming and going for a while now. She's the biggest tease I ever had the bad luck to want in the worst possible way, because I know I'll never make it! It's quite a technique, Lieutenant. She strings you along, making big promises with her eyes and her hands, with small, subtle movements of her body—and right when you think you've finally got it made, down drop the shades and you're right back where you started!"

"She figures you've had MacGregor pandering for you awhile now," I said harshly.

"That's a lot of crap!" he snarled. "She's nothing but a goddamned troublemaker from way—" His voice trailed away suddenly into silence. For a moment his gaze met mine, then slid away in quick panic. Maybe fifteen seconds later it returned reluctantly.

"Be honest, you said, Lieutenant?" he asked in a thick voice. "Honest until it hurts—isn't that what you said? Well, this is hurting a hell of a lot right now!"

"As long as you can feel hurt, you're still alive," I said carefully. "A lot of people might consider that an advantage."

"Yeah!" He grinned ferociously. "You don't need to start rubbing salt into it!" He took time out to light a cigarette with meticulous care. "Okay. So the bitch was right—she was the third, maybe the fourth, girl that Stu brought me. She was the best of the bunch—Stu doesn't have very good taste in women as a rule and Angel was the exception. So what does that make me—legally? I know what it makes me otherwise and I don't give a goddamn!"

"Legally, MacGregor would have a hell of a lot more to worry about than you would if he forced any of those girls into the situation against their will—or paid them off in hard cash," I said. "But I'm a lot more interested in why he did it. What have you got on him that's so bad he didn't have any choice but to jump whenever you said for him to jump?"

"A little matter of personal pride and reputation, Lieutenant," he said in a cold voice. "A small secret shared just between the two of us."

"I'm doing this in an attempt to keep you alive, Kramer," I snarled at him, "and you're making it harder all the time for me to stay interested in the project. You want to play it cute, you can play it alone!"

"I'm sorry," he apologized swiftly. "Stu was a hero, almost as big a hero as me!" His self-deprecating grin wasn't about to fool anyone. "It makes a hell of a difference, Lieutenant—even now people have long memories. I'd take a bet Stu wouldn't have his big sales job if his war record, garnished with Korea, hadn't accelerated his promotions."

"If I want the story of MacGregor's life, I'll ask him for it," I grated. "What did you blackmail him with?"

"It's relevant, Lieutenant!" Kramer sounded almost hurt. "I'm telling you the only way I know how—this hero bit is important in other ways, too. You take the four of us, for example. We were kind of unique in our own small way—buddies through hell and high war—heroes all, reliving our triumphs and tribulations."

"A shining example to American youth," I said frostily. "It takes an old buddy hero to blow another old buddy hero to bits?"

He grinned amiably. "Now you got it, Lieutenant—the big secret. Stu MacGregor's no hero—just one big fake. I didn't meet up with him until toward the end of World War Two—how he'd survived is anybody's guess—and by that time the European sky was about as tame as Main Street. A couple of times when we did meet up with some real opposition, Stu nearly panicked, but the rest of the bunch were veterans by then, and nobody really noticed because it wasn't important—except me.

"But Korea was different, and how!" His voice openly gloated over the memory. "Stu had a flameout the wrong end of Mig Alley, and everybody figured he was only a memory when we got back to base—all except one guy who swore he'd seen Stu bail out and land safely in a small clearing. So we sang a couple of choruses of 'I Used To Work In Chicago' that night in the mess—it was his favorite among the classics—then turned his picture toward the wall and forgot he ever existed.

"Then, six months later, during a big infantry push, one advance unit overran a small POW stockade. The gooks had cleared out a couple of hours before, but left the prisoners in the stockade. There were twenty-three of them, Lieutenant." His voice dropped to a somber note. "One of them was still alive and the rest had been bayoneted to death. Guess who had survived—good old Stu MacGregor! The way he told it, the gooks started the massacre an hour before dawn—he'd had a bad attack of dysentery and hadn't slept at all that night. He was huddled against the outer wall of the stockade when they started in with the bayonets. Stu told it real good, how for a while he'd been simply paralyzed with terror while he watched them stack the bodies in a heap in the center of the stockade. Then later, the primeval urge for survival forced him to crawl into the bottom of the pile and pray they wouldn't set fire to the pyramid of corpses after they'd finished. How he kept on imagining he could smell gasoline seeping through the bodies piled on top of him, and every fragmentary noise was the rasp of a match about to incinerate him."

"For surviving, you blackmailed him?" I grunted.

"That's right," he said grimly, "but not the way you mean it. Maybe two weeks after Stu was back with the squadron, an infantry captain was waiting to see me at the base after I got back from a routine patrol. He was a very nice, very tough guy named Jacobs. It was his outfit that had overrun the stockade. We had a couple of drinks out of my own private bottle, then he pulled a sealed envelope out of his pocket and gave it to me. The handwriting didn't look right somehow, but it was addressed to me by name, as commanding officer of the squadron. I made some corny crack about the pony express, then he told me where he'd gotten it.

"They'd searched all the bodies in the stockade for dog tags and any personal possessions. He'd found the letter on one of the bodies close to the top of the pile. I started to open it and he said he'd prefer I waited until after he left to do that. The address was written in English but sure as hell a gook had written it. And there was something else Jacobs figured I should know. Every single corpse in that pile had been emaciated—guys of six foot two, three, hadn't weighed more than ninety-five pounds. They'd all been on a starvation diet for a long time. He'd been gone all of five minutes before I remembered Stu didn't look any different than he had six months back—not more than by a couple of pounds, anyway.

"So I opened the letter and it had been written by a Chinese liaison officer—a major in their intelligence corps. In their early interrogations they had approached each prisoner separately and offered him food and survival if he'd gather intelligence from the other prisoners for them—turn traitor, to be precise. Every man, bar one, had refused. Then there was detailed chapter and verse on the information Stu had gotten for them. In the last paragraph, the guy said they had promised him survival and they wouldn't break their promise—however, he felt it only proper that Stu's commanding officer should be informed of his traitorous activities. I guess you could call it a Chinese double play, huh, Lieutenant?"

It was my turn to stare at Kramer with my mouth hanging open for a few seconds. "So you kept that letter and used it to blackmail MacGregor, instead of handing it to the proper authorities for action?" I asked him in a stifled voice.

"Why not?" he said, shrugging nonchalantly. "What good would it have done anybody if they'd stood Stu up against a wall and shot him?"

"You still have that letter?"

"I sure do," he said with a grin.

"You don't consider it to be a sufficient motive for murder?"

"Maybe." He shrugged. "But Stu doesn't know where that letter is. It's no good killing me off until he's sure he can get hold of the evidence and destroy it at the same time, is it?"

"I wasn't a real, honest-to-God hero like you, Kramer," I said carefully. "But I was in Army Intelligence during the war. If I put in a report about this, your situation wouldn't be too much different from MacGregor's, would it?"

"It's a lousy bluff, Lieutenant," he said tolerantly. "A private conversation isn't evidence. I'd obviously deny all of it—it puts you in the same boat with Stu. I figure you both need that letter before you can do a goddamned thing."

"It doesn't surprise me that someone tried to kill you, Kramer," I snarled. "Now I'm only amazed you've managed to stay alive for so long."

"And I intend to keep right on living." He laughed derisively. "With the help of a real smart cop like you, how can I miss?"

CHAPTER EIGHT

Polnik was waiting for me on the back terrace when I came out of the house, with that wistful, puppy-dog expression on his face which always means he's about to ask a question of momentous import.

"Lieutenant?" His gravelly voice rasped across my eardrums like coarse sandpaper.

"Sergeant?" I said, trying hard to keep it polite.

"If you don't mind—" His sloping forehead rippled alarmingly for a moment. "I was just curious—not like it's any of my business and all, but when I'm working on a case with you, it always—well, maybe not always, but—"

My reason perched on the edge of a bottomless void for a horrifying moment, then slowly toppled outward.

"Are you trying to say something, Polnik?" I yelped in anguish.

"Yeah!" he said nervously. "I was just curious, Lieutenant. That blonde—you know—stacked? The one they called Angela or something—you took her home last night?"

"What about her?" I snarled, still hovering on the brink.

"Well ..." He shifted his feet uncomfortably. "I was just kind of interested if you'd maybe interrogated her already yet?"

"The answer's yes," I grunted, "but not in the way you mean, Sergeant!"

It was a near fatal error because now I had him all confused again. Any time now that clunking noise inside his head would start up and we'd both be in real trouble.

"Lieutenant," he said, his voice quavering on the edge of total confusion, "you mean there are *two* ways of doing it?"

"I'd like to stay and explain, Sergeant," I said in a kindly voice, "but I can see my bus coming right now."

If I didn't run back toward the Healey, I walked at a record-breaking pace. When I reached the car, I yanked open the door and slid into the driver's seat with one hand reaching for the key, planning for the fast getaway like the bank guards were already pouring out into the street.

"I'd love to go driving with you, Lieutenant," a soft voice said, "but I really wanted to talk."

My hand stopped in midair, quivering, then I turned my head and saw Sally Kramer was sitting in the passenger seat, watching me with an amused look on her face. She'd changed the silk robe for a sleeveless blue velveteen blouse and matching pants, and I figured nothing but a Kramer could drive a beautiful redhead like this into the arms of a Phillip Irving.

"You seemed to be in a dreadful hurry," she said. "Maybe I should leave it until some other time?"

"No hurry," I said. "Just do one thing for me. If that kook of a sergeant asks you did I interrogate you in the car—for both our sakes, tell him a definite, final, and irrevocable *no!*"

"Of course," she said blankly.

"What did you want to talk about?" I relaxed against the upholstery and found a cigarette. She shook her head when I made like a gentleman and offered her one.

"I wondered what progress you're making with the case," she said, and her voice wobbled unsteadily midway through the sentence.

"It's coming along fine," I said airily.

"Do you know who killed Red Hoffner?"

"Not yet—not for sure," I parried.

"Do you have many suspects?"

"Too many!" I grinned wryly at her. "That's one of the problems."

She ran her hand through her long red hair in that unconscious, practiced gesture. "Including Phillip Irving?"

"Sure."

"And me?"

"Right again."

"That's what he told me over the phone." The tremor in her voice had rapidly gotten worse. "I wouldn't believe it, that's why I wanted to ask you myself!"

"We've got plenty more than just you two," I said bitterly. "Right now we're lousy with suspects and motives—it's almost too much of a good thing."

"I bet it was that she-devil who told you a pack of lies about Phillip and me!" she said fiercely. "I never thought I could hate anyone so much, Lieutenant, that I'd wish them dead. But now I can't get it out of my mind, it's become an obsession. One moment I see her lying dead in the middle of the street, victim of a hit-and-run. Five minutes later, I'm visualizing a crowded elevator with her packed tight into the middle of all the people—then they all get out and she keels over gently to the floor. She had a coronary, you see, and she's been dead ever since the first floor."

"That I like," I said gravely. "It has a kind of poetic value, like a sonnet."

"Then it's the middle of the night and I see this horrible man climbing into the window of her apartment, a knife in his hand. He's an escaped maniac, a rapist, and—"

"That's the one you like best?" I finished for her.

Her lips smiled but her eyes didn't change their troubled look. "I guess I sound either stupid or just plain funny," she said tautly. "The trouble is I can't explain to anyone else how very real this all is for me."

"I'd try not to let it go too far," I said vaguely. "I can understand why you and Angel don't get along, but it isn't all that desperate, surely?"

"I hoped you would understand," she said tightly. "I kept trying to convince myself that maybe you would. Something terrible is about to happen soon, Lieutenant. I feel it coming, I know there's nothing can stop it, don't ask me how. But when it does happen, it will have been all her fault. With her lies and her cheap vulgar tricks, she makes stupid fools out of intelligent men!"

"Why don't you just try and take it easy, Mrs. Kramer?" I said politely. "I'm sure everything's going to be just fine! We'll get whoever tried to kill your husband, and killed Hoffner by mistake. You just relax."

"Thank you so much, Lieutenant," she said in an expressionless voice. "You've been very kind, and very patient, listening to the hysterical ravings of a stupid woman." Her lips twisted into a grotesque parody of a smile. "Something else that may amuse you, Lieutenant—it's only in the last day or so I've come to realize how stupid I've been for so long—and now it's too late to do anything about it."

She pushed the door open and slid out of the car in a deft movement so she was gone almost before I'd realized it. I craned my neck and watched her walk back toward the house with swift strides. I had that eerie feeling like the one you get the first time you hear Chinese music—your ear rejects it out of hand but your mind insists that it has to make sense somehow, even without any melody you can latch onto.

Then I realized it was a little after six—it would take almost an hour to my apartment with the downtown traffic at its peak. My date was on the surgical point of eight, I remembered. It felt like it had been a long hard day and I couldn't quite figure out why. I twisted the key and the Healey's motor chattered into sudden life. The hell with it! I thought happily as I turned onto the long, straight road, I have given the Sheriff more than his due, and if he doesn't agree, he can call me Robin Hood. With a heigh and a ho for the open road, and Johnny Jones with that ripe body, and wonderfully sullen face that I was going to light up like a Christmas candle. I could hardly wait yet.

I made it on the precipice-edge of eight—maybe a whole minute after—still wet behind the ears from the shower and all out of breath. Some cretin on the highway had figured an empty bus for the street where he lived and turned straight into it. The traffic tie-up had stretched for miles and it was seven-thirty before I'd gotten into the apartment even. My thumb exerted a discreet pressure on the buzzer, and then I waited nervously, still not having had enough time to get the unnerving Angel out of my system.

The door opened and Johnny Jones stood there, looking at me with those limpid hazel-flecked eyes. "You're late," she said accusingly.

"I'm sorry, honey, I had to stop by on the way for an amputation," I apologized. "Otherwise it would never have happened. It won't bother you if I limp a little when we dance?"

That vulnerable lower lip pouted at me for a moment, then quivered with laughter. "You're a kook," she said almost fondly. "I hate sensible people!"

"Like Phillip Irving?"

"Especially like Phillip Irving," she said emphatically. "You want to come in and make us a drink before we go?"

"I figured you'd invited me for the weekend," I said in a disappointed voice, "but never mind."

"On a Wednesday?" she croaked.

"I'd be gone by Tuesday," I assured her, as I stepped inside the apartment, "but don't feel embarrassed, the invitation probably got held up in the mails."

The living room decor was in very good taste, but then I took another look at Johnny and the rest was merely blurred background. She wore a stunning, heavy silk black dress with about the widest V neckline I'd ever seen. It started at the edge of her shoulders and reluctantly centered about two inches below where her cleavage started. The dress continued on down, naturally, and real tight around her waist, then blossomed into an elegant full skirt. There was a matching jacket draped across the back of a chair, and I mentally shuddered at the thought of how much the price tag must have been. I was glad it had been my year to buy a new suit, and in a moment of insanity last month I'd paid two hundred bucks for the tailored cloth I was presently wearing.

"The absolute beauty wearing the absolute," I said reverently.

"What was that crack about me wearing the absolute?" Johnny said uncertainly.

"In a dress, honey," I reassured her. "Where do I make the drinks?"

She studied my face critically for a couple of seconds. "Al, you're looking straight at me, right?"

"Right!" I said enthusiastically. "What a magnificent, breathtaking view it is."

"You're going to have to make a big effort," she said determinedly.

"Shift your gaze about six inches to your left."

I shrugged disconsolately. "If you insist." Then almost immediately a glittering profusion of bottles and glasses, dominated by a massive silver ice bucket, dazzled my eyes.

"You see it now, don't you, Al?" Johnny said encouragingly. "Remember, that's the bar. You just take five paces forward and you'll be able to reach out and touch it. I would like a martini on the rocks, please, and you can skip the vermouth."

"Why bother with the word *martini* at all?" I asked curiously.

Her lips pursed together for a moment. "I just can't stand people who drink straight gin," she said in a disapproving voice.

A short time later I was sitting uneasily on what I vaguely imagined to be a genuine Louis XIV chaise longue—if Louis ever had time to chaise longue around the court—and I couldn't quite convince myself that the inlay wasn't real fourteen karat gold. My cloud nine, out-of-focus (except for Johnny) vision was fast vanishing under the impact of the furnishings. That ice bucket was solid silver—I'd seen the hallmark—and I figured what else could you make those wonderfully soft, deep rugs out of, except mink? So they dyed it pale green—with this kind of money who needs to be ostentatious?

Johnny was sitting real close to me on the plush royal blue upholstery of the chaise longue, happily sipping her gin on the rocks, with one firmly-rounded hip pressed contentedly against mine.

"You sure have a beautiful apartment here, Johnny," I said cautiously. "I guess Irving pays real well, huh?"

"Are you kidding?" She smiled slowly and secretively, while the magic seemed to leap out the window in all directions. "I couldn't afford to rent the kitchen even, on what he pays me! I'm strictly a working girl, Al."

I had a sudden bleak memory of something she'd said across her reception desk—something about having a strict rule to check the credit rating of any prospective associate. There are times when Wheeler is dull, I thought savagely; and other times when the slob is extremely dull, and this looked like it was one of the latter.

"You should excuse the question," I said coldly. "But how come you do live in this apartment with all its expensive furnishings if you're only a working girl, honey?"

"I'm just lucky, I guess," she sighed happily. "The furnishings belong to the apartment, and somebody else pays the rent."

I snarled. "He must do something real interesting for a living—like own half of Beverly Hills?"

"He?" She turned her head toward me abruptly and that kookie hairdo brushed against my face like a high-tension cable swinging free. Her gleaming white teeth—generously donated by some cannibal ancestor—nibbled her lower lip thoughtfully as she looked me in the eye.

"Al?"

"Yeah?"

"You were thinking bad thoughts," she said solemnly. "Things like my dear old daddy pays for the apartment, and he's no relation?"

"Well," I grated, "you laid it all out for me, didn't you?"

She moved fractionally on the blue velvet, so now our thighs joined our hips in a kind of seamless invisible welding job.

"I have one wealthy aunt," Johnny said slowly. "This apartment belongs to her and I'm minding it until she gets back—she just doesn't trust strangers."

"Where's this aunt gone?" I said suspiciously.

"Overseas for a couple of years." She grinned faintly. "I doubt if she'll get back here again—my aunt is a nut!"

"You dare mention Brazil, and I'll slit your soft white throat from ear to ear!" I snarled threateningly.

"Where else would my Aunt Charlie go?" she asked in an innocent voice, then squealed in sudden anguish. "Al!" Her eyes reproached me sadly. "Don't you ever do that again! Well, not hard, anyway—you've got pointed fingernails, or something."

"I believe every word you say, honey doll," I told her.

"I don't imagine you'd happen to have a picture of your dear old aunt in the apartment someplace?"

"It just so happens I do," she said, her voice a little frosted around the edges. "But it just so happens I don't feel inclined to go look for it. You'll have to take my word for it, Al." Her face was suddenly only a couple of inches away from mine, and as I closed the vital gap between our lips, she slid into my arms like a missile come back to roost on the launching pad. That lower lip was made to be bruised and I figured hopefully I was the guy made to do the job. I'd only just gotten started when her mouth slid away across the side of my cheek, and sharp white teeth nibbled experimentally on my ear lobe.

"Al—honey?" she whispered throatily.

The subtle fragrance of her perfume had all my nerve ends pulsating at the same time. "What is it, Johnny?" I murmured.

"I'm hungry," she sighed softly. "Please, can't we get the hell out of here and go eat?"

It was the stuff from which the great loves of history have been woven—Dante and Beatrice, Romeo and Juliet, Johnny and the nearest Chicken Inn. I would have pretended deafness in that ear and ignored the whole thing, except that those cannibalistic teeth were nibbling a little harder all the time on my ear lobe.

I took her to the Enchantment for dinner, trying hard not to think about the last two weeks of the month when I'd have to exist without eating. By the time we'd reached the brandy and coffee stage, I fully understood how Johnny managed to keep all those wonderful curves so jampacked with vitamins. I held a match while she lit a cigarette, and watched as she leaned back in her chair and sighed blissfully.

"Such beautiful food, Al," she said dreamily. "I bet you eat here all the time."

"Oh, sure," I said nonchalantly. "Every year—it's a regular annual event with me. The other three hundred and sixty-four days I spend picking my way through trashcans. It makes an exhilarating contrast to all this—you'd be surprised."

"Hey!" she said suddenly and sat bolt upright.

I looked nervously over my shoulder. "What is it? —your Aunt Charlie, the nut—or something?" I asked anxiously.

"I just remembered—what did you do to Mr. Phillip Irving this morning?"

"Nothing," I said, firmly resisting the temptation.

"You must have done something!" Johnny insisted. "Me, he doesn't even notice—but after ten minutes with you he's running around in small circles all day, making urgent calls to all points of the compass, and everything?"

"You wouldn't care to translate that into English so I can understand it?" I asked hopefully.

"Sure," she said obligingly. "He was acting like you'd just analyzed him and told him he was a real worm, not just a fake who'd been conditioned to act like one. I never saw him so nervous before. He was on the phone three, maybe four, times to his girlfriend, and they talked for about twenty minutes each time."

"His girlfriend?" I queried.

"She's the only woman in his life," Johnny said casually, "but she can't be his mother because she doesn't have the same name, and she's married. He always gets me to call first and ask for Mrs. Mitchell Kramer, with strict instructions to say it's one of the retail stores calling if she happens to be out. You wouldn't figure a jerk like Irving would have it in him, would you?"

"Who else did he call today after I'd gone?" I asked.

"You mean who didn't he call," she corrected me. "A couple of airlines, maybe four or five shipping agencies. He must be getting real wild and thinking about a vacation, huh?"

"I might be able to get him one real soon," I suggested, "for free—accommodations, American plan, a chance for regular exercise, and even free movies once in a while."

"Sounds wonderful!" she said. "Where is this place?"

"San Quentin."

Her lower lip pouted at me and I achieved instant memory loss without even trying. Phillip Irving disappeared out of my mind, like that! The waiter presented the tab and took away approximately four days' salary in exchange.

"You want to come back to my aunt's apartment, Al?" Johnny asked interestedly. "Or will we go listen to your hi-fi and its five speakers all sneaking up on a girl at the same time?"

"Why don't we try my apartment first?" I said reasonably. "If we get bored with the hi-fi, we can always move over to your place."

"You think of everything," she said admiringly. "I wish I could have been like that—it would've saved my mother worrying and she might even have slept nights."

There was the necessary interlude from door to door in the Healey, and then maybe thirty minutes after we'd left the restaurant, we were inside my apartment. While Johnny was satisfying her feminine curiosity with sharp, penetrating glances into every corner of the living room, I stacked the hi-fi machine with records. A few seconds later the elegant, educated music of Ellington filtered through the five wall speakers into the room.

"How about I make us a drink?" I said. "Martini on the rocks, with no vermouth?"

"I don't think I want another drink, Al," she said absently. "Is that a couch or a handball court?"

"It's just a little old couch, like any other little old couch," I said, very offhand. "When you've seen one, you've seen 'em all."

"No, sir!" Johnny shook her kookie hairdo at me for more emphasis. "Not this one—you could lose a troop of cavalry in the middle of that monster and spend weeks searching for them!"

"Well," I said brightly, "I must remember to get me a troop of cavalry, huh?" I tried for a fast switch in the conversational trend. "You sure you don't want another drink? I have some genuine, French-type, Napoleon-like brandy."

"Not for me, thanks," she said vaguely, her eyes still riveted to that damned couch. "But you make yourself one, if you want."

"Fine," I said. "Won't be a moment. Isn't that Duke out of this world?"

"Maybe he cut the record from the center of your couch?" she murmured thoughtfully.

It seemed like a good time to get myself a drink. I went out to the kitchen and made myself a reasonably conservative corpse-reviver. I tried it on for taste, size, and quality, then carried it back with me into the living room. Things had been happening since I'd been gone, and I was crazy to leave in the first place. Johnny didn't seem to have moved from where she was standing before I'd gone to the kitchen, but now that wonderful black silk dress was neatly draped, along with the jacket, across the back of an armchair. She stood nonchalantly in a delicate beige slip which had been sprayed with lace across the bustline and hem.

"I could have opened a window, honey," I said, "but I think you had much the better idea, all the same."

"I'm not feeling the heat, Al," she said, frowning in concentration. "It's just that I don't want to crush my dress romping around in the middle of that thing." She pointed toward the center of the couch.

"You're not only the absolute beauty, but you've got brains to go with it," I said in awe. "Such a practical attitude is so refreshing—refreshing, hell, it's downright titillating!"

She gave me a sharp look. "I'll thank you to skip the vulgarity," she said primly.

"That's a beautiful slip, honey doll," I said quickly, making a mental note not to say "hell" any more in her presence. I strove for just the right—sympathetic but casual—tone. "It would be an awful shame to see it get crushed."

"It's nylon, Al—no problem."

"Who can tell the exact moment when nylon just might become a problem?" I said gloomily. "I mean, why take a chance?"

"Maybe you're right, Al! I mean all this lace is real delicate."

"Sure," I said, and my voice cracked as I said it.

Johnny bent forward cross-armed, then straightened up again, peeling the slip up and over her head in a smooth, unbroken movement. The slip was draped carefully across the back of another chair, then she stepped up onto the couch gracefully and bounced gently on the soles of her feet.

"You can't be too careful about the springs," she said solemnly.

Being a reasonably polite character I wanted to answer her, but my vocal chords were suddenly paralyzed along with the rest of my body. Johnny leaned forward slightly and came up on tiptoe for a few seconds, looking down at me from a height advantage of maybe nine inches. A wicked, triumphant gleam showed in her eyes as she savored her complete victory.

"What's the matter?" she gurgled throatily. "Cat got your tongue?"

I suddenly remembered with quick remorse how I'd never really believed that teacher in sixth grade who told us geography could be fun. From the crown of Johnny's kookie hairdo right down to the pink soles of her elegantly shaped feet, it was fun, fun, fun all the way. Her bra and panties were obviously part of a matching set with the discarded slip, and both of them looked gloriously inadequate for the herculean tasks demanded of them.

Her full, creaming breasts seemed about to burst loose from the confining bra at any moment, as they jiggled complacently along with the gentle, springy movement of the rest of her body. The brief panties were nothing more than a froth of coffee-colored lace, slung low across her hourglass hips and worn strictly for decorative purposes only. Still traveling south, I experienced new adventures and delights in the alabaster whiteness and delicate sculpturing molded into the tapering arch of her thighs. Her dimpled knees seemed to wink at me encouragingly as the hot blood pounded through my veins, destroying the total paralysis in less than a second.

Johnny leaned further down toward me with both arms outstretched invitingly, and the combination of gravity with the sudden upswinging surge of twin Olympian peaks was too much for nylon and stitching. There was a faint snapping sound and the bra floated gently down toward my feet.

"Hi, there, Al," Johnny said throatily. "Welcome aboard!"

The urgent, jarring sound of the phone left me quivering in mid-stride, like a mountaineer who chickened out half way up Everest. Johnny sighed gently and straightened the arch in her back.

"I guess you'd better answer, Al," she said regretfully.

"Are you out of your scintillating mind?" I asked in a croaking voice.

"You're a police lieutenant—a cop," she said listlessly. "If that's cop business on the other end of the line, the phone will keep on ringing once every five minutes until someone answers."

"So let it ring!" I growled.

"If you think I'll happily sink into the center of this monstrous couch of yours, Al, with the blissful thought that the phone will ring at least once every five minutes, you're a lot more stupid than I figured!"

"Yeah," I said flatly, because her logic was irrefutable. "You know something?" I said in a broken voice. "We could have gone to your apartment instead?"

Ahead of me lay the arid desert that separated the couch from the small table beside the window. I plodded wearily across it and finally lifted the phone.

"Why don't you get the next camel train straight back to Outer Mongolia—whoever you are?" I snarled into the mouthpiece.

"Wheeler?" The last faint hopes twitching inside my head committed instant hara-kiri as I recognized the bull-like voice of Sheriff Lavers.

"Sheriff?" I groaned.

"You'd better get out to the Kramer house right away," he said tightly. "All hell has broken loose out there."

"Like what?"

"Polnik didn't make too much sense when he called about five minutes back," he said crisply. "But I know this much for sure—Mrs. Kramer is dead, killed with a forty-five slug!"

"Who did it? You have any idea at all?"

"Sure, we know who killed her all right." His voice sounded suddenly tired. "Her husband!"

CHAPTER NINE

It took maybe an extra five minutes to drop Johnny outside her apartment building on the way out to the Kramer house. Somehow that vulnerable lower lip had lost all its arrogance when she kissed me goodbye, the moment before she got out of the car.

"Like Romeo and Juliet, even!" she said, smiling bleakly. "Talk about the star-crossed lovers!"

"I'm glad you're not thirteen anyway," I said. "That would be a problem for a cop. I'll call you, honey, as soon as I can."

"You do that thing, Al," she said miserably. "Tell that nasty old sheriff of yours you have a right to some private life and the rest of it is none of his business!"

I watched the gentle roll of her hips under the sleek fit of the black silk dress as she crossed the sidewalk. Then I barreled the Healey out from the curb.

The ride out to the Kramer house, with only myself and my unfulfilled desires for company, was like a ride across the Styx with Charon pointing out the sights of interest. When I arrived there, I saw the Sheriff's car rolling along the rough track maybe a hundred yards ahead of me. Lavers was halfway into the house by the time I'd parked and caught up with him.

"So I was right the first time?" he said tightly. "Irving and Mrs. Kramer!"

"How the hell can you know that right now?" I asked him.

"What else?" he snarled.

Polnik met us in the front hall with a stupefied look on his face, even more so than usual, that is.

"So what happened?" the Sheriff said venomously.

"Cheez! I don't know, Sheriff," the sergeant said in a traumatized voice. "Around ten-thirty, Mrs. Kramer said she was going to bed and told us goodnight. We was sitting out on the back terrace having a—a talk, when she left us and came inside the house. About a half-hour later, Mr. Kramer said he was going to his den to do some paperwork. So I took a walk around the outside of the house to see everything was okay, like the outside doors were locked and everything, and then came back onto the terrace. The next thing I knew I heard the sound of the shot from inside the house and—"

"What time was that?" Lavers barked.

"Three, four minutes after midnight," Polnik answered promptly. "When I got inside the den there was Mrs. Kramer lying dead on the floor with a slug through her head—and Mr. Kramer was slumped in a chair with his face buried in his hands. I guess it was the shock, but for a while there I figured maybe he'd lost his mind." Polnik was obviously a lot happier now he'd had a chance to say it—it was a profound thought and he was pleased with it.

"At least Kramer's got a mind to lose!" the Sheriff said ungratefully. "Where is he now?"

"In the living room, Sheriff," Polnik said in an aggrieved voice. "I got him out of that den as soon as I could and kept him in the other room. I figured—"

"Never mind what you figured!" Lavers roared. "Show us the body first!"

The sergeant led the way through the house to the den, fumbled in his pants pockets for a while until he finally found the key, then opened the door. It was exactly the same room I'd been in that afternoon, with the corpse stretched out across the rug making the only difference.

Sally Kramer lay on her back, her long red hair cushioning her head. Her eyes were wide open and her lips drawn back from her teeth in an expression of total fear. She still wore the blue velveteen blouse and matching pants she'd changed into that afternoon. I remembered her talk in the car, like Chinese music with no melody, but underneath were the rhythmic and tonal patterns of logic if you had the patience to understand.

The dark hole high in her forehead, just beneath the hairline, was an ugly reminder of the inevitable brutality of death by violence. For a guy who'd seen more cadavers than he cared to remember, I had a peculiar queasiness about this one. Somehow I felt responsible toward Sally Kramer, as if I'd failed her badly in some way I didn't understand.

"The gun was lying on the floor right where it is now when I got in here, Sheriff," Polnik volunteered. "I didn't touch it."

It was a .45 service Colt and I wondered just how Sally Kramer had gotten hold of it—although in this damned house I figured guns were probably put out in the bathrooms along with the guest towels whenever people were visiting.

"All right," Lavers grated. "We've seen all there is to see in here. Let's go talk to Kramer!"

He was sitting in an armchair in one corner of the room, a drink in his hand and a look of complete desolation in his eyes. As we came into the room he tried to smile politely and didn't make it.

"I don't want to bother you, Mr. Kramer," Lavers said gruffly, "but we have to ask some questions, you understand? There is possibly even more than the death of your wife involved in this right now."

"Sure." His teeth chattered for a few seconds, and he hastily gulped liquor from the glass. "I understand, Sheriff."

"You want to tell us what happened?" Lavers prodded.

Kramer nodded again. "Sally said she was going to bed sometime around ten-thirty—we were out on the back terrace with the Sergeant then. She went into the house, and I had another drink with the Sergeant, then went into the den to do some paperwork I had stacked up waiting."

The fractional side sweep of the Sheriff's steely gaze toward Polnik at the mention of the word "drink" had reduced the Sergeant to a state of squirming neurosis. I grinned at him encouragingly, figuring the Sheriff was playing this like some heavy out of the silent movies, and he needed to be cut back down to reasonable size.

"I was in the room—I don't know how long—maybe fifteen minutes, maybe less—when the door suddenly opened and Sally came in. She was still fully dressed, and carrying a gun in her hand." Kramer shook his head hopelessly.

"Where did she get the gun?" I asked.

"From my top bureau drawer," he said in a low voice.

"You remember when we searched the museum to see if anything beside the S-2 mine was missing, Lieutenant? You had me going that night—made me realize fully for the first time that I was in real danger. So when I had my back toward you, I lifted the .45 and rammed it down the waistband of my pants."

"Your wife knew you had the gun in the bureau?" Lavers snapped.

"Sure," Kramer said bitterly. "She was scared to death somebody would get into the room in the middle of the night and attack me—she said. So I told her there was nothing to worry about, we had protection, and I showed her the gun."

"You must have been keeping a very observant eye on Mr. Kramer down in that basement, Lieutenant," Lavers said icily.

"I certainly did," I said cheerfully. "But it's nice of you to mention it, Sheriff. Thank you."

His face caught fire and he was about to deliver a broadside, then suddenly thought better of it. "Go on with your story, Mr. Kramer," he growled.

The hero shrugged his shoulders miserably. "I can't describe it, Sheriff. It was like being suddenly plunged into a nightmare while you're still awake. Sally just stood there, pointing the gun straight at me while she talked. She seemed to be in a completely hysterical state—her eyes had a kind of glazed look—and she called me every filthy name she'd ever heard."

A sudden tremor made his body shake uncontrollably for a few seconds. He emptied the glass, then placed it carefully on the small table beside the armchair. "I'm sorry." He cleared his throat sharply. "She went back through our marriage and how I'd never even tried to see things her way, not once in the whole time. How I was nothing but a bum, surrounding himself with other bums, living in drunken debauchery. It went on and on and on—I thought I'd go out of my mind just listening to her.

"Finally she said she had a chance of a new life—the kind of life she wanted—with a man she could love and respect."

"Phillip Irving?" Lavers asked triumphantly.

"Phillip Irving," Kramer repeated. "But I was the stumbling block, the only thing that stood in their way. I tried to talk about divorce, but she laughed in my face. It wasn't enough to be free—she needed my money, too. That was how they'd planned it all so carefully—she had taken the S-2 from the museum, and Irving had bought a cheap alarm clock and wired them together into a time bomb. Once the order of our flying the other morning had been decided, they'd sneaked out onto the back terrace, then across to the hangar, and planted the bomb in the plane. They'd just gotten back to the terrace when they saw Angel coming out of the house, so they went into a clinch. Better Angel should think they'd sneaked out there to get some secluded necking than realize they'd been away from the house."

He rubbed his fingers irritably across his face. "But their plans had misfired, she said, and Hoffner had been blown to pieces instead of me. Somehow she'd gotten it all figured out as being my fault entirely. Her voice got higher and higher as she talked on and on. I didn't listen to all she said, there was a hell of a lot of repetition in it. Finally she said she couldn't wait any longer to be free of me and my drunken friends and my loose women and so on—if a time bomb couldn't kill me, then maybe a bullet could."

Kramer lapsed into silence for a few seconds, his eyes staring unseeingly ahead of him as he relived those last few seconds of Sally Kramer's life.

"She took a step closer toward me," he said in a low voice, "and lifted the gun a fraction. I saw her body stiffen and suddenly I realized it wasn't a nightmare or a bad movie on the late show—this was for real. My wife was going to shoot me and at any moment from then on, she'd pull the trigger and a piece of lead would go hammering through my body."

The thumb and fingers of his right hand pinched his face with deliberate savagery. "Maybe it would have been better if she had killed me," he said in a toneless voice. "But at the moment, I didn't stop to think—all I knew was that I wanted to stay alive. I jumped her—grabbed for her wrist and pushed it up into the air, away from me." He shook his head slowly. "I don't remember it at all clearly," he said. "I know we struggled—the gun went off—and the next thing I knew was Sally falling to the floor with that hole in her forehead."

His face suddenly fell apart as the tears rolled down his cheeks. "All I know is I killed her!" he whimpered hysterically. "It was my fault! Now she's dead and it should be me lying there on the floor with a hole through my forehead!" He buried his face in his hands, then rocked backward and forward in the armchair, his whole body shaking violently.

"The doctor should be here any minute," Lavers said in a low voice. "Give him a sedative and calm him down a little. He's been through a hell of an experience!"

I needed a drink but with Lavers in his present officious mood it was obviously out of the question, so I lit a cigarette instead.

"Sergeant," I said to Polnik, "where's Cliff White?"

"The mechanic, you mean, Lieutenant?" he deduced brilliantly. "In his own room in back of the garage. He came over when he heard the shot, but I kind of bulldozed him out of the house again—I had my hands full with Mr. Kramer right then."

"Sure," I said. "How did he react when he heard what had happened?"

"You mean the mechanic, Lieutenant?" Polnik said cautiously.

"That's right," I agreed. Lavers had unnerved him already, and there are times when you just have to be kind to the Sergeant, instead of indulging your feelings and choking him to death.

"I guess he didn't react at all," Polnik said in a worried voice. "Now I think about it, it's not right to have no reaction at all, is it, Lieutenant?"

"You can stop this piffle, Sergeant!" Lavers thundered. "Do something useful for a change. Call the office and tell them I want Phillip Irving brought in and booked as an accessory on a conspiracy to murder."

"Yes, sir," Polnik said briskly. He took a couple of fast steps toward the phone, then turned back toward me for a moment. "Now I remember, Lieutenant," he said happily. "There was just a little bit of reaction when I told him Mrs. Kramer had tried to kill her husband, but she'd been killed herself when they struggled for the gun. He—"

"*Sergeant!*" The veins corded in Lavers's neck as he shouted at the top of his lungs. "Didn't I tell you to call the office? What the hell do you think you're doing now?"

"He what, Sergeant?" I asked loudly.

"Well"—Polnik looked almost embarrassed—"he just looked kind of disappointed!"

The Sergeant hurried toward the phone in a shambling, Cro-Magnon shuffle, and I suddenly felt a piercing cold across the back of my neck. When I turned around I saw it came from the icy stare of the County Sheriff.

"When I tell the sergeant to do something, he does it," Lavers growled. "He does it first, you understand, Lieutenant? Only then may you engage him in pointless conversation!"

"Yessir," I said smartly. "It's a question of the various social strata living and working together in harmony—this can only be achieved if there's a place for everybody, and everybody knows their place."

His head quivered ominously. "I can send you back to the homicide division at nine tomorrow morning, Wheeler! Maybe it would do you good—maybe you've been a big fish in a small pond too long?"

"Sheriff," I said wearily, "can I ask you a question?"

"If it's pertinent," he snapped.

"Was it something you ate?" I snarled at him. "Or you figure you can handle this better on your own, without having me hang around?"

"I think if I'd handled it on my own from the start—played through my hunch about Irving from the very first—then this might never have happened!" he said grimly.

"So you don't need me here anymore? I can go?"

"I would regard it as a favor," he said coldly.

So I went out of the house, filled with a false hope it still might not be too late to take up with Johnny about where we'd left off so abruptly. Then I checked my watch and realized it would be at least three A.M. by the time I made it back to her apartment. To wake her out of her sleep in the middle of the night and try to recreate the mood we'd had wouldn't be just stupid, I realized, but downright criminal.

It was a long, lonely drive home in the Healey to an empty apartment where a trace of Johnny's perfume still clung to the air and figured to drive me slowly insane—a sniff at a time. I had a quick heart-to-heart session with the other Johnnie I knew—an elegant gentleman by the name of Walker—then went to bed gently reeking of the best anesthetic I know. But even so, I didn't sleep real well, there were too many things bugging me.

The phone woke me around a quarter of nine and it was my gentle boss, Sheriff Lavers Legree calling.

"We haven't been able to find Irving yet," he said abruptly. "I've got a pickup call on him, of course, but he wasn't at his apartment last night and I can't imagine he'll show up at his office this morning. I want you to find him, Wheeler!"

"I thought I was due back at the Homicide division this morning?" I said curiously.

He made a few vague rumbling noises that I could interpret any way I liked, from an abject apology to a cold in the head.

"Forget it!" he said finally. "I may have been a little abrupt last night."

"You really don't like this Irving, do you?" I asked him.

"My personal feelings have nothing to do with it," he said in a furious voice. "You find him, Wheeler, and find him today!" He hung up before I had a chance to argue.

When I was all cleaned and shaved and dressed, I went out and had some breakfast, put some gas in the Healey, then drove out to the engineering plant again. The same girl Friday who shared nightmares with me—and from the look of her eyes in back of the tinted glasses, last night's had been a dilly!—escorted me all the way from the reception desk to the impressive office on the top floor.

MacGregor looked at me curiously as I sat down. "Back again so soon, Lieutenant?" His eyes were cautious. "You've got a new funny story—is that it?"

"I'm not real sure what I've got," I said. "You heard what happened last night?"

"I still can't believe it," he said in a low voice. "Sally dead—about to shoot Mitch with a .45! It's something that doesn't happen to people you know, Lieutenant."

"It happens to people all the time, whether you know them or not," I said morosely. "You worry me, MacGregor, you know that?"

"I wouldn't have thought so—not since the time you bloodied my nose and beat me into the ground a little—about six inches, as I remember?" He grinned wryly. "One of these days I'd like to try that again."

"It's the thing that's really bugged me from the very beginning," I said plaintively. "I never met so in many schizophrenics at the one time in the one place, you included."

He shrugged his immense shoulders easily. "I don't get it."

"You served in the Second World War, and then again in Korea, right?" I asked.

"Sure."

"I was in Army Intelligence," I said. "I still have a couple of good connections there. If I tried, I figure I could have your complete service record pulled and checked inside six hours, with a call to Washington."

"I believe you, Lieutenant," he said mildly. "Why bother telling me all this?"

"Because I want you to know that I can and will check it, so there's no point in you lying to me," I said coldly. "You flew with Kramer in Korea?"

"Who else? The four of us flew together all the time."

"Was he as big a hero as everybody seems to think?"

"I guess so." He thought about it for a moment. "In a war you get all kinds of pilots, but with fighter pilots you don't get too many variations, I guess. You get the guys who like to fly and don't like to kill—Red was one of those, a superb pilot who got sick in the stomach every time he'd shot down an enemy plane. You get the guys who like to fly and will willingly kill when they get the chance. That would include Sam Forde and me. Then there's the last and very special category—the guys who like to kill.

"Nearly all of them will become expert fliers if that's the only way they can get to kill some more. That's Mitch Kramer, and that's also a big hero, because he kills more efficiently and builds a bigger reputation. It's a kind of complex thing, Lieutenant. In Mitch's category you need an overdeveloped ego. A colossal vanity that'll override any other consideration—pity, compassion, fear, uncertainty. Only the egomaniacs survive in the long run." For a moment he looked almost embarrassed. "You had me going there for a while—sorry."

"It was great!" I said sincerely. "Were you ever taken prisoner in Korea?"

"Sure," he said easily. "I had a flameout much too far north and had to bail out. Mitch gave me cover all the way down, but once I hit dirt I was strictly on my own, of course. A gook patrol grabbed me ten minutes after I'd landed."

"How long were you a prisoner?"

"I was one of the real lucky guys," he said happily. "Seventy-five hours, and then there was a big push, and the stockade was overrun by an infantry outfit."

"The gooks just left you there for them to find?"

"Hell, no!" He shook his head decisively. "Some of these infantry boys were very smart. A certain Captain Jacobs knew from his forward patrols in the area that there was a prisoner-of-war stockade. So he split his force in half, moved them up in the middle of the night on either side of the stockade, then moved them fast a half-hour before dawn. The gooks never really knew what hit them, and I guess if it hadn't been for Jacobs, I wouldn't be here now."

"Was there a Chinese interrogation officer in the stockade?" I asked casually.

"How the hell did you know that?" MacGregor sounded amiably surprised. "There sure was—a miserable little bastard who used to try and argue that sex for pleasure was just another proof of American decadence. I told him he was the living proof of his ancestors' decadence and spent the next six hours pegged out in the hot sun for my trouble."

"Just seventy-five hours?" I prodded. "You're sure it wasn't more like six months?"

He opened his desk door and took out a small bronze plaque. "You don't want to believe me, take a look at this," he said, good-humoredly, then placed it on the desk.

The plaque had an etched inscription that read: "To Captain Stuart

MacGregor for his unique achievement in having used a three-day pass to fraternize with the enemy and then return safely to his home base.... From your old buddies, Mitch Kramer, Red Hoffner, Sam Forde."

"If you still don't want to believe me, Lieutenant," he said grinning, "you could check with Mitch and Sam."

"I believe you," I said sincerely. "Thanks for your time, Mr. MacGregor, you've been very helpful. I have a feeling your split personality has made a very successful integration."

"Well—thanks," he said in a stunned voice.

"See you around," I said, and headed toward the door.

"Hey, Lieutenant!" he yelped. "You never did get to tell me that funny story."

"You don't know how close I came to it," I admitted. "But it wasn't really very funny at all—I don't think you would have laughed, Mr. MacGregor. You know how some jokes are in very bad taste, but somehow you don't realize it right away?"

CHAPTER TEN

On the way back into town, I stopped off at a drugstore for a cup of coffee, and used the pay phone afterward. I called Irving's office and heard the phone ring four times, then the click as somebody lifted the instrument.

"Phillip Irving's office," said a cautious voice that sounded like a steel fence being sprayed with buckshot.

"Polnik!" I said disgustedly. "What the hell are you doing there?"

"You must have the wrong number," he said defensively. "There's no Sergeant Polnik here, this is Phillip—"

"This is Lieutenant Wheeler, you primeval procrastinator!" I yelled at him. "Let me speak with Miss Jones there, will you?"

"Oh! It's you, Lieutenant?" He was happy for some reason—who could tell what was fermenting under that shaggy skull? "There ain't no girl here, Lieutenant—or I'd be busy interrogating!"

I slammed the phone down in his ear and I was five miles away from the drugstore when I felt guilty about the whole deal. I should have been more sympathetic—Polnik had made his first, unaided joke.

I'd figured for sure Johnny would be in the office, but as she wasn't there, she was probably home in her aunt's apartment. Once I started thinking about Johnny Jones it wasn't easy to stop. My mind backtracked to the first sight of her sitting at her desk in Irving's office—then moved forward through the whole relationship with a loving attention to detail. It was fascinating when I thought about it, I realized, so fascinating I might just as well stop off at her apartment on my way downtown.

Pressing a buzzer is a technique in its own right which I respect. I used the authoritative approach on Johnny's buzzer this time—a long, loud, imperative squawk, followed almost immediately by another squawk exactly the same. It's nicely intimidating to the occupant, calculated to make them feel that Nemesis has finally gotten their number.

Maybe ten seconds later, Johnny's muffled voice called out nervously, "Who is it?"

"Special delivery!" I yelped in a gruff voice and thumped the door panels gently with my knuckles, like I just couldn't wait to get back to the sleet and snow. I heard the click of the lock, then the door swung open and Johnny's eyes widened in surprise when she saw me.

"Al?" No beacon lit in her eyes. "What do you want this time in the morning?"

"Special delivery," I said brightly, "and here I am!" I brushed past her into the apartment before she had a chance to object. "How about some coffee? —or even a martini without the vermouth?" I suggested.

Johnny was wearing a baby doll pajama outfit with cute bikini briefs, and the whole deal was put together in pale blue, completely transparent nylon. It was an awe-inspiring view, like Grand Canyon yet.

"I'm sorry, Al," she said coldly. "You can see I'm not even dressed yet. I'll have to ask you to leave now—and call me first the next time, will you?"

"Heard from your aunt lately, honey?" I asked nonchalantly.

"Don't fool around, please!" A tartness came into her voice. "I don't want to be rude but—"

"I'm in love with a real vulgar guy?" I finished the couplet for her, helpfully. "Just give me a couple of minutes, Johnny, then I'll be gone like the breeze."

I started walking, and her voice started objecting in back of me, but I didn't listen too hard. It was a three-room apartment and the kitchen was empty, and that left the bedroom. That was empty too, except for the magnificent, king-sized bed which was fit for a queen as well. So that left the bathroom. The door was locked from the inside so I tapped on it gently and yodeled, "Come out, come out, wherever you are!"

I heard the quick patter of naked feet and then Johnny arrived in the bedroom. "Are you out of your mind, or something?" she yelled at me. "If you don't get out of here right now I'll—"

Meantime I kept up a steady hammering on the door, but it was a full minute later before the door opened and Phillip Irving emerged with a sheepish look on his face.

"Well, well, well!" I said coldly. "If it isn't Aunt Charlie—the nut from Brazil!"

Irving's eyes glistened moistly behind the square-cut lenses, while his fingers plucked nervously at the lapels of his suit.

"Lieutenant," he quavered, "I'm innocent!"

"Keeping a girl like Johnny—with all those free-flowing curves—in a lavish love nest like this, and you're innocent?" I gurgled.

"You know what I mean!" he said. "I never planned to murder Kramer, with or without Sally's help! As for that time bomb!" He nearly gagged at the thought. "Fireworks terrify me—even the ones that don't go bang! I could no more plan to murder Kramer than—"

"Yeah," I said thoughtfully. "I'm inclined to believe you."

"—fly in the air!" he continued wildly. "Why won't anyone believe me? I'm innocent, I—what did you say?"

"I said I believe you," I snapped. "But Sheriff Lavers won't believe either of us. So we've got a problem."

"Thank heavens someone thinks I'm innocent!" He sank limply onto the bed, a quivering nervous wreck.

Johnny sat down beside him, and gently cradled his head against her more than adequate bosom. There looked as if there still could be room for me, too—it made for an interesting speculation.

"I'll make a deal with you, Irving," I said harshly. "You stay holed up in this apartment with Johnny for the next twenty-four hours and I'll pretend I never even saw you. Maybe I can take the heat off in that time."

"Thank you, Lieutenant!" he said hysterically. If I'd been any closer, he might even have tried to kiss me. "I swear I'll stay right here and not move an inch outside the door."

"If you skip out on me, friend," I said gently, "I'll find you again and run up and down your face with spiked boots."

He shuddered violently and sought the sanctuary of Johnny's mountainous protection again.

"Tell me one thing before I go," I said. "If you had managed to marry Sally Kramer and finally get your hands on her money, would you have kept this apartment going?"

"I—er—don't know," he mumbled. "Really, Lieutenant, what concern is it of yours?"

"I kind of liked Sally Kramer, that's all," I said slowly. "She played me some Chinese music once and it's only now I can begin to understand the melody. I guess it's all a question of slant. Her bad luck was getting mixed up with a creep like Kramer in the first place, and a creep like you in the second place. I'll be back sometime tomorrow." I walked toward the living room slowly.

"I'll see you to the door," Johnny said, and got up from the bed so fast that Irving's head slammed painfully against the footrail.

She caught up with me at the front door, sliding neatly between the door and me, then sagged a little forward so I could feel the weight of her breasts tight against my chest.

"I feel sort of stupid," she whispered. "You knew about the aunt all the time?"

"Not until this morning," I said. "I wondered why you weren't at the office, then I just plain wondered. What did he say after you told him you'd made a date with me for last night? 'Find out what he's thinking, if he suspects me of being implicated? Sleep with him if you have to,

Johanna, my dear!' And we were so close when that phone rang," I said sadly, "and you couldn't damn well wait for me to answer it."

"I can make it up to you," she whispered softly in my ear. "You understand my situation, Al, don't you? It *is* a beautiful apartment and he does pay the rent, but once all this is over he's definitely going on a long vacation—alone!" Her sharp teeth nibbled my ear lobe excitedly. "Once he's gone, you could come and stay for some of those Wednesday-to-Tuesday weekends of yours!"

"I don't think so, Johnny," I said. "You're getting too fat already, which is fine for Irving's mother complex, but not for me. That jazz you gave me about him calling Mrs. Kramer all the time, and spending most of yesterday calling the airlines and the shipping agencies—was that true?"

"Sure," she said bleakly, her teeth a long way from my ear lobe, and her weight now pressing away from me against the door.

"You wanted to tip me off—maybe you hoped he was guilty, huh?"

She moved away from me about four or five feet, her eyes smoldering with frustrated fury. "That's ridiculous!" she snapped.

"You'd have to have a reason," I said wonderingly, then I grinned at her evilly. "Sure, I just remembered. I bet the lease on the apartment is all paid up maybe a year or more ahead—Irving is a cautious guy and he'd want to avoid any trouble. With him in the gas chamber or the pen, you'd have this lovely apartment all to yourself, right?"

"You're out of your mind!" she grated.

"We can soon check," I said helpfully. "I'll just go ask Irving."

Her sharp nails clawed into my arm before I'd taken a couple of steps. "All right!" she hissed. "But only because I figured you'd be a lot more fun to have around than that cream puff!"

"I was just curious, honey," I said honestly. "You want to open the front door for me?"

Her face was livid as she savagely jerked the door open wide. "It's not that I'm taking a moral attitude to the whole deal," I explained, as I walked past her out into the corridor, "it's just that you're getting a little too fat for me, honey, and any day now you'll start to slump." The door slammed shut in back of me with enough force to move the whole building a couple of inches.

The rest of the day kind of dragged. I didn't want to go near the office and answer Lavers' impatient questions about why I hadn't found Irving yet. While I was out of sight he'd figure I was still looking, and that suited me fine.

I called Angel's apartment before lunch and she didn't answer. During the long wasted afternoon I called three or four more times and there was still no answer. I guessed it must be a big day for modeling underwear but it was no consolation. Around five-thirty in the afternoon when I called from a bar three blocks from where she lived, she finally answered.

"Hi, Angel," I said brightly.

"Hi!" That familiar rasp was back in her voice. "Who is this?"
"Al Wheeler."
"Well!" There was a little more warmth. "How are you?"
"Just fine," I said. "You heard about the Kramers?"
"I've just been reading about it," she said in a somber voice. "It's too dreadful to think about—poor Mitch! Poor Sally, too!"
"You want to hear the detail that didn't get into the papers?" I asked hopefully. "I'm just sitting in a bar, wasting my time, about three blocks from your place."
"I'd sure like to hear it, Al." She laughed self-consciously. "I sound like a ghoul, even to myself. But come right on over—I'll have a drink ready and waiting for you."
"Sounds great," I told her. "About five minutes."

It took a little longer but not much, and then Angel opened the door and suddenly it seemed a hell of a long time since I'd last seen that hauntingly provocative face and the mocking blue eyes that were just a little too big. Her fractionally overfull lips parted in a smile of welcome.

"My house is your house," she said huskily, "so come right on in. We can even do the bacon and eggs bit again, if you want."

She wore a gold silk shirt with a stand-up collar and a pair of orange velveteen pants that were tighter than tight. She looked radiant somehow, like a new universe just exploded into being.

"You look great, Angel," I said with open admiration. "Like you just had some good luck."

"Don't you dare mention good luck to me, you brute!" she said good-humoredly, massaging her velveteen seat tenderly. "It's only since this morning that I've been able to sit down again!"

I sat carefully on that nervous-looking couch while she brought the drinks across and actually sat on the couch beside me.

"Thanks." I took the glass out of her hand. "Aren't you nervous, sitting so close to a man, Angel? You could get your glittering little wings scorched."

"You keep on like this, buddy boy," she said easily, "and you won't have time to finish your drink even—never mind the bacon and eggs!"

I kept on looking at her, I just couldn't help it—she had an aura, a new radiance which gave her an even greater impact than before. The thrust of full, deep breasts against the gold silk shirt was somehow even more exciting—as though her strong femininity had finally broken through the last barriers of repression—or maybe I was just steadily losing my mind.

"Well?" Angel said impatiently. "Tell me!"

"What?" I lifted my eyes from the swelling billows of the gold silk shirt reluctantly and looked at her animated face. "Oh, sure! About what happened at the Kramers' place last night?"

"What else?" She sighed heavily. "I should have remembered those beady eyes of yours, buddy boy! You just concentrate on facts and leave the fantasies alone."

I took a moment out to light a cigarette. "It just wasn't true," I said flatly.

"*What?*"

"About Sally Kramer and Irving planting the time bomb in the plane," I said. "About Sally trying to kill him, either."

"Al!" Her dark blue eyes had suddenly grown enormous as she stared at me. "Do you realize what you're saying?"

"It's very confidential," I said soberly. "I wouldn't tell it to anyone but an angel."

She leaned back against the couch and closed her eyes for a moment. "You throw your shocks around like they're candy!" she said breathlessly. "Now tell me the rest of it before I die of curiosity!"

"I'll level with you, Angel," I said. "I didn't come around just to have a drink and a chat, and maybe bum one of your magnificent dinners for free." I looked at my watch as if each second was vital. "Ten minutes from now I have to leave and go pick up the real murderer. Do you want to come along?"

Her body jerked back into an upright position again. "You mean it would be all right if I did? But why me, Al?"

"Because I figure you have a right to know who it was that planted the bomb in the plane," I said seriously. "It should be exciting with loads of drama—almost as good as staying home and watching television!"

"Try and stop me!" She took a deep breath and her golden bosom sparkled in a shimmering cascade of light.

"Can't you tell me now?" she said eagerly. "Do I have to wait hours and hours?"

She seized my hand in hers, apparently without even being aware of what she was doing, and pressed it hard against the firm contour of her left breast. "Come on, Al!" she said huskily. "You can tell me—an angel always keeps a secret, you know that?"

My hand was pressed even harder into her firm, unyielding flesh. "You just want to be coaxed a little, is that it?" she purred throatily. "You want to get real close and whisper your secrets to the golden Angel?"

I pulled my hand free of hers and got onto my feet. "I can't tell you yet, Angel." I smiled apologetically. "But I'll spell it out for you on the way."

"Well, fine!" She stood up, smoothing the front of her blouse gently. "Are we going very far? Will I need a coat?"

"We're going to the Kramer house," I told her. "So are some of the others."

"Then I don't need a coat," she decided. Her eyes flashed. "So what are we waiting for? This is exciting!"

I spooned her into the passenger's seat of the Healey, then climbed in behind the wheel on the other side of her. Ten minutes driving saw us out of the downtown traffic, so we could talk without too many distractions.

"You remember the night before last?—the big bacon and egg night, Angel? When I asked you about Stu MacGregor?"

"I most certainly do." She rippled with laughter. "I told you, this morning was the first time since then I've been able to sit down."

"You told me how MacGregor tried hard to encourage you to play house with Mitch Kramer?"

"I remember," she said, nodding.

"How you wondered what kind of hold Kramer must have had over him?"

"I still do," she said seriously.

"I found out," I said in a smug voice. "Yesterday I wore Kramer down—scared the hell out him that if he didn't come clean, we couldn't save him the next time the murderer made an attempt on his life."

She shivered slightly. "Stop making me nervous, Al! You seem such a nice guy on the surface, but underneath you're tougher than steel and meaner than a cougar! You'd have to be, to wear Mitch Kramer down."

"They can all be cut down to size sooner or later." I grinned confidently.

The full recital of Kramer's story about MacGregor's traitorous activities in Korea comfortably filled the next ten minutes.

"Wow!" Angel exclaimed softly. "What a lousy rat that Stu MacGregor is!"

The right-hand turn onto the rough track up to the Kramer house was just a little way ahead.

"He's something more than that, Angel," I said softly. "He's a lousy, murdering rat!"

"What?"

I swung the nose of the Healey onto the track and eased it down to a crawl. "Sally Kramer and Irving was an absurd proposition right from the start," I said contemptuously. "Oh, sure, she played it up and even gave Irving some unexpected kicks—like the time you saw them together on the back terrace—but it was strictly a good cover job for the real man in her life."

"MacGregor?" she said tautly.

"Right!" I parked the car in back of the Corvette that nobody ever used as far as I could see. "We're a little early—MacGregor won't be here for another half-hour yet. I just want to check a point with Cliff White. Why don't you go on into the house and say hello to Mitch Kramer? I won't be five minutes."

"All right," she agreed, then swung her long legs out of the car. "Hell!" she said feelingly. "Stu MacGregor! I would never have figured that one. I have to hand it to you, Al. You're a genius."

"Just a cop," I chuckled, "but maybe you're right!"

"See you soon." She headed toward the house and I kept on going in a direct line toward the garage.

Lights showed from the small apartment that had been built onto the back of the garage, so the mechanic was home anyway. I rapped on the door and a moment later it swung open. Cliff White looked at me sullenly. "What do you want?"

"Five minutes of your time, Cliff," I said.

"A cop?" He shook his head slowly. "For a while there, I figured you was different, but you came out just the same as the rest of them after a while."

"She meant a hell of a lot in your life, didn't she, Cliff?" I said quietly.

His dark eyes gleamed with suspicion. "I don't know what the hell you're talking about!"

"Mrs. Kramer," I said. "Last night, just as I was leaving around six, she sat in my car and talked to me. I thought later it was like Chinese music." I explained the involved theory while he listened with a rapt expression on his face. "When I saw her body lying there inside the house," I went on, "I had a feeling I'd failed her somehow. If I'd told the County Sheriff last night what she said to me about hating Angel so much, and realizing only then how stupid she'd been for so long but it was too late to do anything about it, he'd have figured this proved she was about to try and kill her husband at any time—and she did."

"Mrs. Kramer couldn't hurt a mouse!" White said passionately.

"The Chinese music—if you don't understand it, you give it the meaning you think it should have," I said. "If you take the three things Sally Kramer said to me last night and play them with a different slant, what do you get?"

"Yes, what?" he said abruptly.

"Her fear of Angel doing harm to her—she knew something terrible was going to happen to her soon—and only now did she realize that Phillip Irving was a creep, and he had no intention of even trying to protect her from the conspiracy about to take her life."

"You *are* different from the rest of the lousy cops," White said slowly. "You're on her side!"

"Right," I agreed. "Now both the sergeant and Kramer said she left them out on the terrace around ten-thirty and said she was going to bed. Kramer didn't go to the den until a half-hour later, and according to his story it was a little while after that before she came into the den with a gun in her hand. I don't believe it. I think she sneaked out to visit with somebody—somebody like you, Cliff?"

"Yeah," he said huskily. "We got along just fine, she was a real lady, that Mrs. Kramer. Last night she told me how scared she was, but it was hopeless because if she tried to tell the police they just wouldn't believe her. Then she saw him walk into the house from the back terrace, and she raced back to the house so he wouldn't find her missing."

"That's all?" I said dully.

"That's all, Lieutenant." He nodded gloomily. "I see what you mean—it doesn't help any."

"I'll just have to play it by ear," I said dismally. "If I could get hold of just one teeny-weeny piece of concrete evidence!"

"I could lie a little," he growled.

"Thanks, but it wouldn't help," I said. "You hear some Chinese music in a few minutes that'll be me trying to fit a melody!"

CHAPTER ELEVEN

They were sitting together in the living room when I walked into the house. Kramer got up onto his feet and grinned at me.

"Nice to see you again, Lieutenant. Angel's been telling me some of your revelations on the way down. I hope that's okay—I mean, they aren't top secret or anything?"

"That's fine," I said. "You look better tonight—a whole lot better, Mr. Kramer."

"Thank you." He carefully wiped the grin off his face and sank back onto the couch again. His eyes watched me suspiciously.

"MacGregor—Stu MacGregor!" He shook his head. "It seems impossible, Lieutenant!"

"Like that wonderful story you told me about his six months as a prisoner in Korea," I agreed casually. "That plaque you gave him to commemorate the occasion was real cute, I thought."

"Oh—that story?" He smiled tentatively. "I didn't honestly think you'd take it seriously for a moment, Lieutenant. It was just a gag to break my own tension at the time."

"Like Angel's story about MacGregor being blackmailed into pandering for you—that was just a gag, too?" I said.

"That was true, Al!" Angel said tautly.

"Kramer just agreed the whole story of him blackmailing MacGregor was just a gag, honey," I said. "So what did he use to pay off Stu for his pandering? Candy bars?"

Her dark blue eyes were cold and watchful as she looked at me indignantly. "If it isn't true about Stu MacGregor, why did you feed me all that garbage on the way out here?"

"I figured it might keep you amused," I said. "You looked radiant tonight, Angel—a real angel almost. You know what you reminded me of?"

"No," she said icily.

"An expectant bride—they always have that look." I smiled benevolently at the both of them. "Just how soon do you plan on getting married?"

"What the hell are you talking about?" There was an edge to Kramer's voice. Maybe he was more worried than he looked—I hoped.

"That was the deal, wasn't it?" I asked blandly. "Like you told me once before, Mitch—you don't mind if I call you Mitch?"

"Of course not," he snapped. "Go on with what you were saying!"

"Like you said," I repeated, "Angel is a tease, and that's the price you got to pay if you want her fair, golden body—marriage!"

"Did you trick me into coming out here with you just to insult me?" Angel said savagely.

"There's a lot more to it than that, honey," I assured her. "With Sally nicely out of the way, of course the two of you will get married. That way, Mitch will have all those golden curves for his very own, and the comforting knowledge his wife can never testify against him about the time they planted that bomb in the plane."

Kramer came onto his feet angrily. "You've gone far enough with this kind of crap, Lieutenant!" he shouted. "Get the hell out of my house!"

I lit a cigarette and looked at him thoughtfully. "Don't you want to hear the rest of it? I figured you'd be fascinated."

"All I want you to do is—"

"Sit down, Mitch!" Angel's voice crackled. "Let him rave on—we should get a few kicks out of it, even!"

Kramer reluctantly sank back onto the couch and glared at me balefully.

"I had a fascinating talk with Stu MacGregor this morning," I continued. "He was telling me about a very special—and quite rare—category of fighter pilot. 'The killer' was his definition. He's the guy who *likes* to kill; it takes a colossal vanity, an ego inflated to the point of egomania, to belong in this category, Stu said. If I wanted a classical example of the type, he cited Mitch Kramer."

"So what?" Kramer grunted.

"You never gave a damn about your wife, her feelings, or ambitions until she started an affair with Phillip Irving," I said harshly. "Then the egomania took over. To you, it was intolerable Sally could prefer a creep like him to a superhero like yourself. So she had to be punished, and so did he—but Sally mostly, because she had been your wife and had committed the unforgivable crime in your book—rejected you for somebody else."

"You're sick, Al," Angel said venomously. "You belong in a nuthouse!"

"Not me, Angel," I said, "not you, even. It's Mitch who's real sick in the head."

Kramer shifted restlessly on the couch. "So you've got some wild theory about me wanting to punish Sally," he said impatiently. "Anybody's entitled to a theory, I guess, however stupid! But why don't you try tying yours in with a few facts, then see how it stands up?"

"Great!" I said enthusiastically. "You want to give me a fact!"

"That time bomb was set to explode when I would be flying the plane," he said. "If you hadn't come along at the right moment, I would have flown it and been killed instead of Red Hoffner!"

"Unless you already knew it was in the plane," I said slowly. "Then you could fake it—toss it out so it exploded in midair harmlessly. When you came down, you could say you just suddenly heard a ticking sound and found the bomb only seconds before it was due to explode."

"Okay." he sneered. "In that case you think I'd be stupid enough to have it connected before I took off?"

"Sure you would," I said. "Because of the risk of someone finding it inside the plane before anyone had used it—like your mechanic for example. If he had found this one, all set to blow, it would have done just as well as an actual explosion. Everyone would see the timing device was set for when you would be flying the plane, so it was still an attempt against your life."

He shook his head slowly. "I still think you're out of your mind, Wheeler! So how did I get it into the plane?"

"With Angel's help," I said calmly. "Then if anyone saw the two of you in or around the hangar, they'd leap to the obvious conclusion why you were there. It so happened that Cliff White did see you both leaving the hangar—but who'd suspect a man of planting a time bomb inside his own plane, set to explode while he would be flying it himself?"

Kramer bounced onto his feet again: "If I'm going to listen to any more of this bezazz, I need a drink!" he growled. "How about you, Angel?"

"Not right now," she said tautly. "How about the Lieutenant?"

"Not right now, either," I said.

Kramer went across to the bar, then snarled out loud a little time later. "Never in the right place when you want any goddamn thing in this house—I'll have to go get a fresh bottle of bourbon!"

He stomped out of the room and the silence came creeping up around us slowly.

"Al?" Angel said softly. "Are you serious about this crazy theory of yours? Is it for real?"

"Honey," I said reproachfully, "you should know that better than I do—you helped him plant the bomb! And, depending on your outlook it wasn't a bad deal. In return, you get to marry a million dollars or so, and I guess that's one hell of an improvement on modeling underwear!"

"All those dirty little men with their grimy fingernails," she said softly. "God! How I hate them!"

"You've only got two big problems if you do marry Kramer, anyway," I said encouragingly.

"What?" she snapped at me.

"That you never look at another man, and he never looks at another woman," I said soberly. "Because either way, it means your days are strictly numbered, Angel!"

Kramer came back into the room with a fresh bottle of liquor in his hand, made himself a sizable drink, and brought it back to the couch with him. "I just thought of something while I was out there," he said icily. "If your theory's correct, I let Red take off, knowing he'd be blown to bits!"

"I'm sure it worried you a lot," I said truthfully. "Because Hoffner was an old buddy of yours. But in the last analysis, old buddies are expendable if it furthers the cause of Mitch Kramer—right?"

"I could never do that in a million years!" he grated.

"I don't think it was your intention," I said. "My guess is when I suddenly appeared from nowhere and said I was a cop, you panicked for a moment, then suddenly realized this was perfect—a real live police lieutenant to witness the attempt on your life. So you kept stalling the others about flying, using me as the excuse, while you waited for the plane to blow up on the ground. Then Hoffner jumped the gun and the only way you could stop him was by telling everyone—including the cop right beside you—that there was a time bomb in the plane, ready to blow any minute. Compared to that, sacrificing Hoffner would have come real easy, right?"

Kramer shook his head disgustedly. "You got a million answers for everything and they're all wrong. So what happens after the bomb, huh? Tell me that?"

"You make damn sure the cops know about your wife's affair with Irving," I said. "Angel was useful there—dreaming up a story about them being highly indiscreet out on the back terrace—while I'm right there to hear the story. Your one real danger was if I hooked onto the steaming undercover romance between you two. That's why Angel had to be Stu's girl, and when White said he'd seen the two of you coming out of the hangar, it wasn't so good.

"So when I took Angel home and questioned her about it, she came out with a wild story off the top of her head, that Stu had talked her into it. Then she dressed it up a little, making him a panderer, forced into it by some dark blackmail threat Mitch Kramer held over his head. When I followed it up with Mitch—you'd have already briefed him, Angel, naturally—he topped it with an even wilder story."

"It's been fun in a macabre kind of way, Al." Angel made a production out of stifling a yawn. "But now it's getting a little dreary. Can't we change the subject?"

"There isn't much more," I said firmly. "With a police guard around the house, and the County Sheriff's office working hard trying to find out who tried to murder him, it was a perfect setup for Mitch to murder his wife—then reverse it as he did last night, and say she tried to murder him."

Kramer shook his head sullenly. "I wouldn't bother arguing with you, Wheeler"—he almost spat the words at me. "You're insane!"

"You did a pretty good job on that, Mitch," I told him. "A little hammy in places but nobody was about to critically appraise your performance. You had Sally saying all the right things in the right places—how she'd stolen the S-2 from your basement museum, then Irving had wired it to a cheap alarm clock, and they'd sneaked off the back terrace into the hangar and hidden it in the plane. And something I thought was rather cute—you freely admitted stealing the gun from your own museum, keeping it in the bedroom, and nobody thought twice about it. That was pretty tricky, Mitch."

There was a nervous tic starting to pulsate steadily under his right cheekbone, so there was plenty of tension built up inside, but he was a million miles from a crack-up yet. Angel was pretty tense too, the nails of one hand steadily gouging into her thigh through the tight fabric of her orange pants. The trouble was I didn't have anything more to throw at them.

"Are you all through now, Lieutenant?" Angel asked, almost as if she was psychic.

"Don't you think it's enough?" I said with a confidence I didn't feel.

"It's garbage!" Kramer said violently. "The dirtiest garbage I ever heard in my whole life! That you can stand there and say I'd let an old buddy of mine like Red Hoffner be blown to pieces without lifting a finger to help him! I should smash your face into little pieces for that, Wheeler!"

"Try looking into the mirror, Kramer!" I snarled. "That's the face you really want to tear into little bits, and you won't feel any different about it the rest of your life!"

His face distorted in violent fury. "Get out of my house!" he yelled at the top of his voice. "Get out now—or I won't be responsible for what happens!"

"You know something else, Mitch?" I sneered at him. "You got another big problem for the rest of your life, too. Redheaded women—you won't be able to stand even looking at them. They'll keep reminding you of Sally the whole time. But wherever you go, you'll see them, all right!"

He came off the couch in a sudden violent lunge at me, his hands reaching for my throat. I grabbed the lapels of his coat and swung him sideways until he was way off balance, then let go. He went skidding across the floor on his side and smashed into a heavy rocker which brought him to an abrupt stop.

"Mitch!" Angel yelled sharply. "Stop it! Don't be an idiot! You're doing just what he wants you to do!"

"After you're married, Mitch," I said in a leering kind of voice, "and maybe getting a little bored with the golden girl, you could get Angel to dye her hair red—say, every Friday night? That way you could—"

He came up onto his feet, gibbering with a blind and terrible rage that made him almost unrecognizable as the man sitting on the couch two minutes before. His eyes gleamed redly at me, mirroring the malignant hate in back of them.

"All right," he whispered. "So I got to teach you, too, Wheeler?" His right hand pawed inside his coat for a moment, then reappeared holding a clumsy-looking gun with an oversized barrel.

"You never learn!" he said thickly. "Not until it's too late! Nobody fools around with Mitch Kramer, Wheeler! You should have learned that simple fact of life by now!"

"Mitch!" Angel said in a taut-strung voice. "Don't!"

"Shut up!" he snarled at her. "You're only good for one thing, baby, and for that you don't need to talk!"

Angel stood up from the couch and started to walk toward him slowly. "Mitch honey?" She tried for the throaty sexiness in her voice and missed badly by around an octave. "Don't you see, honey?" she pleaded.

"This is exactly what Wheeler wants!"

"Get out of my way!" he hissed at her. "I'd as soon shoot a broad as anyone else, you chiseling teaser!"

"Angel!" I said tautly. "Stay right where you are! That's a Verey flare pistol he's got there. He must have gotten into the basement somehow when he went out for that bottle."

Kramer threw back his head and howled with laughter. "I got five, maybe six, keys to that basement, you dumb cop! When I gave that stupid fat man the second key, he figured he had my museum sewn up real tight!"

"Mitch—honey!" Angel pleaded. "Stop it now, before it's too late!"

He took a lurching step toward her and lifted his head to see her better; she shrank away instinctively from the craziness that burned like a bright fire in his eyes.

"You," he spat the word at her contemptuously, "with your cheap, little tricks for exciting a man into a frenzy, then quitting cold on him! A two-bit whore's got more honesty than you'll ever have!"

Angel's body shook uncontrollably and she began whimpering like a child, one hand thrown up in front of her face so she didn't have to look at him.

"The golden girl!" He chuckled evilly, "All glitter and dazzle on the outside—and nothing but ice inside. What you need is a little warmth and fire burning in your guts, Angel! Give you a brand-new explosive personality!"

There was a sudden scraping sound from the doorway, and Kramer's body went rigid as he listened. A couple of seconds later, Cliff White stepped into the room, dragging his stiff leg painfully. His dark eyes burned like coals in the white face as he stared at Kramer.

"You crazy little punk!" he said contemptuously. "I've owed you a long time for this leg of mine you smashed—and I figure it's about time you got what's coming to you."

A hunted look showed for a moment in Kramer's face as Cliff advanced slowly and steadily toward him. Kramer was turned toward the girl and me, the Verey pistol pointing in our direction, but he kept shooting side-glances to see how much closer Cliff had gotten to him with every step.

I felt the sweat roll down my face as I waited for the break. Cliff's dragging steps sounded awful loud in the quiet of the room as he got closer and closer. Then Kramer's nerve suddenly snapped.

"All right!" he screamed hysterically. "See how you like a burning rocket in your guts to go with your lousy leg!"

As he swung toward Cliff, my right hand dived toward the belt holster. For one frantic moment my moist palm slipped on the butt—then my fingers gripped tight and yanked the .38 clear of its holster.

Kramer suddenly lunged at Cliff, thrusting the Verey pistol toward his stomach, and the mechanic knocked the barrel away from him with a powerful sweep of his arm. It all happened at the same moment.

I triggered the .38, aiming at Kramer's chest. His finger must have been tightening on the flare pistol's trigger as Cliff knocked his arm to one side.

There was a thunderous roar, a pop, and a loud hissing sound, followed by a dreadful scream of agony. Kramer was already toppling sideways to the floor—the two .38 slugs had gone in under his armpit into his chest.

Angel threshed wildly on the floor, her screams filling the whole house with agonizing, unbearable sound. That murderous hissing noise kept on steadily and all the time the white-hot magnesium buried deep in her intestines burned brightly. I didn't hear Cliff White move— I stood spellbound with horror, unable to drag my eyes away from the demented writhings of Angel. The first I knew was the gentle tug that pulled the .38 out of my hand.

Cliff knelt down beside her, his stiff leg splaying out at an awkward angle. There was a merciful tenderness in his face as he put the barrel of the gun to Angel's head and pulled the trigger.

We stood by the garage waiting for the Sheriff and the ambulance. It was only fifteen minutes since the burning horror had exploded inside; now it seemed like a couple of hours—maybe because we'd savored every second outside in the fresh air.

"Once that rocket starts, you can't put it out, anyway you try," Cliff said. "It was better for her not to endure any more pain than she'd already suffered."

"Sure," I said. "Cliff, just one thing I'd like to ask you."

"Go right ahead," he said easily.

"You remember the first time you mentioned my pistons needed adjustment in the Healey?"

"Yeah—it's worse now," he grunted.

"I couldn't even hear them at all then," I said. "You must have very acute hearing, huh?"

"Nothing special," he shrugged. "It's training—a good mechanic develops a keen ear for some things, that's all."

"Kramer said they used a cheap alarm clock as the timing device on the bomb," I said carefully. "I guess that would have a pretty loud tick, huh, Cliff?"

"I guess it would," he acknowledged, "but you wouldn't hear it over the noise of the engine."

"I guess not," I agreed. "But Kramer and the girl hid it in the plane around two—three A.M. So the guy who checked the plane over inside the hangar on a routine maintenance—you'd figure he would have heard it."

"I guess he would," he said in an expressionless voice.

"I was just curious, Cliff," I said, "wondering if my hunch was right. Maybe the guy did find it and pulled it out of the plane. There couldn't be any doubt what it was. Then he looked for the time it was set to go off. He'd know the order of flying that had been fixed the previous night—so he'd have no trouble figuring exactly who the bomb was meant for, right?"

"No trouble at all," he said woodenly.

"What did he do then?" I wondered out loud. "Put it right back inside the plane?"

"What is a mere man to flout the ways of Providence?" Cliff asked soberly. "It's people interfering in the scheme of things all the time that causes half the troubles in the world today!"

THE END

Alan Geoffrey Yates Bibliography (1923-1985)

As Carter Brown/ Peter Carter Brown

Series:

Al Wheeler (no U.S. edition unless otherwise stated through to *Chorine Makes a Killing*)

The Wench is Wicked (1955)
Blonde Verdict (1956; revised for the U.S. as The Brazen, 1960)
Delilah Was Deadly (1956)
No Harp for My Angel (1956)
Booty for a Babe (1956)
Eve, It's Extortion (1957; revised as Walk Softly Witch!, 1959, and further revised for the U.S. as The Victim, 1959)
No Law Against Angels (1957; revised for the U.S. as The Body, 1958; 1st U.S. Wheeler)
Doll for the Big House (1957; revised for the U.S. as The Bombshell, 1960)
Chorine Makes a Killing (1957)
The Unorthodox Corpse (1957; revised for the U.S., 1961)
Death on the Downbeat (1958; revised for the U.S. as The Corpse, 1958)
The Blonde (1958; reprinted in the U.S., 1958)
The Lover (1958)
The Mistress (1959)
The Passionate (1959)
The Wanton (1959)
The Dame (1959)
The Desired (1959)
The Temptress (1960)
Lament for a Lousy Lover (1960) [includes Mavis Seidlitz]
The Stripper (1961)
The Tigress (1961; reprinted in the UK as Wildcat, 1962)
The Exotic (1961)
Angel! (1962)
The Hellcat (1962)
The Lady Is Transparent (1962)
The Dumdum Murder (1962)
Girl in a Shroud (1963)
The Sinners (1963; reprinted in U.S. as The Girl Who Was Possessed, 1963)
The Lady Is Not Available (1963; reprinted in U.S. as The Lady Is Available, 1963)
The Dance of Death (1964)
The Vixen (1964; reprinted in the U.S. as The Velvet Vixen, 1964)
A Corpse for Christmas (1965)
The Hammer of Thor (1965)
Target for Their Dark Desire (1966)
The Plush-Lined Coffin (1967)
Until Temptation Do Us Part (1967)
The Deep Cold Green (1968)
The Up-Tight Blonde (1969)
Burden of Guilt (1970)
The Creative Murders (1971)
W.H.O.R.E. (1971)
The Clown (1972)
The Aseptic Murders (1972)
The Born Loser (1973)
Night Wheeler (1974)
Wheeler Fortune (1974)
Wheeler, Dealer! (1975)
The Dream Merchant (1976)
Busted Wheeler (1979)
The Spanking Girls (1979)
Model for Murder (1980)
The Wicked Widow (1981)
Stab in the Dark (1984; Australia only)

Larry Baker

Charlie Sent Me (1965; revised from Swan Song for a Siren, 1955)
No Blonde Is an Island (1965)
So What Killed the Vampire? (1966)

BIBLIOGRAPHY

Had I But Groaned (1968; reprinted in the UK as The Witches, 1969)
True Son of the Beast (1970)
The Iron Maiden (1975)

Barney Blain (no U.S. editions)

Madam, You're Mayhem (1957)
Ice Cold in Ermine (1958)

Danny Boyd

Tempt a Tigress (1958; no U.S.)
So Deadly, Sinner! (1959; reprinted in the U.S. as Walk Softly, Witch, 1959, 1st U.S. Boyd; different version of the Wheeler title)
Suddenly by Violence (1959)
Terror Comes Creeping (1959)
The Wayward Wahine (1960; published in Australia as The Wayward, 1962)
The Dream Is Deadly (1960)
Graves, I Dig (1960; revised from Cutie Wins a Corpse (1957)
The Myopic Mermaid (1961, revised from A Siren Sounds Off, 1958)
The Ever-Loving Blues (1961; revised from Death of a Doll, 1956)
The Seductress (1961; published in the U.S. as The Sad-Eyed Seductress, 1961)
The Savage Salome (1961; revised from Murder is My Mistress, 1954)
The Ice-Cold Nude (1962)
Lover Don't Come Back (1962)
Nymph to the Slaughter (1963)
Passionate Pagan (1963)
Silken Nightmare (1963)
Catch Me a Phoenix! (1965)
The Sometime Wife (1965)
The Black Lace Hangover (1966)
House of Sorcery (1967)
The Mini-Murders (1968)
Murder Is the Message (1969)
Only the Very Rich (1969)
The Coffin Bird (1970)
The Sex Clinic (1971)
Angry Amazons (1972) [includes Randy Roberts]

Manhattan Cowboy (1973)
So Move the Body (1973)
The Early Boyd (1975)
The Savage Sisters (1976)
The Pipes Are Calling (1976)
The Rip Off (1979)
The Strawberry-Blonde Jungle (1979)
Death to a Downbeat (1980)
Kiss Michelle Goodbye (1981)
The Real Boyd (1984; Australia only)

Paul Donavan

Donavan (1974)
Donavan's Day (1975)
Chinese Donavan (1976)
Donavan's Delight (1979)

Max Dumas (no U.S. editions)

Goddess Gone Bad (1958)
Luck Was No Lady (1958)
Deadly Miss (1958)

Mike Farrel

The Million Dollar Babe (1961; revised from Cutie Cashed His Chips, 1955)
The Scarlet Flush (1963; revised from Ten Grand Tallulah and Temptation, 1957)

Rick Holman

Zelda (1961; 1st U.S. Holman)
Murder in the Harem Club, 1962; reprinted in the U.S. as Murder in the Key Club, 1962)
The Murderer Among Us (1962)
Blonde on the Rocks (1963)
The Jade-Eyed Jinx (1963; reprinted in the U.S. as The Jade-Eyed Jungle, 1964)
The Ballad of Loving Jenny (1963; reprinted in the U.S. as The White Bikini, 1963)
The Wind-Up Doll (1963)
The Never-Was Girl (1964)

Murder Is a Package Deal (1964)
Who Killed Doctor Sex? (1964)
Nude—with a View (1965)
The Girl from Outer Space (1965)
Blonde on a Broomstick (1966)
Play Now... Kill Later (1966)
No Tears from the Widow (1966)
The Deadly Kitten (1967)
Long Time No Leola (1967)
Die Anytime, After Tuesday! (1969)
The Flagellator (1969)
The Streaked-Blond Slave (1969)
A Good Year for Dwarfs? (1970)
The Hang-up Kid (1970)
Where Did Charity Go? (1970)
The Coven (1971)
The Invisible Flamini (1971)
The Pornbroker (1972)
The Master (1973)
Phreak-Out! (1973)
Negative in Blue (1974)
The Star-Crossed Lover (1974)
Ride the Roller Coaster (1975)
Remember Maybelle? (1976)
See It Again, Sam (1979)
The Phantom Lady (1980)
The Swingers (1980)

Andy Kane

The Hong Kong Caper (1962; revised from Blonde, Bad and Beautiful, 1957)
The Guilt-edged Cage (1963; revised from That's Piracy, My Pet, 1957; published in Australia as Bird in a Guilt-Edged Cage)

Ivor MacCallum (no U.S. editions)

Sweetheart You Slay Me (1952)
Blackmail Beauty (1953)

Randy Roberts

Murder in the Family Way (1971)
The Seven Sirens (1972)
Murder on High (1973)
Sex Trap (1975)

Mavis Seidlitz

Honey, Here's Your Hearse (1955; no U.S.)
The Killer is Kissable (1955; no U.S.)
A Bullet For My Baby (1955; no U.S.)
Good Morning, Mavis! (1957; no U.S.)
Murder Wears a Mantilla (1957; revised for U.S. as same title, 1962)
The Loving and the Dead (1959; 1st U.S. Seidlitz)
None But the Lethal Heart (1959; reprinted as The Fabulous, 1961)
Tomorrow Is Murder (1960)
Lament for a Lousy Lover (1960) [includes Al Wheeler]
The Bump and Grind Murders (1964)
Seidlitz and the Super Spy (1967; published in the UK as The Super-Spy, 1968)
Murder Is So Nostalgic (1972)
And the Undead Sing (1974)

Unrelated Novels/Novelettes (all non-U.S. unless otherwise noted)

Death Date for Dolores (1951)
Designed to Deceive (1951)
Duchess Double X (1951)
Forever Forbidden (1951)
The Lady Is Murder (1951; reprinted as Lady is a Killer with Murder by Miss Take, 1958)
Three Men, One Love (1951)
Uncertain Heart (1951)
Your Alibi Is Showing (1951)
Alias a Lady (1952)
Blackmail for a Brunette (1952)
Blondes Prefer Bullets (1952)
Hands Off the Lady (1952)
Kiss Life Goodbye (1952)
Larceny Was Lovely (1952)
Meet Miss Mayhem (1952)
Murder Sweet Murder (1952)
She Wore No Shroud (1952)
Sssh! She's a Killer (1952)
Chill on Chili/Butterfly Nett (1953)

BIBLIOGRAPHY

Cyanide Sweetheart (1953)
Dead Dolls Don't Cry (1953)
Dimples Died De-Luxe (1953)
Judgement of a Jane (1953)
Kidnapper Wears Curves (1953)
The Lady Wore Nylon (1953)
The Lady's Alive (1953)
Lethal in Love (1953; reprinted as The Minx is Murder, 1956)
Madame You're Morgue-Bound (1953)
Meet a Body (1953)
The Mermaid Murmurs Murder (1953)
Model for Murder (1953; different from 1980 Al Wheeler title)
Moonshine Momma (1953)
Murder is a Broad (1953)
Penthouse Pass-Out (1953; reprinted as Hot Seat for a Honey, 1956)
Rope for a Redhead (1953; revised as Model of No Virtue, 1956)
Slightly Dead (1953)
Stripper You're Stuck (1953)
Widow is Willing (1953)
The Black Widow Weeps (1954)
Felon Angel (1954)
Floozie Out of Focus (1954; reprinted with A Bullet for My Baby, 1958)
The Frame is Beautiful (1954)
Fraulein is Feline (1954; reprinted with Moonshine Momma & Slaughter in Satin, 1955)
Good-Knife Sweetheart (1954)
Honky Tonk Homicide (1954; reprinted with Chill on Chili & Butterfly Nett, 1955)
Homicide Harem (1954; reprinted with Good-Knife Sweetheart & Poison Ivy, 1955; with Felon Angel, 1965)
The Lady is Chased (1954; reprinted as Trouble is a Dame, 1957)
A Morgue Amour (1954)
Murder—Paris Fashion (1954)
Murder! She Says (1954)
Nemesis Wore Nylons (1954)
Pagan Perilous (1954)
Perfumed Poison (1954)
Poison Ivy (1954)
Shady Lady (1954)
Sinsation Sadie (1954)
Slaughter in Satin (1954)
Strip Without Tease (1954; reprinted as Stripper, You've Sinned, 1959)
Trouble is a Dame (1954)
Wreath for Rebecca (1954)
Venus Unarmed (1954)
Yogi Shrouds Yolande (1954; reprinted with Poison Ivy, 1965)
Curtains for a Chorine (1955)
Curves for a Coroner (1955)
Cutie Cashed His Chips (1955; revised for U.S. as The Million Dollar Babe, 1961, as Farrel series)
Homicide Hoyden (1955)
Kiss and Kill (1955; reprinted with Cyanide Sweetie, 1958)
Kiss Me Deadly (1955; reprinted as Lipstick Larceny, 1958)
Lead Astray (1955)
Lipstick Larceny (1955)
Maid for Murder (1955)
Miss Called Murder (1955)
Shamus, Your Slip Is Showing (1955; reprinted with A Morgue Amour, 1957)
Shroud for My Sugar (1955)
Sob-Sister Cries Murder (1955)
The Two Timing Blonde (1955; reprinted with Honey, Here's Your Hearse, 1957)
Baby, You're Guilt-Edged (1956; reprinted with Pagan Perilous, 1959)
Bid the Babe Bye-Bye (1956)
Blonde, Beautiful, and – Blam! (1956)
The Bribe Was Beautiful (1956)
Caress Before Killing (1956)
Darling You're Doomed (1956)
Donna Died Laughing (1956)
The Eve of His Dying (1956)
Hi-Jack for Jill (1956)
The Hoodlum Was a Honey (1956)
The Lady Has No Convictions (1956; reprinted with Slightly Dead, 1959)
Meet Murder, My Angel (1956)
Murder By Miss-Demeanour (1956)

My Darling Is Deadpan (1956)
No Halo For Hedy (1956)
Strictly for Felony (1956)
Sweetheart, This is Homicide (1956)
Bella Donna Was Poison (1957)
Cutie Wins a Corpse (1957; revised for U.S. as Graves, I Dig!, 1960, as Boyd series)
Last Note for a Lovely (1957)
Lethal in Love (1957; different than 1953 title)
Sinner, You Slay Me (1957)
Ten Grand Tallulah and Temptation (1957; revised as The Scarlet Flush, 1963, Farrel series)
That's Piracy, My Pet (1957; revised as Bird in a Guilt-Edged Cage, 1963, as Kane series)
Wreath for a Redhead (1957)
The Charmer Chased (1958)
Cutie Takes the Count (1958)
Deadly Miss (1958)
Hi-Fi Fadeout (1958)
High Fashion in Homicide (1958)
No Body She Knows (1958; with Slaughter in Satin, 1960)
No Future Fair Lady (1958)
Sinfully Yours (1958)
A Siren Signs Off (1958; with Moonshine Momma; revised for U.S. as The Myopic Mermaid, 1961, as Boyd series)
So Lovely She Lies (1958)
Widow Bewitched (1958)
The Blonde Avalanche (1984)

As Tod Conway (western stories)

As Caroline Farr (house name shared with Richard Wilkes-Hunter and Lee Pattinson)

The Intruder (1962)
House of Tombs (1966)
Mansion of Evil (1966)
Villa of Shadows (1966)
Web of Horror (1966; reprinted in the U.S. as A Castle in Spain, 1978)
Granite Folly (1967)

The Secret of the Chateau (1967)
Witch's Hammer (1967)
So Near and Yet... (1968)
House of Destiny (1969)
The Castle on the Lake (1970)
The Secret of Castle Ferrara (1970)
Terror on Duncan Island (1971)
The Towers of Fear (1972)
A Castle in Canada (1972)
House of Dark Illusions (1973)
House of Secrets (1973)
Dark Mansion (1974)
Mansion Malevolent (1974)
The House on the Cliffs (1974)
Dark Citadel (1975)
Mansion of Peril (1975)
Castle of Terror (1975)
The Scream in the Storm (1975)
Chateau of Wolves (1976)
Mansion of Menace (1976)
Brecon Castle (1976)
The House of Landsdown (1977)
House of Treachery (1977)
Ravensnest (1977)
The House at Lansdowne (1977)
Sinister House (1978)
House of Valhalla (1978)
Heiress Of Fear (1978)
Room Of Secrets (1979)
Island of Evil (1979)
A Castle on the Rhine (1979)
The Castle on the Loch (1979)
The Secret at Ravenswood (1980)

As Raymond Glenning (stories)

Ghosts Don't Kill (1951)
Seven for Murder (1951)

As Sinclair Mackellar

Prompt for Murder (1981)

As Dennis Sinclair

Temple Dogs Guard My Fate (1968)
Third Force (1976)
The Friends of Lucifer (1977)
Blood Brothers (1977)

As Paul Valdez
(stories & novelettes)

Hypnotic Death (1949)
The Fatal Focus (1950)
Outcasts of Planet J (1950)
Jetbees from Planet J (1951)
Escape to Paradise (1951)
Fugitives from the Flame World (1951)
Kidnapped in Chaos (1951)
Killer by Night (1951)
Suicide Satellite (1951)
The Time Thief (1951)
Flight Into Horror (1951)
Murder Gives Notice (1951)
The Corpse Sat Up (1951)
The Maniac Murders (1951)
Satan's Sabbath (1951)
You Can't Keep Murder Out (1951)
Kill Him Gently (1951)
Feline Frame-Up (1951)
Celluloid Suicide? (1951)
The Murder I Don't Remember (1952)
Kidnapped in Space (1952)
There's No Future in Murder (1952)
The Crook Who Wasn't There (1952)
Maniac Murders (1952)
The Mad Meteor (1952)
Operation Satellite (1952)

As A. G. Yates

The Cold Dark Hours (1958)

As Alan Yates

Novel:

Coriolanus, the Chariot (1978)

Stories & Novelettes:

Client for Murder (*Leisure Detective #7*, 195?)
The Corpse on the Carpet (*Leisure Detective #8*, 195?)
Farewell, My Lady of Shalott! (*Action Detective Magazine #6*, 1952)
Hush-a-Buy Homicide (*Leisure Detective #9*, 195?)
Margie (*Action Detective Magazine #5*, 1952)
Merger with Death (*Leisure Detective #12*, 195?)
Murder in the Family (*Leisure Detective #11*, 195?)
Murder Needs Education (*Action Detective Magazine #2*, 1952)
Murder! She Says (*Detective Monthly #2*, 195?)
My Love Lies Murdered (*Action Detective Magazine #7*, 1952)
Nemesis for a Nude! (*Leisure Detective #10*, 195?)

Genie from Jupiter (*Thrills Incorporated #14*, 1951)
Goddess of Space (*Thrills Incorporated #20*, 1952)
No Pixies on Pluto (*Thrills Incorporated #22*, 1952)
Planet of the Lost (*Thrills Incorporated #17*, 1951)
A Space Ship Is Missing (*Thrills Incorporated #16*, 1951)
Spacemen Spoofed (*Thrills Incorporated #23*, 1952)

Autobiography

Ready when you are, C.B.!: The autobiography of Alan Yates alias Carter Brown (1983)

Follow the previous capers of Al Wheeler from the irrepressible...

Carter Brown

The Wench is Wicked / Blonde Verdict / Delilah Was Deadly $19.95
"All fans of crime fiction should take this opportunity to rediscover Brown and Al Wheeler, and experience what kind of stories kept readers happily turning pages when paperbacks originals ruled the market."
—Alan Cranis, *Bookgasm.*

No Harp for My Angel / Booty for a Babe / Eve, It's Extortion $19.95
"With succulent descriptions of succulent women, two-fisted action, twists and turns, and Wheeler's irrepressible attitude, there's nothing *not* to like..."
—Kristofer Upjohn, *Noir Journal.*

No Law Against Angels / Doll for the Big House / Chorine Makes a Killing $19.95
"Al Wheeler is hilarious with his endless sarcasm, never completely in control but somehow being three steps in front of the bad guys and the reader... a must read."—*Paperback Warrior*

The Unorthodox Corpse / Death on the Downbeat / The Blonde $19.95
"These are all tightly written tales... plenty of action and the plots are straightforward fast reading, laced with humor..."
—Ted Hertel, *Deadly Pleasures.*

The Lover / The Mistress / The Passionate $19.95
"With humor, smart dialogue, sexy women, and mysteries with a Python's grip, these Al Wheeler novels deliver unique entertainment!"—George Kelley

The Wanton / The Dame / The Desired $19.95
"These novels are genuinely, intentionally, funny, there's a quick wit at work here and the dialogue is crisp, one liners come at you like a Bob Hope sketch."—Paul Burke, NB

The Temptress / Lament for a Lousy Lover / The Stripper $19.95
"There's plenty of delightful hardboiled dialogue and a certain amount of sleaze. The emphasis is on fun..."
—*Vintage Pop Fictions*

"A mix of sex, violence, mystery, and police procedural all wrapped in a pure pulp bundle."—*Just a Guy That Likes to Read*

STARK HOUSE PRESS, 1315 H Street, Eureka, CA 95501
griffinskye3@sbcglobal.net / www.StarkHousePress.com
Available from your local bookstore, or order direct via our website.

www.ingramcontent.com/pod-product-compliance
Lightning Source LLC
LaVergne TN
LVHW010157070526
838199LV00062B/4392